De

on the

Slopes

(Book 5 in the series)

by

G J Bellamy

Other books in the Brent Umber series:
1   *Death Among the Vines*
2   *Death in a Restaurant*
3   *Death of a Detective*
4   *Death at Hill Hall*

Sarah & Tom series - Coming soon

COPYRIGHT

Published by G J Bellamy

ISBN: 9798782107017

G J Bellamy
gjbellamy.com

PREFACE

Dear Reader,

Here is a very brief note because I have no wish to keep you from your story.

This book might be set in a mythical and highly fictionalized US state - let's call it Transatlantica - where, and I humbly apologize for this, stories are recorded with British spellings. Can you believe it?

So, you'll find grey instead of gray, flavour instead of flavor, and I have little to offer in defense/defence for this international outrage.

Why do this? - you might ask if you're a US reader. The answer is simple. The US is a dynamic place and is the only venue where certain elements of the story could be played out (and this goes for the rest of the series, too.) However, from my mother's knee I have learnt British English and it's the way I speak and write.

I could never pass myself off as a US national, lacking the intimate knowledge which comes from having grown up in or having travelled extensively through the US. Even if I had attempted to use US spelling and phrasing, you'd undoubtedly smell a rat and the story itself would be diminished. Neither of us would be happy with that.

Therefore, please look upon the following work of fiction as a story set in the USA but narrated and recorded by someone with a British accent.

Enough from me, I think, except to say, I hope you enjoy the story.

G J Bellamy

PS. Transatlantica is about 150 miles due East of Nantucket.

Death on the Slopes

Chapter 1

Sunday, February 1st

*S*wwwish… the snowboarder tracks through the trees on fresh powder in the frigid, biting, early morning air. Soft, soft back country powder - away from the lifts and the slopes that will be congested in a few hours and already dotted with early risers, eager for freshly groomed snow.

Down…. swwwish…. threading between the scented cedars and pines like a needle, quick and sure. The hard metal edge of the board creates a spray of fine snow.

Out in the open again, the boarder twists slightly into a wide curve that throws out a mist of billowing granules to cloud the air behind his fast moving figure - a rocketing figure now followed by a swollen contrail of white dust.

Whoosh…whoosh… a whistling skier appears out of nowhere and, faster than the snowboarder, cuts a second pair of tracks alongside the board's single mark. Two tracks are now clearly distinguishable - the mark of one thick board lying beside those of two narrow planks.

The skier closes the gap. Two dark figures speed across a dazzling white surface under a brilliant blue vault. One chases the other - traversing a slope, in among more trees, sailing over a rocky outcrop, both landing expertly on the sloping surface beneath, and then they are onto a long downhill run, a double black diamond descent. At an insane angle and a crazy speed, skiing ripper gradually gains on boarding shredder.

The slope flattens out onto the top of a wide ridge that divides two valleys. On one side, at the top of a cliff, the boarder comes to a stop to look out over a 170-foot drop and away into the snow-covered distance. A few seconds later, the skier joins the boarder and they stand in silence together. After a while, they begin to talk.

Below them, at the foot of the cliff, a jumble of massive boulders protrude from the thick blanket of snow. A little way out from the rocks lies a snowy and dead flat, open field - the spring flood plain of a now frozen river. Beyond the foreground, the forever view is one of giant sky and an undulating, dark green, alpine forest, heavily plastered with snow.

The vista usually humbles the viewer and all the problems in the world can be forgotten in twenty miles of unspoilt distance. The wind is brisk and sharp and distant clouds will arrive in an hour bringing a brief, light snow with them.

Say Goodbye - that is the name of the cliff. Skiers and boarders have thought about jumping it for years but have decided it cannot be done. Some things are just too dangerous. Besides, that valley leads south-west and away from the resort. A buddy would need to be waiting on a snowmobile by the river to collect the jubilant, successful jumper or take away the remains.

To those who have become familiar with one of nature's greatest glories, an urgent problem can thrust aside the spell of awe and beauty. The skier says something and turns away to look into the distance. The boarder hastily unstraps boots from bindings and picks up the board.

Without warning, the board swings to hit the skier. Stunned by the force of the blow, but without falling, the skier is set in motion, finds a slight decline which accelerates the movement, and slides towards grave peril. The boarder gives another helping push and, in three seconds, the skier has gone over the cliff's edge.

The boarder hurriedly erases footprints before strapping on the board again. The single figure heads south-east across pristine snow, down the slow and easy trail that leads out of the back country and towards the resort.

The previous night in a town called Brophy

"How much does he know?" asked the man sitting in the corner of a settee.

"He can't know anything. He's just guessing… that's all it is - just guessing," replied the younger man who was seated in an armchair opposite.

They paused their conversation as a woman came into the room. She said hello to the younger man before sitting on the arm of the settee.

"What's up?" she asked.

"We've got a problem."

"Oh? It looks serious. What is it?"

"Karl Saunders suspects something," said the younger man.

"Karl? Like, how can he know anything?" said the woman.

"He doesn't," said the man next to her, "but he's suspicious. He's got no evidence and nobody's squawked but he's looking. He thinks it's lift passes or a few bucks under the table. He's got no clue what we're doing but we can't have him getting any closer."

"I'm not going to prison over this. Nope, no way," said the younger man.

"You're right," said the man on the settee who pointed his finger emphatically.

"Can't we buy him off?" asked the woman.

"Ah, come on. Think about it," said the man. "If it had been anyone else we'd probably do just that but not Karl."

"Okay, so what do we do?" asked the younger man.

"We deal with the situation and do it soon. We do whatever it takes because none of us want to go down for this. You get me? We've got a sweet deal going and nobody's going to stop it."

"Yeah, you're right. There's too much at stake," said the woman as she got up. "It's a real shame. I liked Karl."

"So forget about him. Just leave it to us and we'll get it sorted. It'll be easy."

Friday, January 30th

*M*aria's house really did need fixing up. The essential required repairs were a new roof, furnace, and back door with a screen. The first two had to wait until the warm weather came but, towards the end of January, Brent successfully hung the new back door which feat both pleased and mildly surprised him.

To modernize the rest of the house - well, it needed everything really, but at least most things functioned properly so they could be left for a while. Brent brought in his friend, Paul Blake, to redo the plumbing in the upstairs bathroom and install a new shower unit. After he had finished his part, the bathroom floor was tiled. When that was done, Brent painted the room. Maria could not have been happier with her new, sleek bathroom.

This Friday morning, Brent was once again painting and decorating at Maria's house. For some reason that he did not fully understand, Maria had insisted on keeping the colour scheme in the second bedroom exactly the same as it had been before. Brent suggested a few changes but she was adamant it should remain the same. The walls were and would be again a dark pink and a new chocolate-brown carpet was to replace a worn one of the same colour.

While he was painting, he could think of nothing but bubblegum. He came to loathe the colour and felt it was beginning to affect his eyesight.

"Ah, that looks so beautiful," said Maria, as Brent who, close to finishing, was applying careful strokes of white paint to a section of the woodwork.

"You like it?"

"Sure, I do."

"I still don't understand why you didn't choose something else."

"Why change when you have the perfect colour? It just needed freshening up a little. Besides, it all ties in with the lampshade."

He looked at the lamp. It had a brown pleated shade with pink inlets and a fringe of golden tassels.

"You decorated the room to match the lamp?" asked Brent.

"You got it. I'll show you why." Maria switched the lamp on. "Oh, it looks like nothing now, during the day, but at night it's just gorgeous. This is my favourite lamp."

Maria looked so pleased that Brent forgot his aversion to the particular shade of pink.

"The only thing that matters," said Brent, "is that you get the room looking the way you want it."

"It's just how I want it. I love it. Thank you so much, Brent. Oh, yes. I came up to say lunch will be ready at noon."

"What are we having?" he asked. Brent began painting faster than he had before.

"Couscous alla Trapanese. It's got red snapper, tomatoes, and almonds. You'll like it."

"I'm sure I will. It sounds delicious. Trapanese? Where's that from?"

"Trapani. It's a place in Sicily. Don't forget to wash your hands. I gotta go look at it."

After lunch, it crossed Brent's mind that Lieutenant Greg Darrow had failed to call - again. Nearly two whole months had come and gone without Brent working on a single investigation. The Hill Hall case was the last one in which he had participated. It had ended way back in early December. Brent knew the police to be as busy as usual because he and Greg spoke on the phone every week or so.

There had been one near-miss case in early January. An eighty-year-old man had been shot dead outside a funeral home while many family members were inside, solemnly, emotionally, or, at least, reverentially, viewing the body of their departed relative. Brent had not only started on that particular case, he was also physically present in the Homicide Department in the process of familiarizing himself with the details by reading the crime scene report when the murderer arrived to surrender herself to the police.

At ninety-four years old, the aunt of the victim proved to be the oldest murderer ever processed by the Newhampton police. With her admission of guilt being accompanied by the evidence of the revolver that the aunt brought with her, wrapped in paper towels inside a plastic shopping bag and tucked next to her on the cushion of her wheelchair, there was now no reason for Brent to continue working. He left the department feeling slightly conflicted. What had begun as the exciting prospect of a new investigation ended thus abruptly. He could not help but be disappointed that the case was closed before it had even begun for him.

After having eaten his delicious lunch, Brent left Maria's house to drive home - his house was only a few blocks away. It could not have been duller. The dull grey clouds made it a twenty-five-watt bulb kind of a day. The snow that had fallen last week no longer looked fresh or white because dirt had started to accumulate on top of it. Winter was beginning to look messy and disreputable. It was also cold and windy. Spring felt so very far away. To Brent, it seemed the world was now entering the darkest middle section of the tunnel of winter and that it would be a good idea for him, personally, to go into hibernation. He had nothing interesting to do.

Brent parked in his driveway, got out of the Jeep, and looked at the old, tired snow. Out of nowhere, skiing came to mind. He stood still for nearly a minute lost in contemplation and, by the end, concluded he was going on a skiing vacation. He rushed into the house, full of excitement with his new idea.

Ghost Hawk Ridge Resort was the destination Brent selected. The resort's website thoroughly convinced him it was the place he should be. The resort was four hundred and fifty miles away and, Brent thought this highly significant, it was going to be sunny there for all of the following week. Day time highs were forecast to be between 13-20° Fahrenheit and overnight temperatures between minus four and plus eight. He had no worries about snow - the resort had already received two hundred and four inches with another eight to ten inches expected through Saturday night. That was an impressive amount of fresh, white snow by any standard.

Brent got caught up in the cachet so professionally conjured by the promotional materials. He learned Ghost Hawk had just installed a new, high-speed, six-person ski lift which brought the total lift capacity of the resort up to twenty-eight thousand per hour. The highest usable part of the mountain had a vertical drop of 3,857 feet. There were a total of seventy-one runs, plus one hundred and eleven miles of back-country trails. Some of the trails and slopes were rated double black diamond - the most challenging of them all.

He booked a flight for Sunday morning and made a reservation in a beautiful hotel right at the foot of the slopes, adjacent to the resort village. He would be staying until late next Friday. Brent further discovered he could rent or buy all the ski equipment he needed while he was there. It was a joyful sound for him to hear his printer fire up and then spit out all his tickets and receipts.

What he absolutely needed to do before he went on vacation was to buy a good quality ski jacket, ski pants, and accessories. He found he could get those things from a store not twenty minutes' drive from where he lived. While he excitedly put on a jacket to go and get a ski outfit, he remembered there was another, very important thing he must do. Brent sat down at his computer to log in to the resort's website again. He booked some beginner's ski lessons. As soon as this latest confirmation printed off, he was out the door and into his Jeep in seconds. He drove away smiling.

Chapter 2

*F*or the next two days, Brent devoured countless videos on skiing and snowboarding to see how it was done. In the process, he became familiar with many of the technical terms and slang connected with those two sports. He opted for skiing rather than snowboarding but he intended to try both, if he could, while he was there.

That decision was solidified while he was in the store, being aided by a helpful and knowledgeable sales associate named Franky who guided him in selecting items he would definitely need later. However, there were also some items the value of which Brent could not quite see at present. Base, mid, and outer layers, neck tubes, gloves, and a beanie hat - those he understood; sun cream, sunglasses, and goggles he did not until it was explained to him. Boots, Brent was easily persuaded, were better purchased beforehand for a comfortable, fine-tuned experience on the slopes. Ill-fitting rental boots, Franky informed him, could ruin a day's skiing and, as Brent was going for a week, it was a no-brainer to buy them now and have them fitted. Brent, like putty in Franky's hands, did exactly as the salesman suggested.

Ski boots, when not actually attached to skis, win fourth place for the most awkward footwear worn by humans. The bronze medal goes to flippers when not in the water, with the silver to ice skates when not on ice. Winning gold are deep-sea diver boots which weigh in at around forty pounds the pair. When Brent first tried on a pair of ski boots he felt for sure as though he were being fitted out for deep-sea diving as he lurched about the store.

The custom fitting of the boots, conducted by the custom boot-fitting gentleman, named Quincy, began with a technical difficulty.

"What kind of skiing do you do?" asked Quincy, as he, Brent, and Franky stood in front of the ski boot display rack, seriously contemplating the problem before them.

"Well," answered Brent, "I hope very soon to get down a slope without falling over. I went skiing once before and I spent more time spread-eagled in the snow than I did in actually skiing. This time, I'm going to have lessons."

"Ah," said Quincy with sudden enlightenment. "These are the ones you want, then, but we should pick out your skis and match the bindings now. That way I can tune everything so you'll have no problems later. You need to do that if you're going to take skiing seriously. It'll take about an hour. When are you going?"

"On Sunday."

"I can do it right away. It will save you a lot of time on your trip."

"That's true… Um, I have a question. What are bindings?"

"They attach the boots to the skis. Like, I don't mean to be rude or nothing, but you really should let me pick this stuff for you because I don't want you to leave here and have a bad experience. You see, if you get into the sport, you'll want a set-up that'll last you for a few years and one you'll be happy with."

"Are you saying I shouldn't pick what I want because I like the colour or the cool factor or the price?"

"You got it, Brent."

"Then show me your selection."

"Thanks."

Quincy picked up a pair of bindings. He and Brent walked over to where the skis were located. Franky wheeled the cart containing Brent's growing pile of clothing and equipment to the check-out.

A pair of skis were added to the bindings and boots. Brent would not have chosen any of them individually - based on looks alone - but when he saw them together, they worked in a disparate kind of way. Mental assent was about the only 'contribution' he could make because he understood nothing of the technical side of the equipment.

"So, Brent, the way I see it is like this. You look like a fit guy and you're getting lessons. Okay, so if you get a good instructor and catch on quickly, you'll be on the green slopes the same day. By the end of the week you'll be on the blue slopes. That's when you'll realize your technique sucks but you'll be getting the idea of how to fix your bad habits before they become ingrained. You'll buddy with someone or you'll be back to the instructor for more lessons.

Let's say you do all that and skiing's your thing. Going forward, you put in about twenty days a season. Nothing extreme, but in there somewhere you'll want to try black diamonds. After five years you'll be wanting to upgrade this set-up if your skills continue to improve. As long as you're on piste this set-up will do you fine. It's comfortable and forgiving now and it'll handle a little bit of freeriding on powder. Are you with me?"

"I was until the end. What is piste, exactly?"

"Those are the groomed slopes. If equipment is put on the snow to smooth and grade it, that's piste."

"Okay. What about freeriding?"

"Completely off-piste. It's also called back country or big mountain where you'll do your own thing. You'll find as many snowboarders out there as skiers. Don't confuse it with freestyle which incorporates man-made structures. That's all the acrobatic stuff you've seen around jumps, half-pipes, and rails."

Brent smiled. "I can't see myself doing any of that any time soon."

"No, I guess not," said Quincy. He picked up a ski and looked at it appreciatively. "This is a good, ninety-six millimetre ski and you'll be happy with it. Those bindings are very reliable. Some of this stuff breaks over time but this brand and type of binding always has the least number of issues. You just step in and step out. Now the boots… They're not the best but they're the best value for the money. Nice and comfortable with the right amount of flex for what you'll be doing. If you want, we can swap any of these for something else but it'll run you a lot more money to get a little extra performance and you'd need to be an expert to notice the difference."

"As I'm a beginner and don't know anything, I think we should go with your choice. Is rental equipment that bad, then?"

"Not really. It depends on the place and how the equipment's maintained. The real problem is you can't tweak it or get exactly what you need because of the line-up of people behind you who are really anxious to get their stuff and just go."

"So, what do we do now?"

"Boots first. Take a seat up on the platform and remove your boots and socks. We'll do the mould for the custom footbed first."

"Footbed? Is that a type of insole?"

"That's right. A custom footbed takes care of any hotspots you'd have with the factory footbed. It also stabilizes your foot in the boot and helps with the alignment of weight distribution when you initiate a turn."

From start to finish, Brent was in the store for nearly two hours. When he left, he was the proud possessor of a complete ski outfit with all accessories, including a helmet, ski poles, and bag. He was truly ready for his first lesson.

Almost from the time he got home, Brent was wearing his new ski boots around the house to break them in. He sat down at the computer wearing the monstrous objects with a golden yellow beanie perched on his head while trying to absorb the finer points of Snowploughing, Stem Christies, Parallel turns, and Carving. From there he got lost in the effects of weather and snow conditions upon skiing. He had not realized there was so much to learn. The people in the videos did everything effortlessly, making it look easy.

By late Saturday night, he had reached, in a purely academic way, expert level. With a hundred new terms in his mind, he packed his bags and checked he had everything he needed for the trip.

Early on Sunday morning, February 1st, Brent left for the airport to catch his seven-fifteen a.m. flight.

After disembarking from the plane, he went to the bus terminal to catch the shuttle to Ghost Hawk which was a ninety-minute drive away. He could tell that many of the other passengers on the bus were obviously skiers and snowboarders by the clothes they wore. Brent realized suddenly that he looked as they did and, in that same moment, further realized that they could all ski or ride while he could not. He found it amusing to be such a secret fraud.

The entire bus journey seemed to be uphill. The whole region was covered in blindingly white snow spread over an endless succession of hills. After forty-five minutes on a fast highway, a series of big signposts appeared, one after the other, indicating the way to Ghost Hawk and Brophy, population nine thousand, the town that lay next to the resort.

The bus left the highway and turned towards the town. Brent could feel the anticipation building within him. He noticed something similar in a few other passengers who began to crane their necks for a sight of something. Most of the skiing types seemed unaffected. Clearly there was quite a distance to go before the resort would come into view.

At first, the shuttle bus passed by side roads to many small towns and villages. As the road continued to climb, the terrain became more rugged and wilder and intersections fewer. After a while, Brent realized he had not seen a commercial farm for some time. Still the bus climbed and some of the turns in the road were precipitous on one side with sheer rock walls on the other.

The bus had climbed a ridge only to come down several hundred feet into a valley. The road now ran past a lake. A few small farms dotted the open, flat scenery. In the middle of nowhere, a huge sign declared, "Century Burgers - 1 mile - The best burgers any time, any altitude"

The bus flashed past Century Burgers and Brent noticed there were about fifty vehicles parked around the establishment. *Does that mean they're exceptional or all that's available in the area?* he thought to himself. As it was approaching noon, he thought ruefully that he could have used a high-altitude burger about then.

From the warm comfort of the coach, the upland country looked and felt different to the country just an hour further south. The unyielding rocky hardness of it was obvious. There was also a rareness that Brent could not isolate and identify. If anything, it was the solitary feel of the landscape, as though one could escape from everyone and everything by simply walking a hundred yards away from the road to be swallowed up in an endless series of pine tree copses, gullies, cliffs, and other snow-rounded forms. Total anonymity and invisibility were mere steps away but that was allied with the certain failure to survive unless properly prepared. The rareness, then, was that this land between the settlements was not civilized and settled. It was dangerous - and the realization came as a surprise to Brent, a city-bred man.

The bus sped past the lake and, for the first time, several of the more experienced skiers and riders began to sit up and take notice. Then, Brent saw a mountain range in the distance but it was not on his side of the bus so he only got an intermittent, partial view as the vehicle went around bends. On either side of the road, chalet-style properties began to appear. Soon, single vacation properties and sub-divisions came to dominate, interspersed with houses and businesses belonging to local inhabitants.

The bus turned towards the sunlit mountains and Brent had a complete view at last. The mountains were, in fact, a long, wide ridge, undulating into a series of sharp peaks with the closest, and by far the tallest, forming a great, natural buttress against the rest of the mountain range. Brent could see nothing to suggest ghosts or hawks. What the visible white pistes among the dark green lines and pools of fir trees did suggest to him was a zebra. He could not take his eyes off the great mountain. He wondered why an idea of a little over forty-eight hours duration had seized his mind so completely and impulsively. He was glad he had acted because now he was going somewhere and doing something.

Brent knew he was very close when the bus turned again, putting the mountain on the opposite side to him once more. Nearly every passenger was now looking out of the same side. Brent could only see a framed portion of the lower slopes through the window. He saw a red dot coming down one of the white lines. It was a matter of moments before he saw dozens of dots in yellows and blues but mostly greys or blacks, zig-zagging down in a seemingly slow, lazy, side-to-side way.

The bus pulled into the terminal in the centre of snow-covered Brophy. Brent disembarked, reclaimed his bags, and found a taxi to take him to the large, modern Aurora Hotel at the foot of the slopes. The snow-ploughed streets leading to the establishment were busy with pedestrians - many in brightly coloured winter clothes.

To get to the Aurora, the taxi crossed a bridge over the pretty Chute River, frozen at present with small drifts of snow on top of the ice. Brent was impressed by the town, the resort, and with the vibe he saw and sensed through the car window. The blend of old and modern buildings, the decorative features added to the new, well-made infrastructure, and the dominating and stunning backdrop of the snowy mountain range itself combined together beautifully to give the obvious scenic reasons why the place was growing in popularity.

He had chosen the Aurora because it was ski in/ski out. The check-in at the large hotel was quick and painless and so, armed with a map and several pamphlets, Brent went up to his room to unpack his bags and find out where everything was located - particularly the slope where he was to receive his first lesson at two o'clock. Finding the spot, he realized he had a 500-yard walk in his ski boots ahead of him. Brent was unable to ski there or anywhere - yet. Hopefully, by the end of the day, he would be able to ski back. An extra feature about Ghost Hawk was the night skiing under lights on a few select slopes up until 9:00 p.m., which was when the lifts stopped running. This additional enticement of skiing at night had decided Brent on the resort in the first place. It was now a little before one and definitely time for lunch.

All four restaurants within the hotel faced the slopes and three of them had large, outdoor patios where skiers could lounge in the open. The patios were very busy when he arrived but Brent managed to get a small table on the inside almost immediately. His table was at the back of the room but he had a clear view through the glass wall sectioning off the patio and, further, to the busy slopes beyond.

Chapter 3

Sunday afternoon

$\mathcal{A}$s a newly arrived outsider, without the distraction of conversation with friends or family, Brent was free to be an amateur anthropologist and study the affluent class at leisure while he was in the restaurant. Had there been a second observant anthropologist present, that one would have concluded that Brent was of the same class. Although he was wealthy, Brent never considered himself as "belonging" among other wealthy people. It was new to him, he was alien and newly arrived to it, and Brent had no wish to be accepted into a social class based on wealth alone.

Although he had acted upon an impulsive thought to go skiing and could easily afford the expense it entailed, he was there for the sole purpose of learning to ski and to enjoy the thrill of it. Not for one moment had it entered his mind to attach himself to that strata of exclusive society that frequented expensive hotels and resorts. Had he acted less impulsively, by planning a trip six months earlier, he probably could have coerced a couple of old buddies to join him. Then they would have shared a rented chalet for a few days and tried to learn to ski together. It would have been a lot cheaper than Brent's actual trip and probably a lot more riotous fun would have been had. .

Brent continued to observe the restaurant crowd, particularly those occupying the patio. He noticed a lot of posturing. The serious skiers were undoubtedly scattered among them but there were also the ones who table-hopped, slapped people on the back, and laughed loudly in exaggerated ways. Cliques had formed, that was obvious to him. Many people seemed to know many other people. He wondered on what basis did this particular slice of the wider but wealthy skiing community form and congregate? Skiing for pleasure? Competitive skiing? He could not tell.

The food was good, although expensive. He finished up quickly and headed back to his room to get his gear. It was time for him to go skiing.

It was a tough decision for Brent to make. Whether to walk to the beginner slopes in ski boots or change and wear regular winter boots but then have nowhere to put them. If he had brought a backpack with him he would have had an easy solution. He decided he could not risk losing his regular boots by leaving them lying about while he was having lesson - then, he would have nothing but his clodhopping ski boots in which to go to buy new regular ones. That idea did not bear thinking about. So, he just set off as he was. The man in his brand new four thousand dollar skiing outfit started to walk to his lesson and he found it very hard, slow, and slightly absurd going, but he got there in the end. He established a fact en route. The skiers he had seen from the bus had seemed to have been descending slowly. Up close he realized how fast they were moving. A few snowboarders and skiers raced down, holding Brent's fascinated gaze as his steps slowed to properly take it in. He was so glad he had come.

The nomenclature for most of the slopes in the resort was mostly themed around wild animals. The easiest green slopes were named Deer Spring -1, 2, 3, etc.. There were long blue slopes grouped together under the title Wolf Run. Cougar Pounce encompassed a complete range of slopes from intermediate to advanced. One insane but popular drop was called Knife Edge. Bear Tracks presented a mix of difficult terrain from blue to double black. Blister was the area where they kept the bumps - the moguls, rollers, half pipes, and rails.

The easiest slopes for beginners was a sweet gentle winter-world of its own. The broad slopes were named Giraffe, Hippo, and Panda. Brent was to go to Hippo slope for his lesson. It was easy to find because it was marked by a six-foot-high, multicoloured, three-dimensional hippo standing on top of a mound with a short, wide and easy slope in front of it. A slow surface lift with a continually moving rope was to one side of the run.

Brent trudged up the hill towards a small group of people who were also in the process of arriving. His companions for the next two hours were five children between the ages of six and eleven, a tall youth who was probably fifteen but looked to be about twenty-eight, and two ladies who were senior citizens. The instructor for the group was Lotta. She was probably in her mid-twenties. She organized everyone into a line so that she could face them.

"Great! Everyone is here…. Hi, my name is Lotta, and we're going to learn how to ski and it will be fun." The instructor was smiling brightly. "First, we'll do a warm-up and get our circulation going."

The nine beginners duplicated the arm swings their instructor performed. Brent, smiling, looked along the line. Everyone looked happy to be there except the fifteen-year-old and Brent realized this warming-up exercise was also a good way for the instructor to learn what she was up against attitude-wise.

There followed an explanation of the ski equipment with particular attention paid to how the bindings functioned. After the explanation, it took a ragged minute or two but the entire line was now on its skis.

"Today we're going to learn how to parallel ski. An important part to get right is posture. So, you'll want to start out standing like this."

Lotta turned sideways and, with bent knees, she leaned forward slightly. The line copied her. Immediately, the lady at the right end of the line toppled over in the snow, taking her friend down with her. She in turn bumped a small boy, who also fell. The domino effect stopped and no one was hurt. The two women laughed, the boy, as he sat up, shook his head with all the disdain an eight-year-old could muster.

"Okay," said Lotta, apparently unfazed at the sight of three sprawling students, "we're ahead of ourselves but getting up after a fall is one of the things we have to learn today. So, let's learn that now!"

As the lesson progressed, it became apparent that two of the children needed semi-constant attention, as did the lady who had fallen over. The disinterested youth left the group part way through without saying a word to anyone. The rest did their best with varying degrees of success. A small girl was getting everything right - nailing it and naturally so. The second best student was Brent who struggled at first with the innate fear of falling which, he soon realized, was hampering everything he was trying to accomplish. He got control of his fear to a certain extent by forcing himself past it. This made things easier. He quickly began grasping the concepts of balance and shifting weight from one ski to another to manoeuvre or initiate a turn. He was getting it.

The two hours came to an end. Parents collected their children - three being enthusiastic and two apathetic. The two women wobbled away uncertainly on their skis, smiling and talking loudly. Brent gave Lotta a fifty dollar tip and, having thanked her profusely, skied uncertainly away towards a green slope that possessed a ski carpet lift - a conveyor belt for people wearing skis.

The floodlights came on as the day darkened towards evening. Brent fell twice on his first run down the relatively short, gentle training slope. He fell once on his second and ceased to fall thereafter. His turns were getting better. On the incline, he wanted the carpet lift to move faster, so anxious was he to glide down the hill again, but not so fast when it was time for him to get off - which seemed to him to be a most perilous undertaking although he was gradually getting the hang of that, too. It was after five when he decided to try the adjacent slope which was also a lot longer.

The only slopes to be lit were one green and three blues because the serious skiing was finished for the day. It being Sunday night, most of the day-visitors had already left which meant the slopes were less crowded than earlier and the green slope was emptier than the blues. As a consequence of these factors, Brent got the four-person chair - a quad - to himself. He managed to get on it without making a fool of himself and lowered the safety bar.

The sun had gone down and the temperature had dropped. Sitting still as the chair on the cable swayed upwards, Brent felt the impact of the cold wind above the treetops. He was glad to be wearing his snug ski outfit. Although he was enjoying the ride, as a total newbie he now began to worry about exiting the lift. Although Lotta had explained getting on and off a chairlift to him, he had yet to try it for himself. Lift the bar, raise the tips of the skis at the landing platform, and clear the area quickly - that much he remembered. As he approached that's what he did.

What new skier Brent had not reckoned upon was the almost instantaneous quality of the transition from being comfortably seated to suddenly skiing. It was as though he had forgotten everything he had just learned. Brent managed to get clear of the lift area and, after wobbling perilously for about twenty feet, fell over on the icy, slick snow around the lift. While getting up, he could not remember the last time he had felt so embarrassed. His one urgent thought was to move away from the scene as fast as possible so that everyone present could forget he was ever there.

He stopped at the top of the run and realized that what had looked doable from the bottom of the slope now looked life-threatening from the top. He wondered if he had gone up the wrong slope, it looked so different. He now also understood that not all slopes in a colour category were created equal. This green one, gentle at first, disappeared to reappear further down after its steep, middle section. Brent watched as skiers and boarders nonchalantly disappeared over the edge without a care in the world.

While he hesitated, two ski patrollers arriving from different directions met one another nearby to where Brent stood. They wore distinctive red and black outfits bearing a prominent white cross as found on a Swiss flag. This sight caught Brent's attention not only because he had never seen a ski patrol before but also because he could tell something was seriously wrong. The man was shaking his head, clearly unable to accept what the woman was telling him. She looked anxious, too. The patrollers slowly skied away together, crossing laterally to another slope. Whatever news had been communicated had to have been bad. Brent thought the order of magnitude of the news was in the realms of a coming lay off of resort employees or someone having had a bad accident - someone they both knew.

Whatever their problem was, Brent put it out of mind. He had his own problem to face - how to get down the hill in one piece? Choose a line, Brent remembered what Lotta had said. He chose the easiest looking path to zig-zag down and determined to come to a halt at the edge of the dip to see what lay ahead of him.

He made it to the edge. The slope seemed shockingly steep. After a deep breath, he set off, turning frequently and trying not to pick up too much speed. About halfway down he began to enjoy himself and went faster. He wiped out, got up, and went as fast as before. He wiped out again and got up again. At the bottom, he skied straight for the chairlift once more. He was now, officially, having a blast.

Each time at the chairlift, he talked to other skiers and boarders. A dad with his nine-year-old son gave him a few tips as they went up in the chair together. They lived in Brophy and the man owned a business selling, renting, and servicing snowmobiles. Brent thought that when he came back - he had already decided he would - he might give snowmobiling a try.

By six-thirty, Brent was hungry, tired, and the new boots which had been comfortable earlier were now starting to pinch. One last run and he would call it a day so that he could get an early start tomorrow. Then, or before then, he hoped to find a private instructor.

On this last ride up, he puzzled over something he had seen. The lift operators - lifties - had become quiet and sullen whereas earlier they had been smiling and friendly. Something had definitely happened and Brent wondered what it was that would affect both lifties and patrollers alike.

Brent made the last run a good one - for him, anyway. He went over the edge without hesitation and, although a couple of boarders flashed past him, Brent was going as fast as anyone else. However, while watching him, the word 'elegant' was not what sprang to mind. When he reached the bottom he skied back to his hotel, passing two large SUVs from the Sheriff's Office parked opposite the six-person chairlift. The vehicles were empty. Brent assumed the deputies would be talking to the lift operators so he went over to investigate. Upon arriving, he found the deputies had already gone up the hill.

"Hi, can you tell me why the deputies are here?" asked Brent when he found a resort employee. The man in his twenties seemed preoccupied.

"Uh, there's been an accident. They've gone up to check it out."

"A serious one, I guess. What happened?"

"I, uh, don't know. We're not supposed to talk about it. You a reporter or something?"

"No, I'm just curious at all this activity."

"Okay. If I did know, word is, I can't talk to anyone. I gotta go."

"Thanks," said Brent.

"No problem."

Somewhere in Brophy

"It was easy," said the younger man excitedly.

"Yeah, so I guessed. Any problems?"

"None. I hit him and he just went over the edge. Easy, like I said."

"Good. No one saw you?"

"No one. Absolutely no one. I came back and blended in with the crowd like I'd just shown up for a first run. We're cool."

"The deputies dropped the ball. They didn't get there until really late. I went up to Say Goodbye to take a look when they arrived. That was after the body had been recovered. Clueless, they didn't know what to do. The body had been moved and the snow on top was all churned up by the gawkers. A couple of deputies who'd come up top to find witnesses were out of luck - nearly everyone skied away. It was funny, no one wanted to get involved. So they didn't find any witnesses at all. We're in the clear and it totally looked to everyone like an accident."

"Hello, Mary?" Sheriff-Coroner, Jebb Bates, had called Dr Mary Denver. They both lived in Brophy.

"Jebb! I just walked through the door. I haven't heard from you in a while. How are you and the family?" The doctor had a strong, pleasant voice perhaps shaped by her love of singing.

"We're all doing fine, thanks. And yourself? And how's that new grand-daughter of yours?" Sheriff Bates spoke unhurriedly in even tones.

"It was a lovely visit and Michelle's as cute as button. She's putting on weight nicely and even sleeps through the night sometimes. Janie's doing the proud mother act really well. Dave looks like he's shell-shocked but he's okay, he'll survive."

"That's good to hear. I'm happy for them.... Listen, I'm sorry to do this to you, but I need an autopsy done tomorrow."

"Oh, no. Was it the skiing accident? I heard there'd been one but that's all I heard."

"Yep. Karl Saunders went over Say Goodbye. We've contacted his parents and they're coming into town tomorrow afternoon."

"Oh, that's a real shame. I know his name but I didn't know him to talk to... That's such a pity... Wait, though, wasn't he ski patrol?"

"He was. It's strange he should have had an accident. We have to do the autopsy anyway but I need to rule out foul play. After that, we'll be looking to see if it was suicide or not."

"I'll do it tomorrow morning. Do I need to visit the scene do you think?"

"No, there's no point. That's a real mess, believe me. We got called in late and the resort's rescue team got to Saunders first. They'd moved him before my guys arrived. Luckily for us, one of the snowmobilers who found him took a pile of photos."

"I don't understand the rescue team, they know better than to do that," said Dr Denver.

"You would think, but no. There was some confusion over the call. The snowmobilers couldn't get to him immediately. They thought he was only trapped in the rocks at the bottom of the cliff. They didn't think he had fallen off the cliff. They only notified us of that later. When the rescue party arrived they were told deputies were on the way so they didn't call it in. They thought they'd do everyone a favour and bring the body out because it was so difficult to access the site. A snowmobiler went with them to help."

"I see," said Dr Denver. "So I guess everyone was stomping all over the place."

"Exactly. By the time my guys arrive, that was about an hour later, there's a crowd at the top of the cliff and more snowmobilers at the bottom. Any evidence was totally compromised. It was not worth securing the scene. Deputies searched at the bottom and came up empty. On top of the cliff, my guys tried to get names of skiers and boarders to sort out who had arrived first at the cliff top but most of them started skiing away. The ones that stayed hadn't seen anything."

"Jebb, I'll do the autopsy tonight. You don't want this getting worse than it is already."

"You will? I owe you one, Mary."

"Where is the deceased being kept?"

Chapter 4

Sunday night

*I*t was close to eight when Brent went down to the Aurora hotel's Crystal Room which was, of its four restaurants, the establishment's most formal dining room. It lacked a patio but made up for it with picture windows oriented towards the mountainside. The room was about a quarter full. Brent was now well-dressed in smart, casual clothes.

From his seat and with a menu in hand, Brent looked outside at the brightly lit slopes in the great pool of darkness that surrounded them. Most of the mountain had disappeared into the night except for the roughly rectangular illuminated block that rose up towards the invisible peak. His waiter approached.

"Good evening. Is there anything I can get for you?" The name on his badge was 'Toshiro'.   He seemed to be a pleasant, polite man in his early twenties.

"What are the portions like? I only put in half a day's skiing but I can't believe how hungry it's made me."

Toshiro smiled. "They're pretty good. The salads could be larger. I'll make sure you get plenty, though. Are you ready to order?"

"Yes, I think so. I'll have French onion soup, coq au vin with creamed potato and broccoli, and the salad… I'll try the collards, roasted sweet potato and cashews. That one sounds interesting. Have you tried it?"

"Ah, yes, I have. You'll enjoy it. Would you like something to drink?" asked the waiter.

"Water's fine… Oh, a glass of Chardonnay, please."

Toshiro tapped the order with notes into a point-of-sale device.

"Thank you," he said. He transmitted the order to the kitchen and then went to get the wine.

While he waited, Brent reflected on his day. He found it quite amazing that he was now sitting in what was essentially another world to the one he normally inhabited and was participating and progressing in an activity he had never seriously contemplated before. When the wine seemed to be a long time coming, not that Brent was in any hurry, he looked towards the bar which was next to the kitchen area. He saw Toshiro returning to his table with a glass on a tray.

"Sorry about that," said the young man as he placed the glass of wine within Brent's reach.

Brent looked at him as he did so. Whereas the waiter had been bright and pleasant a few minutes ago, he now looked stressed and anxious.

"So, Toshiro, what exactly is going on? Staff around the resort are looking upset, just like like you are right now. Tell me about it."

"Ah, I'm really sorry…. I'm not permitted to discuss certain things."

"Okay…. Will the patios be busy tomorrow at lunchtime?"

"The patios? Ah, yes, you should be good. They'll be busy but they won't get slammed like they did today."

"Slammed… I haven't heard that term in a while. I used to wash dishes and wait on tables for a living."

"Is that right?" Toshiro glanced at Brent's expensive clothes.

"Which restaurant does the best burgers? I've been wanting one ever since I passed Century Burgers on the way in today."

"They do make good burgers and they're worth stopping for. By the slopes, Snow Leopard does the best burgers and, if you want, you can sit outside. That's in the hotel here. In town there are the usual chains; the nearest is in The Village."

"Excellent, now I'm all set for burgers…. Are you busy at present because I need to find a private ski instructor for tomorrow?"

"Right. That's kind of difficult for me to say at the moment. I have another table to look after and…"

"That's fine. You have to do your work. I get it."

"Thanks for understanding. I'll be back with your soup in a few minutes."

While the waiter was gone, Brent began to evaluate what had happened. Skiing accidents were not unusual although fatalities were, yet even those had to be anticipated to occur sometimes. So why, then, was there such a pervasive, marked reaction among the staff? And why was the management limiting talk on the matter? Brent became determined to find out.

The waiter returned with Brent's French Onion soup.

"Here's your soup, sir."

"Thanks."

"About the lessons. I'm only supposed to promote the resort's instructors when asked. I can refer you to the website if you wish to book lessons for tomorrow. I had a quick look and there are a few slots open at the advanced level."

"I see," said Brent. "Actually, I think I can say with confidence that I have graduated from Hippo level."

"Hippo level…? You mean the beginner's slope?"

"That's right. I only started today and I don't know what I'm supposed to do next. Carving, I think."

Toshiro smiled widely. "Oh, I get it. You can find group lessons to help you, there's plenty available."

"No, I would like private lessons to correct any bad habits I might develop early on. I think I can pick it up quickly if I'm shown how in a one-on-one setting."

"That would be expensive. Are you looking for a day, a week…?"

"I'm here until Friday lunchtime."

"Okay, so five days…Um…?" The waiter went quiet again.

"What's the matter?" asked Brent.

"There's a lot going on and I'm not free to speak at the moment."

"Okay. What time does your shift finish? We could meet afterwards and I can pay you for the inconvenience"

"Ah, thanks, but it's not that. Anyway, I don't close tonight so you and my other table are my last customers… probably about nine."

"Good. I'll get on with my soup and you'll tell me where we can meet when you bring the next course."

Brent enjoyed his dinner. For dessert, he had a slice of superb Black Forest cake. He had arranged to meet Toshiro at a coffee shop in The Village which was open until ten.

The bill included a fifteen percent gratuity added to the price of the dinner. The waiter was glad and surprised to find a hundred dollar bill when he cleaned up Brent's table.

Brent arrived early at the coffee shop in The Village. He bought two teas and settled himself at a table by the window. The place was nearly empty. As he waited, he tried to calculate how many coffees the business had to sell to cover what he guessed the rent would be in the prime location it occupied. He was unable to arrive at a firm number but he reckoned on a thousand coffees a week to break even. That was ten cups an hour every hour the place was open. It all hinged on what was the profit per cup of coffee after all product costs and wages were deducted. Toshiro arrived during these deliberations.

"Thanks for the tip, man. I appreciate it. And yeah, I'm sorry I'm late.   The manager wanted to talk about something and I couldn't get away." He looked anxious again.

"Don't worry about it. So, Toshiro, who died today?"

"You found out?"

"No, I surmised. I have seen various resort staff looking upset. I saw two vehicles from the Sheriff's Office. Now they may have put in a routine appearance for all I know but not when it's coupled with the stress levels I've been witnessing."

"Yeah… well… it's going to come out, anyway. Somebody I know died in an accident today."

"Oh, I'm sorry to hear that…. Did you know this person well?"

"I did…. We hung out together sometimes… a lot, actually. There's a group of us employees who hang out together during the season."

"That must be hard for you…. all of you. How did it happen?"

"This is the crazy thing. He's ski patrol and a really good skier…. Like, he was on the Olympic team at one point but he only made it as far as the next gen development squad….

That was a while ago. Anyway, there's this drop that's called Say Goodbye. It's like a cliff, about a hundred and seventy feet high… No one can jump it and walk away… He fell off it. He didn't try to jump he just fell over the side. That's what I don't get. None of us get it. He was never stupid about skiing. He's got a rep as Mr Safety he was so down on skiing improperly and strict about staying within limits and all that kind of thing. It doesn't make any sense."

"You're having difficulty accepting it, I can see. There'll be an autopsy and the matter will be cleared up. Perhaps he tripped and slid off."

"Like, that's possible, I'm not saying it isn't. But if I had to rank all the people I know as to who would have a dumb accident, Karl would have been at the bottom of the list."

"Does that make you suspicious, then?"

"I don't know what to think…. Look, I can't believe it's happened. I suppose I'm in denial."

"Maybe. My guess is that he was a friend but not a close friend of yours."

"I suppose you could say that."

"So you're upset but your mind is not overwhelmed with emotion. It's bad and you wish it hadn't happened but…. there's something else that's wrong here or am I misreading the situation?"

"I don't know."

"I'll come clean… I have a card here somewhere… Oh, that's right. I left them behind… Wallet!" Brent looked in his wallet and found a single business card but, better than that, he took out his Private Investigator credentials and placed them on the table. "There, that's me. It's a horrible photo. I've never liked it."

"You're a private investigator?" Toshiro processed this new information. "You couldn't have been called in already." He shook his head slightly in disbelief.

"No, of course not. I'm up here for the skiing only but the way you describe this incident with Karl has got me thinking."

"You're thinking of investigating it?"

"No, not really. Unless you tell me something more to get me interested. There's another matter at the back of what you said which has got you so anxious. What's that about?"

"Okay. It's Freedom Sports Investments, the company that owns the resort. They've told everyone it's an accident before the authorities have had a chance to say anything. They're going to make a public statement tomorrow and announce it as an accident, hoping it'll be forgotten by the weekend. They're trying to brush it under the carpet. It's all PR and they don't care about Karl."

"How can they do that? The authorities will have to follow due process," said Brent.

"Small town politics, big national company, and a sheriff who's up for re-election. Nothing can ever look bad for business."

"I really don't know anything about what goes on here but it seems to me you're jumping to a conclusion."

"Yes? Well, we'll all say accident because we've been told to but I'm afraid this won't be looked into properly. Excuse me a moment, I've got to send a text." Toshiro rapidly typed a message.

"If it's not an accident that only leaves suicide, manslaughter, or murder."

"Not suicide," said Toshiro abruptly.

"Ah… Well, tell me about it if you feel like you need to."

"No, I shouldn't even be talking this much. You're on vacation and I could be wrong."

"Are you the only person with a suspicion or do others think the way you do?"

"I might be extreme…. I don't really know yet. We're all processing this at different speeds. What you should know is that Brophy is a company town and we don't all love the Company…. It's very complicated."

"Okay. Let's leave that for a while. What about skiing lessons for a Hippo-class beginner?"

"Sure. There are plenty of people who can teach you how to ski one-on-one. Most of the instructors are kind of tied to the Company. Their hourly rate is eighteen to twenty-five an hour. For a day's private instruction, the Company charges around seven fifty for the day."

"Assuming an eight-hour day," said Brent, "the instructor gets no more than two hundred and the Company makes five-fifty. Is that right?"

"You got it."

"Wow. So, if I offer five hundred then both the instructor and I get a break and the Company still makes money from the hotel, the rents and the lift passes?"

"Exactly. The going rate for someone at your level would be four hundred. Anyone with a level one SIA certification would do." Toshiro looked at his phone again before quickly typing a short message.

"SIA… I can't work out the acronym," said Brent.

"Snowsport Instructors Association. Level ones can teach to intermediate skiing or boarding, though most are better at one or the other. Level two-a is skiing, two-b is boarding. They'll take you up to advanced level. Three-a and three-b and you're in elite territory. There's a bunch of separate credentials for different disciplines up to competition level."

"If you know all about that," said Brent, "have you looked into being an instructor?"

"I have my level one," replied Toshiro.

"Then you could be my instructor."

"I'm not teaching at the moment. I work most days in the equipment repair shop and work a few restaurant shifts to get a full week in."

"Toshiro, every time you reply to something I've asked you I feel I should also be asking another twenty questions to get the full back-story. Still, that's none of my business. You're not available so is there someone you could recommend?"

"I'm available tomorrow. Monday's my day off until the evening when I pick up a restaurant shift but I can't do the rest of the week. I can get someone else for those days. Would you be okay with that?"

"That's fine by me," replied Brent. "What time do we meet and how much is the pay?"

"Four hundred like I said. I have a season pass because I work for the Company so there's no extra cost to you. It's good to start early because the trails are in the best condition in the morning. Eight o'clock outside the hotel? Is that alright with you?"

"That's perfect. It means I'd better be heading back now. I'm so tired I can barely keep my eyes open. I think it must be the exercise and the altitude."

"Yeah, takes a day or two to get acclimatized. People call me Tosh, by the way."

"Pleased to meet you, Tosh. I'm Brent." They shook hands. "I'll see you tomorrow, then." Brent got up to leave.

"Sure thing. And don't forget, it's going to get cold overnight and tomorrow morning."

"Hi, Greg."

"Hey, Brent... Aren't you supposed to be on vacation?" The Homicide Lieutenant was very much enjoying a sprawl across a settee in front of a gas fire with simulated logs.

"I *am* on vacation and it's great. However, something has happened and I'm sorry to be bothering you but I need your advice."

"Sure. What's up?"

"There was a skiing accident here today. There's a chance, maybe a slim one, that it wasn't really an accident. I mean, a very experienced, safety-conscious skier literally fell off a cliff. It's been explained to me that the resort here would prefer an accident to a homicide."

"You gotta get hold of the autopsy report," said Greg. "If there's anything in there then you may have something. If not, I'd drop it."

"I don't know if it's been done yet. I looked up the legislation for this state and the only public record of an autopsy is a summary report without notes, photos, and what-have-you. Even that won't be issued for a week or two - that's my guess, anyway."

"What's the set-up with the county?"

"You mean the Sheriff? He's the Coroner, too, but the actual autopsy is performed by a Medical Examiner. My big difficulty is how to approach the Sheriff. Any ideas?"

"Tread carefully, I think. No one's going to appreciate you swooping in and showing them how it's done. Somehow, you have to get them on side…. Now, if you want, have whoever it is you're sweet-talking to give me a call and I'll explain to them how annoying you are sometimes but at least you kind of know what you're doing."

"Thanks, Greg… Do you like fudge?"

"Can't stand the stuff. Far too sweet for me."

"And I was going to get you some Butter Rum fudge because you're such a nice guy. I'll bring you back one of those moose hats instead so you can wear it around the department."

"You know, that might not be such a bad idea. At least the new trainee I've got might actually listen to what I'm saying to him. I swear to you, Brent, this guy knows the manual forwards and backwards but in everything else he's lost. It's so aggravating. Anyway, enough of my griping. Have the Sheriff or whoever you grab hold of give me a call here or in the department and I'll see what I can do."

"I'll do that. Thanks again, and goodnight."

"Before you go… How's the skiing coming along?"

"I don't know how well I'm doing but I'm really enjoying myself."

"Oh, good. I used to ski up to a few years back…. Maybe when you return we'll go out together."

"That would be so good. We'll definitely go. Does Maggie ski?"

"She won't go. She used to snowboard but she never kept it up. I tried a board, too. Give me skis every time. Though some of the stunts those guys do are pretty amazing."

"I might get to see some of that action. There's a competition being held here at the end of the week."

"I've seen a few of those way back when. I prefer to watch them on the TV now… So, you take care, Brent."

"You, too, Greg. Goodnight."

Chapter 5

Monday Morning

*B*rent was up early and, as he got out of bed, he found he was quite stiff and sore from his previous day's activities. A few stretching exercises seemed to allay the worst of it, though. He was also hungry and so soon went down to a restaurant. Once settled and with a good view of the alpine scene outside, he ordered the largest breakfast he could. This was unusual for him. Today, he began with pancakes swamped in maple syrup and cream not only because he liked them but also because he had read that downhill skiing burned around five hundred calories per hour.

The view of the mountain and the snowy wooded hills that receded into the blue of the distance was lit by the fresh morning light of the low slanting sun just clearing the horizon. The light was startlingly brilliant. It picked out and sharpened distant details as the long shadows created by features in the terrain and trees began to recede before the rising sun.

At eight, when skiers were starting to head to the chairlifts, Brent exited the hotel via its ski path in the company of several others. Had Tosh not waved, Brent would have skied past, looking for him.

"Hey, Brent."

"Hi, I didn't recognize you," said Brent, skiing up to him less certainly than he had been skiing the previous day. "How did you know it was me?"

They both looked vastly different from the night before. Brent was wearing a black helmet and gloves, goggles with a large bronze coloured lens because it was sunny, and a black neck-warmer. He looked quite strikingly distinguished in his burgundy over dark grey jacket with a hood, black ski pants, and dark grey ski boots with subtle orange flashes. Black and grey skis completed his ensemble.

"Ah… I kinda knew you would be looking sharp."

"Thanks, but I think it's my wobbling that gave me away. Honestly, I was better last night than I am this morning."

"Did you choose your skis and bindings?" asked Tosh, sounding slightly surprised.

"No. I went to a local store in Newhampton and a guy named Quincy picked them out and set everything up for me."

"I know Quincy. He's put together a sweet package for you."

"Has he? That's good to hear. How do you know him?"

"Quincy's worked here before. He always comes up to ski at least a couple of times a season and we hang out together."

"Small world. I suppose that's to be expected."

"Are you ready to ski, Brent?"

"I am. What do we do first?"

"We'll go over to an easy slope and get a nice spot to ourselves. I'll assess where you're at and we'll take it from there."

They began to ski away.

"Good. The sooner we get moving the better. It's cold out here. I saw the temperature was only 6°."

"That's for Brophy. It will be -2° up top right now. Though it'll warm up once the sun gets on it properly."

"I take it you use the word warm as a relative term only?"

"Yeah. You'll get use to it." Tosh smiled.

Brent was wondering if he would get used to it. Although comfortable while they had been standing talking, he had noticed the bubble of warmth from the hotel being stripped away until only the layer of fabric on the outside of his jacket tenuously kept the frigid air out. As they began to move, Brent began to forget about the cold. Skiing away, they headed towards the green slope Brent had first tried on his own the previous evening.

"I saw the report of Karl's accident on the news," said Brent. "There were very few specifics given. They simply said it was under investigation."

"What does that even mean…? It means a deputy is filling in paperwork somewhere until he gets the coroner's report. Then it'll get recorded as an accident."

"I get the strong impression that you, and people you know, have concluded it was not an accident."

"Yeah, there's a lot of chat going around," answered Tosh.

"Hm… And what is the basis for your conclusion? As you explained it last night?"

"Pretty much. It's, like, impossible for him to have gone over the cliff by accident."

"Not impossible… not really, but so unlikely as to seem impossible. Was anyone skiing with him at the time? Any witnesses?"

"He wasn't found until three in the afternoon when a couple of snowmobilers caught sight of his red jacket. The snow was pretty deep at the base of the cliff but he had hit a rock. To see him from above where he landed, you'd have to be standing right at the edge. That's why no one saw him until late."

"Late? Then he went out early?"

"Yes. The lifties say he was one of the first people up before eight and just as the public were coming in."

"Do you have the names of these lifties?"

"Why? Are you going to talk to them?"

"Might as well hear what they have to say."

"Okay… I should get your phone number."

Tosh nonchalantly tucked his poles under his arm and took off his gloves. He brought out his phone from an inner pocket as he skated on his skis. Brent gave him his number and Tosh sent Brent a text. Having exchanged numbers, they moved on again.

"Do you live all year round in Brophy?" asked Brent.

"I've lived here for twelve years."

"So you must have moved up here with your family."

"Yeah. My mom and dad run the Paper Crane restaurant in town."

"Do they…? We could go there sometime."

"Have you any idea what it's like growing up in a family that runs a Japanese restaurant? You want to eat anywhere but at home. Like, the food's great and you'd enjoy it but for me…" Tosh went quiet.

"You did it again. It's a definite habit of yours."

"What is?" asked Tosh.

"You'll answer a question but instead of giving an ordinary or superficial answer, you reply in a way that leads to something you don't want to talk about and so you stop abruptly."

"I suppose I do if you're noticing it."

"Putting a few tiny pieces together, I would say that you have some unresolved issues with your family."

"You totally got that right."

As Tosh seemed disinclined to say anything further, Brent did not presume to ask anything more. They arrived at the slope and went up on the carpet lift.

For an hour, Tosh had Brent doing nothing but short turns and stops without the use of ski poles so that Brent could focus on positioning himself correctly, according to the changes and bumps in the skied-over snow's surface. The instructor watched carefully and whenever Brent deviated away from accepted practise he shook his head. At first, Brent saw Tosh shaking his head very frequently.

After every few turns they would stop and meet. Tosh had Brent put his hands out in front of him. Tosh did likewise so that they were palm to palm. Then he would push on Brent's hands to explain and demonstrate the rhythm of the turn and how Brent's feet should be placed, mimicking the sequence in a kind of pedalling motion. He made Brent repeat the sequence of pushing motions describing the turn he needed to make. Slowly, Brent was realizing what he should be doing instead of what he was actually doing.

In the second hour, Brent was put to skiing longer runs with ski poles and to varying the width of his turns. Tosh nodded approval a couple of times. Brent also learned how to steer with his feet, the hockey stop which he loved for the spray of snow it produced, and how to traverse slopes. By the end of the hour they were standing once more at the top of the hill.

"So, Tosh, I've been wondering. Why do you not work full-time as an instructor? You're very good and you have your certification."

Toshiro looked completely at home on skis. Every economical movement he made suggested he put in minimal effort but did just what he needed to do to get around on the snow. He wore a blue jacket and his skis were bright blue and white. The rest of his outfit was black.

"It's a long story…"

"I just knew you would say that," said Brent.

"Okay, okay, but I'll tell you if you want."

"Go right ahead," replied Brent.

"Yeah, why not? My parents, particularly my dad, want me to work in their restaurant with the idea that I take over running it one day. My older brother was supposed to do that but he's now a public accountant. He lives in Newhampton. My older sister - she lives in Fulwell - she's a nurse practitioner and kind of wants to be a doctor one day. She's studying for it. My younger sister can't fry an egg and wants to make a career in music. She's sixteen. I'm twenty-two, big bro Jason is twenty-eight, and Louise is twenty-six."

"I envy you having a big family," said Brent.

"Well, let me finish, and you might see it differently. So Jason was to take over the Paper Crane but then he decided it was accounting for him instead and he bailed. Mom and Dad supported him because, hey, he was going into a profession. So his education got paid for and he got Dad's blessings and he and Mom are proud of him… rightly so. He's doing very well.

Louise was up next but, after a year of everyone assuming she would run the restaurant, she gets career fever, too. Fair enough. Next up is me. Only at the time I was fifteen, that's seven years ago, and I had no idea what I was doing with my life. I only wanted to ski and nothing else. Without discussing anything, Dad is assuming I'm going into the biz. Would I mind? Not really, but then everything changes.

Before all of this, Ghost Hawk is either being planned or getting built, and then, when I was fifteen, it was opened to the public. The whole town wanted the development and the boom times it would bring. Lots of jobs, business opportunities, and money would come rolling in. Dad says I've got to work in the restaurant and eventually take over the business.

To cut a long story short, it didn't happen like that. I did start working in the restaurant more and more like dad wanted but the Paper Crane nearly closed. You'd think it would have done well, but no. Whereas it used to be a go to restaurant, it got totally forgotten because of all the new restaurants now crammed in around the slopes. You know, there are now three Japanese restaurants in town and the one farthest from the slopes loses out - and that's the Paper Crane.

My dad… he's so stubborn; he toughed it out and eventually turned the restaurant around. It does okay now but nothing like it used to."

"Am I seeing a connection here?" asked Brent.

"Oh, yes. Finally, I get my act together and I decide I want to get into digital media development, maybe game development, too. Of course, I decide my future career exactly when the family has zero money for anything other than basic necessities. I'm not complaining, but now that I've made a career choice, I can't do it. I'm the one who has to run the restaurant."

"Can you cook?" asked Brent.

"Oh, yeah. I've been working part-time in the kitchen for ten years and Mom and Dad both taught me pretty much all they know. Of course, I did grunt work most of the time."

"Sorry, I interrupted you."

"That's okay. The big deal for me is I don't want to work in a restaurant that's only just getting by. It's worse than that, though. Planning permission has been given to build another hotel. That's got to be another three restaurants or more right there."

"Okay," said Brent. "So, you don't want to let your parents down, you don't see the restaurant flourishing, you don't want to do the work because you feel like you've paid your dues already, and you want to build an independent career for yourself like your brother and sister have done. The problem is, there's no spare money in the family to support you and, even if there were, you could not ask for help from your parents. Yes, you were completely right in saying it's a long, complicated story. And, I still don't know why you're not working as a ski instructor."

"I'm coming to it but you needed all the background first. My dad and me, we're not talking at the moment because we've had some really bad arguments… Anyway, I'm out on my own now and it's tough scraping by in Brophy because the rents are so expensive. The price of real estate has gone way through the roof and the kicker is, the Company pays little better than minimum wage for most of the jobs."

"Which are the better paying jobs that you could do?"

"Level two instructors and above make okay money. Like I said, I'm only level one. The Company doesn't pay much at that level and a lot of the work's part-time. You don't get paid for the time between the lessons. Wait staff can do well here because of the tips. I could work as a sous-chef but that would just kill my parents if they found out. The best I could do was rental equipment repair and that's steady shifts at an okay rate."

"What happens in the summer?"

"There are projects being developed for the other seasons, too…. There are some beautiful trails around here and a couple of good rivers to kayak. This place is so pretty in summer."

"I can imagine it… although, I meant my question from your perspective."

"Oh… I work landscaping and construction. There's always plenty to do."

"Okay… Now, what would happen if we skied down this slope as fast as we could?"

"You saw the signs that said, Slow Area. You could get your lift pass cancelled for being a danger to others."

"Yes, I read about that. Do you agree with that policy?"

"Sure. It makes sense."

"What about the roped off areas between the different slopes. You think we should take short-cuts through them if we're not hurting anyone?"

"No. They're there for everyone's protection. What are you getting at?"

"Well, Tosh, you just told me a long, complicated story that is interwoven with the development of the resort, the expectations of your family, and your own expectations. It sounds like you have a good work ethic but you haven't caught a break yet. I know you're a good instructor because you pay attention and notice details. You can cook, ski, repair equipment, do gardening, and construction. Presumably you're good with computers and are creative, too. You can do all those things but you consider yourself to be stuck in a rut. You're not but you believe you are. Now there's an additional problem. Your friend just died and you don't or can't believe it to have been an accident. Correct?"

"I don't think it was an accident."

"You just told me that you keep all the rules on the slopes because they're sensible and put in place for people's safety. If you're right that it wasn't an accident, it means there was a skier here yesterday who broke all the rules in the worst possible way. He came into your town, climbed your mountain, and did about the worst thing one person can do to another. Tosh, if it wasn't an accident, it was probably murder. Have you thought about that aspect?"

"Uh, like, not really."

"Well, I have. It means that yesterday, on these slopes, the murderer went up in a chairlift, followed Karl, and shoved him over the edge of the cliff with the deliberate intention of harming or killing him."

Tosh was very quiet as he looked away across Brophy and into the sunlit distance. Brent continued, saying,

"I think, if it *was* a murder, you and I should find out who the murderer is," said Brent.

Tosh turned quickly."How can we do that?"

"I think we could do it. I'd absolutely need your help because I don't know anyone in town or at the resort. I only have a few days… although, I could stay longer if necessary."

"I can't help because I've got all kinds of shifts lined up. Besides, I don't know what to do."

"Okay, how about this. I'll ask you a question, then we'll continue with the lesson, and you'll give me your answer in an hour's time. After that we can work out where we're headed."

"I guess… What's the question?"

"First, if you haven't already, don't tell anyone I'm a private investigator. Okay?"

"I won't tell anyone."

"Second… Hold on a moment… I'm not used to these pockets yet… Here's five hundred in advance for giving me your answer. This is besides what I owe you for the lesson." Tosh hesitated.

"Go on… take it. There are no strings attached."

Tosh took the cash from Brent and thanked him with a slightly embarrassed air.

"Third, the big question. Do you, personally, want to catch the murderer?" Brent waited a moment before continuing. "Now, if you don't mind, I'd like to be skiing a little faster than we've been doing so far. As solid as the lessons have been, I don't think you're pushing me hard enough."

"I can change that all right," said Tosh, breaking into a smile.

Chapter 6

Late Monday morning

*B*rent progressed because Tosh kept him focussed on learning and practising what he had been taught. Without this enforced discipline, Brent, on his own, would have taken to flying down the slopes as fast as he could and thereby learning haphazardly or the hard way. Naturally, such progress as he was making was slow but at least it was sure. This last hour went by quickly. Once in a while, Tosh looked preoccupied.

"Do you want me to answer now?" asked Tosh. They were at the bottom of the slope, standing side by side.

"Yes, sure," replied Brent.

"You gave me time to answer so I could realize something on my own… I might know the murderer. And, I think, you wanted me to think it through. Like, a friend of mine might have killed Karl and I might have to suspect ten friends first before the killer's found… or even if he isn't found."

"That's right. You might lose some friendships over this either way. There's a personal cost to you if you get involved."

"Yeah, I totally get it…. Can I ask you something first?"

"Sure."

"Well, it's about how the investigations are done. I've watched a ton of cop shows and I know it wouldn't be like that. How do you get people to talk? How would *I* get people to talk?"

"Who do you think killed Karl?"

"Like, what! How would I know?"

"From all the people of your acquaintance which name would you pick first?"

"You want me to just say it? I don't know that I want to do that."

"See, you have thought of someone already." Brent turned to face Tosh. "In skiing, you have to overcome a fear of falling. That is absolutely basic otherwise skiing won't be fun and there'll be no progress. In interviewing people, the basic scruple to overcome is that you might come off as offensive or as overstepping a mark… in other words, appearing to be rude. It's not a person's public opinion you're looking to discover - people give those out all the time. It's the unstated knowledge they might have and their deeply held beliefs that you're after. I'm struggling with a fear of falling, you will be struggling with a fear of offending someone, whether it be a friend or a stranger. If you can overcome that, then you will get the information you need. The motivation for you is to achieve justice for Karl and that overrides so many lesser considerations. No murderer should be allowed to get away with it."

"I can see that… You talk like I said I was going to help you."

"Well, of course you are. You wouldn't have asked me how to get people to open up if you were dead set against getting involved."

"Am I that obvious?"

"It's not about being obvious. The skills required are not even that special. You feel like you don't have an aptitude to get information from people but that's because you've never had to. Let me ask you something. The name you're withholding, what is the basis of this suspicion of yours? Jealousy? Money? Long-standing feud?"

"It goes back to a snowboarding competition."

"It does? I didn't even think of that aspect.... Do they hold competitions here?"

"All the time. Next week is for skiers and boarders. This week is a boarders' week with Slaloms, Half-pipe, Slopestyle, Big Air, and Boardercross. We host a real mix - community events up to national qualifying competitions."

"Okay... Was Karl a national team hopeful? I think you said he was."

"Yeah. He was sixteen at the time and was a year into the program when he broke his leg in an accident. He missed a season and it put him back so far that he never caught up."

"Karl Saunders. They said on the news he was twenty-nine. So you were nine at the time and not even living in Brophy. Where are his parents living?"

"They live in Fulwell and have a chalet up here. I guess they'll be coming in this week."

"Yes, I suppose they will. Are either of them Scandinavian or German?"

"His mom's Austrian. She got a silver for Downhill in the world cup. That was in the eighties."

"Ah, then skiing was in his blood."

"Kind of.... He was a boarder first and only took to skiing after the accident. The fixed position of the boots on the snowboard caused problems with his bad leg and he found two skis easier to use."

"Got it. Did he go into skiing competitions later on."

"Oh, yeah. And he was very good but he had lost the competitive edge."

"Do you go in for competitions?"

"Sure, I do. We all do… meaning my friends."

"Okay. I have to get a good picture of Karl in my mind. He's ski patrol, ex-snowboarder, very safety conscious, and a good, solid skier. Did he officiate in competitions or anything like that?"

"No, I don't think he did."

"Then, I guess, a guy who works here now, lives locally, who's primarily a snowboarder, aged about twenty-seven to thirty-five, caused Karl to have an accident. That's the basis of the long-standing feud. Karl would be the one to have the grudge but the other guy doesn't want to be blamed for the incident so he turns it around on Karl and blames him instead."

"How did you work that out? He's thirty-one."

"You gave it away. You said the feud arose because of a snowboarding competition. For Karl, his last involvement was thirteen years ago and you weren't present. I just guessed an age range at the time of fourteen to twenty-two for the guy who did… What did he do?"

"He cut across the course during a racing event. To avoid him, Karl swerved, went out of control and hit a tree… The guy's name is Dustin Packard. He's a liftie."

There was a silence between them.

"You got the name out of me," said Tosh.

"No. You gave it to me freely. I never asked you for his name again."

"That's splitting hairs… You got me talking all around the incident and explaining Karl's background so the barrier to giving up Dustin's name kind of shrank down to nothing."

"That's right. Just get people talking and they'll tell you more than they realize. You can do that. Only, don't hammer away at the same question. Now, if someone's resistant and wants to hang on to some information, they'll provide clues in the way they avoid giving it up."

"I'll never remember all that in the moment."

"You're going to teach me how to carve soon. I'll never remember straight off everything about how to do it no matter how many times you explain it."

"Okay," Tosh smiled, "I get where you're going. You teach it - I learn it."

"Sure, you can. Out of the people you know, who is absolutely the least likely person to have murdered Karl?"

"There's a few. Nasir, Lexi, Lotta…"

"I know Lotta," said Brent, "not very well but I agree with you. She seems like a very nice person. We'll get her story… Or, rather, you will get her story."

"We're going to tell her what we're doing, right?"

"Absolutely not. Now later, we might have to bring her or another person or two into the loop but, for now, it's just you and me working the case and we'll see if Lotta can help us. Nobody else should know anything about it."

"You got a plan then?"

"Yes, but it's not much of a one. I need to talk to the Sheriff and the Coroner… How's that set up here? Is it a Sheriff-Coroner or Sheriff only?"

"I don't really know. Dr. Mary Denver does police work, I know that. Maybe she's the coroner as well. She's our family doctor."

"Fantastic! What a gift. It means if I get no information from her you can try." Tosh did not look so sure about this. "Okay, the Sheriff. What's his name and what kind of person is he… or she?"

"Jebb Bates. He's okay."

"Ah, no, Tosh, no. There are hundreds of thousands of words in the English language and you cannot get away with using only four of them to describe a human being. Age, size, and disposition would be a good place to a start."

"He's about six-four and in his fifties. He's a friendly guy most of the time but he has a short fuse if he thinks anyone's playing him for a fool. A lot of visitors who party hard don't take the hint when he says 'Turn down the music.' Then he *makes* them turn it down."

"So he goes out on patrol?"

"At the weekends, he does."

"How many deputies are there, then?"

"Don't know exactly but I think there must be about thirty of them."

"And still he goes on patrol? He must be quite conscientious… or a micro-manager."

"I know a couple of deputies who only ever say good things about him."

"Then why do I have the impression that he's in the pocket of Freedom Sports?"

"I didn't mean to say he's corrupt or anything. What I meant was, he's like a lot of people here. He thinks what's good for the Company is good for Brophy. Because the election is next year, he'll be wanting Karl's death to be an accident for two reasons. Just a natural bias, I guess."

"I can see that. So, if we go looking for a killer, Sheriff Bates will be unhappy about it."

"Yeah, that's probably right. I don't really know if he would suppress anything but I don't think he'll be rushing to find the murderer, either."

"All right. We're getting somewhere. Can I do some carving now?"

"Okay, we can do that."

"Good. Let's do this, then. You teach me carving for half an hour. Then we'll go get an early lunch because I'm so hungry and I'll be buying. Do you think we can get Lotta to join us?"

"I don't know her schedule. Mostly, she teaches on the beginners' slopes."

"Well, give her a call."

"But I'm not ready."

"You'll pick it up. We're just going to have a chat with her. That's all it is.

Now your pay - the standard rate is twenty-five an hour for surveillance for an eight hour day. You continue to work your regular shifts and I'll pay you the daily rate. You'll be picking up what information you can while you work. Outside of your shifts, you'll introduce me to some of your friends and acquaintances and generally give me directions so I can poke my nose into other people's business. At the end of the week I'll pay a bonus. It will be at least a thousand. You bail and there's no bonus. Tosh, you have to find a way to make it work."

"Like, I don't want to be paid for this. He was my friend."

"I know. You probably think you shouldn't be benefiting by Karl's death. But you're not. You'll be working for me in trying to find the killer... If that's at all possible. The deputies and paramedics get paid. The coroner or medical examiner gets paid. You'll be doing a job as crucial as their work is on this case and you'll be doing that while holding down your regular jobs."

"Putting it like that... okay, then... Brent, I think I can cut out my restaurant shifts if that helps any."

"Yes, it would. Okay, that's settled. While we're skiing, I'll try to work out a cover story for myself that doesn't sound too weird."

Chapter 7

Monday lunchtime

"*H*i, Lotta. I'm Brent Umber," he said, getting up as the ski instructor approached the table inside the Snow Leopard restaurant. He pulled out a chair for her.

"Oh, hi! I didn't connect that you were in my class yesterday when Tosh called about lunch." She sat down. "Hi, Tosh. You okay?"

"Getting through it. How are you doing?"

"About the same. This is awful…" she turned to Brent. "It's such a pity it happened. He was a nice guy. Did you know him?"

"No, I never met him. I only know Tosh up here through the Paper Crane."

"Are you, like, in the restaurant industry?" she asked. Her question sounded pointed.

"Only as a consumer now. I used to wash dishes as a teenager and, fortunately, I moved on from there. Would you like to order? For some reason, I can't stop thinking about food."

"You're burning a lot of calories," said Lotta. "Take a few healthy snacks or energy bars with you. You want high carbs and protein."

"Is that what you do?"

"I always take something to nibble on in case I need it," she replied. "Generally, I load up before I go out. Eating in restaurants all the time is way too expensive despite the discounts we get."

"I do the same," said Tosh. "It's like, if you get a good breakfast in, it sets you up for the whole day."

"I would agree, normally," said Brent. "It didn't work for me this morning. Still, I haven't actually got tired yet. I just feel empty all the time. Ah, here's our server."

"Hi, guys. What can I get for you?" asked the waiter.

They placed their orders and Brent was assured that a 3 Spot Burger combo would be more than enough for him. While Lotta looked out over the patio for a moment, Brent turned to a hesitant Tosh and raised his eyebrows. The young man swallowed before speaking.

"You know, I can't help being suspicious about this whole thing with Karl."

Lotta turned back immediately. "What do you mean?"

"I don't think it was an accident. Do you?"

"Well, that's what they're saying on the news," she said emphatically.

"I was just wondering if you had any ideas about it being something else."

Lotta frowned and appeared to be struggling with this new concept.

"I couldn't help thinking things," she said at last. "I mean Karl... of all people. How could *he* have an accident?"

"I know," said Tosh. "It's unbelievable."

"This is all new to me," said Brent, "so take what I say with a grain of salt. I can't help thinking that pushing a person over a cliff would be an easy way to get rid of someone."

"Oh, no. It can't be that. Who would do such a thing? It couldn't be one of us, could it?"

"It's hard for me to say," replied Brent. "Someone with a grudge, I suppose."

"Oh, yeah… I guess that's possible… But it's horrible to think about something like that."

"I know," said Tosh. "It doesn't bring him back. But no one should get away with murder."

Despite the seriousness of the conversation, Brent felt a slight inward smile rise up as Tosh echoed back the words Brent had said earlier.

"That's true," said Brent. "Here comes the food. I am so looking forward to this."

While they were eating, they talked about several different things unconnected with Karl's death. When they were finishing up, Brent suggested they take their drinks and go to sit outside. After they were settled, Brent began fully to appreciate relaxing outside under a sunny winter sky surrounded by snow.

"I noticed something while you two were talking," said Brent. "You're both local and you make a distinction between locals and non-locals. What do you call visitors between yourselves?"

"Townies," said Tosh, "or tourists."

"Or fudgers," said Lotta who smiled as she spoke.

"Fudgers?" responded Brent, amused.

"Because tourists always hit the fudge stores when they visit," replied Lotta.

"I see… So, am I fudger?"

"No," said Lotta. "You're more of a townie… Oh, yeah, how's the skiing going for you?"

"It's fantastic," said Brent. "I messed around yesterday evening, trying to put all your good work into practise. As for today? You'll have to ask my boss here."

Lotta looked to Tosh for an answer.

"It's early but Brent's teachable and he has quite a passion for skiing as far as I can see."

"That's important," said Lotta. "It all begins to click after a while. You're from Newhampton, right? They have a few ski hills around there. You can get some practise in."

"Yes, I will," said Brent. " I feel like I've found a niche for myself in skiing. Speaking of niches brings to mind the lift operators who were working yesterday. I've an idea to talk to them."

"But that's like sixty people," said Lotta. She began to look at her phone.

"Is it? That would be too many. I was thinking of just the lifts where Karl went up and, say, the lift on either side."

"You're serious about this, aren't you…? Why not wait for the Sheriff to investigate?"

"The Company won't want it to be a murder," said Tosh.

"Yeah, right. I get it. Like, are you two going to do your own investigation?"

"Thinking about it," said Brent. "Tosh explained a lot to me. I think it's worth looking into. If it's an accident, and I hope it is, then we're doing nothing worse than wasting our time."

"How can I help?" asked Lotta. There was an intense look in her eyes.

"Just keep your eyes and ears open."

"I did already. You're a private investigator. I searched your name."

"Ah, very good. My cover's easily blown, I suppose. Let everyone else find out for themselves, will you? What gave me away?"

"Tosh inviting me to lunch. That made me curious but I didn't think anything more about it. Hey, a free lunch is a free lunch. Then, you're asking questions. Like, Brent, everyone is going to know. Like we all say, there are no secrets in Brophy."

"Okay. So here's the deal I offered Tosh. Two hundred a day and you can work your regular shifts. This runs until Friday when you'll receive a bonus of at least a thousand. Bail and you lose the bonus. I need both of you to be my eyes and ears because anyone, as you just demonstrated, can look me up. I want to stay out of the picture as much as possible."

"I'm in," said Lotta. "What do I need to do?"

"Talk naturally to everyone you know. Try to be consistent in what you ask from person to person. You want to understand what they saw and when they saw it. You also need to separate opinion from fact. What we're looking for is someone who doesn't want to engage in conversation or a person who is too dismissive of the notion that Karl might have been murdered. If you're conversing over social media use private messaging."

"This is so cool," said Lotta. "What else?"

"A murderer only ever wants to present himself as a normal person who has a strong alibi. He or she only wants their story to be believed. You're not to challenge anyone's story…. That reminds me. Send me a text as soon as you find something. I need updates to either include or exclude a person as a suspect. If you can, keep some kind of notes on what seems relevant. The three of us will need to have a daily debriefing session - nothing formal - text messages will do."

"Got it," said Lotta. "So, I'm going to keep quiet about you, and I'm totally giving everyone else the third degree without looking like I am. Is that okay?"

"Hm, maybe… be careful not to repeat a question the same way. Think of a different approach and try to rephrase it or, better still, just drop it. If you create any pressure, the person you're talking to might think something's weird and react badly. You know what I mean?"

"Totally."

"Last thing. Safety first. While you're doing your regular work you should be fine. While you're investigating, you could be talking to a murderer so I want both of you to check in frequently to let me know where you are and who you're with."

"That sounds like my dad speaking," said Lotta with a slight smile.

"He obviously cares about you. Now that I know you, I care about both you and Tosh. This is not a game. It's work and it's serious work."

"This is awesome. I gotta go. Thanks for the lunch and the work... and for including me in this."

"Glad to have you on board," said Brent.

"See you," said Tosh.

Lotta left the table. There was a long silence.

"What's up?" asked Brent.

"I don't know.... You hired her on the spot."

"What else could I do? It was unlikely anyway that I could have remained anonymous for very long. Lotta seems talkative. How soon would it have been before she spread the word that a private investigator wants to talk to people about Karl's incident?"

"About ten minutes. But it's not only that... I thought I was doing okay," said Tosh.

"And then I jumped in. You did do okay. You gave her something to think about. So now we have to give her space to do just that and not be looking for an immediate answer from her. If she thinks of a person who might fit she'll let us know. Lotta might want to talk to that person first. I know I would."

"Okay…. Something else crossed my mind. Do you think I could have done it? Or Lotta?"

"I'm pretty sure *you* didn't. I don't know enough about Lotta yet to say one way or another."

"I asked because I realized I don't have an alibi," said Tosh. "I went snowboarding early yesterday morning."

"Do you have a motive?"

"No." Tosh shifted in his seat.

"Then you probably didn't do it."

"Wow. Do you suspect everyone?"

"Of course. Are you friendly with Dustin Packard?"

"Not really. I've know him for years but we've never hung out together much unless it's a big group meet."

"Talk to him today. Before Lotta does, if you can. As he's a liftie and works in a defined area, try not to ski straight up or head towards him as though you're looking for him specifically. Try and meet by accident."

"I see what you mean. Why do you want me to talk to him before Lotta does?"

"Because I trust you. Lotta's a little bit of an extrovert and you're not. She might dominate a conversation to get her point of view across while you would prefer to listen rather than talk. Ask your questions naturally and be patient for the answer… or no answer. Watch out of the corner of your eye to see how Dustin reacts. That's important."

"Okay… I like how you're doing this. It's not one size fits all. I'm comfortable with that."

"I know a private investigator who is the quietest guy you could imagine but he knows how to size up a person and get them talking. They tell him what he wants to know in the end without even realizing they're doing it. He trained me and he's patient. You can do it, too. Just be patient. There's no rush and, in your situation, you can always go back to the person. Can we ski now?"

"Sure... Uh, about lessons for the rest of the week, I've got a couple of names I can give you."

"Good. I think it had better be half days from now on. I need to see the Sheriff and the Coroner to find out what they're up to."

"You could see Dr Denver tonight... I mean, she works in a walk-in clinic on Monday evenings. You could probably just go and see her, couldn't you?"

"I might.... It depends if she's done the autopsy or not.... The state requirement is for an autopsy after an accidental death but we don't know if Dr Denver's performing it or not. I'll try to see her anyway."

"Like, what will you say to her?"

"I have no idea. I had hoped you would come up with something. Excuse me a moment, I have to make a call."

"Hello, Maria, it's Brent - calling as promised."

"Hello, Brent. Are you okay? Are you dressing warmly like I said?"

"Yes, thanks, I'm fine and warm. Are you okay?"

"Me? I'm fine. It's you. I'm not the one who's trying to break his neck."

"I gave you my word I wouldn't do anything risky," said Brent. "At present, I'm just wobbling around on very gentle slopes."

"Good. Keep it that way. If you bust a leg and I have to look after you, don't expect any sympathy from me. Why do you want to go skiing, anyway?"

"For excitement, enjoyment, and the challenge of achieving something I've never done before. And, it is so beautiful up here."

"Ah, it's a waste of time. But it's your time to waste. If you're enjoying yourself, then I can't complain. Just take care, honey, that's all I'm saying."

Brent smiled. "Okay. What have you been up to?"

"Well, Brent, I really don't know what to do. After you painted the spare bedroom, I thought to myself, 'What kind of idiot am I?' You know why I thought that? It's because I've got my favourite lamp in a spare bedroom. So, you know what I did? I put the lamp in my bedroom. But it was no good. It didn't go. So, this is what I thought. I'll make the second bedroom my bedroom. It's about the same size so everything will fit nicely. Only, I got a problem." Maria went quiet after her explanation.

"And the problem is?"

"I can't move the beds and furniture around on my own. Could you help me?"

"As soon as I get back we'll get it done… Do you mean that huge wardrobe?"

"It's not that big. We can manage it."

"That thing's got to weigh a ton."

"Me and Dino got it up the stairs thirty-four years ago. Sure we can move it when it's on the same floor."

"Are you sure? I don't want you getting a strain."

"Listen to you talking to me like I'm an old lady. Don't you worry about my end of the wardrobe - you worry about your end."

"Okay, then… but if I have to look after you because you strained your back, don't expect any sympathy from me."

"Ahh…!" Maria laughed for some seconds before speaking again. "That's so funny."

"I should be going," said Brent. "Is there anything I can bring back for you?"

"Well, if it's so beautiful like you say, then send me a postcard. That's all…. Oh, yes, yes… Do they have fudge there?"

"They do," said Brent, smiling to himself. "What flavours do you like?"

"Chocolate with walnuts... maple's okay... my favourite is butter rum but it has to be real rum in it.... Other than those, you choose something nice and I'll probably like it."

"I'll do that. Oh, yes. I have another bit of news to tell you. I might be working on a murder case here. Although, I don't know it is a murder, yet."

"You're joking... How did you manage to get involved in that?"

Brent explained to Maria the story so far.

Chapter 8

Monday afternoon

"*F*resh powder is the absolute best to ski on," explained Tosh, as they stood, yet again, at the top of a green-rated slope. "It's fast and forgiving. There's no better feeling than putting your own tracks across a completely clean surface. It's magic if it's not too deep."

"And I'm not ready for that?" asked Brent.

"No. Not for a while. You're doing okay, though. You're easy to teach. The next best snow condition is when the snow's like butter. Very slick, very fast - you just glide." Tosh made a corresponding hand movement.

"What's this we're on?"

"We call it Chop; most places call it Crud. It's good, too, and has its own challenges… as you know, right?" Tosh smiled. Brent half-heartedly smiled, remembering a couple of recent falls. "'Though this slope's getting kind of messy now, but it'll be groomed tonight. Tomorrow it'll be nice. Nils will bring you out here. Wednesday to Friday it'll be Marv. He's good. He sounds so laid back like he's almost out of it but he knows what he's doing."

"Okay…. Look, a ski patrol. Do you know them?"

"Yeah. That's Lexi, she's local, and he's a management guy. I don't really know him."

"What's this? Another layer of complexity or is he a supervisor?"

"No, he's a regular patroller. The Company is really down on anyone getting free rides on the mountain. They bring in their own people from other resorts to monitor what the rest of the staff is doing."

"Like a company spy?" Brent looked mildly shocked.

"Not exactly. We all know who they are and most of them are decent. Their extra job is to watch the rest of the staff to make sure no one's running a scam."

"Scam… That has to be lift passes."

"You got it. There's other stuff but that's the biggie. It all stems from about ten years back. Fake tickets, borrowed tickets, lifties looking the other way - you name it and it went on here. The parking lot in the afternoon was a joke. Tourists were openly selling on their day tickets after they'd used them in the morning.

The funniest thing was people walking up the beginner slopes. They'd be on snowshoes and use the higher lifts all day for free because no one ever checked tickets on those areas, then. All that was happening when there were three different clubs operating here.

After the clubs got bought out by Freedom Sports, a lot of the employees working the scams got rehired and kept their old habits. Really soon afterwards, there was a big purge. About thirty people got canned. Even that didn't get all of them.

So everything got cleaned up. Now, tickets are scanned and photo ID checked. All the patrols have scanners to make sure nothing like that ever happens again. Each season, the Company brings in a group of patrollers and supervisors of their own and they report to some dude at head office."

"I see. That's interesting… Do they ever catch anyone now?"

"It rarely happens. Usually, it's like a really dumb scheme and the people working it always get caught."

"What happens then? Are deputies called in?"

"No, hardly ever. It's small stuff anyway. The Company makes them pay full price for a ticket, pulls their passes, and then bans them for the rest of the season."

"I see…. Is there a computer store in town? I have to get a laptop otherwise I'll be forgetting things."

"Oh, yeah. Go to Chop Suey's. I know the owner. You want something basic? A Mac or a PC?"

"A basic PC would do."

"You'll save some bucks if you go refurbished. I can call him if you want."

"Could you? That would be helpful and refurbished would be fine as long as it's not an old clunker."

"Sure."

Tosh took out his phone and made the call.

"Hey, Felix. It's Tosh… Where you been, man? The season's going fast… Yeah, don't give me that… Listen, I got a friend who needs a refurb laptop today. What have you got…? The i5 will do. Pick out a good one… … Hold on, I'll ask."

Tosh turned to Brent. "He has to go somewhere at six-thirty so if you're there before then, he's got a nice one for three hundred cash or three-twenty-five plus tax."

"I'll be there," said Brent.

"Felix…? Yes. Load it with an office suite and put it aside for Brent Umber. And, yeah, throw in a mouse and a bag… Come on, you're tripping over those bags… I'll buy you a beer… Okay, good, it's a deal." He ended the call. "You're all set," he said to Brent.

"Thanks. What was that about a laptop bag?"

"He often gets them for free when he buys in off-lease computers. Felix likes to squeeze a few extra bucks out of a sale but he's cool."

"Sounds like you used to work there."

"I did. Probably will again. Okay, Brent. Let's get down to business. When you're carving, you're rolling your knees and ankles about right although you need to lean over a little further…"

The lesson continued. Tosh set himself so as not to slide and began to demonstrate, once more, how Brent should position himself throughout a whole turn. Then he had Brent do it while he watched. They took to doing actual carved turns and so worked their way down the hill.

"I was thinking," said Brent, when they had come to a stop, "is there anyway I could get to see this Say Goodbye cliff?"

"No. The upper section down to it is way too gnarly for you. From the cliff down to the resort is an easy ride but getting to it? No way."

"Could you go, then? We need photos and video. I'd like to see the exact point Karl went over the edge."

"You mean now? I guess I can do that. I might even catch Dustin on the way over. He usually works the Bear Tracks quad lift. What will you be doing?"

"I'll put in a couple more runs on my own and then see if I can get to talk to a few employees."

"Don't worry about the rental guys or the repair shop. I'll be in there tomorrow and I'll get all I can from them."

"That's good. I'll hunt around and see what I can find. How long do you think you'll be? It's nearly three now."

"An hour at least. I'll check in like you said."

"Okay. I haven't heard from Lotta yet but I suppose she's still giving lessons."

"That's right, she is. I'll meet you down by the sixer."

"The six-person lift? Yes, that'll be fine."

Brent finished his last run down the green slope and skied over to the more populous area in front of the hotels. He did not yet know it but his skill level was improving constantly. He was already looking less like a beginner and more like a skier halfway through his first season - albeit with a few wobbles here and there as he went across icy patches. At least he could stop and turn and was well advanced in attempting carving but he knew he needed to put in a lot more work.

Travelling over the flat surface while looking for a likely candidate to interview, Brent became less conscious of how he was skiing and more oriented to how he would get to where he wanted to go. Innately, his body was handling the mechanics of simple skiing while he glanced at the terrain in front of him and then looked ahead to the milling groups of people. Brent had so far found it nearly impossible to approach a liftie for a quiet talk as they were always busy whenever he saw them. However, he did see a ski patroller standing by herself. He headed towards her.

"Hello. Do you have a moment?" asked Brent who came to a stop which, if it was not particularly elegant, at least it allowed him to stop roughly where he had intended.

"Hi, yes, I do. How can I help you?"

"I think I saw you yesterday. It's about Karl's parents. Do you know if they're coming today or if they've arrived already?"

"I'm sorry, I don't."

"They must be hit really hard by the news. My name's Brent, by the way."

"I'm Vicki. I don't know what to tell you. We're all trying to cope with it."

"I'm sure you are. I really wish there was something I could do to help."

"Were you a friend of Karl's?" asked Vicki.

"Not really…" Brent pulled a slightly funny face. "More like a friend of a friend."

Vicki nodded, accepting his statement.

"Were you there when he was brought back?" asked Brent.

"I was. We were on top of the cliff when the rescue team arrived to get him."

"It's an awful business. It's upsetting for the whole community. Has anyone laid flowers on the cliff?"

"Yes, they have. Someone also put white painted skis there, too."

"Ghost skis… on Ghost Hawk Mountain. That seems quite fitting," said Brent. He paused for a moment. "I'm surprised the deputies didn't rope off the area."

"They still haven't but then they got there late. We were already bringing him out when they arrived."

"How did that happen… them arriving so late?"

"I think they were notified after the rescue team was en route. You see, we had no idea it was a fatality when the snowmobilers first called it in and they didn't have any equipment for rock climbing. We all thought it was some guy at the bottom retrieving a ski or something that had fallen off the cliff and then he'd got stuck or broken a leg climbing over the rocks. We'd no idea he'd gone over because of the position of the… excuse me."

"Sorry. It's upsetting. Did you know Karl well?"

"I knew him but I never worked with him. I'm new here this season and we always seemed to be assigned different parts of the mountain or we were on different shifts."

"Look, thank you so much for sharing all of this. If there's anything I can do to help, my name's Brent Umber and I'm staying at the Aurora. Not that I think I can do very much."

"No, it helps to talk it out. All my co-workers know the story already but I still feel like I have to talk it out. Like, go over it because it's going over and over in my mind. I just feel kind of raw at the moment."

"It'll pass. Take care, Vicki."

"Yeah, you, too."

At four-thirty, with the daylight fading, the first thing to greet Brent upon entering Chop Suey's - the computer shop - was the loud, old-fashioned bell on the old-fashioned door. The store was warm with cozy lighting. A man in the back responded immediately by calling out in a high-pitched voice,

"I'll be out in a minute."

The second and third things that came to Brent's attention simultaneously were the extraordinary amount of extravagantly patterned, hand-woven, woollen pieces in piles on tables and hanging on walls, accompanied by the overpowering smell of patchouli. Last to be noticed by him were the computers and monitors on other tables with their accessories on shelves and in racks. He crossed the old, pale wooden floorboards to try and make sense of a large square piece in bright red with an attractive black geometric pattern. It proved to be a well-woven poncho. The price on the ticket was twelve hundred, which amount raised Brent's eyebrows. His eyes travelled across adjacent piles and he realized the inventory was the output of several different weavers because of the variety of distinctive styles and colour choices.

While waiting, Brent checked his phone. He had received text messages from Tosh and Lotta. Both of them had been talking to people but neither had anything newsworthy. Tosh had added that talking to people about Karl Saunders was easier than he had expected it to be. Tosh also sent some photos and clips of Say Goodbye. They weren't ideal but they gave Brent a pretty good idea of the place. Tosh had been unable to see Dustin Packard.

"Are you Brent Umber?" The possessor of the voice appeared suddenly, wearing a woollen chullo hat in a vivid brown and cream pattern and with its strings hanging loose. He was about forty, wore glasses, and had not shaved for several days.

Brent turned and said, "I am. Are you Felix?"

"Yep. Be with you in a sec." He bobbed out the back again.

A few minutes later he returned carrying a laptop and set it down on the counter for Brent to look at.

"There you are." Felix spoke with some degree of pride. "All loaded and ready to go. Take a look."

"Thanks, I will," replied Brent. He took a few minutes in the quiet of the store to look over the installed programs and check the processor and the amount of RAM installed. Felix pottered about behind the counter, tidying things.

"Looks good," Brent said at last. He handed cash to Felix who counted it. "Do you have two businesses operating from here?"

"We sell all the textiles at the weekend market. They're left here during the week to save everyone the trouble of hauling them all over the place. Also, we sell online."

"I saw a few hefty price tags."

"Many wealthy people come into town at the weekends and they want to take home a unique souvenir. Price doesn't seem to matter to some of them. Though I got to tell you this - the stall rents are high and a lot of work goes into those pieces." Felix scratched his head through his woollen hat.

"The amount of work, I can appreciate. Why are the rents high?"

"The Company runs it… Here's the bag for your laptop." Felix placed a bag, mouse, and charger on the counter and began neatly to pack away the various cables. "Yeah, you have to qualify as one of their select vendors to get in. As soon as they slap a title on you like that, you know it's going to cost a lot and it does."

"Why not start up an independent market?"

"There used to be a beautiful market here with very reasonable prices. You could get all kinds of deals. It's too far away from the hotels… the main ones. Now it looks really sorry. Those that could went to where the sales were at, which meant the original market died because of a lack of quality and selection."

"That's a shame. How do you feel about it?"

"Me? I don't know. What can you do? Become a capitalist or stay out of the system. I'll tell you one thing, though. That move took all the fun out of doing the market because the stakes are that much higher. It's become a rat race where you have to sell, sell, sell."

Although Brent could not envisage Felix as a particularly aggressive salesman, he could understand and sympathize with the notion that a little bit of Brophy culture had died because of the Company maximizing its profits.

"What do you think? Will the accident hurt business?"

"It might… Not for long, though. People will forget it soon enough. It's such an unbelievable shame. Karl was such a nice guy. Like, honourable. You know what I mean?"

"I do, although I never met him. I know Tosh liked him. In what way honourable?"

"Like, he would treat everyone equally and with respect. You could just plain trust the dude in anything he did or said."

"He must have been a close friend. I'm so sorry it happened. I guess it's hard to accept and that's why you said it was unbelievable."

"In one way, yes. But I'm having a hard time with it being an accident. When it came to skiing, Karl never made a mistake. He was such a solid skier. And the first time he wipes out or whatever, he dies? That's unreal. I totally don't get it."

"But I heard he had an accident years ago."

"True but totally not his fault... Not his fault at all."

"I see. But if, as you say, he was a good, technical skier and was very unlikely to have had an accident, what *did* happen?"

"Don't know. Don't want to go there."

"Where? You're thinking it was deliberate?"

"Man, I just can't take thinking about that kind of thing."

"No, quite right, too. Must have been a freak accident of some kind. I suppose the Sheriff will get it sorted out eventually."

"Don't know about that. He's a nice guy and all but he's no Sherlock, that's for sure."

"Then what do you think will happen? We know there'll be an investigation, an autopsy, and the findings will be put into reports. Why does that process require exceptional skills?"

"You don't know Brophy. This is a beautiful place but, since the Company came in, nothing moves without its blessing. Whatever is found that might be bad business won't see the light of day. It's as simple as that. The Sheriff would have to really want justice and truth to look past the town's business interests. I just don't know he's got it in him to do that."

"I get it... Tosh made a similar comment."

Brent was about to say something more when angry shouts could be heard in the street outside. Both he and Felix turned towards the source of the commotion but they could not see anything through the store window.

"I wonder what that's about?" said Brent, as he walked towards the door.

Before he got there, a male figure, dressed in dark winter clothing with the hood up, walked quickly past the store window. Brent went outside and looked both ways along the street. A second similarly dressed figure was hurrying away, crossing the street some thirty yards distant, heading in the opposite direction. Brent came back inside.

"What's going on?" asked Felix.

"Who knows? The other guy stomped off as well. Did you recognize the man who walked past the window?"

"Yeah, I did. He's a quiet kid as far as I know."

"Perhaps they were both on their phones and bumped into each other."

"Probably… Anyway, Brent. Is there anything else you need?"

"No, I don't think so at the moment." Brent picked up the laptop and put the strap of the carrying case over his shoulder. "But if I do think of something, you'll be here every day?"

"During the week I'm open from ten till six. Come in whenever you like."

"I might just do that. Take care, Felix, and thanks for the computer."

"Well, thank you for dropping by."

It was now after five and Brent took a chance on being able to see Jebb Bates. He took a taxi to the Sheriff's offices situated on the outskirts of town. From the outside, the long, single-story building of recent construction was reminiscent of a fortress - partly due to its narrow windows and tan-grey stone exterior. By contrast, the large, blue-glass entrance was reasonably spacious. Inside, the foyer was exceptionally clean - marred only by winter mats to stop the snow and de-icing agents being tracked through. A second, locked door required Brent to state his business via an intercom to an unseen person before it would be opened to him. Through the glass door, Brent could see a glassed-in counter but beyond that, he could see nothing. A curt yet indistinct female voice sounded from the device on the wall next to him.

"Good afternoon. Please state your name and business."

"Good afternoon," said Brent to the silver metal grille of the intercom. "My name's Brent Umber. I was hoping I could see Sheriff Bates for a few minutes about Karl Saunders."

There followed a very long pause. Brent guessed it was being decided what to do with him.

The door in front of him clicked loudly and, at the same moment, the disembodied voice spoke again,

"Please step through and take a seat. Someone will see you soon."

"Thank you," said Brent and opened the door. Inside, he found he was the sole occupant of the waiting area.

Brent knew he was not the most patient of people but, at fifteen minutes into his wait, he decided he had been forgotten or hung out to dry for some obscure reason. The glass over the countertop was heavily tinted and the office area beyond had subdued lighting. It gave the impression that the dim figures he could see occasionally moving about were working in cave-like darkness. He got up to walk about because his muscles were stiffening to the point where he could no longer sit comfortably in a chair. Also, he was ravenously hungry again. He wished whoever it was who had been assigned to him would hurry up.

Two other people came in together. There had been an accident and a traffic officer was sought to record details of the accident and take photographs of the damage. The traffic officer appeared in seconds flat and whisked the newcomers away. Brent found that alacrity mildly irritating.

At the twenty-minute mark, a glass panel slid open at the counter. A deputy in uniform with braided fair hair consulted a paper on a clipboard. Brent believed her to be the possessor of the disembodied voice.

"Ah… Mr Umber… what can we do for you today?" After an initial stare, she then only half paid attention to Brent while she wrote something down.

"I'd like to see Sheriff Bates. Is he still here?"

"You don't have an appointment. Why don't you tell me your concerns?" She sounded bored and patronizing.

"Are you the deputy assigned to the case?"

"No… they're out at the moment. How can I help you?" She made her question sound like it was her final offer.

"I think Karl Saunders might have been murdered and I'll speak to no one except Sheriff Bates about it."

Brent finally had her full, engaged attention. She stared at him for some seconds before saying, "He might be busy but I'll see what he says." She closed the glass panel.

It took only three minutes for the woman to return to usher Brent through the security door and metal detector. The woman walked ahead with Brent following her towards the Sheriff's private office.

Jebb Bates' office was an open photograph album. Multiple pictures of immediate family and single photos of more distant relations - the family likeness was quite pronounced among many of the subjects - were ranged across a credenza behind him. Hanging on the wall were approximately ten police-in-uniform portraits and group shots. One was an easily recognizable but youthful Bates in a cadet's uniform. Several shots of him skiing and fishing from a boat were also there. Brent estimated that, at least superficially, Jebb Bates was an open and approachable kind of person. The Sheriff's life and loves were on display for all to see.

The Sheriff was large enough to make his chair seem too small for him. When Brent entered, Bates looked up from what he was reading and fixed his brown-eyed gaze of appraisal on him. He had a faraway look as though he were staring at some distant object. As Brent had discovered with many police officials, Bates' face was impassive and gave the impression that he was thinking, 'I have seen it all and heard it all. Nothing impresses me.'

"Take a seat, Mr Umber." He waited until Brent was settled. "Am I to understand you have some information?"

"I do but it is not in the nature of evidence or testimony. I've come to you because I have heard, and I wholeheartedly agree with it, that there is a strong possibility Karl was pushed off Say Goodbye." Brent took out his private investigator credentials and passed them across to Bates. "That's me. I've spoken to a few people who knew Karl well and they can't understand how such an accomplished skier could make such a simple error. From my perspective, I would rather it were an accident - as I'm sure you would, too. I've been wondering if you've received the autopsy report back yet and if it hinted at anything?"

"Who are you representing?" asked the Sheriff.

"If anyone, I suppose it would be the people of Brophy. Honestly, it is only me interfering when I should be skiing. But this accident bothers me - I can't really say why."

"I understand how disturbing it might be but I want to reassure you that everything is under control. We're conducting a thorough investigation and only when it is completed will we be able to determine what happened. At present, it looks like an accident to me."

"So the autopsy's been done and I can take it there were no signs of violence. And, I guess, there was no evidence of drugs or alcohol being involved. But Sheriff Bates, a simple shove in the small of the back could send someone flying and there would be no trace of it."

"Well, that's true. But we don't have any evidence so there's nothing much for us to do. I'd hate it as much as the next guy if Saunders had been murdered and we couldn't prove it. But we have no indication of that so far. We can't proceed on guesswork."

"I can and I have. I work by making guesses and looking for motivation. I hate to blow my own trumpet, but I've produced results in four recent murder investigations."

Bates was quiet for some moments and was clearly assessing both Brent and his statements.

"That may be so but we don't have a murder investigation."

"Then, if I poked around looking for motivation based upon my hunches and gave you my findings in a week or so, you'd be fine with that?"

"Hmm... You put me in a difficult situation. Your licence is not valid for this state because you didn't arrive here while working on an existing case. Now, as a private citizen, you still have a lot of latitude. I can't stop you from conducting inquiries but, if you do step out of line, I will arrest you. Having said that, and by your coming to see me, I get the impression you may have good intentions. If I thought Saunders was murdered, I'd throw everything I could at finding the murderer but we just don't have anything to go on and I don't think you'll find much, either."

"Thank you for clarifying the situation and for your time," said Brent. "I am going to look into the matter and, as I said, whatever I discover I will share with you. Goodbye."

"Goodbye, Mr Umber."

Once outside the Sheriff's office, Brent saw from the map on his phone that it was only a moderate walk to Dr Denver's clinic and, in between, he could stop at a restaurant, have something to eat, and be able to type up his notes.

Chapter 9

Monday evening

*T*he clinic was a space shared by several Doctors and it was Dr. Mary Denver's turn to stay late and see patients until seven-thirty when the clinic would shut. Brent arrived at seven-fifteen. The receptionist seemed faintly displeased by Brent's presence as he was not a patient and she could imagine no valid reason for his being there. She had alerted Dr. Denver that a man was in the waiting room asking to speak to her privately but that he would not say what it was about. After five minutes or so, a door which led into an inner sanctum opened.

"Ah, Mr Umber, is it?" A woman wearing a white lab coat and with short, iron-grey hair walked purposefully towards him

"Hello, Dr Denver," said Brent, getting up. "Thank you for seeing me. I know you're busy so I'll be brief. These are my credentials." Brent handed his PI licence to her which she carefully scrutinized and which gave her pause for thought. "It is about the accident," he added. "I've been to see Sheriff Bates and I'm not here for information as such. I'm here to discuss something with you and get your opinion. That's all it is."

"I see... We had better go to my office, then."

Brent thought she did not look enthusiastic about his request.

Dr Denver's office had several attractive plants which caught Brent's attention.

"Your plants look very nice. I bought one of those a few weeks back. They're supposed to be easy to keep."

"Which one?"

"The zamioculus zamifolia."

"Oh, yes. It almost takes care of itself. I mist once a day between waterings because the central heating drops the humidity right down this time of year."

"That's good to know. Your plant is doing very well."

"Please, take a seat."

"Thanks… I'll come to the point. I have worked on several murder cases in the past. I came here yesterday for a week of skiing. Since being here, I've spoken to several people in Brophy and they are of the opinion that Karl Saunders was very unlikely to have had the type of accident he apparently has had. This has made me think a great deal about the event and the assumptions surrounding it.

You obviously know the details of the accident and to a greater depth than I do. I assume that the autopsy has not revealed any signs of foul play or drugs or alcohol." Dr Denver gave no sign that she would speak about her report. "As that is so, it seems it must be ruled to be an accident."

"Naturally it would," said Dr Denver.

"Yes. Call it a quirk in my nature but if I look at the matter assuming that a murder had been committed, then I should be able to see some interesting points that bear out my theory."

"And what did you find?"

"The first interesting point is that Karl Saunders had just started his shift. He went up in the lift and should have started his regular patrolling route of the main slopes. Why, then, right at the start of his shift, was he way out on a remote and difficult slope all alone while he's supposed to be working? Did he go there for a challenging run and then a little bit of solitude? I've been told he was a straight-up guy so why was he goofing off at the very beginning of his shift? Having gone down that far slope, skiing past the Say Goodbye cliff, he would have had to go all the way back over to the lifts before he could start his regular patrolling duties.

The second interesting point is that this cliff seems like the perfect place to commit a murder. It's difficult to get to and it's off the beaten track. I haven't been there but I understand it cannot be overlooked - cannot be seen from any other vantage point. With the cliff area being quiet and remote, and with the murder taking place at an early hour, the murderer can distance himself from the crime scene with very little chance of being observed.

Third point. If the murder was planned, the actual method used leaves no trace. An autopsy can be performed and no evidence of violence will be seen. Pushing someone leaves no marks.

Fourth point. The place where the body landed effectively concealed it from view for some considerable amount of time. Eventually, as the day wore on, enough skiers and boarders would arrive at the top of the cliffs that all evidence - all tracks and traces, would be obliterated. Within an hour or two, the crime scene is compromised and can yield no usable evidence.

You see Dr Denver, a murderer could have thought of all those points. Yet there would have been two, I would say, relatively slight risk factors for the perpetrator. The first and greatest would be that another skier or boarder actually sees the murderer leaving the top of the cliffs and recognizes him or can identify him again because of some distinctive clothing. The second risk is that if indeed Karl and the murderer are the first to run down that particular slope, two sets of tracks lead to the cliffs but only one set leads away.

Let us say that a third person comes down the slope. They cannot fail to miss the tracks indicating there are two people ahead of him somewhere. Say the third person bypasses the cliff altogether. Time-wise, he will have gained on the murderer and is now following a single set of tracks. He might even see the murderer ahead of him and pursue, as a skiing exercise, to catch up with the guy in front. If he did catch up and actually knew the murderer, he might stop that person and say, 'Hey, what happened to the other dude? He didn't go over Say Goodbye, did he?' That is my theory and it amounts to a near-perfect murder scenario - if it happened at all."

"That is fascinating," said Dr Denver. "I could visualize all of it as you were speaking… I think you got a little too fanciful at the end there but the rest is so plausible."

"I know I embellished at the end but that's because I wanted to round it off completely."

"What did Sheriff Bates say when you explained your theory?"

"Unfortunately, we didn't get that far. I'm afraid he sees me as an interloper and I can't say I blame him. Even I would resent me poking my nose in. And I know it is just a theory and he needs evidence and eye-witnesses."

"Then why did you tell it to me? I can't see what I can do."

"I know you have your office to uphold and a limited report will be published eventually, but I was just wondering if there was any small detail, anything at all, that might tend to support a murder hypothesis?"

Dr Denver sat back in her chair. She picked up a pen and began to play with it while she deliberated. She said at last,

"I can't recall any of the type of thing you're looking for but I'll tell you what I shall do - and please bear in mind that I have not received all the lab tests back. I'll review the photographs and the lab tests I do have and see if anything unusual presents itself."

"Thank you. I could not ask for more than that. That's perfect. Shall I give you my number?"

"Please do." Mary Denver leaned forward and began to write on a notepad.

Brent was skiing the green slope again under the big lights. His thoughts ranged across numerous subjects, only one of which was whether he should attempt a blue slope tonight or whether he should wait for an instructor to tell him to advance to a blue slope. It would be Nils tomorrow. Tosh had arranged separate meetings with both Nils and Marv tonight but at different venues. Nils he would be meeting around eight at Georgiou's Restaurant - a hangout for Brophy locals - and then afterwards he insisted they should meet Marv at a place simply referred to as 'the House'.

Then he began to think of the types of motivation that could result in murder. Greed, envy, jealousy, pride, fear - which of those delightful goodies has left a man at the bottom of a cliff? From the top of the slope, Brent stared into the inky, featureless night above the lights of Brophy. The light pollution from the stark white of the lights fringing the slopes banished the stars from view. Brent looked directly above himself in the hope of seeing a star. There were none because what the lights did actually pick out faintly was low cloud. Almost at the same moment as he was looking up it began to snow. At first it was a wind-blown shower of hard crystals, like miniature hail, which soon changed to an incessant descent of fine flakes that glinted in the artificial light. It was as if the flour-like snow was being sifted out through a shaken sieve.

The forecast had said it would be sunny all week. He checked his phone again. The daily symbols for sunshine - five in a row - that had been present as recently as yesterday had all been exchanged for symbols of snow - a lot of snow with the threat of a storm. How could they get it so wrong? Brent realized that the temperature had also risen. He noticed he was feeling warmer, almost too warm, even while standing still. He opened up his jacket a little and set off down the slope. He instantly discovered that skiing at night in a heavy snowfall was amazing.

Around eight, Brent was entering Georgiou's with the certain feeling he would soon fall asleep if the restaurant was warm inside. It was warm inside and had a distinctly homey feel with wooden beams overhead, tan walls and wooden wainscotting. When the place had last been decorated could only be guessed at. The chairs and tables were worn and had the patina of regular use and regular cleaning. Tosh was sitting at a table with three men - two about his own age, early twenties, and another closer to Brent's age. When Tosh saw Brent, he smiled and waved him over.

"Hi, guys," said Brent as he pulled out an empty chair. "This is a cozy place. It makes a nice change to the resort… It's so relaxed."

"Yeah, we're here all the time. We call it our parlour. I'm Guy, by the way."

"Nice to meet you, Guy. I'm Brent Umber."

"I should do the introductions," said Tosh. "This is John, and that's Nils, your instructor for tomorrow." They all nodded as they were introduced to one another.

"I guess you can all ski or board," said Brent. "I'll have to try my hardest tomorrow or Nils will be back here with stories of, 'You know that guy we met yesterday? You won't believe how bad he is."

There were a few smiles. "Hey, we all grew up with it," said Nils," so we got all our mistakes out of the way early. No, it's good on you for trying something new."

"That's kind of you to say. You know, my first time getting off a chair I wiped out and I so wanted to curl up and die."

For some reason, the whole table broke up laughing and looked at Guy who, also laughing, said, "Don't worry, man. It doesn't only happen to newbies. I fell off a lift chair last week and these guys won't let me live it down."

"Yeah, that was so good," said Tosh. "He did it in front of everyone."

"Okay," said Guy, smiling, animated, and speaking to Tosh. "What about the time when you took out two slalom gates in one run."

"Yeah, that was pretty bad," admitted Tosh.

"Hey, Brent," said Nils, "we all have stories like that so don't let it bother you."

"Well, I'm finding this fascinating and very reassuring... Do any of you guys want a beer or something to eat? Ever since I've been in Brophy I can't stop eating."

"We've already eaten, thanks," said Tosh.

"Have the beef schnitzel, it's really good," said John.

"I think I will... and beer all round?" answered Brent.

"Yeah, thanks," said Guy. The others all said thanks, too.

John got up. "You want fries or mash with your schnitzel?" he asked.

"Mash, please. What is it you're all drinking?" Brent looked at the beer bottles on the table.

"It's a local brew. Do you want to try it?" asked John.

"Sure."

John went right through into the kitchen and spoke to someone, giving them Brent's order. Next, he went behind the counter and brought out five bottles from a beer cooler. He had the caps off the bottles quickly and, having returned, he passed them around.

"Thanks, and good skiing," said John. They clinked their bottles together in the middle of the table. Brent could tell they were a very close-knit group of friends.

"Do you work here?" Brent asked John the question.

"Uh, no. I have in the past but not for some years."

"I'm deeply impressed. I suppose it's the owner in the kitchen and he trusts you to look after yourselves."

"She, actually," said Guy. "Louise bought the place from the guy who called it Georgiou's. We all kind of help her out."

"You don't see trust like this from where I'm from, Newhampton," said Brent. "I used to work in restaurants and the owners there didn't trust anyone. This is so different... It's nice to see."

"Louise is cool," said Nils. "I lived in Newhampton for a while."

"Did you? Whereabouts?"

"Kershaw. I went to the technical college there."

"I know the area well. They're adding a big extension to the college."

"Really? Where would they fit that in?"

"They appropriated the land next door. Do you remember the strip mall? All torn down and just a hole in the ground at the moment."

"I don't believe it. You mean the Pizza Palace has gone?"

"I'm afraid so. They used to do really good pizza, too."

"I know. I used to live on it... What a sad day."

"Sometimes progress," said Brent, "isn't all it's cracked up to be."

"You got that right," said John. "It's just like this place. Do you know…? Well, I guess you wouldn't, but this restaurant used to have line-ups outside."

"That's right," said Guy. "It was the same with the Paper Crane."

They chatted for a while and Brent was given, by all at the table, a vivid picture of the town living through the inconvenience of a construction boom period as the new resort was built up and out. Then, when it was over, how many of the businesses that had suffered those inconveniences found their existing customer base deserting them for the brighter, shinier, more conveniently placed facilities in the resort and in the area known as The Village. Chain stores and exclusives brands had trumped home-town businesses. Stated or implied, in almost every instance, were the substantial financial losses the various business owners had incurred when their original trade atrophied and the anticipated trade never materialized for them. The business owners were people - people they knew or were related to.

The conversation was interrupted when Louise came up to the table, carrying a plate of food and cutlery rolled up in a napkin.

"Who's this for," she asked, looking round the table. She was about fifty years old and had a nice face.

John indicated Brent with the top of his beer bottle.

"Oh, I'm so sorry!" she said to Brent. "I had no idea I had a real customer. You guys should have told me."

"Don't worry, he's one of us," said Guy.

"I can see you're new to town so… watch these boys," said Louise as she set the plate in front of Brent. Her comment brought forth smiles and mild jeers. "Would you like some mustard with that?"

"I think I would, Louise. Do you have something that has a little bit of a bite to it?"

"I've got just the thing." She tapped him on the shoulder and then hurried away.

"It smells delicious. Please don't watch me eat or you'll put me off my food…. Are you sure you don't want anything?"

"We could get some cheesy nachos for the table," said Guy, looking at the others.

"Is that okay?" asked John.

"Of course, of course," said Brent. John was out of his seat like a shot. "And John," called Brent after him, "bring some more beers." He turned to Nils, "I have to say, this is a very *good* brew."

The talk at the table turned to Karl Saunders and the mood became sombre. The group had all known him well.

"What I can't understand," said Brent, "is why Karl was way out on his own at the beginning of his patrol shift."

"I was thinking that was weird," said Nils.

"Yeah. What could he have been doing?"said Guy as the idea struck him as significant.

"Maybe he was after someone for an infraction," said John.

"That's a thought," said Brent.

"He must have been chasing someone," said Tosh.

"What do you mean?" Guy asked the question while John and Nils looked on with interest.

"I mean, he was probably doing his job," replied Tosh.

"That's a possibility," said Brent. "Let's say a guy's goofing off around the lift. Karl goes over to talk to him. The guy sees him coming and takes off. Karl goes after him… How far is it from the Bear Tracks lift to the Say Goodbye slope?"

"About half a mile or so," said Nils.

"Okay. So Karl goes after someone and, whatever happened, Karl thinks it's worth the effort to catch up with the guy. Would he do that?"

"Oh, totally he would," said Guy.

"There you go. So it means that Karl is either skiing around for his own amusement or he's doing his job."

"That's it, man," said Nils. "That's what's been bugging me about the whole deal. There *was* someone else out there."

"C'mon," said John. "Like, it's possible, but there's no proof. No one's come forward to say anything."

"Yeah, but a lot of guys wouldn't want the hassle," said Guy. "This one saw him fall and realizes it's all because he did something wrong and made the patroller follow him... Hey, it could even look like he killed Karl and who'd want to go through all the questioning that would follow?"

The table fell silent - the silence lengthened.

"Well, it could have happened that way, I suppose, but I just don't see Karl making a mistake like that, going so out of control. I really think somebody pushed him over," said Nils.

"Who would do that? Someone with a grudge?" asked Guy.

Nils leaned forward to say, "It would have to be... I mean, he was pretty chill even when busting someone. It must have been a long-standing grudge." His face changed as though he were having a spasm. "I knew something bad happened and it wasn't just an accident."

"I don't know," said John. "Like, I get what you're saying but... What do you think, Tosh?"

"I think he was murdered."

"What do you say, Brent?" asked Guy.

"I think it's very likely... How much of a management guy was Karl. Tosh has explained that deal to me."

"He was cool about it," said John. "That whole management surveillance thing is only about scams the staff might be running. A couple of lifties don't like it and that's because they used to work a scam themselves. Other than that, you wouldn't know he was doing anything special. He wasn't like a spy or nothing."

"Not like some of them," said Guy. "Total Nazi's."

"You're only saying that because you got busted," said Nils.

"I know, but Smythe was a real jerk about it. Yeah, pull my pass, I get it, but she didn't have to scream at me in public. Give me one or the other but not both."

"Did Karl ever do something like Smythe did?"

"No," said John, "If he did, we've never heard about it."

"Did he used to come in here?"

"Sometimes... It's only Monday so it's quiet. From mid-week on more of us come and the place is a lot busier."

As he finished speaking, Louise called from behind the counter,

"I gotta close now, boys. How many beers was it?"

In an instant, all four Brophy men began to clear up the table. John picked up some bottles by their necks and walked over towards Louise. Brent followed him. While John and Louise sorted out the tally, Brent watched with a slight smile as Tosh wiped the table down, Nils put the chairs straight, and Guy took away the trash and remaining empties on a tray.

Brent settled the bill. Louise was delighted with the tip and was quite profuse in saying goodnight to her customers.

Outside, the five men stopped to talk in a light snow shower. John and Guy soon said goodnight and went home. Brent firmed up his arrangements with Nils - they were to meet early next morning. When he had left, Brent and Tosh started walking to the House. On Main Street they passed a snow removal crew using heavy equipment to truck away the snow from the tall snowbanks which had built up over the last few days.

Their path took them away from the commercial section and into an area that had been mostly developed within the last ten years. There were some individual chalets with their interesting, angular designs and masses of glass. Here and there were older properties in wood or of the pre-fabricated kind.

"What happened with the weather forecast? It went from sunshine to snow every day."

"Yeah, you can't go by it - unless it says there's a snowstorm… then we definitely get one. For everything else they're only about fifty percent accurate."

"Why would that be?"

"It's the mountain. No matter which way the wind blows, it'll catch the moisture in it. It's like a microclimate and, literally, it can be snowing at the top and nothing at the bottom in Brophy. Sometimes it switches and Brophy gets a dump of snow and there's nothing falling at the top."

"Oh… so no more sunshine this week?"

"We'll get snow everyday - that's good for skiing - but we should get a break in the cloud sometime. Depends when this warm front blows through."

"Warm front… I suppose it does feel warmer than it did."

"Yeah… any warmer and the snow would get sloppy."

"Right, right… What exactly is this House we're going to?"

"It's Marv's hang out… I don't know… it's kind of like the unofficial party house. There's always a few extra people crashing there for the night. Cops bust it all the time… at the weekends, I mean. Music's cranked, people drinking outside, drugs inside… although, it's weird… Marv's a guy who doesn't fit into that vibe at all but he's there all the time, enjoying himself watching the others. He doesn't even live there."

"Who owns the property?"

"Some dude who lives in Fulwell. He has a bunch of rentals up here and likes to cram people in. He has this other deal where if you own a chalet, and you're not using it, he'll completely manage and rent it out for you."

"I suppose he wants the rents and doesn't care too much about what the tenants do... as long as they don't trash the place. I think he would mind about that."

They walked on in silence and the style of the residences changed completely. Fourplex and multiplexes dominated this next section and all were very uniform in appearance. Beyond that area they entered a section of duplexes and single residences. There was a definite vacation property feel to the whole area and that feel, Brent thought, exuded the sense of impermanence.

"I want to thank you for opening up your social circle to me. I really appreciate that."

"Ah, no problem. It's for Karl's sake, anyway. So, what do you think... back there, I mean."

"I keep an open mind about suspecting anybody until the very end. That's what I try to do, anyway. Nothing I saw or heard tonight gave me cause for concern. I thought it was interesting the way Nils had some of his thoughts suddenly coalesce into a definite assumption. Guy seemed to accept the theory of murder quickly. John was hesitant. It's about what I expected. What I was relieved not to hear was one of them trying to shoot down the theory as though it were impossible. If I had heard that I would have become suspicious."

"Yeah, I know. It had me worried. Like, I would trust each of those guys with my life and they were all friends with Karl. But I got nervous... You made it all sound like chit-chat. Can I ask you something? I don't mean to pry or nothing but were you really interested in Brophy and the construction, and all that?"

"Yes, I was. I like hearing stories and opinions. During cases I talk to many people and, although I have an overriding objective that I'm heading towards, I very much enjoy the scenery along the way."

"Okay, that's what it sounded like… Nearly there, it's at the end of this block."

"Anything I should know before going in?"

"There'll be a few posers - just ignore them."

Chapter 10

Monday about ten p.m.

*T*he very large split-level house stood on a corner lot. It could probably sleep ten or twelve upstairs. Tosh did not knock but just opened the door as though it were a public place. The main floor was really one big room with different areas reached by short flights of stairs with the only true demarcated area being the open-plan kitchen. Brent knew instantly that this house never could be someone's home. It was as though the architect and builder, anticipating it would become a haunt for a disparate group of young adults, constructed everything to ensure that it was laid out for a big party. The architect may have had sophisticated après-ski cocktail parties in mind while the current occupants had interpreted the space in a different way. There were a lot of large floor cushions scattered throughout and a lot of people sprawling across them or sitting in mismatched chairs. The interior lights were dimmed but the white streetlights reflecting off the snow made the large glass windows front and back quite bright and illuminating.

The smell of marijuana and cigarette smoke hung in the air. Music played in the background. It seemed to Brent that there were about twenty people present as he closed the door behind him. A few of the occupants gave a cursory glance towards the newcomers. Brent's experience with surveillance had given him the ability to know when he himself was being observed. While Tosh and he took off their jackets and boots to add them to the massive pile that was strewn about near the front door, Brent realized that someone had his or her eyes on them and, it soon seemed, on himself in particular. The scrutiny emanated from a seated group of four near the window at the front. He could not make out anything more from his peripheral vision than that the group was composed of three women and a man. It was one of the women who was staring.

"I can't see Marv," said Tosh as he scanned the room.

"Hey, Toshi, Toshi. Where have you been? I've missed you." The patronizing call came from a big man in his early twenties seated in a low-slung easy chair. A buddy, similarly seated across from him, also turned and smiled slowly.

"Hi, Simon." Tosh sounded formal. The two men said no more to each other.

Brent, by now standing close to Tosh, whispered, "School bully, was he?"

"Oh, yeah," said Tosh just as quietly.

"Simon," called back Brent, authoritatively, "is Marv here? We want to talk to him."

"How should I know?" replied Simon who then looked away.

Brent and Tosh walked further into the House to find Marv.

Tosh was acquainted with many of the people present but no one he asked seemed to know Marv's whereabouts. 'He was here a while ago', was the most promising response.

Brent was studying a notice taped to the fridge door which read, 'You bring your own booze and food. Touch any of my stuff and I will kill you.'

"Tosh?" asked Brent. "If this house is this busy on a Monday, what's it like on a Saturday?"

"If you want to party, this is the place in Brophy. Regular tourists don't get in. It's mostly boarders on a normal week but when the competitions are on, it's a crazy zoo in here. Anything goes."

From behind them came a bright, female voice.

"Hi, Tosh. How're you doing?"

"Oh, hi. I'm good and you?"

Brent turned to find an attractive young woman staring straight at him. He also noticed that Tosh had become awkward in her presence.

"Why don't you introduce me to your friend?" she said, smiling at Brent. It was an easily decodable smile and she had come from the front of the house to deliver it.

"Sure. Brent, this is Gloria."

"It's nice to meet you Gloria," said Brent, "very nice. Gloria is such a beautiful name. Guess why I think that?"

She hesitated, "I don't know."

"It's because it's the name of my three-year-old daughter. Isn't that a coincidence? My wife, Josie, likes it, too, because… it was her grandmother's name. Oh, that reminds me. I must call Josie in a minute. I always check in several times a day. Nothing like family, huh?"

"Yeah, I guess not… Just wanted to say hi." Gloria returned to her friends.

Brent surveyed the occupants of the House. He tried to picture several of them in the role of killer. Some were quietly talking. A group of three teenagers were laughing loudly and, using exaggerated movements, described a snowboarding story. Several individuals drifted from one group to another. One man sat by himself with headphones on. All the time, cell phones were being checked. Brent saw

Gloria see something on her phone, laugh extravagantly, and then show her friends what it was. Simon, Brent thought, appeared the most likely-looking person to commit a murder. Brent had turned to Tosh, who was typing on his phone, to speak to him, when someone approached them.

"Yo, Tosh. You looking for me?" A tall, thin man with damp, spiky, brown hair came into the kitchen, wearing a t-shirt, shorts, and flip-flops, and carrying a pink towel.

"Marv, my man," said Tosh, putting his phone away and smiling. "We just want to firm up the skiing lessons. This is Brent. You're teaching him, remember?"

"Naturally, I remember. Eight a.m., Wednesday, outside the Aurora. Standard deal." Marv flicked the towel gently at Tosh who stopped it with his hand. "How are you doing, Brent?"

"I'm doing very well, thanks. They're saying there might be a storm on Wednesday. What I want to know is if the storm does come, can we still go skiing?"

"Depends on the wind speed," said Marv as he rubbed his hair slowly with the towel. "They won't spin the lifts if it's too, too bad. We'll be okay if it's only snow."

"They'll keep Deer Run open as long as possible," said Tosh, "and restart it first after the storm. We might not get a storm at all."

"Marv, do you live here now?" asked Brent.

"Oh, no. I was upstairs in the bathroom checking out the different shampoos these guys have. One of them was amazing so I used it. Here, check it out." Marv put his head forward for both Tosh and Brent to smell which they tentatively did.

"It reminds me of sandalwood," said Brent.

"Smells like a dead animal. Brent's polite so don't play him."

"Okay, I was going to but I won't do that now." Marv grinned at Brent.

"I don't know how you get away with it," said Tosh. "Those are not even *your* clothes."

"You're right, I borrowed them. I guess I'd better put them back before the owner sees me. He might get upset. Besides, these flip-flops are the wrong size but they were the closest fit I could find. And look at this t-shirt I grabbed - I don't even like this band; they're boring. So, are we all set because I'd like to get back to my shower?"

"Yes, we're all set," said Brent.

"Cool. Eight a.m., Wednesday, and we're totally going to be zen about skiing even if there's lightning." They shook hands.

Marv had not gone six steps from the kitchen when someone shouted, "Hey man, that's my shirt! And my flip-flops!"

"It's so cool to meet a brother because this is my favourite band," replied Marv, plucking the front of the shirt as he spoke to a man about his own height. "Did you see them in Fulwell last year? They completely slayed it."

"Yeah, I saw them - but that's not the point. You should have asked me."

"Sure, I would have done that, but I couldn't find you anywhere. I had to come downstairs in a hurry on very important business - these were the first things that came to hand. I guess these shorts must belong to someone else, I thought they were yours. They're not my favourite colour anyway. You got to remember, everyone says you're a chill dude and you would never, ever mind helping out a guy. Are we cool?"

"Just give them back," the man sounded weary.

"Yessir, I'll do that right now. Uh, what brand of shampoo do you use? Here, check this one out. I'm liking it a lot."

"Okay, the debriefing," said Brent, as he and Tosh walked back to the centre of town. "Lotta sent me a string of text messages. She's not heard anything unusual or seen anyone suspicious. She's gone to bed to get an early start tomorrow. The only thing she did note was that two women she knows were reluctant to talk but that's because, she says, they're both that type of person who only thinks about herself and can't stand any kind of depressing news. I asked her if she could visualize either of them as a likely murderer and she said no.

My observation on Lotta's report is that her comment lacks objectivity. Do I need to follow up on these two women because they avoided the subject? Can I trust Lotta's estimation of them?" Brent took out his phone and scrolled to the text messages Lotta had sent containing the two names. "Do you know these people?"

Tosh took the phone and then laughed. "Well, this first one, Lisa, would not, could not hurt a fly. She jumps at the slightest sound and… just no. But this other one, Roxanne - I don't know her very well and yes, I think Lotta's right about her being selfish, but er, she went after someone with a baseball bat about four years ago. Has a real temper. Once someone gets a bad rep in this town you might say hi to them afterwards but you steer clear of them."

"I can see how that would work. The baseball bat attack - spur of the moment or did she plan it?"

"She and a friend went after another girl so it was definitely planned. They hurt her but it was not like they were trying to kill her. I mean, they *could* have killed or seriously injured her but they didn't."

"Who was the victim and who was the other girl?"

"Trina was the girl who got attacked but her family moved away soon afterwards." Tosh hesitated. "Gloria was the friend."

"Wow, Brophy really is a small town - that's the girl we just met at the House, isn't it…? Tosh, do you like Gloria?"

"I used to… maybe I still do, I don't know. We dated for a while but that ended before she attacked Trina. Trina was very nice and didn't deserve what she got."

"Okay, Roxanne and/or Gloria as murderers. Can you picture that scenario?"

"Not really. No, I don't see it. I mean, what would be their motive to kill Karl? As far as I know they didn't hang out with him, weren't dating him, so I don't see either of them murdering him."

"They are duly stricken from the list. I wish we could find out something definite that indicates a motive."

"I was thinking, maybe we're wrong after all."

"Maybe. At the end of the week we can call it quits and know that at least we tested the hypothesis as best we could."

"Yeah… Brent, why do you do this stuff?"

"I have asked myself that question many times. My answer to myself is that I can't *not* do it. A friend of mine was murdered some years ago. Despite discovering who the killers were I could never get enough evidence for either of them to be convicted. That gnaws at me sometimes. I feel as though there is unfinished business I must attend to. So, in a way, all the other cases I've been involved in are probably just me trying to compensate… I should probably see a psychiatrist."

"Naw, you're okay. Maybe you can tell me about those cases, if we get some time."

"Certainly, I will. For now, let's keep focussed on Karl's case. What did you observe in the house we just visited?"

"I got a good look at everyone there. What hit me first was they all looked so ordinary. They were all just doing their thing."

"Including Marv? Is he really my skiing instructor? He should come with a warning label."

"Yeah, I know. He's such a funny guy. He doesn't seem to care what he says or does or who he says it to. One thing I have to tell you. I have never seen him angry about anything, ever. I can't imagine him ever hurting someone. He doesn't see the point of getting angry, or violent, or harming anyone."

"But he must upset people sometimes. Borrowing that guy's clothes when he doesn't even know him - where does he get the idea that's okay?"

"Because, Brent, if you went back to the House right now and asked him for his own shirt he would take it off and give it to you. I'm talking literally here. He's helped out tons of people. He's a total good guy but you can't believe a word he says most of the time. The crazy thing is he would never rip you off. He might find your dinner in the fridge but he'd leave a note behind saying how delicious it was. If he found your wallet he might take a twenty out and leave an IOU. If you went to him and asked for a hundred he'd give it to you even if it means he can't pay his own rent. He just doesn't see things the same way as anyone else."

"Okay, he's different and unlikely to be a murderer. My skiing lessons look like they'll be interesting… and I hope he finds a shampoo he can live with because I refuse to sniff his hair again. Who else was there?"

"No one stuck out more than anyone else. They all seemed natural. But there is Simon. I hate that guy. Of all the people I know, he's easily the most likely to murder someone. He's vindictive, arrogant, and violent but he's also a coward."

"Then shoving someone over a cliff when no one's looking is right up his street?"

"Oh, yeah… The only problem is, I don't think he and Karl had much to do with each other."

"We'll keep him in mind. What about the guy sitting with him?"

"I haven't seen him before."

"So he's probably a tourist side-kick. Was Simon putting on the show for the tourist or was that scene just between you and him."

"Both, I'd say."

"Right. We'll keep him in mind, then."

"Sure… Who did you notice?"

"The man with the headphones," said Brent. "He was listening to a podcast and had his eyes closed."

"Right. I don't know him, either. He was zoned out the whole time."

"He was, except for one instant. There may have been other instances but the one I noticed occurred when Marv stopped in the middle of the room to speak to the man whose clothes he was wearing. Do you know him, by the way?"

"No, he's a tourist. What did the other guy do?"

"He looked up at Marvin because he was standing so close and then he quickly looked at someone else. Guess who it was?"

"I don't know. It must have been you, Brent."

"Ah, no. It was you he was looking at. Probably did so for three seconds. It might not mean anything but are you sure you don't know him?"

"I've never seen him before; at least - I don't remember him if I did."

"He's definitely interesting. Let's take a look at him."

"You took photographs?"

"Oh, yes. I got several of everyone plus a couple of videos. Here he is." Brent handed his phone to Tosh again.

"How come he didn't notice you taking a photograph? How come I didn't notice when I was standing next to you?"

"I can be very sneaky sometimes. Really, it's just a few simple techniques but they require practise. I'll show you tomorrow."

Brent noticed Tosh scrolling through the photos. He studied several but he studied Gloria's photo the longest.

"Does it hurt still?"

Tosh looked up sharply. "Not exactly. Once in a while, I just wish things had been different... Hey, I didn't know you had a family. And you have a daughter named Gloria?"

"Usually I'm quite truthful but, sorry to disappoint you, what I told her wasn't true. I have no wife or family waiting for my call. I made an assumption and thought Gloria hanging around would interfere with the investigation."

"Yeah, it was kind of brash the way she started to make a play for you."

"Oh, Tosh, I would have agreed with you up until you explained your past with her. Now I think all that might have been a show for your benefit."

"No... No, you're not serious?"

"You know her better than I do and you can always ask her. I'm just a tourist who's going to hit the fudge shop tomorrow. By the way, who does make the best fudge in town?"

Chapter 11

Tuesday morning

*T*here had been another couple of inches of snow overnight. To an inhabitant of Brophy that was only a dusting not worth the mention. At the late wintery dawn, the sun struggled to pass through high cloud cover, managing only to brighten some thinner patches. Still, it was enough light to reveal the body of the young man who lay on the surface of the frozen Chute river. He could not be missed with that large, incongruous patch of red dyeing the snow around him. He lay partway under the bridge, having fallen from it. Deputies closed off the area and barricaded the bridge, stopping all traffic.

Close-knit Brophy was hit hard by the news of the overnight murder. A young man, his name currently withheld, had been stabbed several times before being thrown from the bridge. Later, around noon, the Sheriff made a personal appeal for witnesses to come forward. Those who knew Jebb Bates well thought he looked a lot older today.

The authorities may have decided to withhold the name of the victim but, by an hour after dawn, more than a few people in Brophy knew the identity of the man who slept on the river. It was one of their own. A good, quiet kid, many had said. Surprise as to who it was mingled with their fear and outrage. The news spread not like wildfire but haphazardly, like a lop-sided explosion with fragments ricocheting in unpredictable directions. Those living or working near the bridge knew all that was to be known quite quickly. People wishing to cross the bridge and who were now forced into a detour over two other bridges - each a mile away on either side - also learned the reason for their inconvenience. Further away, blissful ignorance prevailed until the news came by personal contact via phone and internet. Mid-morning, the local radio station heavily tipped the balance and ignorance of the event was melting quickly. By one in the afternoon, most schoolchildren knew what had happened and knew who it was. At the end of the school day, parents and guardians came out in droves, rarely seen outside of special events, to collect their children and hurry them safely home.

This wave of dreadful knowledge came into the Aurora hotel just as Brent was exiting it to meet Nils at eight in the morning. The two men got onto a ski lift just as the lifties around them heard the news. When Brent and Nils got off, they passed a knot of boarders who were on their phones and looking worried. Had Brent looked back, he would have noticed something was wrong.

"So, Brent," said Nils, "just ski across this flat and come back again so I can get an idea of how you're doing."

The instructor watched his student while tiny flakes danced in the air around them. They were at the top of an easy green slope in a level area containing a few small mounds and depressions. Enclosing the area was a ring of pines, encased in snow, with branches sagging, and whose ends were already pinioned in deeply piled drifts. A brown and orange rock wall, thirty-feet high, lay behind them.

Before them was the open view of nearer fields, forest, and hills under snow. Isolated snow showers were falling like pale grey streamers but the far distance was entirely obscured by the white precipitation. In unison, everything said 'winter' - and there was a scent to this winter, not of pines but of winter cold itself. At their feet was the long, long slope that seemed to run straight into the main street of toy-town Brophy further below. It was easy to think that one could pick up a house and place it where one pleased.

Brent pulled his goggles down and set-off. He went down a slight dip and up again, pushed across a mound and then returned back to stop in front of Nils.

"This is what, your third day? You've made good progress. What I'm noticing is you're looking a little tense, like you're focusing too hard and willing yourself not to make an error. Is that how it seems to you?"

"I suppose it does. I think I might be anxious about making a mistake and I definitely hate falling over."

"Yeah, that's common. Practice gets rid of most of that anxiety but, even then, some people unintentionally limit themselves by concentrating too hard on the technical aspects of a turn. What I want you to do is assume you're going to make the turn or control your speed properly. Totally drop the fear of falling. Have as many falls as it takes in the early stages. Brent, I want you to fall over today. Can you do that for me?

"Ah, I suppose I can if I have to."

"Good. We got a nice soft covering of snow here so you won't get hurt and I promise not to laugh. We're going to smash any inhibitions you might still have."

"I think I can see what you're trying to achieve."

"That helps. Totally don't hesitate. Be quick, decisive and overplay it if anything. Put some exaggeration into your body position and make it fluid. Don't be creeping up to a turn… blast through it. That's how many kids and teenagers get on so fast. They're not cautious and they take risks."

"Are you wanting me to act like I'm some kind of phenomenal skier?"

"Putting on an act? That's it, that's what I'd like to see. We'll do a few Snowploughs to get you started and then we'll stop a couple of hundred yards downhill. Okay? Let's go."

They set off. Brent threw himself into it and fell over. One fall was so funny that Nils could not help laughing. Brent laughed, too. He imagined Nils now had a new story to tell at Georgiou's and he did not mind that at all. He thought it would begin, 'Man, you should have seen Brent today. He totally wiped out.'

The further they descended the slope, the higher Nils and Brent built up a form of camaraderie and trust between them. They became equally absorbed in their joint effort of imparting and receiving insight. By the time they arrived at the bottom, and Brent was yet to realize it, he had left much of his cautious skiing behaviour on the slope behind him. But that was to be the end of his skiing for the day. Nil's phone rang and the grim news that had followed them up the hill had also chased them down it - to catch both the happy skiers while they chatted, waiting in line at the quad lift.

After the first shock hit them, producing stunned exclamations and then equally stunned silence, Nils began to cry.

"I used to give him skiing lessons… He was a good kid… I just don't get it…. It's like it's all gone insane… insane."

Brent's phone rang. It was Tosh who began speaking hurriedly, intensely.

"Have you heard the news…? It's just crazy. There's been another murder…I just heard the news. I mean, Brent, it's another murder."

"Nils and I just heard it ourselves. I'm really sorry about this. Did you know him well?"

"Know him? Yeah, like yeah… everyone did. What can we do?"

"You have to take time out and grieve. You're at work, I suppose. Just talk to your friends and colleagues about whatever you need discuss and forget the investigation. Repeat back to me what I just said."

"Like what?"

"What did I just say for you to do?"

"Like drop the investigation… talk and stuff."

"That's it. When you're ready you come back in, then we'll find the murderer together. It could be the same person."

"Oh… oh yeah."

"We've got to stop him before anything else happens."

"Ah, yeah… I see. We gotta find him, Brent."

"Tosh. Stay out of it. This is too dangerous for you. Promise me you're dropping the investigation. Say it."

"I don't know…"

"You cannot solve this case. You must leave it to me and you have to trust me."

"Maybe you're right… Okay, I'll drop it."

"Good. Call me if you need me. I've got a lot of things to do."

"Yeah, sure… I'm really sorry, Brent."

"You have nothing to be sorry about. Make sure you call me later."

Next, Brent called Lotta.

"Hi, Lotta."

"Hi, Brent. How are you doing? I'm teaching at the moment. I haven't spoken to..."

"Sorry to interrupt but the investigation is on hold. Please, do not interview anyone and I mean absolutely anyone. You cannot trust anyone. The financial arrangement remains intact. You'll get paid but you must not do anything to earn it. Have I made myself crystal clear?"

"Yeah... I don't get it but... What's happened?"

"You'll hear some very bad news soon. Sorry to sound ominous but the best thing you can do right now is wait for it to come and just teach those children how to ski while you're waiting. That's all I want you to do."

"It must be bad," said Lotta.

"As bad as it gets, I'm afraid."

"Oh, no... I'll get back to work, then."

"Keep in touch, Lotta, and stay safe."

"Nils," said Brent. "Skiing's over for today. Here's what I owe you and next time I come up we'll get together and that's a promise because I was very much enjoying the lesson."

"No, I can't take your money... I didn't deliver and..."

"You delivered but now I have to go somewhere and so I'm breaking off the lesson. It's my choice not yours. So I owe you for the day and that's it - no arguments. Take it, Nils. I'll be offended if you don't."

"Well, thanks, Brent... but I definitely owe you. It's just I can't..."

"I'll go now," said Brent. "Are you coming or do you want to stay here?"

"I think I'll stay... I don't know what to do."

"Okay. Call me if you want to talk about anything." Brent made ready to ski away.

"Thanks, man, for understanding."

Brent nodded to Nils before setting off. He had a clear mission in front of him now and, as he moved away, the wobble had all but gone from his skiing.

In the hotel, Brent hung his ski things on a hanger so they would dry. It was nine-thirty and he thought first to contact Dr Denver to see if she had found out anything. He was picking up his phone off the bed when a call came. He did not recognize the number.

"Hello."

"Is that Brent Umber? It's Felix."

"Felix... How can I help you?" Brent detected a slight hesitant shake in Felix' voice.

"I got your number from Tosh. It's about the murder of Alex Simpson." Felix paused.

"Okay. Do you know something about it?"

"No, but you might."

"Might I? You'll have to say what it is because I don't think I even met him."

"Yeah, well... He's the guy who went past the store window yesterday. You went outside, right? Yeah, so, I was thinking, you might have seen the murderer - the guy who was doing all the shouting."

"You're referring to the other man walking away? That could very well be... I'll go and see the Sheriff. Do you want to come along, too? We can both give our statements. This is the kind of thing they like to hear as they piece their case together."

"You mean, we have to see them?"

"Yes... Do they make you nervous?"

"Kind of... I'd like to stay away."

"Okay, then, that's fine. I will have to state that you saw Alex and I'm sure a deputy will come round to get a statement from you."

"That's cool. I can do that..."

"It's bad, isn't it? You saw him alive yesterday and now he's gone and he didn't deserve to die."

"That's it... Yeah, that's it right there... I hate violence and to think... It's like two of them, man... In two days! I mean, what's goin' on?"

"The Sheriff's office will find out and that'll be an end to it. My guess is they're connected. Felix, you have to be calm and objective. Think safety for yourself and for those you care about. Do you have any kind of plan?"

"I'm staying home. The slopes aren't safe, the streets aren't safe... I just can't go into the store."

"Do what you need to do but understand that this situation will be dealt with. I have to go. Call again if you think of anything else."

"Sure, I'll do that. Stay safe."

"You, too, Felix."

Brent called the walk-in clinic but discovered Dr Denver was not due to work there today because she was working from her offices in her house. Brent got her address and phone number.

"May I speak to Dr Denver please? It's Brent Umber and tell her it's extremely urgent that I speak to her. Can you do that for me now, please? I'll wait."

"I'm sorry, Dr Denver is with a patient at the moment. She only returns calls in the afternoon."

"Okay, goodbye."

Brent called the reception desk and asked them to get him a cab immediately. He put on his ski jacket, picked up his laptop, and headed out through the door. He stopped at the ATM machine in the reception area and made it dispense thick wads of money.

Chapter 12

Tuesday morning continued

*T*he cab arrived. It was an AWD Ford Explorer - a vehicle well suited to winter road conditions in Brophy. Brent sat in the front after telling the driver he wanted to go to Dr Denver's office.

"Ah, Dan. Do you own this vehicle?"

Dan, a man in his fifties, hesitated and sounded suspicious when he replied, "Why do you want to know?"

"I need a driver and a car today."

"Oh. Well, yes, it's my vehicle. The plates belong to the company."

"How much do you need to book off for the day?"

"Three hundred plus fifty cents a mile. I stop at ten o'clock."

"Here's three hundred. Book off now, please." Brent counted out some cash and put it into the drink holder between the front seats.

"Sure thing." Dan pocketed the bills first before calling his dispatcher.

Brent noticed that curiosity had replaced suspicion on Dan's face.

"My name's Brent, by the way. I can't help thinking about this bad deal. A young man getting murdered in the middle of town - it's horrible."

"It is terrible," said Dan. "I didn't know him... I knew his dad, though. We used to play hockey together way back when."

"He must be devastated."

"I don't know... I guess he would be but he lives in Fulwell now."

"Did Alex live with his mom?"

"Yes, he did... He has two younger sisters and an older brother. Gotta be plenty sad in that house today."

"Yes, it will... Dan, I was wondering, were any cab drivers out last night?"

"You mean did anyone see anything? I haven't heard that they did. I guess it depends when he was murdered... Probably after the bars turned out... 'Though that's weird for a Monday. Now, if it were a Friday or Saturday - that I could understand."

"You think it was a drunken fight that went too far?"

"Gotta be something like that, hasn't it?"

"Maybe you're right. It certainly has the look of a brawl gone wrong."

"All I care about is that they catch the guys soon."

"A gang you think?"

"Don't know about a gang. Not local anyway. Had to be a couple of guys - out of town guys maybe. I don't really know. It'd be a first gang-killing for Brophy. Last murder was fifteen years ago and that was a domestic dispute... You investigating this or something?"

"I'm interested and that's why I need your help."

"I get you but you're not a cop. I can tell that right off."

"Are you good at sizing people up?"

"I wouldn't say that but, you know, I think about the fares sometimes - what they do for a living. With some people it's obvious and many tell you quick enough."

"I suppose you know most of the people in Brophy, so you must be guessing about visitors."

"That's true. There's more scope, you see. You know, it's funny, you'd think I'd know every local person but I don't. Some people never take a cab except, like, once in ten years."

"Did that happen recently?"

"Kind of - it was a young gal starting work at Freedom Sports. Picked her up at the bus terminal a year ago. Never seen her before but, as soon as she gets in the car, she says, "It's good to be back." So I asked if she meant skiing or something. We chatted. Then she tells me she was born in Brophy and mentions her family who is still living here. I didn't know any of 'em and I thought I knew this town. So, there you go."

"Laws of chance probably. There's likely to be others who you see all the time. By chance, they'll get in your cab, rather than another, ten times in a row."

"Oh, yeah, and they'd be the ones who don't like to tip... Excuse me - I'm not complaining... Cab driver talk, that's all."

"I can appreciate that." Brent smiled.

"And here we are. Pretty house, isn't it?" The SUV began to slow.

"Yes, it is. And it's one of the oldest I've seen so far."

"Sure, but we've got more than a few older ones. Behind the museum, there's an 1853 log cabin all fixed up and on display. Tiny thing -   I can't see myself going through a winter in something that size. I don't know how those old-timers survived." Dan parked the car in the double-width driveway.

"They must have been a tough breed," said Brent. "I shouldn't be too long." He opened the door and a little eddy of snowflakes swirled into the car.

"Yep, I'll be here," said Dan.

At Brent's insistence, the receptionist called Dr Denver to say he had arrived. The Doctor immediately came to the reception area carrying a file. Brent could see that she had heard of Alex Simpson's death.

"I'm glad you came. I want to show you something." She gestured towards an office door.

As Brent neared the door he stopped and likewise gestured. Mary Denver entered first.

"There is something of interest I'd like you to see. Shut the door, please. I must confess, I cannot unequivocally state what it is but it's worth discussing." They both sat down and Dr Denver opened the folder. On top of the pile it contained were two photographs she had segregated. "Now, with Alex Simpson's death, that mark on Karl Saunders' neck looks more ominous to me." She passed them to Brent.

"Oh, dear," said Brent. "The photographs of an autopsy always make me squirm." He studied the photographs and it was evident that what he saw affected him.

"Many people have the same reaction. Death was either instantaneous or occurred within a few minutes at most. Look at the back of the neck   just beneath the hair. There's a very faint line, slightly off-centre… It is actually a shallow, indented line and it measures two and a quarter inches. The indentation is more pronounced in the middle because of the curvature of the neck."

"I can just make it out," said Brent, holding the photo at different angles. "What do you think would make that kind of mark?"

"Initially, I thought it was produced by his helmet being knocked back off his head. The helmet might have made the mark but then the helmet's rear edge also has a thick radius and a curve to it. Looking at the indentation again, I'm not so sure it was the helmet. It's possible it was damage acquired during the fall. I would expect that but not in a clean, straight line. There is only minor skin abrasion at the site and, at the time I took that photograph, a slight reddening at the point of impact."

"Are you suggesting that he was struck with something with a straight edge... like a ski or a snowboard?"

"I think that it is possible but I'm hesitant to commit to that at present. It could have been produced by his own skis which became detached when he made contact with several surfaces. We have no record of the body in its final position so it's difficult to tell. I have been given to understand from the deputy's report that one ski lodged in a crevice higher up while the other fell with him but landed some four yards away and was partially buried in snow."

"From where they landed," said Brent, "I don't see how they could have hit his neck."

"Very unlikely but still possible. It wasn't his poles. There are no edges on them consistent with the mark.

Whatever object caused the injury, death occurred so soon afterwards that there was insufficient time for bruising to occur. He was struck, the indentation was produced antemortem, I would say perimortem, because, again, there was insufficient time for the tissue to swell. Postmortem, there has been extravasation of blood into the site and it has become a typical yellowish-brown in appearance.

I have already taken a sample of the site and sent it away for independent analysis. The results should be available in two to three days but I've asked them to expedite the report."

"That's good…. Um, I have to warn you I have a bad habit of extrapolating whole stories from the tiniest of clues. Looking at this mark, I would say that a skier or snowboarder was standing behind Karl as he was looking over the cliff and was standing to his left. The assailant would have had to be right-handed and they would have hit him on the right shoulder. The board or ski then followed through with only sufficient force to mark his neck with the metal edge. I say that because if he had been hit full force on his neck with a straight metal edge, he would definitely have a deep cut there."

"Yes… it could have occurred that way. A direct blow as you describe would have caused more extensive damage on the neck."

"Will the analysis show if any metal fragments remain in the indentation?"

"Probably not. I didn't want to do a Trace Metal Detection Test because the amount of residue, if any, would be so slight it would yield no result. I've sent an accompanying note to the lab to say that I need to know the cause of the indentation so they will definitely be looking for the construction materials from a ski or snowboard."

"That's good. Thank you so much for sharing this with me."

"Well, thank you for making me maintain my objectivity. I could not help but think Karl's death was an accident."

"Yes, if it had to happen at all, I wish it had been."

"What are you saying? Are you linking the two deaths?"

"Absolutely, I am. Only if evidence is produced separating the two incidents will I change my mind… When will you be performing the autopsy on Alex?"

"This morning, I expect, or this afternoon at the latest. The Sheriff's office hasn't finished yet. I've been informed of the decedent's injuries. There are numerous wound sites and he was stabbed multiple times."

"This is so terrible… A lot of people have been hit hard by this news… How do you cope?"

She sighed. "I'm expected to cope and that is what I have to do. But I'm as shocked and saddened as anyone else is in Brophy."

"Was he a patient of yours?"

"No. That would have added to my sadness… What will you do now, Mr Umber?"

"I'm paying Sheriff Bates a visit. I have some information for him. When I see him, would you mind if I quote you freely while including your reservations?"

"No, I don't have a problem with that."

"Then, thank you. You have been accommodating and very helpful. Goodbye."

"Goodbye."

Brent got back in the cab.

"Okay. First, let's go to Chop Suey's and then the Sheriff's office, please."

"Sure. Did Dr Denver help you out at all?"

"She did, thanks. Now, Dan, I know you get to hear a lot of inside news about people. Who, in town, would the police immediately think of suspecting of the murder?"

"Well, yes, I guess they'd be thinking like that. Ah, it's difficult… I'd say there's a few of them… maybe six or seven."

"I have a pen, can I use some paper from your pad?"

"Sure, help yourself. Just leave the top sheet, will you? That's my shopping list."

They arrived and spent some time in the parking lot finishing their discussion of possible names. Dan gave Brent eight names which Brent recorded, adding the salient points of Dan's observations to each of them. Brophy, as every town does, possessed some violent, angry inhabitants who, in Dan's opinion, could or would murder someone if they felt they had to. The consistent theme was that they were all known in the Sheriff's office. With one name, Dan felt, it was only a matter of time; the rest, he said, had it in them. When they had finished, Brent suggested Dan go to do his shopping if he needed to. Dan said he would wait. They did decide to get lunch afterwards.

Brent entered the office. As far as he was concerned the usual suspect list had no real meaning unless the Sheriff's deputies invested it with some. They would probably be working their own list to find a lead or something of interest - if they did not already have a likely suspect in mind.

From the moment he entered until the time he began giving his statement, Brent had the distinct impression from the veiled hostility of the people with whom he interacted that he was regarded as an unwanted nuisance.

Deputy Fraser re-read Brent's statement and then got him to sign it. They were sitting together in an open-plan office. The officer leaned back in his chair.

"This person you saw outside Chop Suey's was five-eleven to six-one, about a hundred and seventy pounds, wearing a dark grey winter jacket with the hood up, black snow pants, and dark winter boots and gloves. You didn't see his face. He was walking quickly, had a noticeable bouncing gait, and you thought he might be avoiding cameras." He paused. "You saw a lot of detail in a few seconds… Why would that be?"

"As I said in my statement, I'm a private investigator, so I'm trained to notice things quickly."

"Yeah, I guess you would… What are you doing up here, Brent?"

"I came on a skiing vacation."

"So why are you getting involved in a local matter?"

The pervasive air of slight resentment that Brent had noticed since the moment he had entered the Sheriff's office, resolved itself into a clear and definite cause. Brent was the interloper, the outsider, poking his nose in where it did not belong.

"Because, yesterday, I might have seen the murderer of Alex Simpson. Before that, I believed it unlikely that Karl Saunders had an accident. Do you believe it was an accident?"

"We're waiting on reports and such. It's useless to get into idle speculation."

"That's what I do all the time - idly speculate. I'm an inquisitive guy and I'd like to assist you if I can. If you don't want my assistance just say so."

"We don't want your assistance."

"Good we've cleared the air. Now, if there is nothing further to be done here, I'd like to see Sheriff Bates, if I may."

"Well, I don't think he wants to see you."

"Oh, yes, he does. I have information about something else and he definitely will want to hear what I have to say. He'll find out anyway but the sooner he finds out the better he'll like it. Deputy Fraser, hours, maybe minutes, matter and you have two murders on your hands. I know that for certain."

"Why don't you tell me and I'll decide."

Brent looked at Fraser and realized the man just loved the power his position gave him. He was a true gatekeeper - solely for the purpose of making himself look good. The actual casework was of lesser importance to him. Fraser seemed to represent the ethos of the Sheriff's office. The attitude might be justified but Brent failed to see what the justification could be. He knew he had to be careful with the man sitting opposite him.

"I'll tell you what I'll do. Let's both go and see him - if he's available. If he's not, and I can appreciate that he has a lot to do today, then I'll just let the information come to him in the normal course of events. I've got nothing against you but you did say you didn't want my help."

Fraser sniffed noisily and took a moment to decide. He picked up the phone on his desk and pressed a button.

"Sheriff, it's Fraser. Brent Umber's with me. Says he has information he wants you to hear... Only wants to speak to you... Okay." Fraser replaced the receiver. "Says he'll give you two minutes and that's it. So let's go."

Brent was ushered into the Sheriff's office. Deputy Fraser stepped in also. Neither man was offered a seat so they remained standing.

"Good morning," said Sheriff Bates. "As you can appreciate, I'm busy today. What have you got?"

"Karl Saunders was murdered. A perimortem injury occurred only moments before his fall. It was likely caused by him being struck by either a snowboard or a ski. The indentation is perfectly straight and it is two and a quarter inches in length. My opinion is that the full force of the blow landed on Karl's right shoulder, or back, and then deflected upwards and clipped his neck with far less force but enough to leave an indented mark. Dr Denver can verify much of what I've told you, although she is waiting on confirming lab reports at present. She knew I was coming to see you."

Sheriff Bates stared hard at Brent. He turned to Fraser and said,

"Thanks, that will be all." The deputy left.

When he had gone, Bates said, "Take a seat." As soon as Brent was seated he resumed, saying, "I'm told you saw a party walking away from Simpson yesterday after an argument. Any guesses what it was about?"

"No. I didn't hear any words - only raised voices. It sounded serious - as though a fight was about to break out. Felix heard it, too. Perhaps he understood some of the shouting."

"I know Felix. A deputy's gone to check on CCTV footage and she'll be talking to him."

"I think it likely the person of interest won't be found on camera. When I saw him crossing the street, he did so at right angles when he could very easily have crossed obliquely. Traffic was very light. Although I didn't check at the time, I got the impression he was avoiding cameras. I went back to look today and found he was, indeed, keeping to the blind spots. But I didn't watch him very long so it's not exactly conclusive. Of course, had I known that Alex would be murdered, I would have followed the man."

"Interesting. I suppose you believe the two incidents are related."

"I think it would be too great a coincidence if they weren't. If they're not connected, then two separate individuals are likely to have had violent altercations in two separate assaults. Brophy, I understand, has been a peaceful place up until now."

"Average, I'd say, but well below average for violent crime. We know who the troublemakers are."

"I see. I suppose that, should your investigation lead to a suspect out of state, the FBI will become involved."

"Can't be helped, if that's what it is... Mr Umber, I don't know what to do about you. Frankly, I'm puzzled by your behaviour. We have a local armchair detective who gives us some colourful theories on local crimes but he's in his seventies and harmless. You, on the other hand, are not harmless. You took it on yourself to talk to Dr Denver. I did warn you and you haven't listened."

"I know, but suppose, just for a moment, that I discover a good quality lead that eventually leads to a conviction. You would want that lead even though I'm an irritating guy from Newhampton."

Sheriff Bates smiled. "This is how I see it. I have a stranger coming to me, telling me he likes to investigate homicides when all I know at that moment is that we've had a fatal accident. This same person happens to witness the tail end of an altercation. Maybe you saw the killer, maybe you didn't. It's interesting but it's not proof. I need hard evidence - what you witnessed is not that.

Now this mark on Saunders' neck. It could have been made by his helmet or it occurred when he fell. I don't know and neither do you."

"Dr Denver ruled out it being caused by his helmet."

"Did she?" He paused. "You see, this is what I don't care for - you getting information ahead of us."

"It's not quite that way but I see your point. All I can say is that this is how I operate. I've done recent work on homicide cases for both the Belton and Newhampton police services. I can provide references if you're interested."

"I'm not looking to hire you."

"And I'm not looking for payment. It's my take on civic duty. I only want to help."

"Well, now you've made me curious. Give me your references."

The Sheriff pushed a pen and memo pad across the desk towards Brent. When Brent had finished writing, he passed the pad and pen back. The Sheriff read the names.

"Darrow, eh?" Sheriff Bates' eyebrows went up. "I attended Blaskett's funeral so I followed the case."

"Yes. I was at the funeral, too, because I was involved in that case. It was a very impressive turn out. Officers flew in from all over."

"That's right. I met a captain from Mexico… He was a very interesting man."

The Sheriff dialled Greg's number.

"Good morning, Lieutenant Darrow. This is Sheriff Jebb Bates of Brophy County. I've been given your name by Brent Umber who is sitting in front of me at this moment. What can you tell me about him?"

Greg spoke for nearly two minutes while the Sheriff listened quietly. His face gave no hint as to what he was hearing.

"In addition to the skiing incident, we had a murder here last night… Yes… I see… Very good. Thanks for filling me in… Goodbye."

Bates put the phone down slowly before commenting.

"He speaks very highly of you. Told me how you helped him out both professionally and personally. He went as far as to say that if he were in my shoes, with one possible and one definite murder, he would let you loose on Brophy because he's convinced you would find something useful very quickly."

Brent nodded but said nothing. He was waiting for the Sheriff to come to his decision.

"I have a lot of work to do," said Bates. "If you find out anything bring it to me and not my deputies. Here's my card. Call me. If any deputy leans on you, I'll tell him or her to back off. However, if you break the law…" Sheriff Bates said no more.

"I understand you completely," said Brent who then got up to leave. "Thank you."

"Don't thank me, thank your friend, Darrow."

Chapter 13

Tuesday afternoon

After lunch, at a diner of Dan's choosing, Brent visited the bridge that had become a crime scene. Dan accompanied him. Dan liked to talk.

The road over the bridge was really an extension of Brophy's main street. On the other side of the Chute river, the road intersected with another that roughly followed the river's course. Straight ahead, the road took a couple of gentle bends before it terminated at the wide pedestrian thoroughfare that ran through The Village. Ghost Hawk loomed large, towering just beyond The Village.

The name of Village was a misnomer. It was a retail site laid out like a village and lavishly garnished with quaintness of recent manufacture. It did look very good and many people enjoyed themselves there in a variety of ways but it was not authentic and did not pretend to be so.

Above the store fronts, restaurants, and cafés were condominiums that largely served as rental properties - disguised as part of The Village but which were really camouflaged apartments, the express purpose of which was to accommodate skiers while on vacation. From the bridge, there was only a partial view into the thoroughfare of The Village.

Each end of the bridge was barricaded. A deputy's SUV was parked in the middle with its red light slowly revolving and warm exhaust rising like smoke in the cold air as the snow came down around it. Yellow tape was stretched out and around a section of the railing on one side of the bridge. It was easy to identify where the murder had occurred. More curious to Brent's mind was the additional tape isolating where the now removed body had fallen. It struck him as odd that the demarcation of a murder scene was on water - albeit frozen water. A deputy and a man in civilian clothes were on the river itself discussing something. They looked so nonchalant, as if they were discussing weather or sports, and paid no attention to the churned, stained snow that lay beside them.

"I'll never look at this river the same way again," said Dan.

Brent, suddenly pulled out of his reverie, was slow to answer.

"Yes… It is such a pretty river in the winter… What is it like in summer?"

"Lovely. The water's green and the banks get overgrown. You have to watch out for the geese, though. They make a lot of mess on paths."

"Geese… Why do they call it Ghost Hawk Ridge?"

"Didn't used to be called that. It was always Goshawk Ridge because a lot of goshawks used to nest here. Still see a few of them but not like we used to. Company came in and wanted to re-brand it. Stupid, I call it. They had a poll on the radio at the time. Most people wanted to keep the old name but it got changed anyway. Money talks, right?"

"It seems so… Dan, could you drop me off at the library? I need some quiet to think for a while. You could go and do your shopping if you like."

"If you want, I can do that. I thought we'd be driving around, though."

"We might still do that. I've got another question for you. Does anyone you know seem to be spending more money than they should?"

"How do you mean? Like tipping large or something? There's always someone like that. They get a new job or an inheritance. You don't mean that, though. You probably mean they ain't working but they still have money to burn. Hm, there's a couple of drug dealers who fit the bill. Is that what you mean?"

"Could be. Do you have their names?"

"I don't want to get anyone in trouble."

"I'm not asking you to snitch, Dan. I'm looking for reasons for Alex Simpson's death. Someone killed him. They did it for a purpose. It might be jealousy over a woman, in which case it's likely to be a single man. Could be an insult caused the fight. The fact that Alex was thrown from the bridge makes me think it was two or more killed him. People say he was a quiet kid; a nice kid… Alex *might* have had a secret life that got him into trouble. If that is so, then the reason to murder him would most likely be over money or because he had knowledge of someone else's criminal activities."

"I never heard anyone say anything against him. I don't believe he was involved in any rackets and I doubt it was drugs… Yeah, I don't think it was that… Why are you investigating this? Not that it's any of my business."

"I was having fun skiing and I got to thinking the murderer should be caught."

"That's a good idea. I'm in… except, nothing dangerous, right?"

"Nothing dangerous or illegal. We can be a real pair of armchair detectives or car seat detectives, if you prefer."

"So, you got a hypothesis or something?"

"Not yet. What do you think of Karl Saunders' accident?"

"That was sad. I kinda knew him but only to say hi."

"Did he and Alex know one another?"

"Probably did... Hold on a second. Are you saying Karl was murdered?"

"I'm convincing myself he was. The Sheriff doesn't think so."

"Huh, so you're guessing whoever killed Karl went on to kill Alex but the Sheriff's not buying it? You must know something I don't because it looks like an accident to me."

"I might be wrong. I don't know about you but I'm getting cold standing around. Let's skip the library and go shopping."

"Sure, it's your call." They began to walk back to the cab. The snow squeaked under their boots as they walked.

"Think we'll get a storm?" asked Brent.

"Oh, yeah but it won't be much of one. Half a foot, you'll see. The snow's nothing; it's the wind you gotta watch. I hate white-outs."

"You drive in blizzards?"

"I have done but when the cops close the roads I *never* go round the barriers. If they're open then it's usually fine. People gotta go places. No, it's sudden squalls that irritate me the most. It's worse on county roads. One minute you've got perfect visibility. The next minute you can't see a thing - not even the side of the road."

"I'd hate to drive in that. I like to see where I'm going. It also reminds me of this situation we have here. What do you do in a white out?"

"Slow right down. Pull off the road, if I can, and wait it out."

"Hm, I'm not sure I can slow down - my time's limited."

They neared the supermarket.

"Where are Freedom Sports' offices located?" asked Brent.

"Depends what you mean. Their admin offices are in the north end but close to the slopes. Looks like a bunch of big chalets squished together. They do have an executive suite in the Aurora. You mean those? Because they also have a lot of storage buildings and different operations centres all over the place."

"We'll take a look at the admin building after the supermarket."

"Sure. Mind if we swing by my place so I can drop off my shopping? We'll pass it on the way there."

"Not at all."

Brent sat in the back of the SUV. He had gone into the store and bought some energy bars and snacks. Dan, on the other hand, was doing the weekly shop and appeared to be enjoying himself while chatting to people. Brent got the keys from Dan and went back to the SUV.

Not having access to his usual document templates to lay out the details of the case, Brent simply recorded current information into several blank documents. He knew he had precious little. What did emerge from his deliberations in the quiet of Dan's SUV was that there were three distinct areas for him to consider. The first was the mountain itself. Ghost Hawk was a self-contained world, a bubble, of skiing and snowboarding. People came to enjoy themselves sliding down the slopes. A community of like-minded people had built up around the sport. For Tosh and his friends, skiing dominated their lives. The recreation itself would not obviously give rise to a motive for murder. But regular competitions were held. Competition can give rise to rivalry, and rivalry to jealousy. Brent made a note to ask around about this aspect of the sport.

The second distinct area was the town of Brophy itself. Considered separately, all the usual causes for violent crime would exist in this town as much as they do anywhere. Brent quickly concluded that the deputies would have that aspect covered off in ways he could not. He had no idea where even to begin.

The third area was the Company. In so many ways it controlled or affected the skiing world and Brophy. Very little happened in the town without Freedom Sports being factored into the equation. Brent stared out of the window while his mind slowly worked its way through several scenarios. He decided the Company would not arrange for two murders to occur. Wild conspiracy theories aside, there was no reason for the Company to employ crude methods to be rid of a conscientious employee on the one hand, and a quiet young man on the other. What possible threat could these two men represent to such a large organization?

If not the company as a whole then an individual within the organization might be responsible. Was the Company doing something illegal that needed to be hushed up? Did an individual feel threatened and want to make sure some secret was not publicized? Again, Brent made notes of questions he needed to ask.

He reviewed the crimes themselves. Saunders was murdered, of that he was certain. Brent began to pick apart his certainty to see what it was founded upon. The primary evidence was Karl's reputation of being a careful, safety-conscious person who would not, almost could not, fall off a cliff. Strongly supporting this notion was Karl being at Say Goodbye when there was no good work-related reason for his being present there - unless he had followed someone to it over a skiing-related matter. Everything else Brent could think of was conjecture - valid only if proven to be true.

The mark on Karl's neck was evidence that something had happened prior to his death. Brent knew it did not conclusively prove murder. Someone may have accidentally hit Karl with a piece of equipment and that was what had caused the fall. The person was reluctant to come forward because they could be implicated in a crime. Having not reported the accident promptly, they would look guiltier still if they came forward now. The person would probably determine never to mention to another living soul that he or she had accidentally caused Karl's death. The mark was at best only a partial piece of evidence and Brent realized he had seized upon it as confirmation. He saw that he wanted Karl's death to be a murder and not an accident. He had lost some of his objectivity. Death having unavoidably occurred, Brent now wanted it to be murder so that he could investigate the case. He saw it was as simple as that. He was annoyed with himself over his loss of perspective and continued his exercise with an assumed objectivity he did not truly feel.

The murder of Karl - if murder it was - was one of opportunity. An easy hit and the man died. But how was it set up or was it a mere chance meeting? Coincidence cannot be dismissed. If it wasn't by chance, then someone managed not only to get Karl to ski to Say Goodbye but also to stand quite close to the edge... They talked... but about what?

They talked and Karl looked at the view and then he was hit from behind... Karl had no sense he was about to be attacked or he would never have turned his back on the other person. I think they must have known one another... This was not an attack by a stranger... Karl would have remained facing the individual if a stranger had committed an infraction of the resort's regulations... Infraction - that or another matter was what was being discussed. If not an infraction that had just happened, there must have been another issue that sent Karl chasing after the unknown person.

Brent considered the murder of Alex Simpson. One or more assailants had stabbed him, dumped his body, and had brazenly done so in the middle of town. *The attack looks desperate… as though it were done at the first opportunity. Were the assailants afraid of Alex… Afraid of what he could do or say?*

I'll say it was drugs. Alex owed money to a dealer? No reason to kill him like that - the reverse is true; they'd never get their money from a dead man. Alex going to the Sheriff with a story that would expose the assailant's business? That would do it. Perhaps there's been a recent event that made Alex feel as though he just had to say something… Oh. Karl's death, of course… Did Alex see Karl's murderer at the scene of the crime? That's a possibility… Getting ahead of myself. Back to drugs. Karl sees a drug deal going down on the mountain. He chases after the vendor whom he knows. An altercation and Karl is killed. Assailant escapes and is seen by Alex. Alex also knows the assailant and says something… they argue in the street. Later that night, Alex is attacked and killed by one, two, three people?

They dump the body quickly and scatter. They believe they can get away with it because no one sees them… There's no traffic… Patrolling deputies… I must ask Dan about that. Wish I had a definite time. Maybe Mary will be kind enough to tell me… Poor woman, having to do two autopsies in her quiet town. That has to be tough.

Two murders - one opportunistic, whether contrived or by chance - the other is a desperate, violent ambush… born out of necessity.

Dan emerged from the supermarket with a cart full of bags. Brent was still getting his thoughts down and was just coming to an end when the hatch of the Explorer opened.

"Is all that shopping for you?" asked Brent.

"No. My wife and I couldn't get through all this even if we tried. I got a couple of different neighbours I get shopping for. Seniors - they can't get out so easily in the winter. Did you see the mangoes?" Dan said a little excitedly. "How can mangoes be on sale in the middle of winter? You like 'em? Here, take a couple for in the hotel later. Not in the car, though, eh?" He smiled.

"Thanks, I will… They do smell good. Makes me think of faraway places."

"Yep. Here's a spare bag to put them in." Dan finished up at the back and got in the driver's seat to start the car.

"Dan, I have a question. On weeknights, how often do deputies patrol the streets if nothing much is happening?"

"Weeknights… let me see… They have a kind of circuit going round the downtown area so, Monday to Wednesday, you'd see a deputy's car somewhere on it about once an hour. When they're not there, they check out the ski lifts and a few other places. I think it's normally two cars on patrol. I see them sometimes talking together in a parking lot. Totally different when the nightclubs are open. It gets very rowdy sometimes and there's a lot more deputies on duty."

"Thanks, that fits in."

"You're thinking the guys who got Alex waited for the deputies to pass by and then killed him?"

"It's possible, isn't it? How else did they hope to get away with killing him on the bridge?"

"Local guys then, for sure… Gotta be. Makes me sick to think about it."

"Me, too."

Chapter 14

The Administrative Offices of Freedom Sports conformed to Dan's brief description of them. The façade was of three super-sized chalet units connected together with a single main entrance, oversized windows, and dark grey, faux-wood, vertical siding. Details of the complicated, steeply pitched roof line could not be seen because a foot of snow covered it. At the edges, large lobes of wind-sculpted snow hung down well below the eaves.

As they drove closer, the side of the building came into view. The chalet-style continued for a quarter of the length before the structure became an ordinary, square, office building with rectangular windows let into a wall of large grey panels. The building had three floors. Dan drove into the parking lot which was quite full with employee vehicles.

"Do you know anyone who works in here?" asked Brent.

"Oh, yes," replied Dan. "My son-in-law and my wife's cousin - she's the safety manager. Then there's the guy who runs our hockey team who's in equipment maintenance; there's a neighbour two doors down from me in accounting, and a few others."

"In other words, half the town."

"Naw." Dan thought the remark funny. "What do you want to know?"

"If there's been any recent sign of trouble in the Company. Rumours, long-faces, tense meetings... things like that."

"No, I've heard nothing and I would have been told soon enough. What I do know is the Company is profitable but only through its hotels and concessions. The slopes only break even and some years they lose money. I had it explained to me and I found it a bit complicated... but I never told you any of this, right?"

"I shan't repeat what you say."

"If the first snows are light or late, then they have to manufacture it and the skiing's not so good. People won't pay top dollar for less than ideal conditions. Then, if there's an early thaw the number of visitors drops right off despite what they do. It costs a lot to manufacture snow and no matter how much they make the shine's come off and they can't get the lost revenue back. That's where it kills them. Plus, there's a lot of staff on the payroll and if, at any point, the Company lays *them* off, the ones from out of town are gone for the rest of the season and it leaves operations short-handed. It's a very expensive proposition, skiing is."

"That all makes sense. I didn't realize to what extent the resort is precariously dependent on the weather. Um, you said there was an executive suite in the Aurora. Any idea who works there?"

"Yeah, the top guy, Sam Welch, he's there along with a bunch of marketing and PR types. All the other managers are here, though don't ask me what they all do because I've *no* idea."

"Okay. The snow's letting up... Let's drive round for a while. Show me some of Brophy's highlights."

"I can do that. There's not a lot to see but it's a nice area."

"So how did Brophy get started?"

"Mining and some farming. There was gold and copper here until it played out. There are operational mines about fifty miles north but they're nickel and stuff and there are nearer towns to them than Brophy. Really, since the nineteen-twenties, it's all been about skiing and vacation properties. We were the first place to get developed by people heading out of Fulwell."

While they drove, Brent added to his notes. The security system for the Admin building was adequate but in need of an upgrade. He had noted two security camera blind spots on each of the two sides he had seen. He could get in if he needed to but he could not think of a valid reason to do so at present. Hampering him, should he decide to "visit" the offices, was the lack of equipment he required. Everything he needed was back in Newhampton.

Brent finished updating his notes and looked out of the window at the snow-bound homes they were passing. The sun shone through a gap in the clouds and the snow became almost too painfully brilliant to look at.

He knew he was only wasting time at present because he could not see a way forward. Nothing Brent had seen or heard so far had leapt out at him as a possible line of approach. He was beginning to wonder if the stories he had made up surrounding the deaths were just that - stories.

"Do you ski, Dan?"

"Yep. Used to be pretty good, too."

"Know anyone working on the mountain to talk to?"

"I do. Quite a few people."

"I thought you might. Know a guy named Dustin Packard? He's a lift operator."

"I know him… He's not my kind of people."

"Oh, what makes you say that?"

"Remember that list of names I gave you? He sorta fits in there but nothing has ever come home to him... Wait a minute. Are you thinking about that accident with Karl?"

"I am. Why don't we go and talk to him?"

"Uh, let me see... We can do that. I've got a pass. We'll have to go back to my house to pick up skis and boots, though."

"Let's go, then. I also need to get my equipment from the hotel."

There were definitely fewer skiers waiting for lifts than there had been the day before. Brent and Dan got in a chair almost immediately. This first lift took them to the top of the popular blue and green slopes. From there, they skied across the short distance to the lift that would take them to the top of the Bear Tracks network of runs and trails.

"Do you think he's at the top or the bottom?" asked Brent.

"He'd be at the top I should think. There's a nice lodge up there and, if it's quiet, you could get some skiing in without management really noticing. It's my favourite section. All the runs are good."

As Dan was speaking, Brent recognized Tosh travelling fast down the slope beside the Bear Tracks quad lift. He had to wave for some seconds before Tosh eventually noticed him. The skier altered his course and shot towards Dan and Brent who had halted. He came to a smooth and gracefully controlled stop in front of them. Brent realized he still had such a lot to learn.

"Hi," said Brent. "I thought you were working today."

"I'm on break and I've got to get back."

"Is that Tosh behind those goggles?"

"Hey, Dan." Tosh flipped his goggles up. "Brent got you out of your cab, did he?" Tosh laughed but the laugh quickly died.

"Yeah, it's good to see you. I wish it were under better circumstances. How are you keeping?"

"Good - except for the last few days. It's gone crazy."

"It has that."

There would have been an awkward silence except Brent broke it. "Dan and I are going up to speak to Dustin. Did you see him around?"

"Yeah, I've just spoken to him."

Brent gave a quick sideways glance at Dan before addressing Tosh again. "Is there any point in *our* speaking to him?"

"I'd say no."

"Are you working for Brent?" asked Dan. He looked from one man to the other.

"It's like this," said Brent when he had turned towards Dan. "Tosh and I are convinced that Karl's death looks suspicious. We decided to work together to find out what we could so that we could settle our minds about the accident."

"Ah, I get you. Then you've been wanting to talk to Dustin all along. I gotta say, you've got me *really* interested now." Dan looked as engaged in the matter as he sounded. He clearly wanted to be included.

"So, Tosh, what did you talk about?" asked Brent.

"Yeah, I went over to him and we chatted about Alex for a bit. He said he couldn't believe it and stuff like that. He sounded genuine to me. Then I said, 'Makes me wonder about Karl. Do you think it was an accident?' He, like, went a bit weird... kinda got a little annoyed. He said, 'Of course it was an accident.' Then he said how he'd seen Karl heading over to the Say Goodbye run and how he was the first person going that way as he was cutting the first tracks. Said he hadn't watched him for long because it was starting to get busy on the quad. I said, 'So nobody could have pushed him over?' He came back with, 'Don't go saying that because it's not true. Karl was alone when I saw him and it was a while before anyone else went to Say Goodbye.'"

"How did he sound," asked Brent, "when he made that last statement?"

"Like, in control, but not liking the conversation. You know when someone wants you to stop talking about something but won't come out and say it. Like that."

"Defensive and sullen?"

"Yeah, that's it. I wound it up then because he started working again. I think he wanted me to go... Like I told you, we've never been buddies or anything."

"Good work, Tosh."

"He's lying, isn't he?" asked Dan.

"That could easily be so," said Brent. "If I could get a look at the witness statements, I could cross-check and follow-up by interviewing, or Tosh interviewing, the other guys who were working with him at the time. That way we might be able to prove the truth of his assertions one way or another."

"Wouldn't he get suspicious if we did that?" asked Tosh.

"Undoubtedly, he would... Perhaps I should go and talk to him and the co-workers."

"Yeah... No. You can't, Brent, you're not ready," said Tosh. "It's all difficult blues and black runs up there... unless you take the quad back down."

"I could do that... I guess I'd feel silly but it wouldn't be the first time. I think I'll ask Deputy Fraser to help me."

"Fraser, oh no." said Dan. "Is that who you saw earlier? I can't stand that guy's attitude. Putting a uniform on went to his head and he used to be a really nice kid."

"There are no secrets in Brophy, I see. I have to try and get him onboard. What kind of things does he like?"

"He likes hunting."

"That won't work for me. Anything else?" asked Brent.

"Let me see… He went to Paris last year," said Dan. "Before he went he didn't want to go because it was his wife's idea - their tenth anniversary, as I recall - but when he came back he was full of it. Says he'd like to go back sometime."

"Now that is something I can use."

"Ah, guys, I've got to get back to work," said Tosh.

"We'll talk later," said Brent. "And well done."

"Take care, Tosh."

Tosh adjusted his goggles and skied away. As soon as he was off the flat, he rocketed down the slope. Brent watched the disappearing figure perform the fastest ski run he had seen so far and wondered if he would ever be able to ski as well as Tosh. He also guessed that Tosh had made the decision not to give in to grief but, instead, to go and question Dustin Packard.

"He's always been a good skier," said Dan who was also watching. "If he would set his mind to it, he could make the national team."

"Perhaps he doesn't want to do that," said Brent.

"Ah, they all want to but there's a big price to pay. You gotta put in a lot of work *and* you need a sponsor or two. So, Brent, are you some kind of detective?"

"I'm a private investigator but, as Sheriff Bates recently pointed out to me, my licence isn't valid in this state."

"Oh. Does it pay well?"

"Yes, if you can get steady work."

Brent observed that his answer did not completely satisfy Dan's curiosity but the cab driver did not press for more information and Brent did not volunteer any. They followed after Tosh down the slope, only Brent did so at a much slower pace.

Brent was told that Deputy Fraser was out of the office and no guess could be made as to when he would return other than it was likely to be 'Late, probably.' Brent now fully appreciated the value of the police records he had been allowed to access in the past. Without a list of names - names he could also pass along to Andy Fowler - Brent had no starting point to work with. All he had was conjecture, unsupported theory. There were no anchor points from which to develop real lines of enquiry. He had known that coming into the investigation but knowing it did not allay the growing sense of frustration he felt. He needed to do something.

"Dan, can I bounce an idea off you?"

"Bounce away."

"Assuming Karl was murdered and the two murders are connected, what would you say would be at stake to induce one or more individuals to kill both men."

"That's obvious - money."

"Right. Money. Okay, then. It is not likely to involve drugs because of Karl's nature and probably that of Alex, too. What illegal operations in Brophy would that leave?"

Dan was quiet while he thought. "Well, you've got me there. I can't think of anything."

"Right, so let's make a third assumption while we're in the mood to assume. We will say that there *is* an ongoing illegal operation, only we don't know what. The next question is, who has a lot of money coming in on a regular basis? Bear in mind, that money is coming from illegal activity."

Dan shook his head slowly then puffed suddenly. "Don't know… Who?"

"Who, indeed? I would say the illegal operation is being run through the Company by some of its employees. Is not the Company the only place in town that has huge sums of money coming in? That being so, somebody might have decided to help themselves to some of that cash flow."

"Okay, that sounds reasonable. You mean, there's a bunch of guys ripping them off."

"Yes. It's possible. Maybe Karl guessed something was going on and got killed for asking the wrong questions. Then somebody saw a chance to get rid of him, or they set up the opportunity, and poor Karl gets pushed over the cliff. Alex can identify the killer, who also knows that he has been identified, and so Alex is killed, too. How's the theory so far?"

"It's okay… You've got no real evidence, though."

"True. Now, let's go a step further. Karl has to have been killed by an active and experienced skier or snowboarder. Alex is killed by one or more vicious thugs. Another assumption, I think we need to look for a good skier who has a vicious streak."

"There's a few… I already gave you their names though not all of them ski."

"Good. Next assumption, and I think this is the last of them. Skiing thug or thugs do not also fit the bill of types suitable to run a large scam inside the Company. Lift passes are out because of the security measures in place and even if there is fraud related to them, it would be frivolous in nature or not worth killing for. That means white-collar criminals are running the scam on the inside and the killers are a part of it. It's unlikely the killers were hired. Murdering Alex on the bridge… local knowledge about patrolling deputies was required for that but, in every other way, it was *not* a professional hit."

"Nah, it doesn't look like it. That all sounds possible… I don't know if it's *true*."

"You see, Dan. I'm faced with doing nothing because I *know* nothing or concocting a story and then testing it out.

Also, I really can't see anything else that comes close to being as likely."

"I completely get that... But, Brent, it's all computerized in the Company. I mean, how would that work?"

"Set up a system to siphon out money."

"I don't know how that works... All right, let's say all of that's happening. It could be anyone in the Company doing it. How would you ever know unless the cops went in?"

"Yes. They would only go in if they were called in... You seem to know something about the Company's finances - what are its sales?"

"That was in the news. It was $139 million last year... But what I don't get is how you tie the thugs to the scam."

"Karl noticed something... probably during work hours on ski patrol. He was also tasked with scanning passes and that kind of thing. On top of that, he had to report to head office... where is head office?"

"I don't know... I recall Freedom Sports is part of some bigger conglomerate... or something."

"I can find out. Karl, and a few others like him, reports to head office about potential employee scams. In other words, he's got oversight in this matter but for him it is limited to skiing and boarding activities and, I suppose, lift activities."

"I get where you're going."

"Yes? Whatever the scam is, it requires a few people outside on the slopes to make it work as well as some few people on the inside. That means it is not defrauding the hotels and concessions but only the skiing operations. It is not a few lift passes but something much larger in scale. Something that will make four, five, six or more individuals commit to murdering two people to keep their activity hidden."

"Wow... I feel like we're getting close," said Dan.

"Do you? I don't because I don't know how to test the theory to see if it's true or not."

"Yeah. You know what? It sounds like a TV show but it makes sense."

"Would it make sense to Fraser if I told him?"

"Ha, not in a million years. However, if you want him to break up a fight or go after someone dangerous, he'll do that without thinking twice because he's fearless."

"A man of action, is he?"

"That's right. He was always that way. He faced off against a grizzly bear to save his little sister when he was twelve. Had nothing but a stick in his hand. You should read the story when you have a moment. It was quite something he did there *and* he never bragged about it."

"Then Deputy Fraser deserves respect for his good qualities... I completely forgot about grizzly bears... are there many in the area?"

"No, but one'll wander across the slopes once in a while when it's quiet during the summer. Now black bears can be pesky. They'll get into backyards or go for the garbage cans. They'll do that for a day or two before moving on. If they're a problem the deputies have to do something about it."

"Oh, I see... I think I'd like to see a bear... from a good distance, though."

"Not now you won't. They're all hibernating. You might see coyotes but I don't think you'll see a wolf. I often see coyotes in town at night... I kinda like seeing them."

"We get coyotes in Newhampton. They follow the creeks and they've kind of acclimatized themselves to city life."

"Is that so? I didn't know that."

"Now, back to the theory. If I'm to get anywhere with it what do I do next?"

"You're asking me? I've got no idea *at all*."

"Neither have I, so please think about it."

Chapter 15

Tuesday afternoon

*T*he cab was parked in a lot near the main lifts and facing an open plaza. Dan was texting someone on his phone while Brent, sitting in the back, found it galling to have to wait on others. He was waiting for Dr Denver to finish the autopsy on Alex Simpson, for Deputy Fraser to return to the office, and for Tosh to finish work so that Brent could question him further before telling him to stay off the case again. What he wanted to do was talk to all three of them in short order. Denver, he was hopeful, would provide information while Fraser was highly unlikely to co-operate.

Dan was quiet. Cab chatter came in quietly and intermittently over the radio. The snow had stopped and the sky was a solid pale grey. Brent leaned his head against the window but found the glass too cold against his skin. He repositioned himself. Nearby, the small plaza, paved with pink stones, had been swept relatively clean despite the snow that had kept falling. Beyond the open area, he could see part of The Village with its restaurants and expensive stores. *Fudge*, he remembered.

Brent assessed the danger there was likely to be for someone investigating the cases. It could be quite high. *Would they murder a third time?* he asked himself. He considered that Tosh and Lotta were probably safe because they had not done very much in the way of questioning, particularly Lotta. It came as a surprise to him when he realized he might also be in danger. *Can't be… I've hardly spoken to anyone. Still, if my occupation of PI is known to them I will look suspicious to these people even if I haven't questioned anyone.*

How would they do it? A big scam… yet to be identified but probably diverting funds into private bank accounts. A lot of money and they're active inside and outside the resort… Wonder if Dustin's involved? If he is, Tosh could be on their radar because he was with me at the House and on the slopes… How many of them are there? How good are they?

Brent took out his phone, adjusted the camera settings and suppressed the flash.

"Dan, I've been told the best fudge is to be found right here at a gift shop in The Village. Is that true?"

"Ah, I guess… Martha Graham, a nice woman, supplies the store here and a couple of others, I think. Her stuff is supposed to be good. I never eat it myself. Now if we're talking doughnuts and cookies, then I'm your man."

"Okay, but it's fudge I'm really after. I promised to get some for a friend. What cookies?"

"Ah, chocolate chip or anything with walnuts or pecans."

"I'm going for a walk. As I walk away, could you just watch carefully to see if anyone's following me, please? Sit in a natural position. Also watch out for my return. I'll be twenty minutes. I want to see if I can pick up a tail."

"You're kidding, right?"

"No. I need your phone for two seconds." Dan gave him his phone. Brent changed some camera settings on it before handing it back. "Hold it so the lens is just above the dashboard with a clear view through the windshield, like this. Take a shot every two to three seconds without stopping to look at the results. Try a trial shot now to see if it's all set properly."

"What's going on?"

"I want to see if anyone's following me. If they are, don't make eye contact with them but keep taking photos. Remember, no eye contact. Repeat back to me what it is you're to do."

Dan remembered his instructions perfectly and he took a good sample shot of the area. Brent put his gloves in his pocket and got out of the SUV to begin slowly walking towards The Village carrying his own phone.

Freshly scattered ice-melting granules crunched under foot as he walked. The maintenance crews had been waging war against the persistent snowfall and, although there were thick traces of snow and ice in the crevices between the interlocking stones, the tops were bare and glistening. There were definitely fewer people about than there had been the last couple of days. It came to mind that two recent deaths had to be bad for the resort's business. However, the stores had customers in them and there was still quite a number of people out walking.

As soon as he got into the main thoroughfare, the smell of popcorn wafted in the cold air. A restaurant on the opposite side had unoccupied patio tables with the snow cleared off them. Brent walked over to look at the menu. While he studied the board, he crossed his arms and took surreptitious photos without looking at any particular subjects. He went inside for a moment and stopped a passing waiter to find out what time they closed. He got his answer and left slowly but immediately - looking like a tourist ambling about.

He window-shopped his way past the stores. For a moment, Brent stepped away from a store front to ask a woman who was crossing the thoroughfare if she knew where he could find the fudge shop. The helpful lady explained and, with much gesticulation, pointed further along the row of stores. Brent smiled and thanked her, turning as he did so. No one seemed to be following him but there was a young woman staring in his general direction. She was outside the restaurant with no winter coat on.

Brent bought fudge like the good tourist he was meant to be. Maria was going to be very surprised with the quantity he was bringing back for her.

The return trip was uneventful. Brent stopped at another store and, by the time he emerged, he was eighteen minutes into his tour. He headed back directly, carrying his purchases, to Dan's cab but did so at a leisurely pace. This was the critical moment.

As he casually walked across the plaza, he could see Dan who was playing his part well. The phone was barely visible and you would have to have known it was there to recognize it for what it was. However, Brent could tell that Dan was taking photos. This meant there was probably someone behind him. The last thing he wanted was for the person following to know he knew that fact. Brent first stopped to adjust the way he carried the bag, take two quick, stealthy photos behind him as he did so, and then quickened his pace to draw attention to himself. He approached the passenger side of the vehicle but did not get in when he opened the door. Instead, he bent down to speak to Dan and did so in a clear voice,

"Keeping busy? I need a ride back to the hotel." Almost in a whisper, he also said, "Act like you're negotiating a fare."

"No, I can take you wherever you like."

"Mind if I sit in the front?"

"Jump in," said Dan.

Brent got in the cab.

"Head for any hotel you like but make it one well away from the mountain. Here are some cookies for you." Brent lay a bulging decorative bag on top of the cup holders.

"Thanks, that's nice of you... I got them, you know."

"Good. Two people was it?"

"Yep. One's a local gal. Don't know her name, though." The cab started moving.

"What did they do?"

"It was when you came out of the restaurant. She came out a few seconds later, stopped, then stared after you. Then she dialled a number and went back inside. Had no jacket on, see."

"Okay. She's doesn't have training in surveillance."

"Not like me, eh? Ha. So eleven minutes later, a guy comes running through the plaza and she comes out with her jacket on. He stops and they talk. She points towards the stores while she's explaining something... You, I guess. Then they start walking down the thoroughfare. Five minutes later they come back really quickly. You see where the restaurant juts out, they were standing there on the blind side so you wouldn't see them. As soon as you appeared and turned into the plaza, they came out and were both following you..."

"How far back?"

"Hmm, thirty yards, give or take. Yes, so I got a lot of shots. When you came near the car they stopped, kinda hesitated, turned, and walked away."

"Did they spot you or the cab."

"Oh, yeah, had to. What I haven't said is I know the guy. He's a liftie or he does maintenance. Name's Simon Boltz."

"Simon... he wouldn't be a big, heavy guy, sandy hair with a bit of a sneering attitude - an alpha male type but not much upstairs?"

"That's him. You met him?"

"I did briefly at that place called the House."

"Oh, yeah… Why would he be interested in you?"

"That's what I'd like to find out. Does he come close to getting on your list of possibles?"

"I wouldn't have said so but it wouldn't surprise me, either, if he got into some serious trouble some day… You don't think…?"

"I don't know what to make of it. Looks like there's some kind of network set up. The woman was definitely a lookout. I saw her inside cleaning tables by the window. She calls Boltz to say she's seen me. That means Boltz is very interested for some reason. Let's say he found out I'm a private investigator. What's that to him? Why would he leave the lift to come and follow me? And then bail, as soon as he sees me at your cab? The interesting thing is he has enough smarts to prime a lookout to look for me… Do tourists get robbed?"

"No, hardly ever. It's a safe place… I mean, it *used* to be a safe place… There was some credit card fraud years ago but that all got cleaned up."

"I wonder how many other lookouts there are. You see, if there's some kind of network, then it could be tied in with the scam. What the network wants to know at the moment is what a private investigator is doing in Brophy. A series of informants who are told to look out for individuals that might pose a threat - that's the angle I'm contemplating. They report up the chain of command when they see someone they're looking for. Me, in this instance. The lookouts and spies get paid, not a lot but enough to make them dependant on the extra cash. That's funny, it sort of mimics what the Company does in monitoring employees and in management reporting… That's it! They have an early warning system so that the principle players can bail and not get caught should the Sheriff or the Company be coming after them. That has to be it."

"Ah, no. You're losing me there, Brent. You expect me to believe that half of Brophy is some kind of spy network? I can't believe that."

"It's not half of Brophy... It might be twenty or thirty individuals who just want some extra cash and don't mind how they get it. They won't know anything about the scam. It's like, 'Here's $20. Look for this guy. If you see him there'll be a hundred for you.' Surely there's a lot of people who would do that without asking any questions. It's not breaking any laws as such."

"Put like that, I'd agree - yes, they would... You know, my wife is never going to believe me when I tell her what I've been doing today."

"Maybe keep it secret for a while... Dan, you have to understand, we've got ourselves a dangerous situation here. Do you want out? If you do, I'll pay for you and your wife to go on vacation for a week - two weeks if you want. Won't cost you a cent. I'll cover lost earnings."

"Well, that is about the most generous offer ever made to me. And I thank you for it. But I'll say no. I can't leave town while some scum are killing people and ruining everything. This is my home. I've lived here all my life. I'm not running. Now Judy, my wife, she might not see it quite the same way. In fact, I know she won't so I'd rather not tell her anything, like you suggested. But Brent, we really need to go to the Sheriff with this. We've got evidence of *something* going on even if it's not connected with the murders."

"I agree that we should but who can we trust in the Sheriff's office?"

"Oh, right. They might have someone in there, too. It can't be Bates, though... No, it just can't. He's a decent man."

"Let's hope so because he's the guy we have to see instead of Fraser. The Sheriff is going to get sick of seeing me.

Anyway, that can't be helped. Now, there's a few more things we need to do. Is there a thrift store in Brophy?"

"There is," Dan answered tentatively.

"Excellent. Let's go there now. Take the scenic route while I make sure we're not being followed."

Chapter 16

*B*rent came out of the changing room wearing an ensemble of used but slightly worn winter clothing.

"You know, I wouldn't have recognized you if I passed you in the street. I gotta take a photo of this. You look like a 'Riches to Rags' story or something."

Brent smiled and posed while Dan quickly took a couple of pictures.

"Let's hope no one recognizes me in this. Wait a moment while I change back."

When he came out of the changing room, Brent put his selections into a small shopping cart. He found Dan inspecting an old table lamp in another section and asked him if he was ready to leave.

"Sure. So, you're going to check out a few of the lifties?"

"That's right. I'll keep them under surveillance for a while to see if I can pick up a lead. And Dan, I've been thinking about this carefully. Take me back to the Aurora and we'll call it quits for the day. I was going to see the Sheriff but, you know, I haven't really got anything yet and my theory might be all wrong. I don't really know what's got into me. Mountain air, I think. The murder on the bridge has really stressed me out, too."

"Are you sure? Like I'm all wound up and ready to go."

"Well, here's five hundred for today. You can work out the mileage. I'm too tired to think." Brent followed this up with a yawn. "It must be the warmth in here making me feel sleepy."

"Aw, thanks. Very much appreciated. Now, look, Brent. I've had a great day and I'd have done it for nothing but you know what? You might be right. Maybe that guy was looking for you about something else. I hope the Sheriff gets this all sorted out."

"I'm sure he will. You know, I'll probably end up dropping the cases altogether. I'm supposed to be here learning how to ski."

"How's that going for you? Looked like you were doing okay coming down that blue, though that's an easy one and you took it slowly."

"I must have looked better than I felt, then… I suppose that's something. Are you ready to go?"

"Yeah, sure. Skiing's easy once you get the basics down. Just get the practise in."

They began walking to the checkouts.

"The man born and bred in ski country says it's easy. When did you start skiing?"

"You've got me there… I must have been about four."

"Well, when I was four, I probably couldn't even throw a ball in a straight line and you were already skiing. However, I agree with you about the practise."

Back in his hotel room, Brent put the bag of thrift shop clothes into the closet because he would not be using them. The only item he kept out was a blue, knitted watch cap. His grey and burgundy ski jacket was reversible. The inside being black, it was entirely suitable for what he intended to do.

He sighed as he got ready. This was proving to be a lonely case and it had saddened him in many ways. The loss of life was an obvious cause even though he had never met either victim. He felt he was getting to know them now. Then there was the clear effect it was having on the inhabitants of Brophy. Now it had all taken a sharp turn for the worse. He could no longer trust either Dan or Tosh. No one else had given him cause for concern but both of them had done so in several different ways. Both of them could be spies. At least one of them certainly was, and this, he knew, was not his imagination.

With Dan it was straightforward. Brent really did not fully subscribe to his network of spies theory. He thought it existed but not on the widespread scale he had suggested to Dan. Brent had been followed - that much was true. He had his own photos to prove it and, when he received Dan's photos, it was certain they had both identified and recorded the same people. In that, Brent concluded, Dan was honest.

Where the dishonesty came in was that Dan had to be receiving payment or favour for reporting Brent's whereabouts. It was likely nothing more than that. Each time they had stopped somewhere, it seemed to Brent that Dan used his phone - sent a text message, he now suspected. In isolation, Brent would not have thought it meant anything but when tied to his being followed, Dan's action became significant. It was too much of a random chance for a waiter in a restaurant to come out after him to watch him go shopping, unless they had been forewarned and a photograph of Brent sent to them. That seemed to imply there was something of importance sited on the street in The Village. The only person who could have alerted anyone else to Brent's presence at that time was Dan. And yet, Dan had been surprised and engaged by the turn of events.

Brent decided that Dan had contacted someone who, in turn, contacted the woman in the restaurant. It was she who called Simon Boltz - another operative working nearby. They followed, like the amateurs they were, but left as soon as Brent entered the cab. As far as Boltz and the woman were concerned, they could no longer follow without a vehicle. Alternatively, at least one of them knew that Dan was keeping tabs on Brent so they need not concern themselves any longer. In either event, they had completed their surveillance job which was to protect something in or around The Village's pedestrian thoroughfare. Brent surmised that Boltz knew what it was or, at least, where it was, while Dan did not. Simon Boltz, then, had to be further up the chain of command.

The main reason Brent had even tried the experiment to see if he was being followed was he had realized there was significant risk from the killers and, suddenly, Dan's text messaging became ominous. As Brent had sat thinking of the dangerous situation in the cab, he realized that Dan, the man sitting next to him, might be unwittingly involved in surveillance without understanding the part he played. Dan owed him no loyalty but he had kept a straight face and lied when he realized that his own actions had precipitated what occurred in The Village. He could easily have volunteered that he was reporting to someone. Then, to cap it off, Dan had photographed Brent in his thrift-store disguise. Brent was determined to talk to him at a later date. He would like to ask him, 'Who's your handler?', but he would be unable to trust the answer even if he got one and to do so now would alert the wrong people. The trouble was, who were the right people? Dr Denver was co-operative, Lotta and Tosh's friends seemed so innocent but anybody else, including the Sheriff, was now suspect to Brent.

With Tosh it was very different. Someone could be trading on his naivete and that would mean the young man was in danger. This, too, had come to Brent while he had sat in the cab by the plaza.

The onset of an early winter night is universally detested but always shrugged off as inevitable. Brent welcomed this particular night. At five p.m., he left the Aurora through a side entrance. As soon as he got outside and made sure no one was about, he reversed his jacket and put his watch cap on. The winter air was still relatively mild and he left his hood down to remain aware of his surroundings. He disappeared into the dark, keeping away from all sources of light and all cameras.

The Village was only a short distance away from the Aurora. The area was decoratively and brightly lit and looked very festive. If Brent walked along the pedestrian walkways he could be recognized and he wished to remain incognito. He had hoped to find alleyways servicing the businesses on either side of the streets, particularly the main street, but in this he was disappointed. All available space in the area had been optimized for visitor experience and income generation. The utilitarian side of commerce was discreetly hidden from view and located elsewhere. Deliveries had to be made through the front doors.

What he did find behind the blocks of stores were ground floor community areas for the condos built above the store fronts. To see what lay behind one of the large, multi-use buildings, Brent climbed a privacy fence. What he saw from his vantage point was everything buried in snow - luminous by itself in the shaded areas but also illuminated by apartment lights. From the suggested outlines of round, snow-drifted forms, Brent had to imagine swimming pools, playground equipment, barbeque pits, and open grass within the fenced area. He jumped down again. He did not know what he had expected to find but it was definitely not this.

Brent circled around a large section of the neighbourhood using adjacent streets to approach the main retail area via the plaza he had crossed earlier. Once there, he found a place in a sheltered, darker position opposite the restaurant. He took out his phone to act as a covering reason for standing still in a public place while he scanned the brightly lit interior of the restaurant. Fifteen minutes of observation convinced him he was wasting his time. The woman he had seen earlier had not come into view.

With his hood up and apparently absorbed by something mind-numbingly important on his phone, Brent walked slowly down the main thoroughfare. Pedestrians were fewer than they had been earlier but the area was well frequented. Conversely, the restaurants had become busier while the stores, almost empty, had that 'Can't we just close now?' look about them. A toy and games store bucked the trend. It was still doing a brisk trade even though a murder had occurred within a mile and well within the last twenty-four hours.

Brent had no expectations of what he would find so he was not looking for anything specific. He had counted on something presenting itself. He stopped periodically to look about him in a covert way. No one store looked more menacing or meaningful than any other. He came to a doorway that led to the condos overhead. He went inside through the heavily tinted double doors.

The contrast in atmosphere he found inside the vestibule compared to the carefully crafted exterior came as a surprise. The lighting was low - verging on dingy. There was no carpet, no decorative objects to be seen - only plain off-white contractor-grade tiling and a boring, sandy-brown wallpaper.

It was inconvenient, too. Once through the doors, he was faced with a steep flight of tiled stairs with worn, brass-like handrails and flanked by high, tiled walls. Further up came a landing followed by a shorter, shallower flight. The space would not have been attractive even when it was new.

The area widened considerably at the top, allowing access to two elevators. Here, also, were two corridors - one on either side of the elevators which could only have been about ten years old but looked far older. A bank of mailboxes was installed in the wall to one side. Flyers lay strewn on the floor. Brent decided that if he were coming to consider buying or renting a place in the building it would be at this point he would turn round and walk out. There was nothing really wrong with anything he had seen but it was more the startling contrast between the featureless, uncared for uniformity inside and the highly-crafted and attractive ambience found in the street outside.

Phone in hand, he studied the names on the mailboxes and took several photographs. Most had no name tag attached. On top of a low wall, at right angles to the boxes, were some addressed flyers and circulars. Brent arranged them quickly to get a shot of the names. He was just turning away when the street door opened. It was a man and woman in their forties. In the next moment, three younger women came out of an elevator. The people passed one another on the stairs. Nobody spoke or looked at each other. The place now seemed emptier still.

When they had gone, Brent examined each of the corridors in turn. These passages were lit with warmer, sconce lighting and good carpeting which things made quite a difference to the feel of the place. Some of the doors, Brent noted, had superficial damage from careless comings and goings. The whole inner space spoke in various ways that it was a temporary rental property, with minimal maintenance, and no community.

Brent searched the whole condominium and found it extended over three floors with between sixteen and twenty units on each level. One unit at the top at the very end of a corridor looked cared for. It had plants around the door, paintings close by on the walls, a mat, and a shiny brass knocker. He discovered several more doors that seemed better cared for than the rest. Faint cooking smells emanating from one unit reminded Brent he was hungry and that he also had other things to do before he ate.

Once back outside, Brent continued his tour of The Village. Nothing interested him but he realized there were three more similarly sized condominium blocks he would need to come back to later. He reasoned that if Simon Boltz and the woman were being paid to be vigilant over anything it would probably be found inside one of these condos. He wondered if it was the one with plants and paintings outside and decided it was very unlikely as it drew too much attention to itself.

He left The Village. As he neared the river road he discovered the bridge was still closed to all traffic. Deputies were present and were continuing to keep the crime scene secure. This obstacle meant he had to walk to the next bridge - a two mile detour. He could call a taxi but was reluctant to do so as a mistrust of everyone had firmly settled in his mind.

Brent had no real choice. He needed to be on the other side of the river fairly soon or risk missing Denver or Bates. He hiked to the next bridge. Although the temperature hovered around twenty Fahrenheit, the exercise kept him warm to the point he felt like taking off his jacket.

"Hello, Dr Denver? It's Brent Umber." He had called her while walking and was within several minutes of her offices.

"Hello… You'll be interested to know that I have finished the Simpson autopsy."

"You have? I'm very sorry you're having to perform such duties. I know my sympathy doesn't help you any but you do have my full appreciation."

"Actually, I do appreciate your sympathy more than you realize." Her voice sounded softer than it had before. "Other professionals expect me just to get on with the job. Fellow practitioners who would understand the demands of the work are few and far between. Everyone else either shies away from me, as though I have two heads, or, as a minority do, they want all the gory details." Mary Denver laughed.

"You have a nice laugh," said Brent, realizing she was decompressing after performing the autopsy. "I would stop by and chat if you wanted but I'll just say that I have a professional situation of my own to deal with and it's become a real headache. That's all the griping I'll bore you with." He came to a stop by the side of a building, glad that he would not be forced to view a corpse tonight.

"Ah, I see. Best not come over; I'm still cleaning up. Perhaps we'll have a coffee some other time. Now… Oh, by the way, I spoke to Sheriff Bates and it seems he's far more amenable to the idea that Saunders' death was manslaughter. He also mentioned he's giving you some latitude in investigating the case. Yes, so," her voice became neutral in tone and professionally precise, "Alex Simpson was murdered. He received five puncture wounds, one of which was lethal. Two other wounds would have led to him bleeding to death within an hour if left unattended. The others were non-life-threatening. There were several lacerations on his arm as he defended himself from the attack and his jacket was cut in numerous places which denotes he was struck at about twenty times.

There were two assailants and two weapons used. One was a heavy knife, such as is used for hunting, and this one made the majority of the superficial wounds. The other was a thinner blade approximately four inches long…"

Brent listened to the distressing catalogue of damage that had been inflicted. Initially, Alex Simpson had been taken by surprise by first being stabbed in the back which was a non-fatal wound. He had then fought desperately against two assailants, one of whom got his arm round his neck. It was all over quickly. Dr Denver estimated it to be less than two minutes and probably one when he had either died or was brought so very close to death he was completely incapacitated. Smears of blood on the railing, she had been informed, indicated   he had been rolled over it rather than thrown over clear. Simpson suffered more injuries in the fall but none of them were immediately life-threatening and she believed him to have been dead before he fell.

"… I put the time of death between two and four a.m. this morning. Do you need more details or is that enough for you to work with?"

"Ah, thank you, yes. That's plenty for me. I'm solidly in the squeamish camp."

"I remember you mentioning that before. I've sent samples away for analysis. You realize that the laboratory reports will be coming back over the next four to five business days. You can check back at the end of the week for an update."

"I'll do that," said Brent. "And thank you so much for your help, Dr Denver."

"Don't thank me. We all want closure on these events and I would rather assist you than hamper you."

"That is exactly what I mean by your help. Thanks again."

He put his phone away and walked towards the Sheriff's office. He was saddened and very troubled by the vivid scene of Alex Simpson desperately fighting for his life on a snowy bridge above a frozen river. It played over and over in his mind - fragmented, incomplete, and horrific. After a while, his whirling thoughts made him angry.

Chapter 17

Tuesday night

*B*efore entering the Sheriff's office, Brent took the time to reverse his jacket back to its grey and burgundy exterior and removed his woollen cap, stowing it in a pocket. There was a vehicle in Jebb Bates' reserved parking spot so he presumed the Sheriff was inside. This, his third meeting with Bates, was by far the most critical. Brent had to see him but was reluctant to do so. The case, or cases, could not proceed for Brent without the Sheriff's inclusion. The problem was, Bates could be involved in the murders or he might only be Dan's handler. Suspicion is a deadly thing. Brent was visualizing Bates in every conceivable role, from an evil genius who controlled Brophy from his office with its family photographs, to an innocent officer of the law - one who would be astonished and angry if he knew which direction Brent's thoughts had taken.

The risk might be slight but should Bates prove to be an evil genius, Brent might not be returning to Newhampton anytime soon or, indeed, ever. He decided to call the Sheriff first to see if he could get a sense of how things stood. He took out the card Bates had given him earlier and dialled the number. From across the street, he looked towards the fortress-like building. Not for the first time that day he wondered what on earth he thought he was doing.

"Sheriff Bates, it's Brent Umber."

"So, have you found something?"

"I think so, though I'm not sure what to make of it. Are you with anyone?"

There was a slight pause before the answer came and it was long enough to make Brent wonder what was happening at the other end.

"Not now," said the Sheriff.

"I need to show you something and, I'm going to be honest with you, I have trust issues with everyone in Brophy at the moment."

There was another pause. "I guess you're including me in that statement."

"I have to. It's nothing personal, you understand. Can we meet on neutral ground somewhere?"

"Would a coffee shop or restaurant do you?"

"That would be fine. Not Georgiou's, though."

"There's Destination Donuts. I need to pick up a sandwich anyway and theirs are pretty good."

"Is that the one on Main Street or is there another one?"

"Just the one. Say in half an hour?"

"I'll be there at a table when you arrive," said Brent. "How do you like your coffee?"

"Extra-large, black, two sugars."

"Okay, see you there."

Brent got a table against a wall and was typing on his laptop while eating. Realizing suddenly that he was ravenous, he bought two sandwiches and a bag of doughnuts.

The restaurant was busy with drive-through traffic while inside there was a sprinkling of customers sitting at tables.

Bates came in and saw Brent almost immediately. On his way over, he said hello to people at two different tables and waved while calling out his sandwich order to one of the servers behind the counter.

"Thanks for the coffee," said Bates as he eased himself into a seat facing Brent. He took the lid off and took a sip.

"Ever since I arrived in Brophy, I can't stop eating or feeling hungry. Is there something in the air up here?"

"It's the cold that does it. You like the sandwiches?"

"Yes. They're great, aren't they? Now, if you would take a look at these photos... these are the clearest ten out of what was taken. The woman works in a restaurant but came out to watch me."

Brent passed his phone to the Sheriff. He scrolled through the selection and then handed the phone back.

"Do you know either of them?"

"I don't know the woman. I know Simon. He's a nephew of mine."

"Oh, I see... Would you know why he was following me and why the woman was keeping me under surveillance? This all occurred within The Village precincts."

"I don't. But I can see that was what they were doing... Who took the photos from inside the vehicle?"

"Dan, the taxi driver."

Bates nodded slowly.

"You said, 'He's a nephew of mine,' and not, 'My nephew'. Does that mean something?"

Bates smiled. "I don't really play favourites in the family but Simon is not a favourite nephew. Let's just say there have been issues in the past... There's no law broken here but I guess you see a tie-in with Simpson or Saunders. So let's have it."

"The woman contacted Simon who left his job to come and observe me. The only reason can be that I'm a private investigator. But that's nothing unless I'm investigating something that another person wouldn't want me to be investigating. What am I investigating? Karl Saunders' death. There could be another reason but I doubt it very much.

The woman knew to look out for me. Simon knew to come over immediately when called. Would you say that Simon organized it?"

"He could but it's not the kind of thing I'd expect from him."

"Then if it was not him, and it seems even less likely that the woman is the organizer because of her actions, that means there's a third party issuing instructions to both of them. Would you agree?"

"Sounds logical." The Sheriff rubbed his chin with a thumb and forefinger. "But, ah, they didn't accomplish much here. Did they follow you when you left the area?"

"No. They gave up immediately when I got into Dan's taxi. They also did a poor job because they have no training in surveillance."

"Well, this is an interesting puzzle, then. Let's say they were keeping an eye on you. As soon as you moved away, did a car follow you?"

"I didn't spot one so I'd say no. Which makes me think they were primed to keep me under surveillance only while I was in The Village area."

"That's kind of far-fetched. It also sounds like a random event. The woman sees you, calls Simon… I give you all of that. What I don't get is why she would be looking out for you in the first place. It sounds too random to me."

"Do you trust me?" asked Brent.

Jebb Bates looked at him for a couple of seconds before replying, "No, because I don't know you."

"Totally fair. I'm in the same position as you. I said I would give you everything I discovered because I respect the office you hold and assumed you would fulfil your duties. I believe that is what will happen. At this moment, however, I don't know who to trust. That's why we're here - it's not just for the sandwiches. I have already stuck my neck out - I need to know it's not going to get chopped… otherwise, to be frank, I think I'll be getting on the bus tomorrow morning."

"Yep. I get it." Bates nodded again. "You're tying this in with Saunders and Simpson and you're thinking you could be the next victim if you're a threat to the perpetrators."

"I feel like I have a bullseye on my back," said Brent. "I can put up with it for a while if I know I can trust you."

"You've obviously got more than this… I guess I don't get to hear it unless… What do you want from me?"

It crossed Brent's mind that he had already gone beyond the point of no return with Sheriff Bates. If he were in any way involved with the murders Brent was in trouble. A third murder or death would be hard to sweep under the rug but if the stakes were high enough it could be done. This was a hypothesis Brent did not want to be put to the test. He returned to his initial thought that it might already be too late.

"Make me one of your deputies."

"Ha!" The Sheriff had a big, attention-grabbing type of laugh that caused a couple of patrons to turn round. Smiling, he said,

"Look, I know this is serious but you caught me good. Ah, like, I can do it, but you'd need to meet some minimum training standards. I can't just swear you in. That's a couple of misdemeanor charges for me… I'd have to look up the fines."

"Okay. So you swear me in here and pay me five dollars to make it legal and I'll become a temporary deputy. We can write it now. I won't perform the duties of a deputy and you won't ask me to. But I'll have a signed document that I'll photograph and send to a trusted friend." Brent took out a small notepad and pen.

"You make it sound simple but I'd be risking my job."

"What's the alternative then?"

"I'll tell you what I can do. I'll sign and date a statement that I'm receiving information from you concerning the two cases. We'll put in how far-reaching the case looked to you at the time and to prevent possible consequences from giving the information, you asked me to certify the statement so that a level of trust could be established between us. You'll have it and you'll have safe copies so that in the event anything does happen, the FBI will come knocking on my door and I'll have to answer their questions. That's all I'm prepared to do because I don't break laws. I uphold them."

"This is good. I can go along with a statement," said Brent who then began to write.

With the statement out of the way and a photograph of it already forwarded to Greg Darrow, the two men resumed their conversation.

"What you need to know is Dan is in on this deal. He was with me for some hours before the incident. I didn't clue in at first but every time we'd stop somewhere he would take out his phone and, I believe, send a text message. The big thing is that he had been very helpful all day long. When I asked him to take those photos he was surprised but eager to help. I think he was enjoying himself. This seems to indicate that Dan was deliberately giving location information to someone who has an interest in me. Because of Dan, this unknown person contacted the woman in the restaurant. She then alerted your nephew, Simon.

I got out of the cab to see if I was under surveillance because it had only just dawned on me that I could be of interest to other parties. Dan and his text messaging had eventually made me suspicious of him but what is interesting is that Dan was genuinely surprised by what happened. His reaction convinced me he did not know of anyone else's involvement in what he was doing other than his contact.

Soon afterwards, I thought to alter my appearance so I could avoid being tailed next time I went to The Village. Dan took a photograph of me but without hiding the fact he was doing so. I get the impression that whatever he thinks he's doing, it lies within the law. I even thought *you* might have set him on me."

"No. I've known Dan for years. He's never been in trouble. I have to ask, are you sure about Dan? Could it be a wrong reading of his actions?"

"I'm inclined to be persuaded out of my assessment," said Brent. "It was the speed with which he took the photo of me in disguise that clinched it. It gave me the impression he was doing something extra for someone to show how willing he was. He demonstrated the same zeal in wanting to catch murderers. Does anyone have a hold over him for any reason?"

"Not that I'm aware of… I'll look into that. So you'd say he was under the impression that he was doing something legit in keeping an eye on you?"

"Exactly. In every other respect, he's been friendly and open towards me."

"That sounds like him. I guess you think there's something of interest in The Village."

"Before coming here I took a look around on my own. The only possibility that occurs to me is that something's going on in one of the condos above the stores. I have the impression that the surveillance was to watch me if I came close to some kind of danger zone. Had I done so… I don't know what would have happened next. It might have been anything up to and including my being Brophy's third corpse, I should imagine."

"If you're right... there's money in there somewhere."

"Yes. I think it's Freedom Sports money. My current, working hypothesis is that some employees are defrauding the Company and it requires inside and outside staff to make it happen. I further believe that this network of Intel-gatherers has been in place for a long time. The most likely people they would be on the lookout for would be company employees from head office, FBI agents, tax auditors, IT sub-contractors - anyone with an official capacity or who could get close to the workings of a scam. Such a mandate would make a private investigator of interest to them. If one PI decides to investigate a suspicious incident it would put them on high alert."

"Hm, there's a lot to think about there. I can't see what I can do at the moment except make discreet inquiries... This has me concerned and I think you know why."

"It was why the statement signing was necessary. I'm certain our meeting is likely to get back to whoever it is who's running this enterprise. However, there is something you can do. I have to get information on the inner workings of the Company to see how a scam of any magnitude is even possible. I don't want to disturb the pigeons until we're ready. Do you know Tosh?"

"Not him as well?"

"I'm afraid so but his is a much more complicated situation than Dan's and there's a lot I don't understand as yet. I need time with him to see what more I can find out. As soon as I get what I need about him and the Company, could you please arrest Tosh?"

"Hey, Tosh, are you doing anything at the moment?" Brent had called him. It was now just after nine.

"Hi. I'm not doing much."

"Then come over to the Aurora and I'll buy you a beer. Dinner, too, if you haven't eaten already. You know, the food's really good here."

"Well, I know that but I've eaten, thanks. Sure, I'll come. I'll be about twenty minutes."

"That's good. I'll meet you in the Lodge."

The Lodge was an informal restaurant with a separate bar area. Its décor was that of a log-built Alpine ski lodge. Lining the walls were heavy, pale timbers that looked like whole trees, but which were, in fact, four-inch-wide slices a foot tall and up to twelve feet long. Overhead there was a network of squared timbers that supported circular light fixtures but above these was a suggestion of soaring wooden roof supports quickly terminating into a flat black painted ceiling that also disguised duct-work and electric cabling. Beneath the lights, the place was roomy, hospitable and relaxed. The room ranged over several levels connected by short staircases. It had as a focal piece a massive fireplace with large, irregular-shaped granite slabs surrounding it. The fireplace appeared to be fully functional but surprisingly no fire was burning in it.

Business in the restaurant was slow when Brent arrived and he easily found a secluded table. Having concluded his reports, he sat thinking about what he was going to say to Tosh. Once in a while, his eyes strayed to a group of six at a table on the other side of the room. They were intently discussing something over food and drinks. No laughter emanated from the group.

Brent took out his phone and checked Freedom Sports' website. He looked through the list of executive employees and found a photo of Sam Welch, Chief Operating Officer. He glanced up from his phone to see the real Sam in profile seated at one end of the table across the room from him. Brent further identified the Human Resources Manager, Susan Aislin. The others he could not identify with any degree of certainty because of the way they were seated and because a wooden post was in the way. He wondered what the group was discussing. Was this a regular, after-hours get together or an extended meeting prompted by recent events? Sam Welch looked too miserable and tense not to be discussing what had happened in Brophy last night.

Tosh arrived. Brent waved to him when he hesitated in the main entrance. As he approached the table, Brent thought the young man also looked tense.

"How's it going?" asked Tosh in an offhand way. "Thanks for the beer." He picked up the bottle Brent had ready for him and, ignoring the glass, took a swig.

"Good... Not as good as I would like. What I want is to have all this mess behind me and just go skiing."

"Wouldn't that be nice?" replied Tosh sarcastically.

"Is that directed at me or the situation?"

"I don't know," said Tosh.

"I see. I wonder who you've been talking to."

"What difference does it make who I talk to? It's not your business. You're a tourist. You don't live here."

"You sound a little bit like Simon Boltz. Been talking to him lately?"

Tosh went quiet, stared at Brent for a moment, and then dropped his gaze. "Sorry, I'm just upset."

"Ah, no, I'm not buying that and I have a very good reason to disbelieve you."

Tosh leaned back in his chair and looked around as though he wanted to stare at something, anything, as long as it was not Brent. He did what some angry, frustrated young men do when feeling trapped - he began deliberately and rapidly to twitch a leg.

Brent had not reckoned on the conversation breaking down like this. Something had definitely taken place and he was not sure whether to let it go or try to counter it right now by explaining to Tosh how he saw the situation. It was a difficult choice either way because the stakes were high and, besides, the Sheriff was now involved.

"I think you're finding yourself between the proverbial rock and a hard place. Care to talk about it?"

"What's the point?"

"Okay, so I am on the right track, I think. I would say the point is that you might be the fall guy for a murder rap should it ever be necessary for your handlers to shift the blame onto someone."

There was a long silence in which Tosh looked both scared and shocked - his face blanched.

"Why did you go up the mountain first thing Sunday morning? Who sent you?"

Tosh did not answer. It was obvious from his face that his antagonism subsided as soon as the realization dawned that he might have been made a scapegoat.

"You have to give me names. At the moment, you're in the middle of two investigations but you could soon be converted to prime suspect in one of them or maybe both of them, for all I know. Who is it?"

"I got to think about this." Tosh got up to go.

"No, if you leave here I'll call the Sheriff and have you arrested. It's not up to you anymore!" said Brent tersely. "You have misplaced loyalties. Two people dead... you or I could be next and you're going away to think about it? Sit down, because you get no such luxury." Brent called a waiter over and spoke in a calmer voice.

"Two more beers, please, and I'd like a barbecued chicken pizza with some hot peppers." He addressed Tosh. "What would you like?"

"I don't know… uh, the Classic Margherita, thanks."

"And I think a Greek salad for me, a regular salad… Is that okay?" Tosh nodded that it was. "Two orders of garlic bread, dips, extra black olives… That should do us for the moment."

After the waiter had gone, the two men were quiet.

"I've been an idiot," said Tosh angrily.

"I think you have," said Brent. "I was an idiot once but I decided to change."

The young man remained morosely silent. Brent gave him a quizzical look and said,

"It was you who wanted me to go round to the House to meet Marv. I thought nothing of it at the time. I thought it might be interesting from a couple of angles. It was Marv who told you he wanted to see me, wasn't it?"

"Yeah… that's more or less it."

"Care to describe your relationship with Marv?"

"It's difficult to put into words. I guess… I guess he is, like, so free and easy when I feel so uptight all the time. It's like he lives on thin air and I work hard just to scrape by. I thought he was a friend."

"Some people do seem to get an easy time of it," said Brent. "My guess is that, as soon as Marv learned I was a private investigator, he persuaded you to give up the three days' skiing instruction I'd offered you and to hand them over to him. One reason was he wanted some money out of the gig but the other was he wanted to keep an eye on me. Is that about right?"

"It is. I gotta tell you, Nils has nothing to do with this at all. At all."

"I'm glad to hear that because I like Nils… When did Marv learn I was a PI?"

"Ah, Sunday night. I let him know you were an investigator. You see, I was going to be your instructor those other three days but I had to go in to work at the restaurant on Tuesday to arrange to take time off Wednesday to Friday. I knew Nils had a spare so I called him first and got that set. I thought I was solid for three more days' instruction. But Marv has this thing that he wants to know if any police or government types come snooping around. I know something's going down but I'm not in on it. As for Marv - he's helped me in the past and I'd do anything for him." Tosh took a sip of beer.

"As soon as I got it sorted with Nils, I texted Marv about the lessons. He called me back almost immediately, saying I gotta bring you over to the House. When I told him about the skiing lessons, he asked me for the three days. He said he'd split some of the money with me. I think, okay, whatever, it's no big deal. He's been a really good friend to me in the past and I've still got my shifts at the restaurant. You didn't seem to mind three different instructors so I thought we were cool."

"It would have been," said Brent. "I couldn't help but find several things quite strange, though. I thought it was weird that we had to go and meet my skiing instructor. It was weird that you'd go to a place where you'll meet someone you detest, meaning Boltz. It was also weird that Marv put on that act… for me, I suppose. I guess he acts up sometimes but he made sure he did it for me. Am I right?"

"Yes, he knew you were coming to the House but then he pretends like you'd shown up out of the blue and puts on his crazy, scatterbrained act. That makes me look like a dope in front of you."

"Yes, it would but it didn't, if you know what I mean. It's only a method some people use to control others just because they can. So was it Marvin who suggested you go boarding Sunday morning?"

"Yeah. He said he'd meet me at the top of Bear Tracks at eight-fifteen. I was there but he didn't show up until nearly nine."

"Was Dustin Packard there that day?"

"Yes, but we didn't speak because we never do usually. Might nod to each other but that's it."

"Did he see you waiting?"

"Yes, he did."

"Were you at any time near the Say Goodbye run and what tracks did you notice if you were?"

"I was. I didn't go down it… I don't know, there were only a few tracks - boards and skis. I can't remember how many. Max, maybe two or three of each but that was after I'd been there for a while."

"Okay, this is very helpful. First, does Marv know you're here tonight?"

"No."

"Don't tell him. Do not tell him. Tosh, what has happened between the time I saw you earlier until now - with approximate times?"

"Marv called me round to the House about one. He was totally freaking out about something. As soon as I got there, he takes me to another room and says that you're bad news. Then he starts in and asks what was I doing talking to Dustin Packard - obviously someone had told him about that. Marv then told me to totally stay away from Dustin."

"Why do you think he did that?" asked Brent.

"I don't know. I told him I never normally speak to Dustin but, since I'd been wondering about Karl's death, I thought I'd ask him if he'd seen anything and Dustin said he hadn't. Then Marv completely calms down. Starts smiling and says it's the murder making him jumpy."

"Did he know Alex Simpson?"

184

"Probably. I don't think they hung out together. At least, I've never seen them."

"Okay. Did anything happen around four?"

"Yeah, it did. I'm fixing equipment, minding my own business, and Simon Boltz came in looking for me. He comes up and whispers so that only I hear it and says, "Snitches don't survive in this town." Then he walks away. Like, what did he even mean? Is he crazy?"

"No, Tosh, he isn't. He is one magnificent idiot. He exists in a realm of idiocy that you and I have never come close to inhabiting. That will be the last time he ever bullies you, Tosh. Remember that. He's given the game away... part of it, anyway... And here comes the pizza. I'm so hungry and I've hardly skied at all today. I've been informed it's being out in the cold that does it."

Tosh and Brent parted company with Brent warning him again not to say anything to anyone about their meeting. The young man left far more settled in his mind but also very subdued. The realization had come upon him that, with a high degree of probability, he had been aiding and abetting murderers. Brent had not needed to say anything along those lines and he certainly avoided all details and theories concerning the perpetration of the fraud. Nevertheless, Tosh awoke to the fact that he had unwittingly been drawn into the very thing that he had wanted to investigate - the conspiracy of murder, as it now appeared to be. He fully realized the danger to which he was exposed from both the murderers and the authorities. He took it well enough - quietly, but well enough. He resolved to distance himself from Marv and Simon Boltz as much as he possibly could.

Brent and Tosh had discussed what he needed to do. Brent gave him Sheriff Bates' private phone number to call if an emergency should arise, telling him that the Sheriff was now fully invested in two connected murder cases.

So concerned was Brent with Tosh's welfare that he followed him home without the young man being aware that he was trailing a hundred yards behind him. On his return journey, and after Tosh was safely inside, Brent noticed that the frequency of deputy patrols had increased to about three an hour.

He got to his hotel room at about eleven. It did not take him long to find out that someone had been through his things but, after he conducted a quick survey, he found they had not taken anything. He was unsure when it had occurred and thought it might be anytime since early morning. Several items were out of place in one drawer - the items had been moved and not put back very carefully. He supposed that if he had left his laptop in the room it would have undoubtedly been taken.

If it had not been for the murder cases and the losing of related sensitive information, Brent concluded that it would have served him right had they taken everything including his laptop because of his own past behaviour. He wished, sometimes, that he could go back and erase his past. Once in a while, he felt so ashamed of his former life he wanted to tear it out of himself.

He sat in a chair eating a mango, reflecting upon how amateurish these people were and hoped that such crudeness of operation extended into the fraud itself. That would mean that, once exposed, it would be self-evident what had been going on. Amateurish these people who were running the operation might be but their use of violence and murder signified that they would stop at nothing to protect their interests.

He got up at 5:30 a.m. and, as sometimes happens, a clear path presented itself to his mind - a way through all the muddied, swirling details. It was actually two paths. The first and foremost led to a place where the nature of the fraud became so obviously apparent to him that he could not imagine it being anything else. The second was the road he would have to take to deal with mercurial Marv who, if not the actual murderer, was definitely complicit in one if not both cases.

Chapter 18

Wednesday morning

"*M*y goodness, Brent. What are you thinking of? This is not a proper time to be calling anyone," said Edmond. "And why are we calling at this time of the night? Do we have a scheduled call? Let me check my calendar. No, I see no scheduled night-time call with Brent Umber."

"It is early morning and we're in the same time zone. You're awake and I need your advice on something."

"Whether I am awake or not has nothing to do with the issue. My time belongs to me and not to you. This lack of civility on your part is a habit you must stamp out."

"I've never called you early in the morning before."

"Oh, yes, you have. I was in Morocco and you called me at 4:03 a.m. I remember it distinctly. You wanted me to… Is this a secure line?"

"The line's okay but your moaning isn't. It was 11:03 p.m. for me, Edmond. Anyway, you sound pretty perky right now so, come on, just hear me out."

"You have a warped view of things, Brent. It was the middle of the night for me. Not that you care."

"Edmond, that was a life or death situation."

"Yes, so you say. And which genius got himself in that jam because he didn't think to ask a simple question during what people commonly call office hours? You know, those hours where the sun is actually in the sky. Wait a moment, my coffee's ready. Had you curbed your impatience and thought things through… mmm… I would have been more tolerant of your nonsense. Mmm… So, what's up Brent? Is your laptop stuck in an update cycle again?"

"Okay, so if I was going to hack a major retail outlet to extract some receipts without any audit trail, I think I would do it as a small percentage of each sale or, let's say, one sale in a hundred or some similar ratio. This would be a state-of-the-art system. If I were to do that, what kind of equipment set-up and people would I need?"

"That's a long-term hack. Time-frame?"

"Indefinitely but let's say a few years. It's a ski resort, involving lift passes in particular."

"Very well. You'd need staff on-site. One critical person has to be in IT with full control to implement upgrades, wipe histories, and that kind of thing. You might need a cashier to switch the terminal over to a separate connection that funds a different bank account. That could get very messy, though. The problem I see … mmm… the problem with a percentage of sales is the sequential transaction numbers."

"Ah, are you saying one in a hundred sales wouldn't work?"

"I didn't say that. Anything can be made to work. There are several ways to approach this. Some are messier and more awkward than others. However, I know what I would do."

"Tell me what you would do, and please, make it intelligible."

"I would route all transactions before they are processed for payment to separate off-site servers. Once each transaction is there, it would automatically be renumbered into two sequences. One sequence would be the diverted percentage of non-refundable ticket sales. These would be processed within the parasitic system and beautifully deposited into my accounts. Then, a temporary file is sent back to the terminal to generate a scannable code for the customer to wear to get on the lifts.

The second sequence of transactions is for the rest of the sales. Those would be renumbered and forwarded to the company's servers. The receipts from those are put into the company accounts. When the day is over, any temporary files are wiped from the terminals because there is no corresponding sale. Weekend passes could be handled, too. I'd stay away from season passes. It's easy really."

"That sounds like it might be close to what's being done if I'm understanding it correctly. I'm guessing, but I think the haul is about two to three million each season."

"Very nice, indeed. I'd like to meet the IT guy and have a chat with him. You know, Brent, if they're consistent and don't get greedy, they won't be caught under normal circumstances. You see, once their system is set up, they only need to purchase extra scannable ticket consumables and keep those at the terminals. It's a very elegant little project and there are no pesky inventory counts to worry about."

"Would staff scanning tickets be likely to notice anything?"

"No, I don't think they would. There might be a lag of a second or two at the terminal as each sale is processed. The risk exposure would come if someone physically counted heads going up the lifts for an hour. Then if they matched the count to the company's sales records for that same hour they could see a discrepancy. The result being more heads than sales. Auditors would do that. Tax auditors might, also, although they'd need to factor in estimates for multiple uses of a lift by the same person or season pass holders. That's why, if the percentage diverted is low enough, the parasitic system should never be discovered. Better yet would be to switch off the parasitic system while the auditors are counting. As soon as they're gone then it gets rebooted. Easy peasy."

"Some of what you said fits in with my guesswork. I believe we're both missing an element though. I think there's a need for some lift operators and a few other staff to be involved."

"No, not if it's set up properly.... Ah, wait a moment. Has this operation been running for a while?"

"A decade at least. It started out as a cash-only operation and then switched later."

"Then this is what probably happened. The earlier phase was much simpler and non-electronic. The lift staff were extracting money in unsophisticated ways. The legacy operation was probably worked in tandem with the new, secure system as it was being brought online. The people in charge of the old operation must have got an IT guy in their scheme and he designed the new system to defeat the new security features being implemented. That could be why they're included. It was the lift staff's franchise to begin with."

"I think that's likely to be it. I've discovered that there are a number of lookouts posted in different places. This group is vigilant against surprises."

"Yes," said Edmond slowly. "There are probably trust issues being safeguarded in there, too - you know, between the various members of the syndicate. Brent, I really should try and hack their parasitic server system or whatever they have. Do you know where it is?"

"Not yet and, when I do find it, I'm not telling you."

"Oh, Brent, you're like a centenarian - dithering around behaving like life is over for you. Think of it - a few days' work and we'd be earning some serious pocket money. Fifty-

fifty - what could be fairer than that? We might even get to drain their bank accounts but I'd want sixty points for that part. If we rip them off, they'd never report it to the police, now would they? Of course, they wouldn't. What do you say?"

"Absolutely and finally, no. How is Darlene?"

"She's very well, thank you. February fourteenth is almost here and I feel quite giddy about my marriage prospects. I believe she'll say yes, I really do. When she does, Brent, there will be no more of this calling in the middle of the night, let me tell you."

After Brent got off the phone, he came away knowing he had to get into the company somehow. It had been good for him to talk to Edmond - good to hear the familiar voice of a person he trusted, even if that person *was* slightly crazed. His discussion with Edmond had also clarified and refined many aspects of the fraud so that Brent felt more certain he was on the right track. The remaining, inescapable issue was that, no matter what he did next, it would be known almost at once by the shadowy group of people observing his movements. An idea struck him and he quickly developed a plan. Because he had no printer, he handwrote a note instead. If he was lucky, he might get something significant accomplished before meeting Marv at eight.

After a hurried breakfast, Brent descended to the underground garage and began to survey the reserved parking spots, looking for the one belonging to Sam Welch, the Chief Operating Officer of Freedom Sports and, therefore, Ghost Hawk Resort. It was now just after seven and although some parking stalls were clearly marked 'Reserved' they gave no indication as to which person or organization they belonged to. Guessing that the man he wanted to talk to was the ultimate manager of nearly every member of staff in the building, Brent elected to stake out the reserved spots nearest to the elevators.

Normally, any person, particularly a man, standing around in an underground parking lot, would be viewed as a car thief or worse. If the same man, wearing ski boots, carrying skis and poles, is standing in the underground parking lot of a major hotel at a ski resort while, as is to be expected, communing with a phone, he then looks totally fine. However, as natural as it might have seemed to the various people who walked past him coming from their cars, Brent felt like a complete idiot.

The fourteenth person who was about to pass him was obviously naturally inclined to be more helpful than those who had preceded her.

"Can I help you?" she asked. Brent, who had studied the Freedom Sports management team's photographs on its website, recognized the Director of Safety who was also Dan's wife's cousin.

"Oh, hi. Ah, no, I'm waiting for someone." Brent smiled and then said in a lower voice, "Does it look like I can't find the ski hill?"

She laughed. "Well, that did cross my mind but I didn't want to come right out and say it. Have a nice day." She started walking away.

"Thanks. You have a great one, too."

Brent now knew where the reserved spaces for Ghost Hawk management were located.

At a quarter to eight, a sleek Mercedes SUV pulled into a reserved spot. Brent was about to walk towards it but a woman got out of the driver's side. Within a minute, she walked past Brent, barely glancing at him. It was the Public Relations Director. While she waited for an elevator to arrive, a Tesla pulled in, parking next to the Mercedes. A man got out. Brent approached him for it was, at last, Sam Welch. He saw Brent coming towards him and his face took on a guarded look.

"I don't want to take any of your time," said Brent.

"What's this?" asked Welch. He was a tall man in his early fifties with short, curly blond hair framing a lined, serious face.

"My name's Brent Umber. Here are my private investigator credentials. Also, here is a note that explains a few things. Please take it. I don't wish for us to be seen talking together because your company has a serious security issue."

Welch took the folded piece of paper.

"If you believe I'm some kind of maniac, please call Sheriff Bates and he will explain what it is I'm doing. Good day."

Welch said nothing. In fact, it was pointless for him to speak to Brent's retreating back. He read the note twice before quickly putting it in his pocket. The look on his face proclaimed that his day had begun badly.

The Public Relations Director was holding the elevator door open for him. He hurried over to her. Sam Welch had already resolved not to say much of anything about the guy in the skiing outfit although the PR Director had to have seen them talking together.

Marv was dressed in a bright yellow ski jacket, an orange knitted cap, emerald green ski pants, and dark red ski boots attached to white skis. Brent nearly guffawed at the overall colour scheme that seemed to have been chosen exclusively for the purpose of not matching. Brent, a scrupulously colour-co-ordinated man, would be spending half the day with Marv, a man intent on drawing attention to himself for any reason but style. As Brent drew closer, he observed that several items were top quality brands.

At present, Brent reminded himself, Marv had manipulated Tosh out of three days' skiing instruction for the express purpose of keeping him under surveillance and was, without doubt, involved in fraud. Brent would not have bothered or particularly cared about Marv's activities if it had been fraud alone. That the fraud had led to two deaths meant there was no separation. Involvement in any part meant inclusion in all. If Marv was not a murderer, he was at least a co-conspirator. He knew Brent to be a private investigator but did he also know that Brent was aware of this?

The clouds hinted there would be a storm later on. Brophy expected it. A northwest wind was forecast to push a front across the region but it was still a little way off at that moment. The air pressure had yet to drop and heavy clouds had yet to appear because the system was coming up on the blind-side of the high ridge. From the top of Ghost Hawk, however, a dark line could be seen on the northwest horizon. Meanwhile, immediately above the lower slopes, thin, slow-moving, high clouds allowed pale golden sunshine to filter through. It was a perfect day for skiing - comfortably below freezing and barely a breeze.

"Dude, we'll ski around to see where you're at," said Marv, as he and Brent swayed in the chair going up to a green slope. "Then we'll get focussed… You know, I feel so good about today. It's like the storm's gonna bring a big clearing out of all the bad vibes in Brophy."

"You think it can do that? I don't see how a change in weather will make a difference."

"It's psychological… It puts a break between how things have been and how they will be. I love storms… all that power surging around. Man, it's good, so good... You know, I heard there's as much energy in a thunderstorm as there is in a nuclear bomb. This storm today will be like a slow-burn nuke and we're going to be right in the middle of it. That's amazing... And, and, and," He nudged Brent, "instead of ash being the fallout we get tons of snow to ski on. How good's that? Woo-hoo!" he yelled.

Marv proved to be both an excellent skier, his actions possessing a loose, almost careless, grace, and a patient, insightful instructor who knew how to get the best from a student. While he was in instructor mode, he explained and conversed without extravagance.

"Okay, Brent, you're doing good. We'll go over to Wolf Run and try an easy blue. So far, you've been learning to execute single elements or small combos. Now you've got to put what you know to the test. Don't go too, too fast, stay in control, and ski it like you love it."

The approaching storm had caused some would-be skiers to stay away. The obvious murder of Alex had probably also contributed to the decline in attendance. Even so, many people who had already booked hotel stays had come anyway or were staying to ride it out.

Brent went down the blue slope and tried to 'ski it like he loved it.' He did love it but he knew what Marv had meant - to ski as though that art belonged to him, that he owned it and was content in that ownership. This main slope was incredibly long and, although fairly steep, would not be any great challenge to an accomplished skier.

The first third of his descent had Brent still trying to ski properly. The second third found Brent relaxing, recalling fragments of what Tosh, Nils, and Marv had told him. It became easier to do what he needed to get down the slope. In the final third it was as though something gelled inside and, he could think of it no other way, he was finally skiing rather than learning to ski. Externally, in the way Brent executed turns and such, there was little that was observably different from the man who had started at the top of the slope to the man who reached the bottom. Inwardly, a change had been wrought. Brent now thought of himself as a skier. He looked back up the long, white slope in its extraordinarily beautiful setting to see Marv coming down easily. Brent thought to himself, I can do that.

After two hours, they needed a break. They had got on well together and, in some measure, Brent had set aside thoughts of investigation - but not completely. Marv, despite his ways, was a perceptive man. They both knew that they were scrutinizing one another and the scrutiny produced a growing constraint. Marv ceased to show off. Brent was at a loss as to what to do. If he asked any questions whatsoever, Marv would instantly be put on the defensive. Besides, there was Tosh's situation to consider. Normally, in any situation similar to this, Brent would have been honest and asked direct questions, believing that the person to whom he was talking was in all likelihood innocent. In any case, Brent's primary motivation was to establish their innocence. Today, this approach was denied him. Marv was guilty of something and the only question was as to the degree of his guilt.

"What have you been doing with yourself, Brent? Besides skiing, that is."

"Not a lot. I have to say that the murder yesterday was very upsetting. I hope the Sheriff finds Alex Simpson's killer soon," said Brent. "Can't be good for the town. What do you think?"

"Yeah, sure. It's bad. We never usually have any real trouble up here."

"Do you think it was someone from out of town or someone with a grudge?"

"Don't know. Does it make any difference? The guy's dead and gone. That's the same for all of us. We all die so make the most of it while you can."

"I suppose… I hope Alex had made the most of it. If he didn't then he can't now and that's a real shame."

"Here today, gone tomorrow. Yeah, it's a shame but what can you do?"

"Find the murderers. I think that will begin the healing process for his family."

"Yeah, so we're up here skiing and the storm'll probably kick us off. We should get some more practice in before that happens. What I want you to do now is…"

"Sheriff Bates? It's Sam Welch. I know you're busy at the moment but what can you tell me about a private investigator named Brent Umber? He handed me a note this morning and said I should contact you. I have doubts about his authenticity."

Welch was calling from the quiet airiness of his office - a large, well laid-out, minimalist room that had a view of the slopes and was devoid of personal mementoes.

"I can't vouch for him personally because I only met him this week," replied Bates. "I checked a reference he gave me and he's been employed on several high-profile murder cases. He's an odd duck who's freelancing on the Simpson murder case. Having said that, he seems to know what he's doing. What did the note say?"

"Okay, I'll read it to you…

'Excuse the cloak and dagger delivery. Freedom Sports is being systematically defrauded by a group of your employees with the help of outside agents. There is a strong possibility that this ties in with Alex Simpson's death.'

He provided a phone number and asked me to contact him after three today. When he handed me the note, he said I should call you. So, here I am. If it's true, I want to know all about this immediately."

"Well, he outlined a potential fraud to me and said he was working on it but he never said he would be contacting you. I doubt he's got any hard evidence… Probably he's coming to you to find out if his claims can be substantiated or to give you a heads up."

"I guess so," said Welch. "You see my problem, don't you? If he's correct, who, among the employees, can I trust?"

"I can appreciate that. So why not talk to him like he asks and then you'll have a better idea. I'm pretty sure he'll be doing more cloak and dagger stuff - the guy seems to like that."

"Do you think he really does know something and will ask for a… let's call it a retainer?"

"You'll soon find out if that's his goal… I doubt it, although, I could be wrong."

"Thanks, Sheriff. I see I have no option but to talk to him."

"I think so, Mr Welch. Call me back if you have any problems with Umber. Bye."

At about eleven, the weather began to change. The wind picked up and the sun was obscured. The cloud ceiling was noticeably lower and this put a dull grey wash over Brophy. Brent watched as sunlight in bright patches still grazing distant hills was chased away by the fast-moving front and, in a minute, the patches of sunlight were gone.

"Would you like an energy bar?" Brent offered one to Marv.

"Sure… Thanks."

They both stood looking at the view from a spot near the top of Ghost Hawk. A ski patrol went past.

"It's a pity about Karl Saunders," said Brent.

"Yeah. I've no idea what happened there. I mean, how could a guy like him fall off Say Goodbye? It makes no sense to me."

"I don't know. I suppose the coroner will report it as an accident. What else could it be?"

"Gotta be an accident… Probably a freak one. Like he tripped over a pole or something. I guess we'll never know for sure but that's what it has to be."

Brent watched him from the corner of his eye while he answered. He had watched as Marv had gone to bite on his energy bar, stopped, and then answered instead.

"Yep… These bars are good but they're on the small side, aren't they?" said Brent who timed his question as Marv went for his bar again. Marv took a bite this time and answered with his mouth half full.

"They're a bit of a rip… but they're handy to have. You got the munchies or something?"

"Continuously," said Brent. "Do you want to join me for lunch?"

"Thanks, man, but I've got to be somewhere else." Marv unzipped a pocket and took his phone out.

"Okay, another time… Something I've been meaning to ask you," said Brent who noticed Marv stiffen slightly and do nothing with his phone. "Will this storm affect the competition at the end of the week?"

"No… it'll blow through and end overnight. Likely it'll be sunny tomorrow." As he spoke, he relaxed and began texting without looking at Brent.

"Are you in the competition?"

"Oh, yeah. Snowboard, though. Slalom and Slopestyle."

"How do you handle competing against your friends?" asked Brent.

Marv looked up suddenly with an odd half-smile that was not a real smile. "Oh, man, when you're competing you

totally forget about your friends. You have no friends then."
He shook his head to add emphasis to his last point.

"I've heard you need sponsorships to get anywhere."

"Sure. There'll be a bunch of company reps up here
checking things out. The Black Shark Drinksco rep is already
up here talking to people. She's the one who signs the
sweetest deals and they're actively looking for new talent.
Anyone who signs with Black Shark is solid."

Brent thought to ask if that was where he was going at
lunch - to schmooze or be schmoozed by potential sponsors.
He refrained, though, as he did not want to have it seem that
he was too interested in what Marv did or did not do.

"If you're competing on Friday, won't you want to rest
up or practise instead of teaching me?"

"Nah, it'll be fine. I spend my life on this hill anyway. I'll
be ready for the comp... You gonna watch?"

"I think I will."

"So do that and be sure you drop by the House
afterwards. It'll be total madness there the whole weekend."

Brent thought of a quip but suppressed it. "I probably
won't. I'm leaving late Friday."

"Yeah? Too bad." He put his phone away. "Okay, Brent,
we'll probably get two more runs in so let's do something
different..."

Brent listened carefully to the man who had reverted to
being in instructor mode. Marv looked relaxed as he spoke.
Brent got the impression that Marv now thought he was no
threat, or no longer a threat. Slight though the evidence was,
Brent also believed Marv had been lying about Karl
Saunders.

Chapter 19

Wednesday Afternoon

With Marv gone and while eating an early lunch, Brent called Lotta.

"Hi Lotta, where are you exactly?"

"Hi, I'm at home. Lessons have been cancelled this afternoon."

"Ah, it's the storm, of course. We need to meet up sometime so I can pay what I owe. When would be convenient for you?"

Lotta laughed. "Oh, I don't know, whenever you like. Tonight would be okay but probably tomorrow when the roads have been cleared."

"Okay… I must ask, why did you laugh?"

"You're so polite. It's nice. The people I hang out with rarely go in for politeness."

"I see. I acquired the habit because it doesn't cost a penny and makes things more pleasant. I do have a favour to ask. Are you in any local social media groups?"

"I am on Facebook, if that's the kind of thing you mean. What's this about?"

"I was thinking, if you sent me an invitation to one that would be likely to reach many local skiers and boarders, I could join anonymously. I could post a few innocuous comments first, and then, if I needed to, set a rumour going to produce a result."

"I don't know if I can do that... What type of rumour? About Karl, you mean?"

"It would be in connection with that, yes."

"You hope to catch his murderer?" There was a very long pause. "I guess I could if it will help. I'll ask a moderator to let you in."

"Excellent! Thank you. Tell the mod I'm Miles Fairleigh. I'll be using an email address with that name. And I'll have the user name of... Why can I never think of a good sounding name for these things...? Something like BoardBoy, if it's not already taken. I'm doing this because I hope to scare the killers into action. It might work or it might not. I may not even use it. Even if I don't, this is just between us, okay?"

"Sure. What would you say?" asked Lotta eagerly.

"It's a pretty good rumour, even though I say so myself. But I must keep it a secret at present. I'll give you a heads-up just before I post. Then we can both watch as the action unfolds. But it's not the online comments I'm looking for. It's the offline activity that results from it I'm after."

"Okay, Miles. I've got a reply back from a mod and she's cool with letting you join. I'm sending the link to you."

"Just perfect."

As Brent skied his way back to the hotel in an increasingly boisterous wind, the slate grey cloud that seemed low enough to touch began to release its burden. Snow pellets descended in thick clusters as if hurled down. Brent put his hood up and his goggles over his eyes because the pellets were stinging his neck and face. He tried to hurry along but the wind pressure wanted to push him off track and took his breath away. He went along slowly and laboriously. He was only two hundred yards from the hotel but it had already disappeared from view in the turbulent air filled with ice and snow. When he was a hundred yards away, the snow pellets stopped while the wind now pushed him along. The wind blew harder just as Brent reached the sanctuary of the hotel.

"Wow. Will you look at that?" said a woman by the entrance who had thought to go out.

Brent turned to look. "It is disgusting."

The view was depressing. Increasingly heavy amounts of snow were travelling at such high speed it was perfectly horizontal - a streaming, incessant white procession in the foreground which turned to a flowing grey in the distance. As they watched, the wind died down. The vanguard of the storm had passed. Now it began to snow properly.

Brent was in his room looking out of the window at where the mountain should have been. The wind had died away to nothing. Anything beyond a hundred yards was rendered invisible by heavy snow which had been coming down for two hours without a let-up. Brent thought the sky could not possibly hold such amounts of the stuff. The sky ignored his disbelief and continued to pour down its white contents in much the same manner as, on a smaller scale, a large grain truck offloads its cargo through its tailgate. His thoughts were suddenly disturbed when the call came at 3:01 p.m.

"Hello," said Brent.

"Mr Umber, this is Sam Welch."

"Thank you for calling. I've been interviewing and observing people in the resort and around Brophy and I'm convinced your company is being systematically defrauded. I've discovered this operation while looking into the two recent deaths which have occurred. I don't want to dwell on that part. What I will say is that there has to be at least two high-level managers within your company that are running this scam operation.

If you prefer, we could meet to discuss the matter. My chief concern is that you might be personally involved in this fraud. I know you spoke to Sheriff Bates and he voiced his displeasure at my contacting you about this. Obviously, no charges can be laid until the perpetrators are identified. What I would like is to aid you in identifying them, then for you to stop their activities, and for Sheriff Bates to arrest the murderers. Until I'm assured that you're not involved we have nothing to say to each other. Just so you know, I've sent my notes to two sources I trust and they will be released to the authorities should anything happen to me.

I think I've said enough. Now it's your turn to convince me that you have nothing to do with defrauding the company."

"And what if I choose to say nothing because I find your manner insulting?"

Brent did not answer.

"These are serious allegations but they lack any specifics. Do you expect me to believe your vague statements about people I've known and worked with for years…? I trust these people."

"I understand your difficulties," said Brent. "Please understand mine. It's not my concern that your company is being defrauded. The criminals could be taking twenty million instead of the two or three million I think they're getting and it would make no difference to me. What I am deeply concerned about are the two deaths. The fraud is tied to them. I want no more deaths and I want the people responsible for the murders to be brought to justice. You are a gatekeeper to the information I need. But if you give me no help, I will find the murderers without you."

Sam Welch took some moments to answer.

"Can I call you back on this? I need time to think over what you've said."

"I have no problem with that but, as the lawyers like to say, time is of the essence. I'd appreciate hearing from you in an hour or so. And I caution you not to mention this to anyone. Goodbye."

Brent tried to analyze the possible reasons for Welch's hesitancy. If the positions had been reversed, he mused indulgently, he would have arranged a meeting in a moment. Welch had not done this so what was it that stopped him? Being neck-deep in the fraud himself was the most obvious answer. Beyond that, and chief operating officers usually being selected for their decisiveness, all Brent could think was that Welch wanted to talk to his boss who would be… the CEO and who undoubtedly worked in another location.

Welch called back within half an hour. Brent had done little but watch the snow while he waited as he was unable to focus on anything else. It was a brief call, in which Brent was asked to go to room 1408 that served as an office suite dedicated to the use of Freedom Sports. He went there immediately.

Brent knocked on the door and entered. The very thing he had not wished to see, he saw. Seated at a table for four were two women as well as Sam Welch.

"This is Mr Brent Umber and this is Cynthia Dane, our Public Relations Director, and Mary Hines, Director of Retail Sales. Please, be seated."

"Thank you." Brent sat down, unsure as to how to proceed in the conversation that would shortly ensue.

"Thank you for coming," said Cynthia Dane who was in her mid-thirties, wearing a smart, navy blue business suit, and looking relaxed despite the unique circumstances that had initiated the meeting. She had the only laptop present open in front of her. "We understand you have some disturbing information about the company. Would you mind sharing it with us?" Her voice was pleasant but she clearly meant to control the meeting.

Brent looked at each of them in turn. Mary Hines looked ill at ease but Brent was unable to read anything particularly significant into that. Many people are awkward in meetings and the subject of this one could easily cause alarm. Retail Sales… Director… Could be hands-on which would make her a potential suspect.

He looked at Cynthia Dane and her polished appearance - highly suitable for the company's spokesperson. *She's an unlikely candidate. Can't tell, though. She might be the brains behind it all.*

Sam Welch looked tense and depressed - as though he would rather be somewhere else. Brent thought it extremely unlikely he would bring two other people into the meeting unless he trusted them. *That also counts in his favour. He wouldn't want witnesses if he's involved in fraud… Unless all three of them are in on the scam. I suppose he must be the type of guy who manages by consensus.*

The problem is, can I afford to let this idea, this untested idea, loose at the moment?

"If I were defrauding your company," said Brent, "I think I would have an exit plan in place. At the first sign of trouble, I would close up shop and just disappear. If anyone at this table tells another person or so much as hints that there is an ongoing fraud, two possible things might happen. One is that several employees could suddenly disappear. That would be the least problematic of the two. The other is that one or more of you might end up dead under the bridge in the middle of town.

In some sense, we have already gone too far. Mr Welch, who else have you spoken to?"

"No one but I'm yet to be convinced you have anything. So are my colleagues."

"I suppose you think I'm the scam artist. Very well… I can see we're not going to get anywhere." Brent got up. He thought to say that they deserved to be defrauded but thought better of being sarcastic. They might come around eventually.

"You're leaving?" Welch looked astonished.

"Yes. I had hoped to trade information with you. You give me names and I tell you how it's being done. As we can't get past the trust issue I'll just give what I have to Sheriff Bates. He won't like it when the FBI comes in but that can't be helped."

"Ah, Mr Umber," said Ms Dane, "we *do* want to hear what you have to say and we *are* prepared to help you."

"I don't know that I can trust you. I asked Mr Welch not to tell anyone because, literally, any employee could be a party to this fraud or embezzlement. I came to this meeting and I find he has told two other people." He turned to Welch. "Have you told anyone else?" He could not stop himself this time. "Did you post it on all your social media accounts?"

"I did not tell anyone else. I know you're annoyed but you should look at it from my perspective. This is a complicated business and I do not want the heart torn out of the company. I trust both Mary and Cynthia implicitly. If there is a problem, they will help me identify and recover from it. This is not something I can do on my own. You need to understand that…. Credit me with some sense. You will notice certain managers are not present for the simple reason that their departments are likely to be involved and, if what you say proves to be correct, they may be involved themselves."

"You should have given that little speech first," said Brent. "As far as I could see it, you had completely ignored my warning that our meeting should be kept strictly private. But now that potential damage is done, I will trust you that you know what you're doing, Mr Welch, and may as well lay out the schema of the scam for the three of you to consider. Please remember, all of you, that there will be consequences in relating what is said in this meeting to anyone." Brent sat down again.

It took a long time to get through all the information. His audience was attentive. Brent gave the complete set-up and spoke of the possibility of lift operators being involved. He showed how it was possible to deposit receipts in outside bank accounts using a parasitic server system. He did not tell them where he thought the system was located.

When asked, as he was several times, what proof he had it was taking place, Brent pointed to his one piece of evidence which was the existence of the network of informants and lookouts. They would only do what they did if they were paid and they certainly were protecting something or someone. Pressed further, he stated he had spoken to three such informants, seen two more, and, he believed, knew the name of a sixth.

"Let's say those six get, on average, two hundred a week each for their services. It could be more but, at two hundred, that's over sixty thousand a year. Where's that money coming from? I've checked and it's not drug dealing. Of the six people I know, none of them is a key player within the company."

Sam and Cynthia bought into the premise while Mary appeared to be reluctant. She asked about how it would be accomplished technically. Brent replied that if she went looking for extra cables or routers around terminals she would give the game away. It quickly became apparent that this was exactly what she had been thinking to do.

"If they get spooked, they probably have an exit strategy, which would make tracing their past transactions much harder for us. Also, the principals would likely escape... maybe not for long, unless they leave the country. Remember, there are murder conspiracy charges to be laid. It's not just fraud."

It was a sober discussion. Brent received a complete organizational chart and a long list of names and occupations. Sam said he would forward background details of key personnel when, as he put it, the HR Director wasn't looking.

Sam now openly shared his thoughts as though in a regular meeting. "We need a forensic audit and some kind of specialist team to come in to identify, and eventually isolate this... parasitic system. That's a good term for it. I can't let this go on too long. How much time do you think you need?"

"Technically, I'm on vacation and learning to ski, so I'm officially supposed to be here until Friday night. The group is already suspicious of me. If I extend my stay they will become very suspicious."

"Why are they suspicious of you?" asked Cynthia.

"By virtue of my being a private investigator. Because I, like an auditor or a government official or someone from head office, might ask awkward questions. I have made myself particularly worthy of their suspicion because I took an interest in Karl Saunder's death."

"But that was an accident," said Sam quickly.

"Well... I found some circumstances that are curious and curiosity is not something this group appreciates. So, to answer your question, I hope to finish up by Friday. That means I will give everything I have to Sheriff Bates at that time and I'll give you a heads-up that I've done so. The capturing of this group is best left up to him."

"I'm not sure he has any experience in white-collar crime," said Sam, resting an elbow on the table and holding his chin. "He'll need to bring in other agencies."

"If the group's bank accounts are out of state then he has to," said Brent. "Otherwise, it's his call, I think."

"We have the snowboarding competition Friday and Saturday," said Cynthia.

"Those will be particularly busy days," said Mary. "I can't have terminals going down while the system gets fixed."

"Yes," said Sam. "We need to get this operation stopped with a minimum of disruption. Cynthia, put together a timeline of what we need to do. Once we have an action plan, then I can assign tasks. We'll need to bring in a team from head office."

Seeing that the matter had now been relegated to an item on the agenda of things to be done by management, Brent took his leave but not without impressing upon them once more the need for continuing secrecy, as in, 'Do not even tell your significant others.' He hoped it was a redundant warning. Even as he said this and then left, he felt certain that someone in head office would know everything by the end of the day.

Chapter 20

Later Wednesday afternoon

*B*ack in his hotel room, Brent went over what he had already known, fitting in what he had just recently heard. He reviewed the charts and lists. Although he felt he was progressing, the list of names did not add much to what he had already. The exception was the Information Technology department. The IT Manager, Wesley King, and the Assistant Manager, Bella Downs, looked to be roughly equal candidates for inclusion. They had even started at approximately the same time with Bella Downs being hired first and Wesley King two months later. Either or both could be involved.

What troubled him was that the world of the slopes and the world within Freedom Sports were two entirely different spheres, both socially and economically. He felt that someone had to bridge the gap so that the two spheres communicated with each other.

Marv controlled Tosh within the confines of their friendship. Marv had a free run of the House - as if he owned the place or had a right to be there. Did he also control Simon Boltz? He put the question at the top of his list.

Boltz had hinted, in his threat to Tosh about what happened to snitches, that *he* may have murdered Alex

Simpson. Did he or had he used the statement merely as a scare tactic? Brent knew that it was himself that Tosh was likely to snitch to if anyone. Marv would know it, too, so that nugget of information probably came to Boltz from Marv.

Marv had also been very annoyed with Tosh for talking to Dustin Packard, the lift operator. Whatever else Marv might be, he was not the one controlling the entire operation. Matters had to be reported to someone else. Brent wrote down more questions.

Finally, there was Dan, the taxi driver, who contacted someone other than Boltz. Brent could not imagine it was Marv to whom he was sending text messages. Another question made the list and at this point it began to look to Brent that one person controlled Marv, Dan, and Simon. But who could it be?

Being a marked man meant Brent could not easily go anywhere to investigate without the threat of being identified and followed. He could not trust any taxi drivers but especially Dan. Added to that, the snowstorm was likely to keep him in the hotel for the rest of the day. Even if he could get out and about, he could jeopardize everything if someone spotted him. Then he had an idea. He searched the internet for flight and bus times.

"Vane, how are you?"

"Hey, Brent. Broken anything yet?"

"Kind of you to ask. Not yet and I hope to keep it that way."

"Ooh, you sound serious. What's up?"

"A double murder, I can't go anywhere without being recognized by the group responsible for them, there's a large-scale fraud going on, and I don't know who to trust. Then I thought of you. It's for two or three days' work."

"Wow, Brent. This is what you do on vacation? What do you want me to do?"

"Come out to the Ghost Hawk Resort and be a ghost yourself."

"I can do that class-wise… Short notice, though… This is going to cost you big time, brother."

"Name your price."

"Er, five grand."

"Okay. Fifteen hundred in cash, three and a half invested, and I pay all expenses."

"Brent, I was joking. You can't be doing that!"

"Well, I'm going to. I'm sending you the info on a flight at 7:20 p.m. and you should arrive in time to connect with the last bus to Brophy. If you miss it, get a cab up here so have some cash with you. I'll transfer an advance now."

"I can't ski."

"Pack your stuff and go to the Ski and Surf Sports Store. Talk to Quincy and get your boots custom-fitted - only tell him to get a move on. Tell him I sent you… I know, I'll give him a heads up. Snowboard or skis?

"I don't know. I do skateboarding and I can skate, does that help?"

"Not as much as you'd think it would."

"You're skiing so I'll go with skis, then."

"Okay. Let them pick the equipment for you, it's much easier. Oh, yes! Choose clothing in darker colours so you blend in.

Now, you also have to pick up some items from my house. I'll have Maria get everything ready to go so you aren't held up. Think you can do all that?"

"I'll try. I'm on my way."

Brent bought Vane's tickets for the flight and the bus. He told Quincy what Vane would need and to take special care of her. He gave him a credit card number. He also called Maria.

"Hello, Maria. How are you?"

"I'm fine. Monty says hi. Don't you, puss? He's right here, rubbing against my legs."

"Say hi to Monty for me. Sorry to bother you but I need some things made ready to be picked up today. Vane will be coming round in a few hours to collect them and she'll be in a hurry."

"Oh, what's going on?"

"She's coming out here to help me."

"Is she? Why's that? Are you on to something?"

"I think so. I can't explain now. I need my dark grey business suit, a blue shirt, a white shirt, a couple of conservative ties, a black belt, and a pair of black shoes - loafers, I think."

"Okay, so you'll need the suit bag. What else? Wait, I gotta get a pen. I don't want to forget nothing…. Okay, I'm ready."

"I need my laptop and the regular backpack I carry when I'm on an investigation."

"That's in your closet. Anything else?"

"Yes. There's that small case of cosmetics and stuff - the one I showed you. I'll need that, too."

"The wig box. Yep, I know where that is. Is that everything, hon?"

"I think so. If I think of anything else…"

"Then you'll call to tell me and I'll get it. This sounds good. I wish I were coming out to help. You must have a good plan. But tell me, are you eating enough?"

"I'm eating plenty, thanks. The plan is not that great but I feel I have to do all I can."

"Ah, don't worry about it. You'll do fine. What's Vane gonna be doing?"

"Trailing people and interviewing a few suspects."

"Aw, that's nice. She likes that. She's a good kid. I bet she dropped everything when you asked her to help."

"Yes, she did. Vane's very, very good in many ways. I appreciate her and I also highly value what you do."

"That's very nice. You just keep saying nice things like that because I love hearing them. But you got to let me go so I can get all this stuff ready… Brent, you forgot something. Do you need an overcoat to go with the suit?"

"I probably do. Poor Vane, she has to carry all this extra luggage as well as her own."

"Ah, she'll live. Bye, bye, sweetie."

"Bye, Maria, and thank you."

The blizzard associated with the front had passed through and the weather that had followed was steadily falling snow in a five mph wind. Brent found a weather forecast that was unique in his experience. The forecast stated the snow would taper off sometime before midnight. Thursday's projection was a mix of sun, cloud, snow, ice pellets, falling temperatures, and the possibility of strong wind gusts producing blowing snow and white-out conditions. The forecasters were seriously hedging their bets.

Frustration set in with his enforced idleness. He supposed the case would restart the next day when he met Marv again and Vane started working. It was an odd situation - being taught to ski by a suspect. If Brent cancelled the lessons, Marv, and presumably the group he belonged to, would have their suspicions raised - as if they were not suspicious enough already.

He knew he was in danger and was surprised to feel so calm under that threat. He idly wondered how an attack would be made upon him. Would they choose an accident on the slopes or an attack in the street? Maybe it would come while he was sleeping in the hotel. He was not unduly alarmed but certainly felt that he should start to be more prudent. Many people were becoming aware of what he knew and, at present, his safety could be jeopardized by any one of these many. Tosh, Bates, Dr Denver, Lotta, and the three people he had just met - any one of them might say something to the wrong person… to that someone who ran things. The circle of those who knew could already be wider than he was thinking. There were other deputies present when Brent had seen Jebb Bates and there were two different receptionists connected to Dr Denver who may have overheard conversations or guessed at something. The only way to defeat any potential attack would be to go public immediately. Unfortunately, that was the last thing he could do without jeopardizing the integrity of the pieces he was trying to build into a case.

He mulled over the jeopardy. What was he waiting for exactly? Was he waiting for the Sheriff or Sam Welch to precipitate matters? Jebb Bates would not do anything without evidence. Welch was waiting on Brent. And Brent was waiting for what? He could not see what to do next unless he knew who all the major players were. He received a call from Sam Welch.

"Mr Umber? This is just to let you know that you might be right. Don't worry, we made sure no one saw this but Mary examined a terminal and found some type of a splitter box hidden under a service desk. She couldn't trace where the cables went but she says there is no reason for it to be there. She's worked in IT elsewhere so I believe she knows what she's talking about."

"She didn't touch it, did she?"

"No, and she was very careful but, ah, we had to know for certain."

"I see," said Brent. "Thanks for letting me know but please, be careful."

"Oh, we will. You needn't worry about that. I have a lot to do but I'll let you know if anything more becomes apparent."

Brent was not pleased by this news. That the theory had been partially proven did not offset the danger of the murderers being at large and possibly striking again or escaping or both. Now it looked as though it were only a matter of time - hours or a day - before the knowledge he had been trying to restrict became *common* knowledge. Brent knew he had to do something and do it soon.

Chapter 21

Late Wednesday afternoon

*T*he snowstorm had blocked roads sufficiently that only powerful SUVs were able to get anywhere. Snowploughs had cleared main roads but little else. The big clean-up would come after the snow stopped falling but, for now, there was very little traffic. This did not mean all the people of Brophy had stayed inside. Quite a few were moving about the town - some on snowshoes, several skiers, and some on snowmobiles. Brent, observing such activity from a hotel window, decided he would try to reach the County Records Office before it closed for the day.

The settled snow was, on average, a foot deep with some small drifts up to two feet high. Brent had rented some cross-country equipment from the rental outlet, thinking that this was the perfect time to try it out. It was a minor exhilaration for Brent when he began to ski along in the middle of an unploughed side street. It gave him the feeling that Brophy was having a holiday where such absurd things as this could happen. However, he soon found it hard going in the loose snow but at least he was going somewhere. This was better than if he had stayed inside just staring at the weather. Brent also found a sense of release from the tension that had been building up as he travelled through the quietened town, surrounded by gently falling flakes. It was as if he were inside a pretty snow globe and the feeling simply made him happy.

Arriving at the Records Office, Brent stuck his skis upright in a snowdrift and went inside. Although he banged his boots and brushed off what snow he could before entering, he still managed to trail small quantities of the stuff across the rubber mats.

"Great, you made it. Thanks for coming to pick me up." One of the two ladies behind the counter had her winter coat on and started to lift the counter flap as soon as she saw Brent.

Brent lifted his goggles. "Hello," he said. "Sorry to disappoint you. I would take you wherever you wanted to go but I came on skis."

"Oh, my goodness! I thought you were my snowmobile ride."

"Sorry about that," said the other lady apologetically. "We've closed early and are waiting to go home. We didn't think anyone would show."

"Ah, I see. I only wanted one little piece of information on a property. I can come back tomorrow."

"No, that's fine," said the second lady. "How can I help you?"

"I need a property owner's name."

"Okay… Just be a minute here."

She switched her terminal back on, took off her coat, and sat down. As she did so the sound of a snowmobile coming to a stop outside could be heard.

"That's gotta be him. I'll see you tomorrow," said the lady who was ready to go home. She smiled and headed for the door.

"Yep, take care," said the woman at the terminal. She turned to Brent. "Do you have the address?"

"Yes. This is it. It's rented out most of the time if that helps at all."

"Oh, *that* one - the party house. I hardly need to look it up. It's owned by an LLC. It's eight dollars for the search by the way."

"Certainly." Brent took out some cash to pay. "Have you looked it up recently?"

"Did in December... The Code Enforcement Officer is always after them for something or other. Like trash on the property... I don't mean to pry or anything but aren't you that private investigator looking into Alex Simpson's murder?"

"I am looking into what happened. I wonder, who was it who told you?"

"Ah, Betty did. She's the lady who just left."

Brent now recognized that literally anyone in Brophy could know who he was. Worse than that, they were also aware of what he was doing.

"Okay. So what's your take on what happened yesterday?"

"Oh, isn't awful? I can't believe such a thing would happen here. Just unbelievable. Makes me feel sick to my stomach."

"It is a wretched business... Did you know Alex Simpson?"

"No, but my eldest son did. He even saw him earlier last night, about eleven or something. They met in the street when Alex was heading home. He said he didn't notice anything wrong at the time... Then to think..." She left her thought unfinished and slowly shook her head with a mournful expression on her face.

"Was Alex with anyone?"

"No, by himself... But he must have met someone afterwards, right?"

"I think he had to. Has your son mentioned that Alex was in any kind of trouble?"

"Ah, no. But then I never asked him. So, he might have been, right?"

"He could, indeed. If I give you my number, would you be kind enough to have him call me, please?"

"Sure, I can do that."

Brent wrote out his name and number and, while he did so, the search report began printing.

"I'm Debbie, by the way. Are you thinking that this company is involved?"

"They're probably not," answered Brent. "I was thinking more about the people who hang out there. It seems an odd sort of set-up to me."

"Ah, snowboarders, they've got so much attitude. It's not all of them, mind. There's some who think they can get away with anything… You're right to be looking into that crowd."

"Am I?" Brent was suddenly concerned that the Brophy gossip mill could soon be cranking out fresh material if he was not careful. "I was only thinking that would be one of the few venues open late in Brophy and somebody coming from there might have witnessed something."

"Oh, I get you now," said Debbie, nodding. "It sounds fascinating, being a private detective. But, like, how do you get yourself included in a murder case?"

"I'm not included. I happened to be up here for the skiing when it occurred and I thought I'd look around to see if there were any witnesses to Alex's death or if anyone knew where he was in the hours leading up to it. Should I find anything I'll hand it in at the Sheriff's office. And do you know what? You've helped me immensely."

"I have…? You mean Chris, my eldest, don't you?" Debbie was visibly pleased with herself. "I'll make sure he calls you," she said emphatically.

"Thank you so much and thank you for the report. Is this your ride?"

Another snowmobile had pulled up outside. A big boy about twelve or thirteen got off it and came inside, removing a black, shiny helmet as he did so.

"Hi, mom," he said as soon as he was through the door. "Can we go?"

"You wait a minute," Debbie said by stern look as well as in tones full of maternal authority.

"Hi," said Brent to the boy. "Do the deputies ever stop you in town on your snowmobile?"

"Nah, they're cool. Dad's a deputy, anyways. But it's snowing, right? You gotta get where you need to go."

"We could never snowmobile through Newhampton," replied Brent. "Mind you, the snow we have is nothing in comparison to what you get up here."

The boy grinned. Brent turned back to Debbie.

"Goodbye, and thanks again for your help."

"Goodbye. Think nothing of it. We all want those killers caught and punished."

By the time Brent had left the Records Office, the storm had noticeably abated. It was nearly dark and this prompted him to go back via The Village - to take another look at the blocks of condominiums. On his way, he had to recross the re-opened bridge. The road over it had been recently ploughed so he skied on the sidewalk instead. He stopped at about the mid-point to look down at the river. It came as a surprise that although the sun had almost gone down, the small amount of light reflecting off the snow made the vista quite bright with a strange, muted luminosity.

The Chute itself had disappeared. The steep banks and sheltered surface were now buried under a curving white sweep, two or three feet thick - the snow having fallen into its final resting place or been blown there by the wind. Incongruously, a single post, barely protruding above the snow, possessed a flapping section of crime scene tape. As desolate and thought-provoking as the view was, Brent took time to study the whole area.

It was his habit to check for security cameras and he did so now. The eastern bank - the Main Street side - possessed two that he could see but they were directed away from the river. On the western bank was a park-like riverside walkway, then a road with buildings on the far side of it. Located there were a church, a small office building, and houses converted to professional offices. None of those seemed to have cameras or, if they did, they were concealed and pointed in such a way that the bridge was not overlooked. It became apparent to Brent that where the murder had occurred was indeed a blind spot - unless there was a camera in The Village that happened to capture a distant view of the bridge. He began moving again.

Going uphill on skis took some effort over the short road which ended at the barrier before the main pedestrian thoroughfare of the complex.

The block of shops and condominiums to his right had the best view of the river. He saw a camera at the back of the building. Its primary function was to monitor a side entrance as well as an adjacent garbage collection point but, because of the slope, there was nothing in the way to obscure a direct line of sight to the bridge. The garbage was held for collection in a tall, square privacy fence of upright planks which effectively screened the bins within its gates. Brent skied over to examine the camera. He found that someone had already blown the snow from the area, leaving only a thin base behind.

Brent recognized the camera brand - the model was a good quality, wireless, infra-red camera that may have picked up movement on the bridge but, if it had, the images would probably be indistinct because of the distance. It appeared to be functional. He tried the side door but found it locked. The snow perched on the door's sill was undisturbed.

As the two blocks on either side of the street were configured very similarly, he skied over to the other one. All the cameras he saw here faced the wrong way. Even the camera covering the side door faced in a different direction. There were no garbage facilities here but, instead, two reserved parking spaces for emergency vehicles only. Here, too, the snow had been blown out but there were also the distinctive ribbed track and ski marks made by a single snowmobile. The side door had been used - snow was disturbed around the door. Brent tried it but found it was locked. The same set of footprints led both into and out of the entrance - a man's winter boot, large but not massive. Brent found it curious - this use of a side entrance after a storm. He bent down to examine the prints and guessed they were a size ten or eleven. He smiled to himself as he stood up again, imagining he should be using a magnifying glass and wearing a deerstalker to make the most of such clues. He went around to the front to see if he could discover where the winter boots had gone inside.

The interior of this condominium block was almost identical to the one he had examined before except the carpet was blue. Brent stopped momentarily to collect names from the mailboxes but there were far fewer here than there had been in the block he had visited the day before.

Carrying his skis, Brent walked along the lowest corridor and through the emergency exit door at the end to discover a staircase. One floor down he found the side entrance door with a push bar for easy access out. He could feel how cool it was by the door. The area acted as a sump for cold air which meant some of the snow tracked in by his quarry had barely begun melting. Brent followed his quarry's damp footprints back up the stairs but they petered out between the first and second floors. The man had been in a hurry because he had taken the stairs two at a time.

Once more outside, Brent called Sam Welch.

"Hello. Are you on your own…? I have a quick question."

"I am."

"Have you had any power outages during the storm?"

"We did. Why do you ask?"

"Just a thought. Specifically, what was affected?"

"The main ticket office. Power was cut for a few seconds before coming back on and then everything rebooted."

"I take it there are terminals there."

"Yes, four of them. I was told they were off-line for nearly ten minutes but they're up and running now."

"Thank you."

"Wait a second… You've found out something. What is it?"

During the moment before he replied, Brent thought how quick Welch was to ask for information while not paying for it.

"Ah, nothing much. Thanks, bye."

He ended the call. But he did feel it was something. Brent believed he had narrowed down to a single building the site where the parasitic server system was located. It would be somewhere on the second or third floors. The man on the snowmobile had to have gone to the parasitic servers to physically reset the connection when the targeted servers in the ticket office had gone off-line.

Feeling his luck was changing, Brent called Sheriff Bates.

"Yep," said Bates with resignation when he saw who the call was from.

"I think I may have found an approximate location for the servers used by the gang. It needs more investigation to pinpoint the exact unit."

"And where would that be?"

"I'll tell you but, first, do you know who was involved in the old lift pass scams?"

"That was pretty widespread… I'd say there were about ten individuals at the centre of it but they've all moved away. There were rumours about what they were doing. I think there were a lot more helping themselves besides them. That all got cleaned up so what's your point?"

"I think it likely that those young men and women who were involved but who remained in Brophy are, as a cohort, now approaching middle age. Who among them either has the organizational skills or works in a key position where they could run a much more sophisticated fraud?"

"Interesting question… Me, for one. I was a liftie for a season but I didn't see any money changing hands. A couple of guys sometimes spoke of what they were up to but it was small change. My time was way before it got as bad as it did. After my time? I'd say there's only a couple of people I can recall but they don't fit the bill." Bates had a pen poised over his notebook.

"Okay. I'm trying to build a picture of a person who's got impeccable credentials, used to be a lift operator, is a take-charge kind of person, looks a little better off than they really should be, and is secretive or non-committal about some things."

There was a long silence on the phone which Brent broke.

"You have someone in mind?"

"Yes, I do… Where are the servers?"

"In a condominium in The Village. There are four blocks and it's the one in the southwest corner. You know, the one with the art gallery and perfume shop?"

"I know it… In there, eh?"

"Yes. The terminals went off-line in the main ticket office. This meant that somebody had to go to the parasitic system to fiddle around with it - probably to re-establish a connection or something. The man who did so rides a snowmobile. He went to a condo after the worst of the storm had passed and after much of the snow had been cleared away in The Village. He used a side entrance but I could only follow his wet footprints up to the second floor. There are three floors and the person ran up the stairs. He used a key to the emergency exit that is normally locked to the outside. Using the emergency exit to get in means it would be very unlikely for him, or anyone else for that matter, to be observed."

"Hm... The snowmobile helps narrow it down. Might be the IT guy."

"The Manager is Wesley King and the Assistant Manager is Bella Downs. It could be either of them. I don't know how to check if they used a snowmobile today seeing as I can only get around very slowly on skis at the moment."

"Leave that with me."

"Thank you. Um, I'm sure you understand the trickiness of the situation."

"Oh, yes. It's one big headache."

"I completely agree with that. We have a systematic fraud and two murders have been committed to keep it from being discovered. There's a network of sorts in Brophy. There's no telling how extensive it is or who's involved or how much they know. But you see, knowledge of the murders has to be restricted to only a very few people. By the way, I think we're looking for either two or three individuals. Two, definitely, for the attack on Alex Simpson. I can give you one of the names although I could be wrong."

"You're telling me this last?"

"In the middle because I'm less certain about it being factual - your nephew, Simon Boltz. Somebody helped him but I have no idea who. Remember I mentioned Tosh before?"

"Yes. I wouldn't have thought he fitted into this operation."

"No, he doesn't, really. He's been caught up in it as a fall guy, though, and this is how I see it. Simon Boltz, I'm told, is a habitual bully. Out of the blue, yesterday, he went out of his way to see Tosh and state, 'Snitches don't survive in this town.' This occurred shortly after Alex Simpson was killed and, presumably, it was to warn Tosh against saying anything to you or to me.

I'm pretty sure Simon was acting independently and did this mainly because he despises Tosh and gets a kick out of bullying him. However, it might also be that Simon knows Marv has Tosh lined up for the fall guy for Karl Saunders' death should it start to be officially investigated as a murder - they certainly wouldn't want their fall guy getting too close and confidential with either of *us*!

Whatever is the truth here, I'm pretty sure that Simon also spoke to Tosh the way he did as a form of boasting not only over what he himself might have done but certainly over his being a part of a power structure that controls certain things in Brophy.

This is the last piece I have and it's the most speculative. It seems possible that Marv, who Tosh idolizes to some extent, arranged to meet him at the top of Bear Tracks early Sunday morning. Marv shows up more than half an hour late. If I have it correctly, that would have given him enough time to ski down earlier, with Karl Saunders chasing after him for some infraction or other, to push Karl over Say Goodbye, and then come back around to go up the slope a second time. There he'll meet Tosh and so establish his alibi.

To get his story to sit properly as an alibi, Marv would need a couple of lift operators to say something like they saw Tosh ski away with Karl while Marv was nowhere near the place until later. As you can see - highly speculative."

"Hmm, could have been Marv and Simon who killed Alex Simpson."

"Maybe but we can't know that with any certainty. I'm having skiing lessons with Marv. I had one today and I've got two more in the next couple of days. We're carefully watching each other. He wants to know what I know without asking and I'm doing the same with him. Consequently, we're getting nowhere."

"You're having lessons with the guy?" For once, Sheriff Bates sounded surprised.

"He's very good. He's been a great help to me skiing-wise but our suspecting each other makes for some stilted conversation."

"Watch yourself. Now, listen, I've got to think of a way to play all this and I can't see a clear path yet. You can't go spooking any of these people before I'm ready and I've not got that much to go on."

"I'm being as careful as I can. I certainly don't want to spook them because I'm pretty sure the principals must have some kind of exit plan. They will leave while the small fry gets left to answer for everything. I know I would have an exit strategy so why wouldn't they?"

"Okay. King or Downs runs the computer side of it. They're probably not running Marv and Simon so somebody else is."

"Yes, there has to be one other person to manage the outside network," said Brent. "That would likely be the ex-lift operator we were speculating about. But I've been thinking that over. Wesley King or Bella Downs would be completely in the dark within the company unless someone outside of their department but at the corporate office or another local, top-tier manager could get word to them if a problem arose *inside* the company. Knowing about external investigators and auditors is one issue, being warned of internal reviews and audits are another. I think it likely there is a second person, at least one, *inside* the company who is in on the deal but not at a technical level. This person could also liaise between those within the company and the person running the outside organization."

"Like a personal secretary?"

"Yes, exactly like that. A person in a position to see information in advance of a potential threat, be called into critical meetings or, more or less, know what Sam Welch knows. That information would be relayed immediately to whoever needs to get it. If the threat were serious enough, they would all vanish. This means that the person on point duty would be the one to assess the risk in the situation and would, therefore, be a principal."

"I've got to ask you something. Is this how you work with Darrow?"

"I suppose it is. You mean the theories?"

"Yeah. Like, if I didn't know you were guessing at a lot of this, it would sound like you're telling me what's actually happening."

"I can't stop myself from doing it. The big difference in this situation is that I have no idea who's involved. With Greg Darrow, he's usually handing me a case that has a list of names. I try to find out who's innocent first so then the list shrinks to a few highly probable suspects. I know that technique will get caught out one day but it's worked so far."

"Right. I have to go. Is there anything you need from me?"

"Yes, there is. The murder on the bridge took place in a blind spot. Has CCTV footage been reviewed?"

"Deputy Fraser is leading the case but I know a couple of them were looking at all the tapes they'd got. Fraser says there's nothing to see. Whoever did it, knows all about the camera coverage in Brophy and how to get around it."

They said goodbye. Before returning to the hotel, Brent reflected that the deputies may have missed the camera he had found. He also knew how easy it was to jam a camera's operating frequency. Having done that, two men accompanying Alex Simpson, could leave by a side door, kill him on the bridge, return, and then cancel the jam. He had not wanted to share that particular idea because the deputies would immediately want to shift their attention to The Village itself, which attention could very easily ruin things.

Back at the hotel, Brent put his ski equipment away in his locker. As he walked through the lobby he saw a small display advertising the upcoming snowboarding competition. It was being assembled by a man in his mid-twenties who was working at a catch that refused to lock into place. Brent went over to chat with him. The Black Shark logo was prominently displayed on banners and printed materials which explained how proud the company was to be promoting the event.

"Your company is promoting the snowboarding competition?" asked Brent.

"Like, ah, yeah," said the man. "We're one of the sponsors." He answered as though Brent's question was inane.

"Are you looking to sign up new talent to represent your company?"

"Maybe."

"Are you familiar with the sponsorship program ?"

"I don't know the answer to that one."

"There must be a rep here. Who should I speak to?"

The man stopped what he was doing to look at Brent.

"Deidra Keaton is who you want to see. Before you ask, she's somewhere in the hotel but I don't know where."

"Thanks." Brent walked away. The man returned to fixing the catch.

Brent wished he were not dining alone. As he surveyed the restaurant he realized he was the only one doing so among the other early diners. This time, it did not affect him as much as it sometimes did. As usual, he thought it would be nice to have someone he knew to talk to if only for a little while. He had called Maria earlier in the day and did not wish to disturb her again and, of course, Vane would be arriving soon. In the meantime, at least he was occupied with numerous thoughts about the case. Brent was also looking forward to going skiing for an hour or two because the slopes had re-opened. The word around the hotel was that the wind direction and speed had kept much of the snowfall off the mountain to dump it in Brophy instead.

It was a beautiful soft night after the storm. Earlier, when all the weather's energy had been expended, the crews were on the slopes, beginning to get the runs in shape. A fleet of large tracked vehicles - some with massive ploughs on their front ends - was busy grooming the trails and inexorably moving downhill. When they had gone, all that remained to mark their passage were long, straight lines, as though a giant comb had been dragged across the surface of the snow. The areas at the bottom - the hardest hit - were still being worked at by crews with smaller tractors, snowblowers, and shovels. Indeed, the whole of the town was full of noise - the swollen chorus of snow blowing and ploughing equipment - as Brophy worked hard to dig itself out from under.

While skiing over to the lifts, Brent was still racking his brains as to what it was that should happen next - at least, what *he* should be doing. As he considered the others involved, those with some say as to what action should be taken, he could not see what it was they should do, either. Jebb Bates had sounded slightly overwhelmed. Sam Welch was waiting for the nod to go into action. The fraudsters were laying low. That left only him to precipitate events and he was not sure how to do it or when. Brent going skiing was only his way of deferring making a move. At issue was the lack of clear targets. The IT people, however, were cut and dried or should be anyway. There was no escape for them. Likewise, this was true for Marv, Simon, and others of their rank within the Brophy crime syndicate. But who were the ones at the top of the outfit? There had to be at least two of them, perhaps more. One of those was probably in overall command of the organizational structure and, as yet, Brent had no idea who it could be.

Before getting onto the lift, he made a call.

"Hello, Tosh. It's Brent."

"Hi, I'm glad you called. I was thinking about something." He paused.

"And what would that be?" asked Brent.

"I don't know if it's my imagination or what, but a guy at work started cutting me out for no reason. Like he won't speak to me. Then another guy started picking on me on social media. You think it's anything to do with you know what?"

"Could be that or there might be other reasons. Are they close friends or acquaintances?"

"Acquaintances."

"I think it's likely to be connected to Simon Boltz rather than anyone else."

"That's what I thought. You called."

"I'm looking for someone who now holds a good job or has a high profile or authoritative position but who also used to be a lift operator at the time when many of them were taking cash. Anyone spring to mind?"

"Oh… I don't know. A lot of people have done that job but mostly they were temporary. Like, they did it for a season. I guess you mean someone who worked for a while before moving to a better local job. Difficult… I can't think of anyone at the moment. You gotta know they were quite a bit older than me so I wouldn't have heard them talking about it."

"Of course, that would be the case. Thanks, Tosh. Please get back to me if you happen to think of a name," said Brent.

While waiting in line for the lift, Brent spoke conversationally to two women. They had just arrived from out of state and were going up for their first run. They were happy the storm had passed over without interfering with their vacation. Neither of them knew of the recent deaths and Brent did not mention what had happened. In fact, he found their exuberance infectious and had no wish to spoil it.

Dr Denver called Brent.

"I have some news for you. I just got off the phone with the lab and they gave me a preliminary report. The mark on Karl Saunders neck had a trace of wax in it. They say it is consistent with and presume it to be the type used for waxing expensive skis or boards. Further analysis is needed to determine its exact composition. So, it looks like you were right. I have to think about this situation carefully but I can no longer see the deceased's death as a simple accident."

"Thank you for telling me, doctor. Um, I wonder if I could suggest that you not publish this news just yet. There is a lot at stake at the moment."

"I have to inform the Sheriff."

"Oh, I understand and I didn't mean him specifically. You have to fulfil all the requirements. I was thinking the longer the general public assumes the death was accidental, the better it will be for the investigation. It was just a thought."

"I'll bear it in mind and will mention it when I talk to Sheriff Bates."

"That's excellent, that really is. Thanks."

"I understand. There are no secrets in Brophy, that's for sure. Maybe we can keep one for a little while. Goodnight, Mr Umber."

"Goodnight."

The next run down was one of Brent's most confident and accomplished to date. The added bonus of confirming evidence for his hypothesis provided an extra charge to the thrill. The temperature was dropping again but he found it quite delightful to be under the bright lights that had banished the night from off the slopes which had been impassable two hours earlier. Unnatural though all of it was, the slopes on the mountain now had a distinct aura, making the place feel enchanted. The forms of skiers raced down, some decorated with LED lights, and as they swerved and swayed through shadowy areas, it made for an elfin-land of smoothly dancing gleams that looked almost magical.

Another call came as Brent was sitting on the chairlift. This one was from Chris, the eldest son of Debby, the Records Officer.

"Hello, is this Brent Umber?"

"It is. How can I help you?"

"Ah, like, you don't know me or nothing but you were speaking to my mom. I saw Alex Monday night."

"Have you reported this?"

"I told my dad, he's a deputy, and he said he'd pass it along but I haven't heard anything back."

"Okay. What time did you see Alex?"

"About eleven fifteen. It was in front of Pizza Shack. He was just coming out and I was just going in to grab a slice."

"How did he seem to you? Anxious or worried?"

"No, he was cool. We talked about the competition for like a minute and that was it."

"Pizza Shack is on the corner at the crossroads in the middle of Main Street," mused Brent. "Which way was he heading when he left you?"

"West."

"That's towards the mountain. Was he going home, do you think?"

"I thought so. Like, he didn't say he was but his house is in that direction."

"So he was heading towards the bridge or his house and he stops to get pizza. You chat about the snowboarding competition. He heads off… Was he eating pizza? Was he walking quickly?"

"Yeah, he was eating but he wasn't in a hurry. That's all it was. I wish I could tell you more."

"Actually, Chris, you've told me a lot and I very much appreciate you calling. Thank you."

"No problems."

After his next successful descent, Brent called Lotta.

"You know, I still have your money and it's burning a hole in my pocket. You're lucky there aren't slot machines in the resort."

"Ha… You're not a gambler, are you?"

"If it's your money, yes. If it's my money, no. But, seriously, I'd like to meet up and get this settled."

"I still feel weird that you're paying me for not doing anything."

"You're still helping me out with the little social media scheme we have going. Who is this band, Glider? Every time

I go to post something, you're all chatting and I haven't a clue what you're talking about. I'm probably seven or eight years older than you are and it might as well be a hundred and eight."

"There are people your age on the site. It's just the local scene and you're not yet dialled in, that's all."

"Can't you talk about the weather or something to make it easy for me?"

"Like, *no*. That would be too weird."

"Brophy gets a foot and a half of snow, no one talks about it, and I'm the weird one?"

"You're from Newhampton so it's a big deal for you. We get three of these a year so it's no biggie for anyone who lives here. If the skiing was stopped for any longer than it was, then you would have heard a lot." She laughed. "Anyways, Glider's a red-hot local band and they're going on tour at the end of the month. So they announced today they're doing one last gig before they leave. It's going to be a big bash and we're all stoked."

"Is that this week?"

"Next Friday, so you'll miss it. But you know what's cruel about this? Alex used to be the sound guy at all their gigs. And he won't be there - but, for sure, we're all going to remember him as though he was."

"I see. That's a good way of doing it. By the way, are you working tomorrow?"

"I've got a group lesson in the morning. I might get another in the afternoon. A lot of people changed their plans because of the storm but it should start picking up again. Why do you ask?"

"I was thinking, it would be good therapy for you to keep busy for a while."

"I wish I could. Thanks for the heads up and warning yesterday. It's hard to believe he's gone."

"I know, isn't it? It's an awful thought which puts a hole in one's life."

"Yeah, it does. Do you think these guys will do anything more?"

"I can't say one way or another. I'd like to think that was the end of it and, perhaps, it is."

"Yeah. I don't get why people have to be like that. I mean, why turn to violence? It doesn't solve anything. I hope you find them, though… I'm kind of afraid to ask how your investigation's going."

"I'd tell you but, to be honest, and, for your safety, it's best you don't know."

"I get it… Ah, about this payment. I'm seeing someone tonight. What do you want to do?"

"You're busy so I'll transfer it instead."

"Oh, okay, cool. I'll send you my email address."

The call ended and Brent forwarded Lotta's payment. The next thing he did was to send a text to Vane, telling her to book an appointment for skiing lessons with Lotta's group the next morning. He also cautioned Vane not to mention that she knew him to anyone she met, including Lotta.

Brent then contacted Sam Welch to set up a little ruse he had in mind. Welch was reluctant to accept the idea when he first heard it but, when Brent fully explained the matter, Welch warmed to the notion.

Chapter 22

Wednesday night

With no more pots to stir at that particular moment, Brent returned to the hotel. Already he was realizing that he had skied a little too much today and would be paying for it tomorrow. It was the cross-country skiing and the toll it had taken on his muscles that were the problem. A soak in the tub was in order. He would have gone to bed early but, with Vane arriving late, that was not possible.

He was glad she was coming. He could depend upon Vane to do professional surveillance and she could act with initiative, too. She had picked it all up so quickly. He recalled her early days of training when he and Andy Fowler had showed her what to do and she had taken to it eagerly and seriously. On that first day, she never did spot Andy following her when being trained in counter-surveillance. In later sessions, she did but not that first one, even though she knew what he looked like. The man was a ghost's ghost. She had spotted Brent but not Andy and she could not believe it was possible she had missed him. Yet, after half an hour of trying to catch him out, Andy gave her a verbal list of everything she had done in that time period. Vane become quite theatrical in her 'I don't believe it!' exclamations when she heard him detail her actions to her. It made Brent smile to think of the pair of them - Vane all drama and Andy quietly and inevitably accurate. They could not have been more diverse characters.

When they had finished for the day, Brent had called Andy to ask him what he thought of Vane's potential. "Ah, yes. Vanessa will be good when she's fully trained," he had said. That, coming from Andy Fowler, was high praise indeed.

It was 11:45 p.m when the bus carrying Vane arrived at the terminal. The driver retrieved her gear from one of the luggage compartments. The waiting room was closed so she piled all the things on a bench and waited. The other passengers quickly dispersed on foot or to waiting vehicles. Two cab drivers, one of them being Dan in his Explorer, picked up fares. A third was out of luck, although he looked hopefully at Vane. He drove away when he saw she was talking to someone on her phone.

"Hurry up, Brent. It's freezing out here."

"Zip up your jacket."

"Oh, yeah. It was hot on the bus." Vane zipped up her sleek, black jacket and put up its hood over her grey beanie. She also got her gloves on.

"Nice jacket, by the way."

"You like it? It cost a lot, I know, but it was just beautiful. They said it was warm."

"You have good taste. All clear from where you are?"

"Looks like it. There's a police car parked fifty yards away and the officer in it is looking at me from time to time."

"What age?"

"Late twenties, I guess, although it's difficult to say without staring and he's wearing one of those furry hat things. What are they called anyway?"

"I don't know. Go and ask him."

"Fun-ny. I hope your car's nice and warm."

"Sorry, lady, but I left the car at home. You'll soon warm up with a nice brisk walk."

"You're kidding me?" Vane sounded dismayed.

"I kid you not. On my way."

A shadow detached itself from the shelter of a dark storefront to cross the street. Brent, hunched over, with his hood up, and carrying his Brophy-bought laptop, walked quickly towards the terminal. When he met Vane, they put on a show by first hugging affectionately, followed by Brent acting out contrition for not being present when the bus had arrived - all the while Brent keeping his back towards the deputy's car.

They divided the gear between them before heading towards The Comet Inn. This hotel, where Vane would be staying, was half a mile away.

"First of all," began Vane, "I want to say how sorry I am for saying 'five grand' like that."

"Are you?"

"Yeah, I should have said ten."

Brent smiled. "Your jokes are as bad as mine."

Vane laughed. "Talking of jokes. Brent, you were in a ski and surf shop. You should have gone surfing instead. That is a no-brainer."

"It's winter and I wanted to go skiing. What can I say?"

"It's winter and you should have gone somewhere hot. It is so cold here it's like a freezer. Gah. How does anyone live in this? I thought Newhampton winters were bad enough but this is a whole other level of cold."

"You'll think differently about it once you start skiing. What time is your lesson?"

"I doubt I will. The lesson's at ten. And who's Lotta, may I ask? Is she your new flame?"

"No, she's seeing someone anyway. Lotta's very chatty but she's sharp. She would like to investigate the deaths - which she was doing for the first one. After the second, I took her and a man named Tosh off the case as a precaution.

So I want you to be friendly towards Lotta. Talk to her but not to the point of 'Why don't we hang out together?' friendliness. Give her a twenty-dollar tip at the end of the lesson. That reminds me, I need to give you some cash for expenses. I really don't think Lotta is involved with this syndicate or gang that's operating but I don't want her or anyone else to find out that you and I know each other.

The whole point of your being present is for you to observe people I've made contact with as well as any suspects who need watching. I need to get an idea of how they behave when I'm not around because everyone in Brophy seems to know who I am and what I'm doing."

"Got it. You'd better fill me in. This sounds like another of your unholy messes."

"Oh, yes, it's nice and complicated. First off, and I know I'm repeating myself, we do not know each other and that's for your protection more than anything else."

"Okay. Is anyone tailing you?"

"They're amateurs and no one's doing it consistently. I've noticed several people in different places observing me. Someone went through my things at the hotel. Then there was the incident when I was followed. You'd have laughed if you'd seen them. They were like the Keystone Cops."

"I saw one of those shows. The actors must have got injured all the time! But these people you're talking about, they're responsible for two murders, aren't they?"

"That's right. This is the set-up...." Brent methodically began to explain what had been happening in Brophy. By the time they arrived at Vane's hotel, she had a thorough understanding of the situation and was feeling very warm in her new jacket.

The name of Comet Inn, a smaller but still expensive hotel near the slopes, was entirely divorced from its interior theme of spectacular hunting lodge. Peeled and lightly stained logs of varying dimensions had been used for everything from posts and pillars to tables and chairs. Antique decorative objects were scattered across walls and sat on odd perches. These items mainly consisted of old signs, hunting paraphernalia and trophies, framed prints, with a heavy representation of old winter sporting equipment. The clerk at the reception desk in the three-storey, galleried hall looked unconscionably bright and alert - considering the late hour. His blue fleece top had a logo of a comet shooting past a depiction in outline of Ghost Hawk mountain. Brent was too tired to ask the significance of it but he did wonder.

They got to Vane's room without difficulty and without Brent being recognized. They still had an hour's work ahead of them.

Brent opened his laptop to begin sending to Vane's phone some photos and short biographies of the people he wanted her to watch.

"The first set of photos is of Marv," said Brent. "That's what everyone calls him but his full name is John Marvin Jones. He's the top priority because I believe him to be the highest-ranked. He's smart. He acts out to get attention but he's quite clever. I'm having lessons with him tomorrow and Friday. You shadow him as soon as the lesson is finished in the morning. I'll let you know what lift we're using so, as he comes down, he then becomes your responsibility."

"Okay," said Vane. "You had a lesson with him today. Show me which ski slope you were on."

"This one, Wolf Run number three. But I don't know if we'll be on the same one again."

"Where will I be in the morning?"

"Over here on the Hippo slope."

"Hippo…? Where'd they get that from…? It won't all be kids, will it?"

"Everyone starts at the same place regardless of age. I graduated from Hippo class, so please don't knock my modest success."

"You're a hippo?" Vane burst out laughing.

"I'm hippo class, yes, although it's not anything official. *You* need to be in the same exalted class by noon tomorrow."

"I guess I will… This is crazy… What do I do if Marv skis away? I won't keep up with him."

"Do your best and if you do lose him it just can't be helped."

"Couldn't you put a tracking device on him?"

"I thought about that but he's likely to find it and then he would know it was me. So, no is the answer to that one. However, in my trusty bag are a couple of vehicle trackers. Here, take one." Brent took out a small, square object and handed it to her. "We'll tag Dan's Explorer - he's the cab driver I mentioned. I don't know if it will yield any valuable results but we can try. One thing you should know about Marv, he's easily recognizable by the clothes he wears while skiing… He reminded me of Zach in his colour selection."

"Okay… You know Zach is so big on going into acting now? He's seriously considering taking classes and I'll think he'll do it. But we can talk about him later. So I'm to follow Marv. How long for?"

"Until he goes somewhere where you think he'll be staying for a while. Like an hour or more. He doesn't have a regular job. I asked Tosh and he says Marv only does skiing instruction but, from what I understood, that's not very often.

He is continually short of money. Do you know what's weird? Tosh has never been to his place... Marv's parents live in town - you have their address - and that's the one he uses for official purposes. Other than that, he seems to be a couch surfer. I think it's plausible that he lives somewhere else but hasn't told Tosh."

"Who's next?"

"Simon Boltz is the Sheriff Jebb Bates' nephew. Whereas Marv is weird and entertaining, Simon is not. He's a bully... well, you have his story in my notes. He's one of them who followed me but, more importantly, I think he and an accomplice murdered Alex Simpson. He'll be easier to keep tabs on. He works regular hours in maintenance and he seems to work exclusively at the bottom of the hill. He's not so important because he'll be scooped up when everything breaks wide open. Simon works in several different areas because I've seen him but it's always in and around the lifts without him actually operating the lifts."

"Good, good... now Tosh?"

"Yes, that's him. He's a very nice guy but he's a little bit shy and somewhat naive. I'm convinced he's been set up by Marv to be the killer of Karl Saunders should any verdict other than accidental death be given by the coroner. Read through the notes and you'll get the idea.

Tosh is a low priority. He works in the rental store and his hours are nine to six. Some evenings he works in a resort restaurant. He shares an apartment in a house with two other guys. I met one of them, John, and he seems to be above suspicion. Tosh and his closest friends meet regularly at a restaurant called Georgiou's. The owner is Louise. If you go there, have the beef schnitzel, it's really good. The problem with the restaurant is it's not very busy sometimes and there's no cover in there at all so you can't keep anyone under surveillance without being conspicuous."

"That's a shame," said Vane. "What am I looking for with Tosh?"

"I want to be absolutely sure he's not neck-deep in this scheme."

"He'll be difficult to watch while he's working. I could rent some skis and boots and, like, fuss over them or something."

"You could. A recent development for you to be aware of is that Simon has turned several of Tosh's acquaintances against him. So be extra careful because they are suspicious and probably extra vigilant with him. I would say to keep your distance if you can. Try and get a sense of who it is who's talking to him as well as anyone who is avoiding him and might seem at all antagonistic. Get photos and video of everyone."

"Yes, yes, of course, I will, Brent."

"I know you will but I have to say it because I'm the official worrier in this partnership."

"The worry's unnecessary but I'll get you framed photos of everyone. Who's next?"

"Last is Dan. He drives a black Ford Explorer as a taxi cab - you can't miss him. We'll each take a tracking device and whoever sees him first, tags him."

"Oh, game on. Bet I beat you."

"Ha, you wouldn't under normal circumstances but I have the next two mornings booked off."

"No, you don't get out of it that easily. Let's make it an even playing field, then. If I tag him tomorrow morning I won't say a word. But in the afternoon, whoever loses has to..."

"Before you get too creative, let's stay focused on the mission."

"Chicken."

"I'm a sensible chicken. If I did lose, why would I want to lose twice?"

"Yeah, okay. I'll still tag him first."

"Just let me know when you do so I can start tracking him... You should download the app. I'll send you a link." Brent picked up his phone and started scrolling through pages.

"Anything else to be aware of?"

"There's a snowboarding competition Friday and Saturday. From what I can gather, Tosh and Marv, maybe Simon, too, will be in it. It sounds like a big deal to a lot of people."

"What's my cover story?"

"Make it adaptable. Up here with a friend who had to go back suddenly. You work as... what do you want to be doing?" He looked up at her as he asked the question.

"Movie production assistant. I can make up a lot of stories with that one."

"Good idea... You should have the login credentials by now."

"Got them. Okay, can I throw you out now because I'm so tired?"

"Yes. A gentleman should never overstay his welcome. It's getting late and I've got an early start. Let me know if you need anything." Brent got up to go.

"I'll do that... Thanks for calling me in. This is important and you're going to catch them."

"Let's hope so." He picked up all his gear. "Thank you for coming because I definitely need your help. Goodnight, Vane."

"Goodnight," she said, smiling as she shut the door behind him.

Chapter 23

Thursday morning

*B*rent could not believe how stiff he was when he got up the next morning. His legs felt like jelly and were painful. He vowed never to cross-country ski anywhere ever again. He had to get up but another couple of hours in bed, even half an hour, would have been so, so sweet. He had to meet Marvin, therefore he got ready and breakfasted quickly.

Brent was soon outside and it was still dark and very cold, although the first brightening of the sky was just beginning to show in the east. He was more than an hour early for Marvin but then he was heading in the opposite direction because there was no way he was going to let Vane get to Dan's cab before him.

His choice, born out of painful necessity, was to walk rather than ski. The exercise did ease the discomfort in his legs. Once he got going, he began to feel very pleased with himself, knowing he had stolen a march on her while she slept. He crossed over the bridge and that was when he realized he was, in essence, following someone. It took him a moment to process the fact but there, about a hundred and fifty yards in front of him in the gloom was someone looking remarkably similar to Vane and walking in the same direction. He was certain it was her and she was wearing her nice new jacket. It was obvious that Vane was heading to Dan's house. Brent started jogging.

In a minute or so he drew level. It was definitely Vane. Brent had slowed as he caught up with her and, without looking in her direction, said distinctly, "You tag his cab but it's a draw." Without waiting for an answer, he crossed the street to take a circuitous route back to his hotel.

Marv taught Brent skiing without antics. To an outside observer, that was all they did. They went up the slopes by lift and came down again with many stops and discussions on the way. Brent was learning new things and those manoeuvres he had already learned were being solidified. While they were occupied the sun came out.

Throughout everything they did, tension began to build. To Brent, it seemed that Marv wished to be elsewhere but only remained because he had to. He still communicated easily but only about skiing.

High up the mountain, Brent said,

"This is a beautiful view. I don't think I could ever get tired of it. You can see forever."

Marv said nothing at first. "Come on, let's go," he said finally. He had spoken with some difficulty and took off immediately.

Brent delayed moving, puzzled by the man's reaction, but then he followed as quickly as he could. He had no chance of catching Marv who was skiing fast. The instructor reached the bottom of the slope and turned to watch his student who, only then, was passing the halfway mark.

As Brent descended, it crossed his mind that Marv was becoming volatile. He could not do much thinking about it because he had to concentrate on getting down the hill. As soon as the word volatile appeared among his thoughts, it occurred to Brent that Marv might try to kill him. He got to the bottom and they faced each other.

"Woohoo, Brent my man, you are doing better and better. Yep, there's no stopping you now except putting in a lot of practice. Finish your week here and never come back to Brophy." Marv looked relaxed and in control again.

"I needn't ask why I suppose. That's a shame because I like it here. But you're right, there are ski hills much nearer to where I live."

"That's what I'm talking about. That's it, right there."

"We'll cancel tomorrow's lesson because you have the competition but I'll pay you for it because it's me who's cancelling."

"You're a good guy. I respect you for that."

"Do you want cash or should I transfer it to you?"

"Folding money's good enough. I'm serious about the practice, though. You'll be as good as you want one day. Don't give up on it."

"I like skiing," said Brent, "so I'll keep on practising. Here you go. Be seeing you."

Marv made no move to leave so Brent adjusted his goggles and skied away, knowing he was being watched. He had had no chance to alert Vane. If Brent did so now, Marv would probably notice and become suspicious. Besides, Brent reasoned, an attack might be imminent anyway and he needed to keep his wits about him and not be talking on the phone if it came.

There were few people about and it was several hundred yards to the main lift on a relatively empty track. He kept nearer to the open hillside and away from the fringe of trees and rocks on the other side. It seemed unlikely that anything would be tried here. Brent wondered if he was imagining the threat. 'Never come back to Brophy' - the words crystallized everything but would they let him leave?

*What do they know? Was I seen somewhere near The Village…?
Is Bates trustworthy…? If not him, then who? And what about
Marv? Did Marv simply tire of keeping up the pretence all of a
sudden? Hard to read him accurately.*

Brent stopped and turned round to wave or at least to see
what was behind him. When he did so, Marv had gone. It
meant there had to be another way out in the opposite
direction - one the locals knew about but was not marked on
any tourist map. He called Vane.

"Hi, where are you?" Brent kept looking around him but
there was no one nearby.

"I finished my lesson and I'm waiting by the main lifts.
I'm ready."

"It's a bust. He went out another way and I've got no
lesson with him tomorrow. I'll tell you about it later. For
now, go and buy a burner phone at Chop Suey's. Don't tell
Felix you know me. I'll be calling every fifteen minutes. If
you don't hear from me, get out of Brophy immediately, then
go and see Greg Darrow. Don't talk to anyone in Brophy.
You got that?"

"I get it. Be careful, brother, and stay safe."

"You, too, sister."

Brent skied on. He had nothing to lose now in one sense,
but everything to lose in another. He thought again about
Marv. As he got in amongst other people, his wariness
increased, if anything. *He started acting strangely when all I
said was something ordinary about the view… Why?* Somebody
laughed suddenly and it surprised Brent as though a pistol
had been fired nearby.

*If an attack was coming, why would he give me a warning?
The answer is… he wouldn't… No, he wouldn't do that… Then
why warn me off….? The view… Of course, the view! Maybe Karl
said something similar before Marv, had to have been Marv, before*

he struck Karl and pushed him over the edge… That has to be it…
There's no attack coming… Marv's remorseful and thinking about
what he's done. If so, then he did me a favour… I hope I'm right.

In his suite back at the hotel, Brent set down his wig box, as Maria called it, on top of the glass table. He proceeded to open it carefully. Inside, were numerous bottles and boxes strapped in place. In the centre section were three wigs - black, blond, and sandy coloured. He stared at himself in the box's mirror and then began the process of transformation.

More than half an hour later, when he had finished, he no longer looked like Brent Umber. A black-haired wig covered his brown hair, contact lenses changed his blue eyes to brown. He had also aged himself a little. His face was swarthier and he now had a neat black beard with a touch of grey in it. From a distance, he looked like a completely different man. Up close, it could be seen that he had used cosmetics but it was not obvious.

He called Sam Welch to say he was ready and would meet him outside the Aurora in twenty minutes. He told him to look for a man in a dark blue overcoat at the entrance. When that was done, Brent dressed himself carefully so as not to disturb his face or get marks on his blue shirt.

Attired in a dark blue suit with a dark red tie, he went downstairs to the lobby. He spoke to a man on the elevator about the previous day's snowstorm. In doing so, he pitched his voice deeper. He also let his shoulders sag and hunched over very slightly. When he got off the elevator, he walked slower, too. He felt confidant he would not be recognized. Andy Fowler might see through the disguise and people who knew him well might guess after a while but anyone else would not recognize him. Brent thought of playing a gag on Maria but decided against it. Still, the thought of doing so made him smile to himself.

Sam Welch arrived promptly and Brent went out to meet him.

"I'd never have guessed it was you," said Sam.

"That's a relief. Not too obvious, is it?"

"No, not really and I'm staring at your face. But, ah, let's get this done."

"Yes, let's get started," Brent said as the car began to pull away. "My name's Alan Stanton. I'm an insurance broker who works for Lang, Stanton & Associates. We've been asked to quote on the liability insurance for Freedom Sports. This is a getting-to-know-you visit and you're showing me the office side of things today before I can quote competitively. Your company is anxious to save money on premiums and I'm anxious for the group of underwriters I represent to write the business, otherwise, no commission for me. So far, so good?"

"I've got that," said Welch.

"Okay. That's the easy part. The tricky part is for me to quickly identify someone who looks alarmed at my sudden appearance without explanation. If asked, you're to say that the Corporate Office sent me, without mentioning insurance as the reason for my presence. I won't be going into the IT department but you're to say I probably will. Are we okay so far?"

"Yes. As you explained yesterday, you're to look threatening towards this hidden group to see if you can get a reaction from anyone. Does Sheriff Bates know of this?"

"We discussed that," said Brent. "Do you want to bring him in? He won't like it."

Welch was quiet for a moment. "We'll leave him out of this."

"Very good. There will be no confrontation today. I'll try and record what I can. This whole exercise is mostly so that I can have a good look around for anything that might prove useful. It may all come to nothing. You and I won't be chatty but I will be asking some insurance-related questions. Some of those will sound on the dumb side because I'm to be an outsider trying to get a feel for the place. Got it?"

"Yes."

"Should someone come and ask a direct question and you think the person is a part of the group, be dismissive of me, as though you think my being present is a waste of time. You could question why the Corporate Office sent me - something along those lines. You wanting to be rid of me as a time-waster and my being there as a one-off should calm the person down. Now, this is the important part and I won't be present to hear any of it. Remember exactly what they say and how they say it. Please repeat this last part back to me because it's vital."

Sam Welch did so without omitting anything. He then gave Brent a few names of managers at the Corporate Offices which Brent might need. They chatted a while longer and then fell silent as the car first neared and then pulled into the parking lot of the administrative offices.

Chapter 24

Thursday afternoon

Sam Welch and Brent entered the large reception area. It was tiled at the front in natural brown flagstones. This changed to golden brown carpeting around the reception area. Displays, on the walls and free-standing, stated past skiing glories, the construction phases of the resort, local attractions, current Freedom Sports programs and upcoming events. Brent was surprised at the amount of space devoted to summertime activities and attractions.

Sam stopped long enough at the front desk to explain he would be busy and that he and Mr Stanton were not to be disturbed. The Chief Operating Officer wore a parka over his business casual clothing. Brent, standing by his side, looked very formal in his overcoat and suit. The receptionist witnessed Sam's deferential attitude towards Brent.

The tour of inspection began at ground level in the Maintenance Department. It occupied much of the floor but also shared space with the receiving and purchasing departments. These were located towards the back. Sam gave a literal tour and explained to Brent much of what was to be seen. The area was busy, clean, brightly lit, and a little cluttered. Managers' offices lined one wall and tall dividers separated the various departments while lower ones provided desks with a degree of privacy. Brent could see about twelve people but there were also people coming and going through a pair of heavily used double doors on a sidewall that led to what looked to be a large garage. The two men went over to examine this area.

Sam only went to the admin offices about once a week. His being there accompanied by a corporate suit was a rarity sufficient to elicit comments among the employees. The word quickly spread throughout the building. Everyone made sure they looked busy - even though most had been busy already.

The next floor was better appointed, quieter, and had permanent dividing walls and many more private offices. Here were housed the Customer Service, Accounting, and Human Resources departments. Brent worked this floor at a slower pace because there were so many separate and occupied sections. Sam and Brent did the tour. Sam spoke sporadically while Brent asked the occasional mundane question. The work being performed on this floor was less self-evident. As the two men drifted past each group of workstations or private office, Sam briefly explained what work was being performed while the employees simply continued to work at their desks. Brent guessed that a few emails were now flying between floors and departments.

The top floor was where the IT department was housed alongside the more senior or specialized managers and their support staff. It was quieter still on this floor and the offices were much larger. Brent and Sam stood in front of the elevators talking.

A middle-aged woman in ski patrol gear was coming towards them, heading for the stairs. She smiled at Sam and looked uncertainly at Brent.

"Ah, Jane, a moment please," said Sam to her.

"Of course," she said, regaining her smile.

Sam turned to Brent. "I'd like you to meet Jane Leonard. Jane's our Mountain Safety Manager. Jane, this is Mr Stanton."

"Pleased to meet you." She extended her hand quickly towards Brent and they shook hands.

"It's my pleasure. Do you go out on ski patrol?" Brent spoke slightly slower and deeper than usual.

"Not on patrol but I do have to check on what the ski patrols are doing. I don't want to be isolated from them. I want to keep in touch with what they're experiencing outside of their reports."

"Very commendable," said Brent. "That's a good approach," he added.

"Jane is a highly committed manager and always has been," said Sam.

"Thank you," said Jane, slightly embarrassed by the commendation.

"We don't want to hold you up," said Sam.

"Goodbye," said Jane. The two men said goodbye.

When she was out of earshot, they resumed talking to each other.

"It can't be her," said Sam. "She's outside a lot and isn't included in many operational decisions unless they relate to safety."

"Okay, I'm keeping an open mind."

After that, they toured the office on this floor and met several more managers or directors of specialist operations. Each time, a similar routine was followed. The supervisor seemed natural, nothing was explained of Mr Stanton's presence beyond his name, and Sam was quick to state afterwards that it could not be that particular person for a variety of reasons.

About two-thirds of the way through the office tour, Brent stopped Sam and spoke to him quietly in front of a room. The lights were off and the door shut. There was a nameplate on the wall outside.

"Where is Anita Walters, Director of Marketing Strategy today?" Brent maintained his altered way of speaking to keep in character.

"Anita has two offices. You'll be meeting her later."

"Why two offices?"

"She works closely with Cynthia on public relations and I need her to be present at many meetings. Much of what I do here - what we all do here - is focused on increasing attendance in all our programs. On our busiest days during winter we get to about eighty per cent capacity. Weekdays, we operate at around forty to fifty per cent."

"I see. You have to continually wage war to attract new skiers and retain existing ones."

"That's correct. Then there are our summer programs which represent a real growth area for us."

"I can understand that. I had no appreciation that there were things to do in and around Ghost Hawk once the snow has gone."

"We have several plans in development to increase that attendance. We want to bring more families up here so we're working to address their needs and provide compelling attractions."

"And Anita's presence?"

"Yes, so when there's a new program to be rolled out, that's when she needs to work closely with all the other departments here. It's a waste of her valuable time to be travelling between the two offices for every little thing."

"That makes sense."

They had just finished speaking when a big, burly man sporting a full beard walked past them.

"Sam," he said with a nod.

"Dave, I want you to meet Mr Stanton. He's paying us a visit from the Corporate Office. This is Dave Bassinger, our Mountain Operations Manager.

"Good to meet you," said Dave, smiling.

"Nice to meet you, too," said Brent. "You keep all the trails and runs open? That must have been a challenge yesterday."

"Nothing we couldn't handle but, you're right, it has its challenges."

"Dave's one of our longest-serving employees and knows these mountains like the back of his hand. Don't let us keep you, Dave."

When he had gone, Brent spoke first.

"I know, it couldn't possibly be him," said Brent.

"I can't think it's any one of them, to be honest with you."

"The IT department excepted?"

"That's different. They are obviously involved."

"Have you informed anyone at the Corporate Office?"

"Yes. The chief exec knows and, before you say anything, he's anxious more about the integrity of the system than catching the fraudsters. He's put a team of sub-contractors together to take over IT operations here. They'll be coming up tomorrow."

"I take it that means you're pulling the plug tomorrow?"

"Yes. He and I have done some quick analysis and we think there's up to five million a year being taken. We've had niggling questions about flat sales in various categories in the past and they kind of get answered by all of this. It's not just lift passes - it's package deals, too, we think. We have to draw a line under this quickly and get our PR campaign rolled out while the news is breaking."

"I understand. If I asked for a delay, I suppose you wouldn't give it."

"We can't. The company's reputation is on the line. It's a lot of money we're talking about."

Brent nodded in agreement. He thought that jobs might be on the line, too - specifically Welch's. After all, Freedom Sports was not his real interest except where it interfered with catching murderers. He was now quite certain of the names of two murderers but whose was the third? He was certain that one of two names in the IT department ran the fraud but who were the other two people he believed necessary for the entire operation?

"Okay. I'll walk around the office for a few minutes looking like I know what I'm doing. You stay ready to talk to anyone who seems inquisitive."

"Certainly," replied Sam.

They did just that. Although Sam spoke to several managers, none of them inquired after Mr Stanton, the suit who was wandering around the office.

As Brent and Sam were crossing the reception area, they could see through the glass doors ahead of them a new, white Buick Avenir. The vehicle pulled in from the road and disappeared as it went to park by the side of the building.

Sam stopped. There was a scowl on his face. "What's she doing here?"

"Who is it?" asked Brent.

"Anita from marketing - the one whose empty office you asked me about. She doesn't have any projects at the moment. She has no reason to be here unless…" He looked very annoyed and dismayed.

"Sam, go somewhere else. The washroom or something. You can't meet her looking annoyed. You'll blow it." Sam hesitated. "Go now or it'll be too late."

Brent took out his phone to look at as he stood waiting close by the doors. Sam went into the Maintenance Department.

A woman in her late thirties, wearing a white, fur-trimmed parka, hurried through the two sets of doors. Brent looked at her before she noticed him. As soon as she noticed his suit, she slowed down.

"Hi, there," said Brent affably as their eyes locked.

"Oh, hi… Can I help you?" She asked the question in a bright tone.

"Help me? I get you… You must work here," said Brent slowly. "No, but thanks for the offer. I'm just waiting for someone."

"Are you? A taxi? They can take a while." There was a slight tension in her question.

"No, I'm waiting for Mr Welch. He's in the Maintenance Department somewhere. We just finished a tour of these facilities."

"Did you? I work in both offices but I had to come over here to get something."

"I'm always doing that. I've got a vacation property I visit regularly and I always leave things behind. Annoying, isn't it?"

"I guess so… Did you see everything you needed to see?"

"I did, thanks. It was very interesting… I'm Alan Stanton, by the way." Brent extended his hand as it seemed to be the Brophy custom.

"I'm Anita Walters." They shook hands.

"And what do you do, Anita?"

"I'm the Marketing Manager."

"That must keep you busy. Mr Welch was telling me how the company wants to reach out to families through summer programs. He didn't tell me the nuts and bolts of it but I'm sure you could."

"Don't get me started," said Anita as she laughed. "Promoting the company is my passion." She then asked, in a relaxed but pointed manner, "What do *you* do?"

"Me? I'm in insurance. I'm visiting to get a sense of the place so that when we quote we know what we're talking about. Besides, I like meeting people. It's a good excuse for me to get out of the office but don't tell anyone I said that."

"I won't," said Anita laughing again. She looked very relaxed now and said, "Sorry, I have to go."

"Sure. Nice meeting you."

"Goodbye," said Anita. She walked away to go upstairs to her office.

When she had gone, Brent called Sam, who quickly reappeared from the Maintenance Department.

"Well?" he said. Sam had a slightly vicious look on his face, having brooded over the betrayal while in the other office.

"We're done for the day," said Brent. "You must not speak to her at all. Not a word by email or phone. And certainly do not be in the same room as she is. You're telegraphing all kinds of signals."

"She has betrayed my trust!" he said in a violent whisper. "How am I supposed to feel? She's jeopardized so much."

"Let's go outside," said Brent.

Chapter 25

Also Thursday morning and afternoon but elsewhere

*P*artway through her lesson with Lotta, Vane sent a text message to Brent that simply stated 'I LOVE skiing!!!' The Newhampton girl was fascinated by the clean mountain air and incredibly, almost impossibly, white snow. She had never experienced winter in anything like this way before.

The fascination had started when the sun came up and she finally saw the mountain for the first time while eating breakfast back at the Comet Inn. She had been in Newhampton, travelled into the dark, and emerged in a magic country that was very different to anything she had experienced before. Vane had not comprehended that snow could come down in such vast quantities and look so beautiful. Awestruck, the shock of this new world challenged her dedication to her mission. It seemed of minor importance to be watching the signal emanating from the tracking device on Dan's taxi.

As Brent had done a few days earlier, Vane trudged slowly along in her unwieldy boots towards the beginners' area while being captivated by the skiers swaying down the slopes. The first divergence from Brent's experience occurred almost immediately when she arrived. Vane would soon be a Panda class graduate which, she believed, was eminently more suitable for her. Robbed of her triumph in getting to Dan's cab first, she intended to remind Brent that he was a mere hippo, with hippo-like qualities, while she was a panda.

Vane took to skiing quickly. She fell over many times and was a little disappointed that her skateboarding skills were not translating over. Her sense of balance and readiness to take risks helped but all the ways of controlling a skateboard were different to those needed for skiing.

It crossed Vane's mind that Brent may have fallen for Lotta, his ski instructor, and had yet to confess his hidden passion. She watched Lotta. *It's possible*, she thought, *but I doubt it*. What Brent did not know was that Vane, who had recently had a crush on Brent herself but had got over it, was now hyper-vigilant about his entanglements. She took a proprietary view of the matter. He was her brother in all but family ties and she was not going to let him make a mistake. In particular, she was on the lookout for gold-diggers. It was not so much that she mistrusted his judgment but it was more that when he finally fell in love, she knew he was going to fall hard. With her research out of the way, Vane concentrated on the lessons and being friendly towards Lotta. During the two hours, progress was made on both fronts.

"So what's the deal with this competition tomorrow?" asked Vane after the lesson.

"It's a *big* deal. It counts for points in the national league so a lot of names will show."

"Okay. Are you in it?"

"No, I'm a skier. We have a big competition in two weeks."

"What do you think? Can you get me ready for it?"

"No way!" Lotta laughed, having taken the Newhampton girl's joke semi-seriously.

"Here's twenty for this morning. I'd like some more lessons but I'm on a budget, you know what I mean? What can you do for me?"

"I have the afternoon free. Thank you." Lotta took the twenty from Vane.

"Good. What do you charge to take me up a big slope and get me down in one piece?"

"You mean like for an hour?" asked Lotta. Vane nodded. "Fifty bucks?"

"Sounds good. Three o'clock okay?"

"Sure… Are you up here by yourself?"

"You won't believe this but my girlfriend bailed on me at the last minute. She had to cancel because of family problems or something. I so wanted to come that I thought, I'm not missing out on this."

They began to ski away from the beginner slopes. Lotta matched her speed to that of her wobbling companion.

"I can't imagine going on vacation alone," said Lotta.

"I had to. My schedule is getting really heavy later in the year."

"Oh… What do you do?"

"I'm a movie production assistant or I will be this year. I've worked on TV shows before."

"That's really interesting. What shows?"

"Do you know Two-Way Street Beat?"

"I love that show." They stopped skiing to talk.

"I was in the first episode," said Vane.

"I've seen that twice so I must have seen you… wait a minute, wait a minute… You were the skater girl!"

"Got it."

"Wow, that's so cool. Are you an actress?"

"I'd like to be but I need a lot more training and it's not what you know, it's who you know in the business that counts."

"I've heard that."

They skied on, chatting about movies and skiing.

"There was a murder here. What was that about?" asked Vane.

"It's devastating. I knew the guy who got killed."

"Aw, I'm so sorry to hear that. That's gotta be hard for you."

"Yeah. This is a tight-knit community and it hurts. Alex shouldn't have died. It's unfair."

"I heard it was a gang-related thing."

"No, it wasn't that." A cautious note crept into Lotta's voice.

"Then the cops probably know who did it and it's just a matter of time."

"I hope so." There was a different quality in Lotta's voice that Vane could not place but presumed it related to Brent's activities.

Lotta spoke again. "We have a sheriff and deputies here."

"Do you not call them cops?"

"Some people do. Most of us call them deputies."

"Yes? - unless they're breaking up a party."

"Right! There'll be a few of those this weekend."

"I guess there will. Any interesting ones?"

"In a way. There's this place called the House but I won't go there. It's gross."

"Then I'll pass on it, should anyone invite me."

"There'll be an outdoor party with a DJ on Saturday in the resort. Now that you have got to go to."

They arrived at the lift area. Vane immediately spotted Simon Boltz. To Lotta, she said she needed to make a call. They said goodbye and Lotta continued on. Vane took a few photographs of Boltz. Then she sent a text message to Brent stating her lesson was over and she was ready to trail after

Marv. Vane also mentioned that Lotta seemed to be fine and was like an open book.

Boltz did not do anything of interest. He was wearing a yellow reflective vest and was, therefore, easy to spot if Vane needed to find him again. She bought a hamburger to go and was glad Brent was paying for it considering the 'rip-off price' she paid for what she got.

The difficulties she encountered in conducting winter surveillance were that standing still made her cold and that Boltz might eventually notice her because there was very little useful cover close to any of the lifts. Vane judged that being forty or fifty yards from him and changing position often solved both problems. She practised her skiing as she moved from point to point. What she really wanted to do instead was to go up on a lift and come down a run. Vane tried to calculate whether it was possible to round up all the suspects today so that she could get a whole day's skiing in tomorrow? With a couple of unidentified suspects still to find, as Brent had explained, skiing did not seem likely. On her phone, she looked up ski hills near Newhampton and found several but none that came anywhere close in dramatic scale to where she was now.

Vane watched as Boltz, while laughing loudly, slapped hard a smaller man on the back. The recipient clearly did not want his back slapped. Even at forty yards, Vane was able to consign Boltz to an idiot class of man within her mental filing system of people.

Brent's frantic call came at last which surprised and dismayed her. Vane began worrying about him. It took much effort for her to think clearly. Boltz was still where he should be. What did that mean in reference to what Brent had just said? She struggled to focus her thoughts while waiting out the allotted fifteen minutes. Vane had no intention of calmly going to buy a burner phone while this situation lasted. Brent had only said that to protect her - so that she would remain untraceable in the event his phone was seized. She was scared for him, yes, but it could not be as bad as he was saying because she could see Boltz shovelling snow. Then it must be true that Marv had left Brent. Who did that leave to attack him? There was the unknown third party that Brent insisted took a hand in Alex Simpson's death. To take down Brent in daylight would need two or three of them unless... unless... Vane called Brent ahead of time.

"I'm glad you called," said Brent. "I think I may have jumped to a wrong conclusion."

"You might," said Vane, "but this just occurred to me - suppose the third person is a cop. Cops are armed and can say what they like afterwards to justify their use of firearms. A cop is the only type of person who could get away with an attack upon you in broad daylight. I've seen several of them in town and there was even one here earlier. As far as Boltz is concerned, he's right here and I guess Marv has gone, has he?"

There was silence while Brent digested this information.

"You guess correctly... It begins to fit... Yes, I think it does... They call them deputies, by the way. Okay, I'll look out for that angle but I've calmed down now. How are you doing?"

"Better now I know you're alive. Don't frighten me like that."

"Sorry, it's my over-active imagination taking control. Is Lotta in the clear?"

"I think so. She's nice. She didn't mention you but when I got close to talking about killers she kind of made it obvious to me she was thinking about your investigation."

"And Boltz?"

"The guy's been working the whole time I've been watching him. He looks like a bully."

"He does, doesn't he? Well done, Vane, for that excellent suggestion about being wary of deputies. And how's the skiing?"

"I'm totally going to own it and we're hitting the hills when we get back to Newhampton. Look, can't we wind this up today and just go skiing tomorrow?"

"That's a beautiful idea but we have a way to go yet. You okay?"

"I am now that you are. You can't go scaring me like that again. I'll tell Maria if you do."

"Don't you dare do that. Seriously, don't go upsetting her."

"Oh, brother Brent, have I got a hold over you now or what?"

"I hope you're joking. I'll assume you are. I believe you enjoy torturing me."

"I wouldn't exactly call it torture - more like keeping you in line with a jab or two."

"Maybe I need your corrective measures. I have to go soon to get ready for a certain performance this afternoon. What are you up to?"

"Lotta and a lesson. Later, I'll talk to Dan. I've got an idea, though. Do you mind if I try it out?"

"What is it?"

"I don't like to say until I see if it works or not."

"Okay but nothing risky. We can't rock the boat."

"No, it'll be fine."

They said goodbye and went their ways - Brent to get ready to go to Freedom Sports and Vane, having taken off her skis, intent upon finding a nearby locker to store them in.

Chapter 26

Thursday evening

*B*rent now had a name to consider. Anita Walters as the Director of Marketing Strategy was well placed to observe the inner workings of the executive suite as well as the administrative offices of Freedom Sports. She did not look like a criminal; Anita looked like a middle-class manager in a prosperous company.

"Sheriff Bates, am I a pain in the neck?" asked Brent who had discarded his Alan Stanton look.

Brent did not perceive it but the Sheriff smiled. "I'd say you're like a dull ache, but yeah, you are."

"Do you want to horse trade? I've got a name. I believe you have one. How about a straight exchange?"

"There are reasons why I don't want to do that," said the Sheriff.

"Let me guess what they are. You've known someone for a long time but there's always been a niggling doubt as to how well set up the man has become on a deputy's pay."

"You can fish if you want but I'm not biting."

"Because you've known the guy, you want to give him a break and have him answer a few questions. Sheriff, he will lie to you because he's been lying all along."

"You sound like you know who it is when that's not possible."

"I'm guessing, that part is true. Was Deputy Fraser a lift operator by any chance?"

"Why him?"

"I have one tiny shred of information that points towards Fraser. He went to France on a wedding anniversary trip. Before he went, he let it be known quite widely that he didn't really want to go. Now, who blows that kind of money on a big trip that they don't care about particularly? It can only be someone who has no money worries and for whom a ten or twenty thousand dollar vacation makes little difference. He has said he would also like to go back some time - he unexpectedly enjoyed himself that much."

"You heard about that...? That isn't all of it. He has two rental properties that he and his wife bought."

"In The Village?"

"Not the ones I know about. Why'd you ask that?"

"It seems to me, for the servers to be secure where they are, they'd need to be in a unit owned by one of the gang or someone who can be trusted. They wouldn't like the landlord coming in on short notice to fix the plumbing or anything like that. The unit may not be in their name, necessarily, but could be held by a corporation."

"Look, Umber, Fraser may be clean and I have to check that first. That'll take a while and these are serious allegations. I just don't see him as a killer... The fraud, yes, unfortunately, I can, but not the murders."

"He may have been desperate at the time but you know him and I don't. I'll give you the name I have even though you didn't exactly volunteer yours. Anita Walters. She's the Director of Marketing Strategy at Freedom Sports."

"Aw, shoot... How sure are you about Anita?"

"Ninety-nine per cent. I went into the company today with Sam Welch. We set it up between us that I was there about insurance but made it look like I was from the Corporate Office. I wanted to see if anyone got interested, thinking I might be a danger to the operation. Anita Walters was the only one... Even Sam thinks it's her. Do you know her?"

"Oh, yeah... I wish I wasn't Sheriff today... She's my wife's best friend's sister. I meet her socially all the time... Huh, she's a nice woman... You'll find out anyway so I might as well tell you. She and Fraser were a couple for a long time, back when he used to be a liftie. And you can guess when that was."

"You mean," said Brent, "at the time of the Liftie Lift Pass Scam, for want of a better term? So Fraser went on to marry someone else?"

"Yep. Anita went to college and got some high paying work soon afterwards. She did very well for herself. She came back here and I don't know if she angled for the job at the Company or if it was a coincidence. Anyway, she got hired by them just when they were starting operations - so the timing's right, too."

"When was that exactly?"

"Got to be six years ago... She's currently in a relationship with a lawyer... I'll have to check him out as well.... How is it she didn't recognize you if the group's been circulating photos of you ?"

"I went in disguise, wearing a suit. I wore a wig and made myself look older."

"You did?"

"Yes, a little bit of exposure to amateur dramatics has gone a long way for me. What are you going to do now?"

"I'll have to bring all of them in for questioning… I count six parties, 'cos I don't know which of them it is in the IT department."

"Sam Welch is bringing in a team tomorrow. The mission is to relieve Downs and King of their duties. The company's concerned their computer system could be sabotaged."

"Yes, he told me. Be nice if he thought of the real victims once in a while."

"I agree. Will you coordinate with him and his team?"

"I don't want to but I guess I must, seeing I have to go onto company property. I'll have warrants but I hope to do this with no fuss."

"How will you work around Fraser?"

"I'll deal with him as soon as he comes into the office here tomorrow. I'll start with him and find out where he's at, get the IT people and Anita, then pick up Boltz and Jones… What a day - I'll be arresting friends, family, and colleagues."

"That's got to be hard for you. Ah, don't take this the wrong way, I like Brophy and the resort, but keeping a secret here is like carrying water in a sieve."

"Oh, yes."

"Supposing it gets out that arrests are coming and these people escape?"

"They won't get far if they do. There are only a few roads out of here but it shouldn't come to that."

"I see there's an airfield here and Fraser might not be the only deputy who's gone wrong."

"We can cover all of it." There was a slight hesitancy in the way he answered.

"No, I'm not saying you can't. What I'm thinking is that as soon as you rearrange the deputies' work schedule to arrest six people, more or less simultaneously, the people you're trying to arrest could get a heads up at some time, maybe hours, in advance."

"Are you going to tell me how to do my job?"

"Not blatantly but I suppose it amounts to that. I have several suggestions to make."

"Okay, let's have them," said Jebb in a tired, resigned voice.

Dan's taxi travelled predictably around town. Vane had monitored the tracking device which showed that, when moving, the cab travelled to supermarkets, doctors' offices, residences on the outskirts of town, and back again.

At just before six, a second flashing signal joined the first. Dan's indicator light was orange and Deputy Fraser's was blue. Vane was asked to log out of the account so that Brent could access it. He needed to do this to show Sheriff Bates what was happening which was nothing much of anything at that particular moment.

"Fraser's working overtime on the Simpson case," said the Sheriff, as he studied the map on Brent's phone. "If he's working, he may be sitting for hours and we're wasting our time."

"True. He has two jobs, though. He has to act immediately if there's a chance the fraud is discovered or the murders come home to him."

"I know I said it before but I can't picture him as the murderer."

"That's what I do - create a mental image of the murder. I can't fit Deputy Fraser either because I don't know anything about him. What's he like?"

"He's probably my best deputy. A decent guy - he's sharp, coordinated… Always gets the job done and he's a team player. I couldn't ask for more from him. But, uh, I know what he and his wife earn and I've always wondered where he was getting money from… Not that anything's proved yet.

He doesn't spend like a big spender on drink or anything… Here, I'll give you an example. He has a pick-up truck, a new one, a very nice F150. He spent an extra fifteen hundred on a paint job at the dealer. He didn't say he did, so he wasn't showing off, but we all know that he did. It's that kind of thing - non-essentials that most working people do without - he often buys them. That kind of thing adds up."

"I see… Now *there's* a crime, Sheriff. The price of vehicle paint should be regulated!"

"Oh, yes, I agree with you there. Hey, they're both moving now."

"That's interesting, each of them is heading towards the bridge in town but from a different direction."

"Let's go take a look," said the Sheriff. "That's a handy gizmo you got there, Brent."

Vane tried her little endeavour. The waiter at the restaurant - Suzie - returned monosyllabic answers to all of Vane's leading questions. As she was disinclined to chat, Vane was left wondering what she should do to get Suzie to open up. Then it occurred to her that a young woman, on her own in a restaurant, and she only drinking a juice, would not exactly represent a goldmine in tips to someone in a waiter's position.

"Hey, Suzie. Want to earn a twenty?" asked Vane the next time the waiter walked past.

"Yeah, sure. What do I do?" She smiled.

"Clue me into the nightlife here. Who's cool to hang with? Who parties the hardest? The best clubs. The best bands. You gotta know that stuff." Vane held out a folded bill.

"Yeah, give me five minutes to see to that table and we can talk."

Talk they did. Suzie spoke at length with little prompting from Vane. Eventually, Vane eased the conversation around to the subject of who were the coolest people in town. She kept that particular gossiping conversation going - even bridging two interruptions by customers - until Suzie mentioned Marv's name.

"Isn't he the guy who wears the weird colours when skiing?"

"I know. But he's a snowboarder… Yeah, yeah, he skis, too, 'cos he teaches it. He's a funny guy."

"Joking around? Stand-up comic?"

"It's him. He's off the wall. A lot of people like him, though. He's got a kind heart - everyone says so."

"Then where will Marv and these other people be tonight?"

"Probably at the House. Now that will be so insane. Like, everyone will go this weekend."

"Are you going?"

"I don't know. I'll think about it. You could just go if you want. A lot of wannabes get turned away but they'd let *you* in. Only… you gotta watch yourself, you know what I mean?"

"I hear you. Ah! Look at the time. Gotta run. Thanks, Suzie. See you."

"Yes, see you. And thanks."

Riding in Dan's taxi produced no discernible result for Vane other than he proved to be a friendly cab driver. The only difference she could discern between her short ride and what she had heard about Brent's stint with the cab driver was that Dan did not use his phone at any time.

Vane finished her lesson with Lotta without hearing anything to make her think twice. Lotta had gone home afterwards. It was then that Vane decided to try a green slope on her own. Unlike Brent, she negotiated getting on and off the lift without mishap. However, once on the slope, she realized she preferred learning in a group or with a friend rather than being alone.

As she went down the hill, she tried putting the basics into practice. Unlike Brent's early wipe-outs, which were now almost a thing of the past for him but which had been caused by an excess of exuberance and speed, Vane's problem was that she was skiing too slowly to make a decent turn. Lotta had tried to correct Vane in this, urging her to go faster but now, alone on the piste, she did not feel like pushing herself. Consequently, when her turns stalled, she just sat down rather than allow herself to fall over. Vane got to the base of the hill with only a slight improvement in her technique. She decided against more skiing for the time being while there was a job to be done. Vane realized she needed to focus on one or the other because she seemed incapable of concentrating on both at the same time.

She found Simon Boltz to be very uninteresting for a person of interest. He did his work, laughed a lot with people he knew, had a vague look on his face when not talking, and looked irritated when looking at his phone. Boltz did nothing nor met anyone that furthered the investigation. Vane felt a bit guilty about the amount she was being paid considering the results she was producing. She felt suddenly very flat inside especially since now, from a surveillance perspective, she was at a loose end.

Brent accompanied the Sheriff in his GMC Yukon. A memory of his past aversion to police vehicles briefly washed over him as he recalled his own former criminal behaviour. It subsided quickly as they began following one of the two vehicles. Brent studied the flashing lights on the map as they drove. Dan had taken the river road once he had crossed the bridge. He appeared to be heading out of town. Deputy Fraser, however, was in the parking lot at the foot of the ski hill.

"He's parked his vehicle," said Brent.

"How many vehicles can that thing track simultaneously?" asked Jebb.

"Six, although two are hard enough to follow on a phone. It would need a laptop's bigger screen for more. What do you think he's doing there?"

"I don't know," said the Sheriff. "You'll be walking nearby so that, when he gets a look at you, I'll see what he does."

"What if he spots you?"

"I'll be in a place where he won't see me."

"That's good. Better drop me off away from the area."

"Yep… About here will do you. There aren't many people about. I'll be over there behind those firs with my binoculars in two to three minutes."

"Okay, we'll meet by the bridge in case someone starts following me. If I'm being tailed just drive on."

"Sure thing."

Deputy Clarence Fraser was working the Alex Simpson case by interviewing a parking lot attendant in front of his booth. Deep in conversation, Fraser caught a glimpse of Brent as he walked past.

"Back in a moment," said Fraser to the attendant. He moved quickly to catch up with Brent.

"Mr Umber," called the deputy.

Brent stopped and turned to see who it was.

"Hello," said Brent, smiling after allowing himself a moment to 'recognize' him.

"I've been meaning to catch up with you. This case has got me working all kinds of hours. Anyways, have you found out anything?" Fraser spoke with easy assurance.

"A few things but nothing material," answered Brent. "I think I'm out of my depth here. I should probably leave it to you guys."

"Maybe... We got off to a bad start, you and I. I do appreciate you trying but this is a small town and we kind of know who we're dealing with locally. I'm getting the idea it was someone from out of town and a local guy."

"Do you think so?"

"Sure. It looks to me like it was a street attack that went way too far."

"Could be... How did it start?"

"Don't know that yet. Mary Denver hasn't released the blood-work results yet. It's bound to be drugs. Gotta be an argument about drugs and cash."

"Do you have someone in mind?"

"Oh, yeah. I just need a little bit more evidence and then I can make the arrest... I was kinda hoping you had a lead, to see if it matched with what I had."

"As I said, I don't have anything."

"That's a pity... Can't keep my guy hanging any longer." The deputy nodded towards the attendant. "See you around."

Brent continued walking. They parted with Brent turning several corners and then stopping to see if he was followed. He was not so he was free to rejoin Sheriff Bates.

"What did he say?" asked the Sheriff.

"Does he ever coerce people?"

"Not that I know. He can be hard - a no-nonsense kind of deputy."

"I don't think I imagined it. He only briefly explained the case he's putting together but he says he definitely has an idea as to who killed Alex. The way he phrased it - a local guy and someone from out of town - I thought he meant Tosh and myself. At least, we fit into what he was saying. I don't see how he could pin it on us."

"Interesting... You got an alibi?"

"I was asleep in my hotel room at the time."

"And Tosh?"

"No idea but Tosh has already been set up for Karl's death. It would be a simple extension to set him up for Alex as well."

"If he had a mind to do it, he could make trouble for both of you. Depends if he's got anything or not. He's not said anything to me about this." Jebb tapped the steering wheel with his finger. "I asked around about Dan. Word is, Dan doesn't like Fraser but there's something at the back of it. I reckon they've had some kind of an interaction."

"Interaction... Meaning what? That Fraser has a hold over Dan?"

"I don't know," said Jebb slowly. "I checked Downs and King for snowmobile ownership. Nothing, so it wasn't either of them in the stairwell. There's a lot of snowmobiles in Brophy so we can't follow up that."

"Of course not. How did Fraser seem to you?"

"He looked relaxed - perfectly normal. However, he made a call as soon as you walked away."

"That could have been for any number of reasons. I wasn't followed."

"I need something concrete, Brent."

"I know you do. What about my idea of using social media?"

"Well, you know I can't be involved in that. So, unofficially speaking, if you try it... We'll see what happens."

Almost as soon as Brent left the Sheriff's SUV he received a call from Vane.

"I've got eyes on Marv," she said.

"Where are you?"

"I'm in Destination Donuts. There's a café called Roast Supremo across the street. He's in there at a table with two women. I can just make him out but there's a logo slapped on the window that's in the way."

"Well done, Vane. How did you find him?"

"Oh, you know, persistence, intelligence, extreme skills, that kind of thing."

"And all that is true. Keep after him. Is there anything you need me to do?"

"No, everything's cool."

"Okay. So here's the plan. I'm going to find Boltz even though his shift ends soon. I'm launching the social media campaign imminently and then I'll trail him. Let's see what they do when the news gets out."

"Okay. Brent, does skiing make you, like, really hungry?"

"Does it ever… Get a sandwich while you're watching. They're very good there."

"Thanks, but I already found that out. I'm about to order my second."

Chapter 27

Thursday night

$\mathcal{A}$s soon as food had been mentioned, Brent struggled to dismiss it from his mind. He found Boltz who was putting equipment away in a storage shed. At a distance of a hundred yards, with his coat reversed and hood up, he felt relatively certain he would not be identified by Boltz. While he waited, looking up occasionally, he sent off his first post to begin the campaign.

BoardBoy: Spoke 2 a dude a couple of days ago. Said he'd seen Alex murdered on the bridge. Thought he recognized one of the guys doing it. What do you think? Should he go 2 the cops? Said he didn't want 2 talk 2 them.

KandyKane: OMG!!!! R U serious?

Itsplaytime: if this is for real tell him he's gotta go to the cops

aWkWaRd1: Gotta be making it up. Got any pics?

Elephancy: What's the dude's name?

Brent let the replies flow for a few minutes. He also received some private messages, one of which was from a deputy who identified himself with his name and badge number. Another person asked very similar questions without identifying him or herself.

BoardBoy: Guys, I don't know the dude!! It was a random convo. He went out of town and comes back tomorrow for the competition. Big guy, pale green jacket, ginger hair - you all go talk 2 him. I'm done with the snarky comments.

Brent watched Simon Boltz intently. Annoyingly for him, the man went out of view inside the shed. He was there for some minutes. Then Boltz came running out, hurriedly closed the shed door, locked it, and took off walking rapidly. Brent followed him.

Marv left the café. Vane went after him, barely having enough time to wrap the remaining half of her second sandwich and shove it in her pocket before leaving. He walked fast and Vane nearly had to run after him to maintain a discreet distance.

"Sheriff Bates says he can't get a warrant although he'd like to," said Brent.

"Why not!? There's at least four of them in there. He can get them all at once." Vane was outraged.

"He says there's nothing linking them to any specific crime."

Vane and Brent were in The Village. Keeping out of the cold wind, they had stationed themselves in the entrance to the condominiums of the building that possessed the camera overlooking the bridge. From there, they kept watch on the entrance to the condominiums opposite.

"That's ridiculous!"

They had been there for over half an hour. Brent had arrived first, having the shortest distance to walk while following Boltz. He had been in time to see Anita Walters arrive and enter the condominiums with Boltz following her in by mere seconds. As far as Brent could tell, they had not acknowledged one another. While they went up in the elevator together, Brent had run up the main staircase. He checked the second floor quickly but realized they had gone to the top floor. He had been in time to see Boltz entering suite 308. Walters was nowhere to be seen and so, he had concluded, they had entered the suite together with her going in first.

Brent listened at the door but heard nothing. What did suddenly alert him was a muffled reverberating noise of someone coming up the emergency staircase. He had run back to the main staircase and quietly shut the door behind him even as he heard the door to the other staircase open noisily. Brent had almost flown downstairs, hoping he had not been seen.

Outside, he had met Vane. They had taken cover in the opposite building's entrance. Vane informed him that it had been Marv who had nearly discovered Brent at the door of 308. While they were talking, the lights of an SUV shone along the thoroughfare before turning away as it parked. It was a deputy's vehicle. Brent checked the app on his phone. The SUV was Fraser's vehicle.

All this information Brent had immediately relayed to Sheriff Bates who had asked for photographs. Brent had sent them.

"What more could he possibly want?" continued Vane.

"He thinks it's them," said Brent. "He doesn't need convincing anymore but he does need evidence. Some of that will come through interviews but he needs a starting point. Testimony that puts one of them at a crime scene. Otherwise, if they don't lose their heads, they'll get away with it."

"What can we do?"

"Make them lose their heads. We've got them panicked now. Boltz and another believe they were seen committing murder and that implicates them all. It was stupid of them to meet together like this but it shows they're rattled."

"Marv was avoiding cameras the whole way over here."

"Was he now?" Brent paused for a moment. "Does he have a kind of bouncing gait?"

"Yes, he does. It almost looks like he's walking on a trampoline."

"He's the guy, then. I saw him walking away from Alex Simpson on the day he died. They'd had an argument in the street."

"You think he killed him?"

"I don't know. Must have, I suppose… It's funny, I kind of like the guy. He's a very good ski instructor."

"He should have stuck to that, then… Appearances are funny, though. Boltz, I can totally see as a murderer. I'd pick him out of a random selection of photos and say, 'Yep, he must have killed someone.' But Marv? He looks like a nice guy."

"Looks are deceptive, aren't they? I had a case once where this sweet looking senior citizen was systematically blackmailing three different people. You see, she looked so completely trustworthy and was such a good listener, people confided their innermost secrets to her. She then proceeded to extort money from them. The crazy thing was, she never asked for more than a hundred or so at a time. She would tell them it was for her gas bill or something like that."

"Really? What happened to her?"

"She and I had a long chat. The mad thing was she was horrified when she learned that she was blackmailing people. She had this idea that the person had done something wrong, they should have paid for it, and they might as well be paying her because she needed the money. She insisted she would never have asked money from someone who couldn't afford it."

"And so then what happened?"

"Um, I don't remember."

"Don't remember! You expect me to believe that?" Vane was quiet for a moment. "You helped her out, didn't you?"

"It was a while ago and I've completely forgotten."

Vane laughed quietly and shook her head.

Brent went back to his hotel and Vane to hers as there was little reason for them to keep the condo under observation. It was now seven and he definitely felt like it was dinner time.

As he entered the lobby, he was reminded by the competition display that he had yet to talk to Deidra Keaton. He went over to the reception.

"Excuse me. I'm staying in the hotel and I'm looking for Deidra Keaton. She's with Black Shark."

"I know who you mean," said the young man. He looked down a corridor for a brief moment. "I saw her about fifteen minutes ago. I believe she was heading to one of the restaurants but I don't know which one."

"I'm heading that way myself. Thanks for your help." Brent smiled.

After a quick survey in one restaurant, Brent found her in another. He asked the host to seat him in the same section. There were four people at Deidra's table. Brent recognized one of them as the man who had been struggling with the display stand. The other two, a woman and a man, were both young. They were both probably in their late teens and could easily be visualized as snowboarders. If that was so, then Deidra was probably conducting a getting-to-know-you session over dinner with a couple of prospects who might, if all went well, end up by being sponsored by Black Shark to compete in winter sports.

Deidra was about Brent's own age, appeared to be quite tall even though she was seated. Her naturally blonde hair was tied in a short braid. She was doing most of the talking. Her routine seemed to be to ask an elaborate question and then get a brief response from each of the two teenagers in turn. The other Black Shark employee was relatively mute. He smiled while something amusing was being said or he made the odd supporting comment but at no time did he take over the conversation.

While Brent ate his dinner, he took a moment to write out a note. When his waiter next approached the table, he asked him to take the note to Deidra. He watched as the waiter spoke to the woman and then gave her the slip of paper. She looked puzzled at first and then the waiter indicated Brent. She turned and Brent smiled at her. Deidra gave a weak answering smile before turning back to her table. Her fellow employee had also looked over. He said something and she nodded slightly. The conversation resumed at their table.

Eventually, the Black Shark table broke up. The two women hugged. Deidra shook hands with the teenager. Brent heard her distinctly say, "Good luck tomorrow." The man left also while Deidra came over to Brent's table.

When she arrived, he stood up and said, "Please, sit down. Can I get you something to drink?" At six-one, she was the same height as Brent.

"Ah, no thanks. What is this about, Mr Umber? Your note said you had some business you wanted to discuss with me."

"Yes, I do. Here are my credentials. As you can see, I'm licensed in another state."

Brent watched her as she studied his photograph and carefully read the details on the card. She looked suspicious - a look that Brent had seen many times before with many other people.

"I came up to Ghost Hawk to learn how to ski," began Brent. "On Sunday, there was a fatal skiing accident. In the early hours of Tuesday, there was a murder in town."

"I heard about them. What have they to do with me?"

"Nothing. I've been looking into both incidents because, in different ways, they've bothered me. In the beginning, and not knowing where to start, I wondered if there was any connection with tomorrow's competition or snow sport competitions in general. I decided that I should speak to a company rep who sponsors athletes to get an insider's view of the rivalry between competitors.

Things have kind of moved on from there but I thought, if you didn't mind, would you fill me in with some background information."

"So, this is not a proper investigation?"

"Er, no. Purely personal but it might have some bearing on at least one of these cases."

"Why not? I can't speak to skiing because I focus on boarding in the winter and surfing in the summer."

"That seems like an amazing set-up. Have you done both?"

"For snowboarding, I was on the Olympic team at Sochi, and I grew up on the west coast and surfed a lot. In many ways, the two sports are similar. They're both community-based. A lot of competitive snowboarders talk and share experiences with each other."

"Like a friendly rivalry, then?"

"Exactly. Everyone wants to win, make no mistake about that. But there are so many good athletes who might win in any given competition there's no one person that everyone loves to hate. Because of that, there are so few rivalries that it's not worth mentioning. There have been a couple of exceptions over the years but they were just that, exceptions."

"If the field is so crowded, how does your company go about choosing who represents it?"

"Instead of looking for two or three star performers, we sponsor a much wider group of technically competent snowboarders."

"I get it. That way you make sure there's always going to be a Black Shark sponsored person in the medals."

"You got it."

"That being so, there still has to be some dirty tricks being played by someone, somewhere."

"I'm sure there are but I've literally heard of only half a dozen incidents ever. Believe me, the bad actors get called out by the community so fast… You might as well say it never happens. Now name calling and psychological tricks? That's a whole different ball game. But, you know what? It doesn't work so even that's not too, too common."

"I see… Are you sure I can't get you something?"

"No, thanks, really. I've a busy day tomorrow."

"I'm sure you have. Now, last question because I don't want to hold you up. Is there anyone in Brophy whom you would consider signing?"

"I don't think I can answer that question."

"I'll rephrase it, then. How many Brophy residents would you consider signing to the company?"

"Oh, yeah… three of them. I'm not saying another word so don't ask."

"Marv?"

Deidra smiled. "He could have been good if he'd set his mind to it. I'll be surprised if he's not in a competition tomorrow. To tell you the truth, he's a bit too old for us to consider now. We're looking for long-term relationships that start when a boarder first shows promise. It's about developing talent."

"Ah… How about that? Too old at twenty-four."

"You know what I mean," Deidra laughed.

"I do. Thank you for taking the time to answer my questions."

"No problems." She got up to go. "Bye."

As soon as she had gone, Brent looked up her name on the internet. He discovered she had won a snowboarding bronze medal in the Sochi Winter Olympics.

Brent retrieved a laptop from a locker and went to his room. He decided to get an early night after he had put his thoughts in order. He added to his notes and then reviewed the whole matter. It was all one long, convoluted plot beginning with a fraudulent scheme established within Freedom Sports. At some point, Karl Saunders had become suspicious about something he had seen. Unwittingly, he had alerted the network that protected the scheme. It had been decided to get rid of him. The planned killing of Karl was Marv's responsibility - confirmed by his setting up of Tosh.

What Marv did not know, but it soon became apparent to him shortly afterwards, was that Alex Simpson had seen him on the slopes or doing something suspicious in and around the time Karl had died. Alex had incautiously spoken to someone, not realizing Karl had been murdered. A simple comment had cost him his life. That murder, Brent felt sure, was carried out by Simon Boltz and another. A stab-in-the-back murder. To Brent, that would be the way Boltz would do it. Now the Brophy-based conspirators had all met up in a suite as soon as they believed there was yet another witness to be dealt with.

Oh, to have been a fly on that wall… What am I going to do with them tomorrow if Jebb won't make a move…? I'll go to the Records Office to find out who owns the suite… Do they keep the servers in 308 as well as meet there…? Seems risky if they use the suite for meetings with any frequency… A deputy, a middle-class businesswoman, Marv who's definitely eccentric, and Simon, the bully… what a strange assortment… but not if you scratch below the surface. Then Fraser and Anita are connected to the old fraud. Why do I call him Fraser and not Clarence? They're smart, anyhow… so's Marv… I suppose Simon was there because… Why was he there? He doesn't really fit or am I missing something?

Simon was present at the meeting because he's the weakest link in the chain or he knows too much… It could be something has gone wrong with Boltz because of the supposed witness to the murder… Maybe, Simon made a mess of the attack on Alex. The wounds Alex received sure makes it seem like it was nearly botched. It was supposed to be quick and clean; it turned into a brawl. They believe Simon was seen and he's to blame… He may well end up in a snowdrift out of town somewhere.

Brent was supposed to be going to sleep. Instead, he was wide awake. His phone rang. Jebb Bates was calling.

"I'm at the records office," said the Sheriff.

"They're open late," said Brent. He had nearly said, 'Did you break in?' but thought better of it.

"Debbie…, I hear you've met Debbie already… anyways, she kindly opened up the office at my request. I've been looking into the ownership of suite 308." Jebb paused.

"I've no idea who it could belong to," said Brent promptly.

"It belongs to John Marvin Jones, that's who. And I'd think I'd like to know how he came by the money to buy it. You may not know this but the monthly condo fees in that place are very expensive."

"But why…? Sheriff, I don't understand why he would slap his name on the place where they keep the servers… It must have been Marv who went there on the snowmobile, though."

"I'm coming to that. Debbie has very kindly searched the ownership of all the suites on the second and third floors. She found something. The same company that owns the place called the House also owns a suite on the third floor, number 306. Get this. It's next door to Jones' suite. She remembered the name because you looked it up yesterday."

"White Hill Investments Inc.?"

"That's the one."

"Marv hangs out at the House all the time."

"Yes. It's run like a rooming house. Rents are collected from individual snowboarders. Wouldn't surprise me if Marv rents it and then sublets it to make some extra cash."

"Assuming that's correct, then it's likely to be another of the group who owns the company that owns both properties."

"Well, I'm thinking that will be Clarence Fraser," said Jebb. "I remember when they were first being built and how Deputy Fraser went to the sales pavilion as soon as it opened. He came back talking them up, saying how'd they'd be a good investment but how they cost so much to buy. Since then, he's mentioned those condos a couple of times. For one, he said they were not being as well maintained as they should be. And for two, he said how quiet they were on the inside. That, Brent, sounds like first-hand knowledge to me. The type of knowledge an owner has."

"Yes, it does…. Um, Sheriff, is Debbie overhearing all of this?"

"Ah, don't worry about her. She's my youngest sister."

"Is she? Put her on the phone, please."

"Oh… Okay." Brent could hear Jebb say in muffled tones, "Deb, he wants to talk to you."

"Hello, Mr Umber?"

"I'll call you Debbie if you call me Brent."

"Deal," she said.

"I want to thank you, Debbie, for coming into work at this late hour."

"Believe me, Brent. I don't mind if it helps get the job done."

"I thought you might say something like that. To show our appreciation, and I know deputies and police can get a bit cranky about this type of thing, I'm going to pre-pay a dinner for your family at the Aurora. How many of you are there?"

"You can't be doing that."

"I'm doing it anyway. Are there four of you?"

"Five, but my youngest is nine so she would be half-price. But it doesn't seem right and that's a lot of money."

"It's mine to spend and it pleases me to do it this way. You make sure you all have a good time. Better put Jebb back on before he gets involved and arrests me."

Debbie laughed. "Okay, and thanks a lot."

"I can guess what you just did," said Jebb. "You might be celebrating early."

"I'm not. You wouldn't be disturbing your youngest sister like this unless you were going for warrants."

"Well, well, you got that right. I won't be doing anything with them tonight but I'll have them for first thing in the morning."

"What will it be? Fraser first and then to Freedom Sports with Welch and his team in tow?"

"Yep, I believe so. Then we'll get Simon and Marv. As soon as someone decides to talk, we'll pick up whoever else needs to be brought in."

"Excellent. You have a good night."

"You, too."

Brent sent a text message to Vane, alerting her of the change in the situation. Brent climbed into bed, realizing that they might be able to go skiing together tomorrow.

Chapter 28

Friday morning

*T*he day came bright and cold and the mountain shone crisply white against the blue sky. Deputy Clarence Fraser poured himself another half cup of coffee as he stood in his kitchen. He only had to put his jacket on and go. The sun began to stream through the window. He swallowed his coffee and started for the front door.

"Jen, I'll be back late tonight," he called up to his wife.

His wife came to the top of the stairs.

"Again! How long is this going on for?"

"It's the case. Like I told you, I'm not back to regular hours until I've broken it."

"But you got in so late last night."

"I know… I know. What can I do? But don't worry, I'll make it up to you. We'll do something nice together."

"You say this every time and we never get around to the nice part. What's happening to us? It's not just your job."

"Ah, it is the job. C'mon, you know that. I tell you what we'll do. If I get time over the weekend we'll talk about our future. I've got some plans and we only need a little capital. I don't want to be a deputy forever."

"Are you serious? But you love your job. I know it's stressful, but..." She shrugged her shoulders and held up her hands in disbelief.

"I used to love my job but not if it's going to cause trouble between us. We'll talk... You'll see, everything will be fine. Gotta go..." Instead of leaving, he ran up the stairs to kiss Jen goodbye.

"There, see? I love you and there's nothing to worry about."

"Well, okay, let's have the talk and see where we get with it. Try to be back early."

"If I can, I will. I'll call you later. Bye"

Commuting in Brophy, if it can be termed as such, only takes a matter of minutes even when going from one end of town to the other. Deputy Fraser soon arrived at his place of work. He entered the building at a little before eight, passed through security, clocked in, and then headed for his desk, saying brief good mornings to several others as he walked by.

Later, Fraser stood with a file open on the desk in front of him. He was reading through a report from another deputy. He smiled to himself, thinking of all the time and work being expended on the Alex Simpson case and how it was for nothing. He considered Brent Umber and Tosh again. *It would have been so neat to bring charges against them. That would have shut Umber's mouth. Risky, though. It might have looked like I had a grudge against the PI. Still, he's leaving today and that should be the end of it.* So after all, he need not do anything.

He sat down at his workstation and wrote out a list of things to do on loose paper. There were a lot of things Fraser never committed to his notebook because, as he knew, a deputy's notebook can wind up in court. He paused to consider the red-headed snowboarder reported to have seen what happened on the bridge. Fraser could not remember meeting or seeing anyone who fitted the description. Nobody else had, either, by all accounts. He tapped the end of his pen on the paper. *If only he had a name. The pale green jacket narrows it down a lot.* He looked at a map pinned to his cubicle wall. Fraser was going to send everyone in his network to the competition to look for the guy on the basis that the boarder was a material witness whom he needed to get to first.

He was thinking of ways to deal with the green-jacketed man once he had found him when a wave of anger washed over him. He remembered Boltz' ineffectual slashings at Alex Simpson because he was scared of being kicked. Fraser had stabbed him in the back but missed a vital spot in the moment. It had taken him some seconds but he managed to put Simpson in a choke-hold while Boltz, frightened, froze on the spot, despite Fraser's angry urgings. Simpson had fought desperately hard, he gave him that much. It should have taken twenty seconds, though, not two minutes. He wanted to shout he was so angry with Simon. *Stupid, stupid, Boltz. I should never have trusted him.*

At that moment, Sheriff Bates, accompanied by two deputies, came around his cubicle wall. The deputies had their hands on their holstered pistols, ready to draw.

"Deputy Clarence Fraser, you're under arrest. Put your hands on top of the desk where I can see them and remain still. Don't reach for anything."

"What's this about, guys? You're arresting me?" Fraser had trouble comprehending what was happening as he put his hands in front of him.

"Secure his sidearm," said the Sheriff to the deputy on his right.

"This is all wrong. What are you arresting me for?"
Fraser did not resist as the deputy took Fraser's automatic
from its holster.

"Stand up and put your hands behind your back."

"Look, I… I don't think you should be doing this."

"Comply when requested. Stand up slowly and put your
hands behind your back."

Fraser did so and was efficiently handcuffed by the same
deputy while the other was still at the ready.

Once cuffed, Fraser appeared to accept the situation.
While being patted down, he asked, "What's the charge?"

"I have an arrest warrant for the offences of murder,
conspiracy to murder, and fraud. You have the right to
remain silent. Anything you say may be used against you in
court. You have the right to talk to a lawyer before we ask
questions…."

As his rights were being read to him - Fraser knew them
by heart - he could think of no one else but Simon Boltz, the
Sheriff's nephew.

Anita Walters was quietly arrested by two deputies.
When she heard the charges, she collapsed in her chair,
white-faced and trembling. She was taken away without
incident. Jebb Bates neither wanted to go with the arresting
officers or see Anita when she was brought in for processing.

Four deputies, as well as three IT specialists sent by
Freedom Sports' Corporate Office, arrived early at the admin
offices and swiftly entered to take into custody both Downs
and King. Sam Welch was present to make sure all went well.

Bella Downs immediately began screaming it was all
Wesley King's idea and fault. She kept repeating that King
had forced her to do the work which is what they had called
it between themselves - the work. Wesley King went mute.
Once the two employees were gone, the specialist team

carefully analyzed the servers for any software booby-traps that might have been installed and to see what work was required to keep the system running while disconnecting the parasitic servers.

Six deputies went to the two suites in The Village to execute search warrants. Suite 308, proved to be Marvin's home but he was not there. Suite 306 was found to contain two racks of servers. The deputies who found the hardware had no idea what to do with it. They were afraid to just unplug everything and take it away so they called Sheriff Bates for direction. But neither did he have any idea so he, in his turn, called Sam Welch. At least Welch was able to talk to the team of specialists who were all extremely interested to go and see how everything had been set up.

Whatever it was they did with the parasitic system and Freedom Sports' own servers, the specialists managed everything without interruption to the Company's business. And in that Sam Welch was heartily relieved.

The search was on for John Marvin Jones. Known contacts were interviewed. Deputies went everywhere, stopping and questioning hundreds of people, showing them Marv's photograph. An alert was put out by the local radio station. It was determined he had not left Brophy by bus. Similarly, the airfield was contacted and Marv had not been seen there, either. A state-wide search was then instituted. He owned no car so it was assumed someone was driving him or he had stolen a vehicle.

Immediately after all of this activity and mostly successful takedown of the criminal group, Jebb Bates sat alone in his office at ten o'clock. Career-wise, it was a red-letter day for him. Personally, he could not remember feeling so bad since the time when he was eleven and his dog had died.

Simon had been arrested. Jebb remembered him as a little
boy. It seemed like yesterday. Simon had been a happy little
fellow up until the time he went to school. From then on, he
was always in trouble one way or another. But, before that,
when the chubby four-year-old was bundled up in his blue
snowsuit, making snow angels and throwing snowballs -
that was the Simon he would remember. It was an awfully
long way to reach back in time to find a cherished moment
when he actually liked the boy, but, there it was, and Jebb
determined to remember him that way.

He indulged in more self-reproach. How could this large-
scale criminal venture have been operating in his town and
he not know about it? He had already been congratulated on
a job well done. Although he had accepted the metaphorical
pats on the back, he thoroughly understood that if it had not
been for the guy from Newhampton, he probably would
have continued to miss it. He consoled himself in that he was
no computer expert so there was no way he could ever have
understood what IT specialists were getting up to inside the
Company.

It was not just that, though. The Saunders incident had
looked like an accident and he, Jebb Bates, had been all
wrong. He felt old today, and out of touch. He wanted to call
his wife but she was not happy at present, on account of her
best friend's sister, Anita, being arrested. The feeling Jebb got
was that unspoken words were hanging in the air and the
meaning of them ran along these lines, 'For goodness sake,
Jebb, why did you have to go and arrest her? All you had to
do was tell her to stop.'

Then, to top it all, Fraser, of all people - arguably the best
deputy in Brophy! The man had been right under his nose all
along. The deputy had betrayed all his oaths of office, broken
all allegiances, lied, and then killed or conspired to kill, just

to make money. And he, Jebb Bates, had missed all of that by a good old country mile.

His phone rang. A deputy at the front informed him that Brent Umber wanted to see him.

"Yep, send him in."

"Good morning," said Brent cheerfully. "I've heard a few things and they're all good."

"Yes, they are. It's gone well. And that's almost entirely thanks to you."

"In some ways, yes, but I could never do what I do on my own. Chiefly, it's your operation that brought it to this successful conclusion. I just poked my nose in where it wasn't wanted." Brent smiled. It faded when he realized something was up with the Sheriff.

"Thanks for that," said Jebb.

"Are you feeling a bit down?"

Jebb took time to answer. "Yes, you could say that."

"The personal connections… Yes, that must make you feel awful."

"I've had better days."

"Frequently, as in almost every case I investigate, I feel like I lose a little part of my happier self somewhere along the way and acquire someone else's cares. The result is, I often go into a depression that lasts anywhere between a few days to a week."

"Well, I'd have said I wasn't like that up until today."

"I have observed that police officers often have a professional veneer that preserves them against most routine stuff. The way I work, and the way I am, I usually get very involved in people's lives, even the lives of suspects. I get to know them well or as well as I'm able in a brief amount of time. When one of them is hurt by what has happened or the person proves to be a murderer, it hurts me because it's someone I know who's involved. It's the same for you today only your time-scale of knowing the friends and family involved is much greater."

"Huh. Well, Brent, you've hit the proverbial nail on the head."

"There's a way around it," said Brent.

"Okay."

"For me, the best thing is to get occupied with something. The greatest antidote to post-case depression is to work on another case. The trouble I have is that I'm not called in very frequently to work on homicide cases. You might laugh at this. My most recent antidote was to learn to ski because I hadn't worked on a case since December."

Jebb wanted to get the matter straight. "You mean, you wanted to be busy to keep from being depressed because you had no cases. So you came up here and walked into this mess?"

"That's about it."

Jebb Bates threw back his head and laughed long and loud. He was a true exhibition laugher. He did not laugh explosively very often but when he did the whole office or house knew he had found something funny. It took him some seconds to get himself under control.

"Sorry about that," said Jebb.

"I nearly jumped out of my skin," said Brent, smiling.

"Yes, a bad habit of mine. Well, I can't sit here moping, anyway. That's not what they pay me for. So, Marv Jones got away from us."

"Where can he go?"

"Depends when he went. He might have left Brophy last night."

"That's possible, I suppose... Anyone talking yet?"

"Bella Downs. She's not stopped saying how she was coerced into the scheme, though she's short on details as to exactly how that happened. Everyone else is on the quiet side until the lawyers get started. We're kind of short on criminal lawyers in Brophy, so we're waiting for a bunch to come up from Fulwell. We can't start questioning until they've had their say... FBI's coming in, which I'm glad about because the fraud case is just a little over my head."

"And the murders?"

"We can't do anything about Saunders. I should imagine that Simon will be going down for the murder of Simpson. I'm sure he'll point the finger at someone eventually. They'll give themselves away in the end... bits and pieces, here and there... Never had anything like this before. How I'll hate seeing myself on TV. Gotta be done, though. You know, they're going to ask those awful questions and I'm going to look such a jackass."

"Don't answer their questions. Work out what you want to say before they ask. When it comes up about your connection to the accused, tell them Brophy is a beautiful place to live, work, and play. Say it has a real sense of community and it's a shame that a few people took advantage of the friendly community-spirit present here. You could say that Brophy's a better place now to live in than it's ever been."

"Do you want to speak to the media for me?" asked Jebb, smiling. "I'd swear you in as a deputy for *that*."

Chapter 29

Later Friday morning

*B*rent found himself in the novel position of teaching Vane how to ski. Out of the entire week he had spent on the slopes, he found this time spent with Vane, as they messed about on a green slope, to be the most enjoyable. They forgot the case, joked freely - taking lots of photos - and just skied.

"You missed your chance, boy," said Vane, as they both came to a stop at the bottom.

"I did…? Oh, no, what's his name?"

"Cory, and he's not into skateboards at all."

"Okay… Is that good or bad?"

"I'd say good because he talks about a wide range of things instead of the same old stuff I've heard already."

"That's important. Did you meet him in one of your classes?"

"I did. We study together."

"Is that what it's called these days?"

"No jokes, Brent. Not even bad ones."

"Serious, is it?"

"I'd say semi-serious… We like each other. That's about it at the moment."

"Do I get to meet Cory?"

"I don't know. I can't have Mr Charm scaring him off."

"I could wear a disguise. I really enjoyed that part of the investigation."

"Yes! You didn't show me your photos of you in costume."

"I can do that now." He took out his phone to find the images. "What do you think?"

"That's really good. I'm impressed. She held the phone a little distance from her. "If I didn't know it was you I'd have thought it was someone else… Oh, do you know your wig's not on straight in this one? It's slight but it's noticeable."

"Where! Let me see… I don't believe it. I did knock it getting out of Sam Welch's car when he dropped me back to the hotel, now that I think about it… and I did take a few more photos once I got back. Phew, at least I didn't go through the admin office looking like that - at least, I certainly hope I didn't." A slow smile came over his face. "They would have thought I was really weird."

"Ha, you don't need a wig for that… Come on, bro, teach me to ski like you do. I'm amazed at how good you are."

"Oh, it's easy. You only need persistence, intelligence, and extreme skills."

Vane laughed as he served her back her own words.

Over a perfect lunch under towering Ghost Hawk mountain, the two of them chatted about little things, avoiding the dominating matter of arrests for the most part. Eventually, they came around to it because they *had* to talk about it.

"Do you think someone gave him a warning?" asked Vane.

"That's very likely… He'd only need to hear of one arrest or that arrests were coming and Marv would be on his way."

"If I were in his situation, I'd have no idea what to do. I'd need money… I'd go out of the country, that's for sure."

"Yes, that, or a complete fake ID to step into immediately. I think I'd leave the country, too."

"Where would you go?"

"Somewhere cheap to live… Um, a place where the local authorities wouldn't trouble me. Somewhere warm and where there are also mountains and ski hills. South America, I guess."

Vane did a search on her phone. "Wow, who knew? You have Chile or Argentina to choose from. Look at that for snow." Vane handed her phone to Brent. He saw images of snowy mountains, frozen lakes, and ski lifts.

"Of course, the Andes… I didn't think of those."

"Maybe he's going there."

"Snowboarding's in his blood so he might."

"Now, if I were choosing," said Vane, "I'd want warm all the time. I like skiing but I can totally skip winter."

"Yes… There's something wrong with Marv's disappearance."

"What?"

"I don't see him hearing of the coming arrests last night because he would have told the others. That means he heard of it early this morning and vanished before the deputies got to him. I think he's in Brophy somewhere."

"You do? Think he's dangerous?"

"Best to assume so but, for some reason, I don't think he is. I know he killed Karl… We'll probably never know the real underlying reasons for that. The obvious one of protecting the operation - that's a given - but we don't know the history between them that led up to the murder, making it possible."

"It's probably something ordinary. They had a spat way back and they were weird about it ever since."

"Could be… but not knowing gives the reason some kind of special aura of significance."

"Brent, you're the only guy I know who speaks like that. Where'd you get 'aura of significance' from, anyway?"

"I'll tell you my secret. When I was a dopey teenage criminal, I realized that the people in authority or who did something meaningful with their lives had a much better vocabulary than I did. So I started reading and got myself a dictionary. When I came across a word I didn't know, I looked it up. After a while, I began reading the dictionary itself."

"I do that! Look words up, I mean. But not the reading the dictionary bit."

"I remember how self-conscious I felt when I first tried a few new words in conversation."

"Yeah, yeah, that's how I feel. You know, people don't notice. They just think that's how you are."

"That's true unless you're around friends who know how you used to speak. Paul Blake gave me grief over it. I tried onomatopoeia on him once and he couldn't stop laughing at me."

"That's when the word sounds like what it's describing… Paul's the art guy, isn't he?"

"Right. These days he's an amateur art historian as well as a plumber. Paul's a walking mine of information on American and European art."

"You must have some interesting stories from back then."

"I suppose I do. Maybe I'll tell you a few someday. At present, I'd like them all to be erased from my memory. But that isn't possible."

"You and me, too. So let's talk about what we're doing this afternoon. Are we going to watch the competition?"

"Why not? Should be exciting."

Chapter 30

Friday afternoon

*T*he areas where the competition was to be held teemed with people. Blister was crammed with boarders practising tricks along rails, over bumps, and somersaulting from ramps. Vane and Brent watched, fascinated, until a halt was called to the practising while the competition was being set up. For some unexplained reason, there was a delay to the start. Officials looked to be in no hurry, either. They decided to go to Cougar Pounce instead where the slalom events were being held and then return to Blister later when things had got going properly.

They skied across to the correct lift for the Cougar runs. Brent had not been near this part of the resort before and he found it had a completely different set of characteristics to the other groomed slopes. If Olympic events were ever to be held at Ghost Hawk, many disciplines would use the Cougar Pounce system of trails and runs.

With the competition set to go, it looked very much like an important, national event such as is seen on television. The first race on the card was the Parallel Giant Slalom where two boarders would go head to head. The organizers were doing it this way because of the high number of entrants in the race.

"What do we do?" asked Brent. "Stay up here and watch them set off or ski down and see the winner's moment of glory?"

"Er, Brent. I don't think I can get down the slope. It's too steep for me. I'm not going down on my butt in front of all these people."

"No, I can understand that."

They found themselves a good place to watch the races.

"It's like another world," said Vane. "Some of the outfits are so cool."

"If I hadn't insisted on dark colours, what would you have chosen?"

"See that woman in all white? I really like what she's wearing but it's like she's on show all the time. I think she enjoys that but I wouldn't." Vane scanned the other spectators. "I wouldn't do pink. Once you notice pink, it seems to be everywhere."

"Ah, that's like Monty's whiskers."

"What did you say?" Vane gave him a funny look.

"Um, Monty had been in the house for about three months. I knew he had whiskers because I'd seen them. But I hadn't looked at them properly. I suddenly became whisker-conscious and it was as though I was seeing them on Monty for the first time. I was really shocked to find that he has this monstrous set sticking out way beyond his face. He even has them coming out of his eyebrows… where his eyebrows would be if he had any. For a few days, all I could see when I looked at him were his freaky whiskers - I could hardly take him seriously."

"That's hilarious. I'll have to look at them."

"So far you've told me what you don't like in skier and boarder fashion. What *do* you like?"

"You see that girl among the competitors?" Vane pointed. "She's wearing an olive green anorak jacket with a black stripe inserted down the sides."

"You like that? I can see why you would. It looks like she means business and knows what's she's doing."

"That's it exactly. Don't get me wrong, though. I love my jacket - it's beautiful, and it was my favourite in the store."

"Probably the woman in white will be dressed all in black tomorrow."

"Yes, probably."

Brent began to look at what other men were wearing with more precision than he had before. He thoughtfully admired many of the choices that had been made. Suddenly he exclaimed,

"I don't believe it!"

"What is it?"

"I can't point. Beyond the rope on the other side of the course. I think I've spotted Marv."

"He's here? What's he thinking of?"

"No… it makes sense in a warped way. He's going to get caught and he knows it. Marv's going to do one last run before being taken into custody."

"What a crazy guy."

"It is him. He's got his hood up and he's hiding his face. Wearing a black jacket. Let's go and talk to him."

"Are you serious?"

"Yes. He's only here to do a run or watch the race. He'll be fine."

"Like you know him that well?"

"I think so. Are you coming?"

"I'm not going to miss this."

They trudged uphill carrying their skis intending to go around the competitors' start areas and come down on the other side of the slalom course. As they made their way around the scoreboard, Brent and Vane had a different view down the slopes.

"Brent! Deputies are coming up on the ski lift."

They stopped and looked. On the quad lift chairs coming up, about five out from the exit platform, was Sheriff Bates and three deputies, all of them wearing skis. In the chair behind were another two deputies, both of them carrying rifles.

"This is so bad," said Vane.

"He's seen them!" said Brent.

Marv left the course and began moving quickly uphill carrying his snowboard. Vane and Brent watched him.

"Where are you going, Marv?" asked Brent out loud. It took a moment for Brent to realize what he was doing. "He's going to the upper ski lift to Bear Tracks… Do you think you can keep up?"

"No. You go, but call me. Like, I mean, I want a running commentary."

"Okay."

Brent stepped into his skis and began moving along the level ground. He got quite close to Marv who looked up to see who was approaching. They locked eyes. Marv smiled. Brent called for him to stop. Marv shook his head, got on his snowboard and began moving away.

Brent chased after Marv and, by a combination of skiing down dips and shuffling up the steeper inclines, managed to work his way along the mountain's lateral trail that led to the Bear Tracks lift system. It was an unequal contest. They had started out with a gap between them of twenty yards but this grew to nearly several hundred yards by the time Marv reached the lift to the top of Bear Tracks.

The lift had few skiers on it and so Marv was already well on his way when Brent arrived. He lost time in explaining why the operators should stop the lift immediately. By the time they caught on and agreed it was too late because Marv's chair was already over a shallow section near the top. Beneath it was a drop of fifteen or twenty feet into soft snow. Brent told them not to bother and got in a chair to follow. Out of breath, he called Vane to tell her that he had probably missed him.

"Dustin, my man. Taking it easy, huh?" Marv had exited the lift. Dustin Packard was sitting in a plastic lawn chair by the side of the lift's machinery housing.

"You still here? Now that surprises me." He was in his thirties and had a deep tan. He looked older than his age.

"You know it's all over?" asked Marv.

"I can't say I mind," said Dustin.

"Look, man, I'm sorry I got the House job and everything and you didn't. But the way things have worked out, you can be glad things happened the way they did."

"True. What I'd like to know is, am I going to get arrested?"

"Nah, I don't think so. I never gave your name to Fraser when the deal over Tosh was set up. It was only me who knew you were in it and I haven't told anyone."

"Thanks for letting me know."

"Yeah, it's the least I could do… I wish I'd never got started in any of this."

"None of us had a choice, did we? Not with Fraser running things. I hope he gets everything coming to him."

"Me, too… Deputies are after me. If they clue in to where I am they'll be here in twenty minutes."

"Okay… What will you do?"

"One last run. It'll be a good one."

"Yeah? Might as well at that… You always said you'd never do time."

"No, not me. Shall I tell you something...? I cry about Karl."

"He was a good man. We should have hung with people like him."

"Yep, we should have... Gotta be going. See you on the other side."

"See you, Marv."

The lift was not fast enough for Brent. He had not been up this high on the mountain before and, as did so many other areas around the resort, it had a unique feel to it - very unlike the rest of the range. The top of Ghost Hawk was a powerful place of rugged beauty thrust upwards into the sky. Something of that rawness imposed itself into Brent's mind even while he thought only of catching up with Marv. He got off the lift.

"Mr Brent Umber. Don't bother, you won't catch him."

Dustin had not moved from his chair. To Brent, it immediately struck him that Packard looked like the old man of the mountain in a younger man's form.

"You look like you own this mountain... You're Dustin. I've been meaning all along to speak to you."

"That's me. Maybe I do own it... I can't say I'm pleased to meet you. You've stirred things up but at least there'll be a change for the better now."

"That sounds very enigmatic. At the moment, I'm looking for Marv. Which way did he go?"

"He's gone down there." Dustin nodded to the track on his extreme right. "But there's no point in you following. You can't ever catch him where he's going."

Brent paused for a moment. "Say Goodbye?"

Dustin nodded and Brent understood. He sighed deeply. He had been fearing some such thing. They were both quiet until Dustin spoke again, asking,

"Are you going to cause me trouble?"

"Depends what you mean… Personally, no, I won't. In a semi-official way, possibly. Seeing as we're launched on this frank discussion, I'll ask a couple of questions in a similar vein. Did you know that Marv was going to kill Karl?"

"It was never stated like that. But if I had put two and two together, I guess I would have known what was coming."

"What *was* stated? For you to give Marv an alibi and to say you saw Tosh go down that trail?"

"That's about it."

"Why were you willing to do that?"

"Now there I take issue. I would have lied, yes. But willingly - never."

"What am I missing?"

"You're missing the Fraser factor. Deputy Clarence Fraser. You don't know him but let's just say he had a hold over a lot of people."

"Blackmail?"

"No… Well maybe he did, I don't know. His favourite trick was to drop a little bag of drugs on the floor and arrest the guy standing next to it for possession. He did it to me. He did it to Marv and to three others that I know of. For me, he let me know that next time, it would be a big bag of drugs and I'd be going to prison unless I did what he said when he said it. After that, the payments started. It was never great money, but, hey, every little bit extra helps. So that's how I got to be as dirty as he was. Who do I tell? Who's going to believe me? He paused. "Do you believe me?"

"I think so. It makes sense in a lot of ways. What did you know of the fraud in the Company."

"Nothing. Oh, I knew money was coming out of the Company but I only ever wanted to keep my head down and be out of Fraser's way. That's why I work up here. He's not a great skier so he never comes up this far. Suited me fine."

"What about Alex Simpson?"

"That sickened me as much as it did everyone... Who's going down for that?"

"Simon Boltz, for one. I don't know about the accomplice."

"Boltz, that figures. He always wanted to be a big shot. Hope he's happy."

"Any guesses as to the second killer?"

"I don't know. Fraser, maybe?"

"Okay... Something I don't understand. Why didn't you go to the Sheriff about this?"

The look on Dustin's face changed to one of mild shock.

"You mean, I could have? But... Ah, no!" There was a mournful slur in his voice.

"I take it Fraser put it about that Sheriff Bates was the mastermind behind it all?"

Dustin nodded. "Yeah."

"Then who do you think has been arresting everyone today?"

"I thought Bates was cleaning house and had got tired of Fraser... I hadn't really thought it through because of my own situation."

"Yes, your situation... What to do? You know, Dustin, you look so comfortable sitting there that I think I should leave you in peace and forget we had this conversation. However, there's one thing you can help me with to seal the deal. Please point out the easiest slope. I refuse the shame of going down by lift and I don't yet want to risk breaking my neck on a black slope."

Dustin smiled and nodded. "That one's your best bet," he said as he pointed.

The slope down which Marv slid was super fast and he well knew the route he was taking. He moved with easy competence - equivalent to the best-trained ballet dancer. The scenery streamed past in his peripheral vision. He was leaving it all behind. Marv knew this was his personal best on this slope. If it was not, he had never shredded a run before. He was exultant as it all came together perfectly.

There was no one else in sight - they were far away at the competition. Marv had the mountain to himself. He owned it. A simple twist, a swerve, and a sheet of snow slammed into the firs as he passed. It felt good to do that. He remembered nothing about anything but was fully alive at that moment on that run under that sky. His mind was focussed on one thing alone - to make the perfect jump. It would be a legendary jump. And he, Marv, would be remembered.

It all gelled - all came together. This, his best run ever, was the preamble for the great flight he would take. He did not will his way down, he did not work his way down; Marv shot down as if guided by effortless magic.

He took the short jump over a little cliff and aced it. Perfect landing, everything under control. He picked up some speed on the steeper slope and now headed straight as an arrow for Say Goodbye. He had it in his sights. There ahead he could see the edge section with its little rise and when he hit that just right, he would get an extra lift to make some really big air.

Never had it been done before. No one had ever jumped this cliff. Today was Marv's day to do just that. He lined up exactly with the rise, going flat out, and it came up close so fast. He hit it hard and, then, was truly airborne.

There was no one to see him jump, no one to hear the wolf-like howl of 'Woohoo' as he shot from the top of the cliff. However, Marv needed no audience because, as he rose upwards, he had never been so ecstatic, so sublimely happy in his life. This was not for others - this was for himself. He flew. He rose to the top of the arc he was tracing through the air. The moment had arrived when he sailed weightless - a split second of being perfectly balanced between heaven and earth. All worry had been left far below and behind. He gave thought to nothing but this, his new possession, his supreme sliver of time - he had finally done it. Then, a few moments later, he never worried about anything again.

Chapter 31

Just before sundown Friday

*B*rent tapped on the side window of Dan's taxi, causing the man to jump. Dan was stunned to see him. He lowered his window.

"I guessed, Dan."

"Did you? Yeah, I thought you had… Yep. You know it was Fraser, right? I feel bad about lying to you."

"Then there's hope for you yet. With Fraser gone, there's no one to lean on you anymore."

"He was holding something over me. I'd rather not say what it was."

"That's fine and none of my business anyway."

"Good of you to take it like that… You know, I can't believe how stupid I've been. Why didn't I catch on that what I was doing was like being part of this whole deal… murders included?" Brent did not reply. Dan continued, "I feel like garbage."

"You felt you had no choice. Fraser worked a number of people the same way. It's not you, it was him. Now it's over. I'll be seeing you next time I'm in Brophy, will I?"

"I won't be going anywhere… Thanks, for stopping to talk. No hard feelings, eh?"

"None. Goodbye, Dan." Brent turned to go but stopped. "By the way, those mangoes were delicious."

"They were at that. Be seeing you, Brent."

"Thanks for meeting me, Tosh." They were sitting in a booth in Destination Donuts.

The young man looked exhausted and beaten. Three people he knew had died in the last week and it had ground him right down.

"Yeah, ah, I don't know why you'd want to see me."

"One reason is that I owe you some money."

"No, you don't. I didn't do much of anything except be an idiot."

"I won't disagree with you there but this is yours or you can leave it for the person cleaning the tables." Brent put an envelope on the tabletop.

Tosh hesitated for a long time and then picked up the envelope. "Thanks."

"What are you going to do?" asked Brent.

"I've no idea."

"It's strange how things turned out. I'd planned to go and talk to your dad about his restaurant. I went by his place and I think something could be done there."

"Why would you talk to my dad?"

"I'll probably talk to him next trip up here. You see, I know a guy who needs a break and he's a really good cook. He's taking courses and he wants to build a career and a name for himself. He might think it to be a great opportunity to come up to a resort such as Brophy and work in a Japanese restaurant. I was going to see if I could cut a deal with your dad but I ran out of time. The way I see it is, my man would help turn the Paper Crane into a landmark restaurant again."

"You were going to do that?"

"Yes. I also had an idea about you. Would you be interested to hear what it was?"

"Uh, yes… I would."

"I could pay for you to get your education in digital media development. I'm not sure what that is exactly but if you think it would make a good career, I'd go along with it. The way I see it is that you need to get out of Brophy. Your life here is all jammed up. Are you interested?"

"I can't believe what I'm hearing," said Tosh. "But I didn't do anything… and I lied to you."

"I've got a fairly good imagination. If Marv had not interfered, the week would have gone like this. You, Tosh, would have taught me to ski over four days - discounting the snowstorm. Nils would have given me a full day of instruction, too. By the end of the week, you and I would have been great friends, and I would have sympathized so strongly with your career and family situations that I probably would have done exactly what I've just outlined to you."

Tosh looked like he was taking it in so Brent continued,

"Because of others and their manipulative ways - it wasn't just Marv, you realize - because of their manipulation, you've missed out on that opportunity. That doesn't seem fair to me. I thought to put matters right by offering the same deal as if my vacation had gone the way I just described." Brent paused.

"The offer stands for one week. Here's my email address. I'll pay your tuition directly and send you a rent allowance. You let me know where it is you're going and what you want to do. I guess this will be for two or three years. Just let me know by next Friday and we'll take it from there. I have to go now. Someone's waiting and I've a flight to catch."

"I don't know what to say… Thanks. This is so kind of you… I'm so sorry I messed up."

"Tosh, I know a lot of guys who've messed up and you're just small fry in the brain-dead but functional game. Take care."

"Goodbye, Brent... and thanks for the chance."

Vane and Brent were seated together on their flight home.

"The next time you go on vacation, can you make sure it's just a vacation," said Vane.

"I didn't plan for any of that to happen."

"But my emotions can't take that kind of roller-coaster ride again. One minute we're having fun watching the competition, the next minute the guy I'd followed earlier is dead... I still can't believe it."

"It's what he chose to do. No one forced him to go out like that... I suppose, he thought it was worth doing."

"I don't understand why he did *any* of what he did... He looked like a nice guy."

"He was in a way. I think Fraser was intending to get rid of me, and Marv gave me a heads up... Shows he had a conscience even if he did kill Karl... For me, that show of remorse has gone a long way."

"I guess so... Does any of this put you off skiing?"

"I thought it might but I don't think it has... The hills near Newhampton are going to look pretty tame by comparison to Ghost Hawk."

"Suits my skill level... I spoke to a few boarders my age. They talked and acted just like many skateboarders I know."

"Are you surprised at that?"

"Not really. It was something I wasn't aware of... I won't get home 'til midnight."

"Make that one o'clock. Maria has cooked up a batch of spaghetti bolognese. It just needs reheating and I can't eat it all. I can take you home afterwards."

"Deal. I'm not missing out on that… I hope this eating binge I'm on stops when I get back to normal. I can't ever remember being so hungry all the time."

"Same here. Do you want an energy bar?" asked Brent. "I've got a few left."

"Sure," said Vane.

Epilogue

Brophy mourned, grieved, and went about its tasks as though smitten. After a week of that, it recovered. The business of the ski resort barely missed a step, however. The season was extended by good skiing weather and did not wind down until the middle of April.

The official tally for Brophy's grim week was one accident, with a concise reservation in Dr Denver's final report, one murder, and one suicide. Brent had explained to the doctor late on Friday that the killer would never be brought to official justice but had already served himself a full measure of unofficial justice.

The town's opinion arrived at a different conclusion and winked at the official version. Everyone knew it was two murders and one suicide but as all the matters had been satisfactorily settled, there was no point shouting about it.

Marv's posthumous reputation became something of a mixed bag. Most roundly condemned him for killing Karl Saunders. Some said he paid the right price for what he did. A few just focussed on his jumping Say Goodbye and, to them anyway, he had become a legend. Because they knew the distance from the cliff base to Marv's final landing site, they realized his jump had to have been truly awesome. Within that circle, Marv took on an heroic status as the man who gave everything to make the perfect jump.

Brent thought of contacting Karl's parents to tell them what he knew. He agonized over the decision. In the end, he assumed they believed their son's death to have been an accident. He could not see that showing them Karl had been murdered would be helpful to them in any way. He hoped he was making the right choice.

Sam Welch retained his job. He had to answer some awkward questions and it was a very close call for him. To have had such a fraud perpetrated on his watch was not what the managers in the Corporate Office were looking for in a chief operating officer. But to fire him would have made Welch seem complicit in the fraud and could ruin his reputation. Instead of firing him, which would be followed by suit and counter-suit, it was decided to put the matter behind them all and get on with growing the business.

The fraud trial went on for a long time. The trial judge had difficulty understanding some of the technical aspects of the scheme's implementation. Wesley King entered a guilty plea and received a hefty sentence. Being a willing participant and the chief architect of the systemic fraud gave him little room for manoeuvre. Bella Downs received a much lesser sentence on the grounds of there being mitigating factors in her situation. The first factor was Clarence Fraser who had blackmailed and recruited Bella using his bag of drugs trick. The second was that King was able to threaten to fire her if she did not do as she was told because he was also aware of the threatened drug charges. Unfortunately for her, she succumbed to their lies and pressure tactics. The same arguments were used in both her trials.

The amount of which the Company had been defrauded proved to be less than Brent's back-of-envelope calculation and, therefore, far less than the Company's spreadsheet-driven estimates. It was shown that the outfit began with more modest aims in the first year but, by the third year, the amount extracted went over the million mark, with the final year coming in at 1.7 million.

No one seemed interested enough to ask the question as to whether the gang had had a projected termination date or an exit plan from the scheme. Presumably, they were content to keep milking the cow until caught or almost caught. However, Brent was right on another point. All the principles - even Boltz - had fake IDs in their possession and money stashed away out of the country. The early warning system had worked, up to a point, but failed once it had been identified and bypassed.

Anita Walters pleaded guilty to everything. She was sentenced to twelve years in prison on a conspiracy to murder charge with three more years being added for lesser charges. Simon Boltz got twenty-two years in total by agreeing to testify against Clarence Fraser. Fraser, who pleaded not guilty to all charges, was locked up for life and then some with no parole.

A wealth of evidence came out at trial but very little of it changed how anything was viewed. Of interest in Boltz' testimony was that Alex Simpson had seen Marv coming along the track from Say Goodbye on the Sunday morning of Karl's death. Alex had been sitting down off the track adjusting a strap on his boot when Marv passed by quickly without noticing him. The argument in the street had occurred because Alex had approached Marv to say that he had seen him coming from the area at the time of Karl's death. Marv vehemently denied it.

The gang was forced to act and put a plan together. Boltz called Alex asking to meet him and Marv in the latter's suite. Alex was reluctant at first but Boltz persuaded him by saying Deputy Fraser would be present, even though it was late, to take all their statements. Alex arrived at eleven-thirty to find Fraser, Boltz, and Marv Jones present.

They spoke at length on several off-topic subjects while beer was consumed. When it got around to Karl's death, Fraser pretended to believe Jones' statement that he had not seen Karl that morning. Alex became suspicious to the point that he began to question Fraser's assessment. His suspicions were confirmed when Fraser tried to recruit him into the organization he controlled. At that moment, Marv Jones left the suite.

Alex rejected Fraser's offer. Boltz went on to describe how he was then supposed to spike Alex' drink with a drug known as GMB which would render Alex unconscious or compliant. After that took effect, Fraser and Boltz were to take Alex out into the backcountry and dump him somewhere so that he froze to death.

Alex saw what Boltz was attempting to do with the drug and, on the pretence of going to the washroom, managed to get out of the apartment. Fraser and Boltz pursued him. Alex, by now in a mild state of intoxication, slipped over as he ran across the bridge where his pursuers caught up with him. The trial judge was greatly annoyed with the structure of the plea bargain that Boltz had received and freely expressed herself on Simon Boltz' despicable actions.

The outdoor camera which Brent had found to overlook the bridge had been working intermittently the day before the murder, not at all on the night in question, but then started working again the following day. These conditions were also true for the camera on the side of the building containing the two suites used by the gang. The prosecution argued that the cameras were jammed to allow Fraser and Boltz to remove unseen from the building an unconscious Alex Simpson but that, in the end, the jamming had served the similar purpose of concealing the identities of the assailants on the bridge.

Within a week after Brent's return to Newhampton, Tosh was all set to go back to school after the young man had excitedly explained to Brent the career path he intended to pursue.

Within two weeks of Brent returning home, he received a very friendly letter from Jebb Bates to which he responded in kind. Brent also received another letter about the same time - one he found to contain immense irony. Sam Welch of Freedom Sports personally thanked Brent for his timely assistance. To show the full measure of the Company's gratitude, included in the envelope were two free lifetime lift passes valid for all lifts at the Ghost Hawk Resort that only required activation. Brent shook his head when he held the passes in his hand. Of all the things that Sam Welch could send, he had sent lift passes.

And, in case anyone was wondering, on February 14th Darlene said 'Yes' to Edmond. Brent, in a state of mild disbelief, patiently listened to his friend's exuberant explanation of what happened. This state deepened when Edmond began to relate the series of life events that the happy couple were scheduling, including children. Darlene was thinking of two children, and Edmond three. Brent supposed they would eventually work that out between themselves.

Brent went skiing again at a busy ski hill north of Newhampton. Vane went with him as did Greg Darrow on two occasions. Both men were surprised to discover how good the other was at skiing. Vane got on well, too. She quickly overcame her beginner's inhibitions and picked up the skills she needed so that, by her third time out, she skied as well as either man.

Before the trials began but after Brent had been at home for a couple of weeks, he was reflecting on the case and all that had transpired. In so many ways he had found it very challenging. Even his self-confidence felt challenged when he recalled how blithely he had sat across from Deputy Fraser with no idea that the man was a callous killer.

An answer to one question would forever elude him. He could not see what had alerted Karl Saunders to the fraudulent operation. No one was ever brought to trial for Karl's murder which, having been labelled an accident, was officially laid to rest. Brent concluded that right now, barring that single item, it could truly be said that there really were no secrets in Brophy. Any of the town's inhabitants would tell you the same thing if you asked them.

Epi-prologue

Greg and Brent had a gentleman's agreement. When a case stalled because there were too many potential suspects, Greg would then ask Brent in. By "winding him up and letting him loose," as Greg had once stated, Brent would isolate the guilty parties. Brent, on his part and once let loose, would busy himself in the lives of the people on the suspect list and thereby discover the most likely candidate. Greg Darrow was sometimes alarmed by Brent's methods but, so far, the investigator had done nothing that could not be overlooked.

As the drought in Darrow-supplied cases extended into February, Brent wondered if Greg was side-lining him. He did not mention the matter while they enjoyed their skiing, considering weekend hours to be neutral territory and inviolate. During the working week, however, Brent was thinking he had been dropped out of the scheme of things homicide. He was considering having a heart-to-heart discussion with Greg.

In March, Brent considered Greg to be in breach of their gentleman's agreement and told him so. Greg replied, "What are you talking about? Nothing's changed." Brent had to be satisfied with the cold comfort that such a flat statement could give.

In April it changed. With the advent of Spring and a welcome brightness and warmth in the weather, a case came up. This, of course, coincided with Eric's demands that they get busy fixing up Brent's gardens. Avid, fledgling gardener though Brent was, Eric found it difficult to keep him focussed on the work needing to be done.

One evening in late February, in the kitchen at Brent's house, Eric had handed him a list. Brent had to sit down to take it all in.

"As soon as the snow's gone," said Eric, referencing the list, "we have to get working."

"But there's so much here."

"Always is."

"I might get a case any moment."

"No, you won't. You're always saying that and you haven't had one so far. If you do, then fair enough. Brent, if you want to do this properly you have to be a gardener first and a detective second."

"So it seems. But there's a lot here."

"Funny things, lists. I find that if I start at the top and work down to the bottom they have this habit of getting themselves done."

Brent looked at Eric.

"You think I'm shirking, don't you?"

"That's your choice of words but, since you've said it, yes, I do."

"Ah… My apologies to you. I'm fully committed to the project and I have no excuse to give you."

"That's good and settled, then. Guess what's in the bag I brought?" Eric smiled.

"I would say it was four bottles of your home brew."

"Right you are. We need to layout the front yard and I thought we could do that today. Are you busy?"

"I am now," replied Brent.

As is often the way of things, as soon as Brent was settled and raring to go on a meaningful project, other claims upon his time began to roll in from people he knew. It got to the point where he was actually becoming busy. Paul Blake asked if Brent could give him a hand on a large plumbing job and Brent said he would help.

When he was finally and fully occupied, Greg called about an interesting case that had landed on his desk. Brent dropped everything and went to see him. Eric understood he had to go but did say, "Don't be messing about with this one too long because we've a lot to do and, remember, there are Maria's vegetables to be planted."

Brent's next case proved to be a puzzling one. It differed in so many respects to all the ones he had worked on before. The principle barrier to both him and the police was that every single potential suspect greatly admired or even loved the man who was murdered. He had been such a popular guy.

OTHER TITLES IN THE BRENT UMBER SERIES

Death among the Vines
Death in a Restaurant,
Death of a Detective,
Death at Hill Hall
+ another Brent Umber story coming early 2022.

NEWSLETTER + FREE STORY CYCLE

If you liked this story, a great choice is to sign up for the **monthly newsletter** and be automatically included in the **Free Story Cycle**.

The current cycle of novella length stories is entitled:

The Village of the Sevenfold Curse
- Murder Mystery through the ages

This new series of seven unpublished stories are free - exclusive only to newsletter subscribers. But it doesn't stop there. When one **Story Cycle** ends… another begins.

https://gjbellamy.com

Printed in Great Britain
by Amazon